SOUL OF THE BLADE

SOUL OF THE BLADE

BRENDA J. PIERSON

Crimson Fox
PUBLISHING

TURNER, OREGON

There are so many people who deserve to be listed here — friends and family who've believed in me, even when I didn't.

But the first fruits belong to the Lord, without whose gifts none of this would have been possible.

CHAPTER ONE

Aeo stormed into the king's dining hall, sword bared, a trail of muddy footprints in his wake. It had taken little more than a grimace to send the ornamental guards scurrying away. Those amateurs were supposed to protect the king? They were a waste of good armor and steel.

The massive table, a single slab of cedar polished to a mirror shine, was set with a feast that could have fed a small village. Haunches of meat, loaves of bread still steaming from the ovens, bowls of custards, and more. So much more. Nearly every delicacy Aeo could imagine, laid out before fewer than a dozen posh noblemen. As if the ravages of war couldn't reach beyond the fancy gates of the castle.

He lifted his sword, letting the gleaming steel reflect the firelight. A few of the men glanced at him, but the meal continued more or less uninterrupted.

Aeo walked up to the table and dropped his sword directly on its center. Metal clanged against wood and table settings, upsetting several goblets of wine and splattering pudding on the nearby nobles.

The decadent meal was forgotten. Conversation hushed as every eye turned to him.

"Next time you send me on a contract, at least make it a challenge."

He pulled a bloodstained nobleman's scarf, emblazoned with the crest of Halkron, from his pocket. It followed his sword onto the table. Aeo smirked as the noblemen around the table blanched and fingered their own scarves.

He turned his eyes back to his employer's. The man was short and pudgy, soft from a life of rich food and richer pockets. Aeo could slit his throat and be gone before he even realized he was in danger.

The king of Arata dabbed at his chin, leaving a smear of oil on his face. He tried to imitate Aeo's steely look, to convey power and control. Aeo did his best to contain his laughter. That might work on politicians and sycophants, but Aeo was an assassin. The world's best assassin. Empty threats didn't scare him. Then again, not much did.

The king waved his guests away. They tried to maintain their composure as they scurried away from Aeo, but he just smiled. He could smell their fear even through their suffocating perfumes.

When they were alone, the king leveled his gaze at Aeo. "Do the words 'secret mission' and 'tell no one' mean nothing to you?"

Aeo stepped around the table, helping himself to tender duck and soft, fresh bread. "Please. Anyone could have infiltrated that camp. Your nephew may have been the prince of Halkron, but he was a miserable strategist. Annoying little bastard, too. No one will miss him."

"My sister may!" the king replied, slamming his ham-sized fist onto the table. A moment later he winced and rubbed it. "Don't doubt the harlot's love for her son. He was the closest thing she had to civilization in that barbarian's court."

Aeo rolled his eyes. The king acted like Halkron was some gods-forsaken land filled with heathens and animals, when all that separated its people from Arata's was a river and a slightly darker shade of hair.

"That boy was her life."

"And now he's dead." Aeo licked grease from his fingers. "Because of you, I might add."

"If anyone were to find out I was involved…" The king stood and started pacing, pausing to pick up the bloodied scarf with two fingers. His nose crinkled at the smell. "You were supposed to eliminate my nephew and make it seem as if another Halkronar was to blame. How can that work if you show evidence such as this to anyone you run across?" The scarf fluttered back to the table.

"Are you saying you don't trust those with whom you dine, Your Majesty?"

"I can't afford for this plan to fail," the king replied. He fiddled with his many rings, sending flickers of gold and gems around the room. "Arata desperately needs a reprieve from this war. If my sister learns I had my nephew killed, Halkron will hit us with everything they have. Our army can't stand against that."

Aeo snorted and reached for a goblet of wine. "Families."

He continued to pick at the nobles' plates while the king paced and muttered. Aeo ignored him. The man might be ruler of the richest nation on the continent, but he was an idiot. He only held onto his throne because of Aeo's subtle political influence. Or his blade. Whichever.

While Aeo enjoyed eating the king's feast and watching him sweat, another man entered the dining hall. He was close to Aeo's none-too-impressive height, but where Aeo had the solid look of a warrior, this man was thin like a scholar who'd rather study than eat. He held himself rigidly, the serenity plastered on his features masking the tension of a drawn bow. Aeo kept himself calm by sheer willpower. He might not be afraid of much, but this man never failed to twist his guts into knots.

Even the king, supposedly the ultimate authority in all of Arata, did his best to remain invisible around this man. "Mage General," he greeted meekly.

"Your Majesty," he replied. Somehow he managed to make the title a mockery instead of a respect. "Allow me to extend my regrets at the loss of your nephew."

The king shot a glare at Aeo. "I just received the news myself. How did you hear?"

"I am a mage, Your Majesty. Surely you can't think Halkron is out of my reach."

"Of course not."

Aeo shook his head. *He may as well kiss his boots and offer him the throne at this rate.*

The Mage General looked toward Aeo. He inclined his head

in the tiniest, most insincere greeting Aeo had ever seen. "I trust you are well?"

No thanks to your training, Aeo thought. "I do my best with what I have," he replied.

"And that is all we have ever asked of you." The Mage General turned back to the king, brushing Aeo off as if they had never spoken.

Even though the mage's eyes were averted, Aeo didn't dare release the shudder building inside him. Any contact with the Mage General, no matter how trivial, always left a sheen of cold sweat on his forehead. One look into his eyes and Aeo could almost feel the man's magic intruding into his thoughts, twisting and tearing them apart in order to make him obey. It didn't matter that years had passed since his conditioning had been deemed complete. There were some wounds that time doesn't heal, empty platitudes be damned.

Aeo couldn't hear what the men whispered about, but the king was clearly unhappy about the topic. He shook his head and scowled, trying to argue, but the Mage General grew more animated as he pushed his point. He waved his arms toward the west and pointed to the ground as if to stab it with his forefinger. His eyes grew frantic, fanatical. Aeo knew that look. There was no arguing with that level of crazy. The only thing to do was cower and obey, and that's exactly what the king did. For once, Aeo couldn't blame him.

"I'd hoped it wouldn't come to this," the king said aloud. He didn't look back to the Mage General. Instead, he raised his eyes to meet Aeo's. "I have another contract for you."

"So soon?" Aeo asked. "I haven't even had time to enjoy my coin."

"Your drinking and whoring will have to wait. This is urgent."

Aeo sighed. "Of course it is."

The king glared at his sarcasm, but Aeo just stared back. He took another sip of wine, not blinking.

The king looked away first.

"You say you want a challenge. I'll give you one. You know of the Bok'Tarong?"

Aeo shrugged. "Rumors only. It's supposed to be some kind of enchanted, double-bladed sword. Wherever it shows up, people die. Lots of them."

"Do not discount such legends so quickly," the Mage General said as he approached. The intensity in his expression made Aeo drop his food back to the table. Not even a king's feast seemed appetizing anymore. "The Bok'Tarong is very real."

"If you say so."

The look Aeo received for that made his bowels watery and his stomach churn. Aeo had seen that look—and received the corresponding beatings—many times in the past. His gaze fell to the table as fast as the king's had.

The king cleared his throat. "How would you like to take that blade for your own?"

Aeo paused. The Bok'Tarong… that would be plunder for the ages. And if the rumors were true, no one had ever defeated the bearer in single combat. Once Aeo did, he would never again have competition for the title of best assassin in the world. Not like there was much, or any at all, but still.

Finally, Aeo would have a target who'd well and truly earned his blade in their neck rather than some insufferable noble who'd irritated the wrong king. Aeo had taken great care to ensure no innocent had died by his hands — he had to maintain at least *some* control over his life — but this target was a menace, a harbinger of death. Some even said they were Death incarnate. "I suppose I could do worse," Aeo said.

"And with the Bok'Tarong in your possession," the Mage General added, "the tide of war will turn in our favor."

The fanatical look returned to the Mage General's eyes. He *needed* Aeo to have this sword. Aeo could only guess why, but whenever the Mage General looked at him like this, it never turned out well for him. "What's so special about this sword, anyway?" he asked, forcing his tone to be one of calm and disinterest.

"It is, indeed, enchanted," the Mage General replied. "One of the few enchanted weapons in the world."

"What does the magic do?"

A pause, no longer than the blink of an eye. "Only the bearer of the weapon can be sure of that. The communion between bearer and blade is what makes the magic so potent."

A lot of words to say absolutely nothing.

He was hiding something, Aeo was sure of that much. If this was some plan to be rid of him…

The king, in a rare moment of insight, noticed his hesitation. He stepped in front of Aeo, leveling as firm a gaze as he could muster on him. "Your next target is the bearer of the Bok'Tarong," he announced.

The order reverberated in Aeo's head, the taste of the Mage General's magic souring every word. The words burrowed through his thoughts and into his heart. Whether or not Aeo would have accepted was no matter anymore. The king had ordered—Aeo would obey. His years under the Mage General's tutorage guaranteed that.

Aeo rose from the table and drained his goblet. "Where can I find this man?"

The king shrugged as if he couldn't be bothered with details like that. "Ask around. Commoners love to tell tales. Someone who's seen this sword will want to brag about it."

"That isn't much to go on."

"You say you're the world's greatest assassin," the king replied. For the first time in their long partnership, Aeo heard something bordering on true authority in his voice. "Surely that means you can find one man with a remarkable sword."

Aeo squared his shoulders. If the king would challenge him, then Aeo would show him just how great he was. "The next time I see you, Your Majesty, the Bok'Tarong will be mine."

Before leaving, he "borrowed" a large platter and loaded it with as much food as he could carry. The king scowled, but didn't say anything. Like the coward he was.

The ornamental guards found other things to look at as Aeo made his way out of the castle.

Warm spring air, with a hint of summer's heat, welcomed him into the king's courtyard. Below him stretched Karim, the massive capital of Arata. From this vantage point, atop the lone hill in the area, even the trees of the surrounding forest seemed miniscule. The people scurried like ants on meaningless errands. No wonder the king was so bad at remembering to take care of them.

Leaving the castle behind, Aeo was confronted by the more familiar aspects of normal life—merchants hawking their wares, mothers calling out to children, the smells of meat and bread and sewage and smoke. Aeo much preferred this to the perfumed and sterile halls of the castle.

A few steps off the stuffy nobles' hill, Aeo tossed a piece of duck to a small beggar. She couldn't have been more than seven. An even younger boy, perhaps her brother, peeked out from behind her. Aeo knelt, offering the boy some bread. He was skittish, but Aeo waited. He knew all too well how hard it was to accept food from a stranger when all you're used to is abuse and starvation.

Finally, hunger overcame fear and the boy snatched the bread.

Several of the beggars Aeo fed had the strange, distorted eyes of those suffering from the Coming Madness. Maybe it was just his imagination, but he swore he saw more of them now than he had before the war. Was he doing a mercy to these people by feeding them? Death, even by starvation, had to be better than waiting for the Madness to strike. And once it did, there was no mercy anyone could give. Swords couldn't stop one consumed by the Madness. The lost one traded their sanity for superhuman strength—some even said they could heal from wounds that would kill a normal man. Luckily, most who got that far didn't retain enough mental capacity to remember the importance of food, or that bears and mountain lions didn't make good sparring partners.

Aeo moved away from those poor souls before the temptation to put them out of their misery became too much.

He'd hardly emerged from the castle's shadow when the king's food ran out. Ever since Halkron broke the treaty and attacked Arata, people were being forced into poverty by the hundreds. The streets were filled with war orphans and destitute craftsmen and victims of the Coming Madness like they'd never been before. Stupid as he was, the king was right about one thing — Arata couldn't stand much more of this war.

Aeo pushed those thoughts out of his mind. He had to focus on his mission. This Bok'Tarong wouldn't be easy to find. Arata was huge, and her forests were as treacherous as a harlot with a dagger.

He headed to a nearby tavern. Running across someone with information would be as much a matter of luck as skill. He may as well start here.

CHAPTER TWO

Aeo loved taverns as much as the next guy, but visiting a dozen in half as many days was a little much, even for him.

Karim was a far-fetched dream to this a tiny village lost amongst firs and cedars, yet the tavern was just like all the others he'd visited—dark, smoky, thick with the smell of unwashed humanity, overcooked food, and whatever don't-ask-what's-in-it drink the locals fancied.

With any luck, this should be the last one he'd have to visit for a while. After a month of travel, maybe more, he may have finally found someone who could point him to the Bok'Tarong.

His gaze roamed the room's occupants. They were the usual rabble—a couple of travelers, a few merchants, but mostly local drunks who'd practically grown roots into their favorite chair. A handful of Kingsmen milled around, still hoping to recruit new able-bodied men to the war. From the slump of their shoulders, Aeo figured they knew as well as he did they wouldn't find any.

This land had been emptied of soldiers and countrymen long ago. Since then, the only folks left in places like this weren't the kind of men you'd want to hang your life on in a fight.

His eyes landed on a mousy-looking man in the corner, the opaque lenses of the blind perched on his nose. This must be his man. How many blind men could there be in a no-name village like this?

He sat apart from the others, against a wall and as far back as possible. Any farther away and he would have been in the stables. He jumped at every sound louder than a half-smothered cough. He didn't have anything on the table before him — no ale, not even a crumb to indicate an already finished meal.

Aeo ordered two pints of liquor that smelled suspiciously like pine sap and joined the blind man. "I hear you have some information that can help me," he said, sliding one mug across the table.

The man cocked his head toward Aeo's voice. He didn't reach for the ale, if he even knew Aeo had offered it. "Do I know you?"

"No. I'm just a traveler."

"As am I. I doubt I know anything that can help you."

"I've been told you know where I could find a sword called the Bok'Tarong."

The man stilled at this name. Aeo tried to read his expression, but he'd gone as stiff and emotionless as a statue. "Why are you looking for the Bok'Tarong?"

"That's my business."

He clearly didn't like that answer, but Aeo offered no other. Stubborn silence fell over the table. Aeo sipped at the pungent pine ale and immediately regretted it. Eyes watering, mouth puckered, he pushed the mug away and forced himself to swallow.

"It takes some getting used to," the blind man said.

The silence returned. The man took a long swallow of ale without even a hint of gagging. Aeo could sense the challenge in that motion, but didn't rise to it.

"The Bok'Tarong," the blind man said. Aeo had to lean in close as an overly dramatic, drunken argument broke out at the bar. "If you're hoping to exact revenge you may as well give up now. You'll be dead before you can raise your blade against the bearer."

"I doubt that," Aeo replied.

"So confident."

"With reason."

The blind man paused, as if considering Aeo's words. "Do you understand what you're getting yourself into? The Bok'Tarong is much more than a special sword, and its bearer is far more skilled than even the best of Arata's swordsmen."

"I've fought many of Arata's finest swordsmen in my time. I'm still here, and they're not." He raised his mug to his mouth, peered down at the vile liquor, and put it down again. After a moment, he reached over and placed it on a neighboring table. "As to the sword itself, I know what it is."

"Do you?"

The man's tone made Aeo pause. His question wasn't as simple as it seemed. Did Aeo *know* the truth, or *think* he knew the truth? "It's heavily enchanted. The magic interacts with the bearer somehow, and with the Bok'Tarong's reputation as the most fearsome sword in the world it seems obvious that magic has something to do with it."

Aeo waited to see if the man would approve, or share what he knew of the sword, but he didn't do either.

By this time, the drunken argument had been resolved and a round of off-tune, off-color singing filled the tavern. A curvaceous serving girl came around, offering Aeo more of the disgusting ale and, judging by her smile, something more lewd on the side. Normally he'd have been thrilled to explore those curves outside the confines of her corset, but right now he had more important things to do. Pity.

After another swig from his pint, the blind man sighed. "You're going to hunt the Bok'Tarong no matter what I tell you, aren't you?"

Aeo smirked. He liked this man. "Yes."

"If I tell you the Bok'Tarong is so much more than you know, that it is more dangerous than anything you've ever encountered, and I doubt you stand a chance against it, you'll still try, won't you?"

"Yes."

"You are either insanely brave or just insane. I've yet to decide which."

Aeo smiled. "Let's go with both, then."

The man laughed. "Last I heard, the Bok'Tarong was in the north. But I would expect it to head this way any time."

"Why do you say that?"

A long pause. "A village to the east of here has been ravaged by the Coming Madness. The Bok'Tarong will come for it before long."

"I don't understand. How will this help me find the sword?"

"The Bok'Tarong hunts those touched by the Coming Madness. Find a place where the Madness is prevalent, and the sword will find you."

Aeo sat back. Now that was an interesting tidbit. He'd never heard of anything hunting the Coming Madness before. And yet, that could explain quite a bit of what he'd heard about the sword. Was that its magic, that it was able to cut through the insane power those taken by the Madness possessed and kill them? Was that why it had such a reputation for leaving rivers of blood in its wake?

Fascinating though it may be, it mattered little. Whatever the sword's power was, or whomever it hunted, Aeo was still contracted to kill the man bearing it.

He stood, giving the blind man a nod of respect even though it couldn't be seen. "Thank you."

"Whatever your business is with the Bok'Tarong, it's a fool's errand."

"We'll see about that."

Aeo left the tavern, and the village, behind. He put the sun to his back and set out into the forest, on his way to battle a legend.

THE MOON WAS still high, the village asleep, when the blind man slipped out of the tavern. He moved with more agility and speed than was prudent, but Raeb was more concerned with putting distance between him and the town than maintaining his disguise.

He stuffed his opaque lenses in his pack, revealing solid black eyes with an elongated pupil the color of peridot. The timid demeanor fell off like a discarded cloak as he moved into the trees. Despite the dangers, he was much safer out here than in the village. Trees and deer didn't care about his incriminating eyes, or his history, or remember his passage like naïve townspeople—or strangers approaching him asking uncomfortable questions— would.

Still, the unexpected meeting in the tavern might be exactly what he needed. Whether the man succeeded in defeating the Bok'Tarong's bearer or not, it would slow down the sword. It might give him enough time to disappear.

Of course, the next to wield the Bok'Tarong would come after him, just as they always did.

And he would run, just as he always did.

The pattern had gone unbroken for over two centuries. Whenever one of the Taronese warriors got close to him, he'd either vanish or have them killed. He did his best to avoid the latter option, but sometimes it was necessary.

Sometimes several bearers passed before another tried to find him. But they were always watching for him, always waiting for him to show himself. Then the chase would resume yet again.

Raeb shook the thoughts from his mind and continued through the starlit trees. He'd lost this bearer, for the moment. And if the man from the tavern happened to kill him, so much the better. It would take the next bearer at least a month, maybe two, before finding the sword. Then at least another two months to pick up his trail.

If he was lucky, they wouldn't look for him. But Raeb had

stopped believing in luck a long time ago. It never seemed to work for him.

Except today. Perhaps it was a sign of things to come?

Raeb ground his teeth, shoving the concept from his mind. He couldn't afford to waste time on things like hope. Right now, he had to move.

Two months of relative safety. Maybe even four. Months where he wouldn't have to look over his shoulder every moment of every day. He could rest.

He wouldn't, though. At least not now. He didn't intend to be anywhere near here when the next Taronese warrior arrived.

*
**

LESS THAN A week had passed since Aeo found the village he'd been directed to. The tiny homes were so crowded by undergrowth and covered in moss he'd been within a stone's throw before he even knew he'd arrived.

He hadn't needed to enter the village to know this was the right one. The entire place was thick with melancholy and dread. The residents spent more time scrutinizing each other than speaking. No one got within an arm's length of another, and if someone approached too quickly they jumped as if poked in the back with a dagger. Though the surrounding forest was cool and peaceful, most people stayed behind solid oak doors as often as possible.

Since then he'd been surrounded by people who were moments, or years, away from the Madness. The uncertainty had driven everyone to a kind of madness of its own. Aeo had never seen a person, let alone an entire village, so poised on the edge of self-destruction.

He kept his distance from the villagers and their strange, distorted eyes, but it was like the Coming Madness had permeated the very trees. He couldn't escape the tension or fear in the air. More often than not, he found himself pacing or pushing his way through extra sword exercises just to keep busy. Just to do something—anything—besides waiting.

At long last, Aeo heard footsteps on the deserted forest road. He could only hope it was the Bok'Tarong, finally arriving to end this misery.

He made sure his sword was loose in its scabbard as he crept through the underbrush, keeping low and in the shadows so he wouldn't be seen. Little sunlight reached this deep into the forest, and the sweetness of loam and rot filled his nose and sat heavily on his tongue. Deep moisture made each breath an effort. He pushed leafy ferns out of his way, only to have them spring back into his face an instant later.

He couldn't wait to finish this and get back to the city.

The footsteps grew closer, but they didn't sound right. They weren't a warrior's purposeful stride. They were slower, more shuffling, like those of the old or infirm. Just a peddler, then, or some poor fool lost in the forest.

A moment later, a frail old man came into view. He hobbled down the road as if each step would be his last. His skin was blotchy with age spots and hung loose on his bones. His joints looked stiff and swollen. Yet he was dressed in a warrior's clothes, a baldric with a rosy gold buckle crossing the front of his chest.

Aeo snorted. *This* was his mark? Aeo the assassin, slayer of emperors and dragons, was contracted to kill an old man with a fancy sword? There had to be some mistake. This man couldn't be the undefeated warrior responsible for the hundreds, maybe even thousands, of deaths attributed to the Bok'Tarong.

Aeo waited, still and silent as a serpent, while the man passed by.

There was no mistake. This ancient man was either a thief or Aeo's target. Because slung across his back was the massive Bok'Tarong.

Aeo had never seen a weapon like it. Instead of a single blade extending from the hilt, the rosy gold metal split down the middle and opened into a gentle Y. One blade was slightly longer than the other, their edges wavy like a flamberge. They seemed to stick to the baldric without any kind of sheath or thongs to hold it in place. That confirmed it was indeed enchanted, though Aeo hoped there was more to it than that. A cheap trick to hold the Bok'Tarong wasn't what he'd been expecting.

Aeo didn't move until the man was out of sight. Only then did he creep out of the ferns, brush the rotted leaves and mud from his clothes, and follow him.

He'd never been so grateful for an abundance of trees. The man shuffled so slowly Aeo had to stop and hide several times in order to not overtake him. If the road had been open, he'd never have been able to avoid being seen.

He crouched behind an old fir, just beyond the first of the

houses, while the man entered the village. Aeo wasn't expecting much to happen—a brief conversation, maybe, before the man fled from the Coming Madness.

He didn't expect screaming.

Aeo sprinted into the village, unsheathing his sword as he ran. Could he have been so wrong? Could that old man be such a fearsome warrior that he walks into a village and people die? It might be coincidence—maybe someone had succumbed to the Madness—but Aeo couldn't make himself believe it.

The smells of cedar and wood smoke were drowned by blood and death as he entered the village outskirts. In the seconds it had taken him to catch up to the old man, two men and a woman were killed. Their dead eyes stared at him, empty of humanity, but still marked by the Coming Madness. Somehow that made them even more disturbing.

He knelt beside the bodies. A single slice across the throat to each. Clean kills. Aeo wasn't sure he'd have been able to manage as much in so short a time himself—and he could manage just about anything.

Another scream pierced the air, and Aeo ran toward it. Villagers were scattered through the area, some fleeing, others seeming at peace with their fate. Those who hadn't escaped fast enough littered the ground. Their blood splattered the wooden walls and painted the dirt crimson.

In the middle of all this was the old man and the Bok'Tarong, though he was hardly the same man Aeo had seen on the road. He moved with the grace of a dancer and the strength of a lifelong swordsman. The massive double-bladed sword glinted with rosy gold light as it passed from shadow to sunshine. With each swing, another victim was laid at the old man's feet.

For several breaths, Aeo could only watch in bewilderment. The man had been hardly able to walk down the road just moments ago. Now he was working that sword so brilliantly Aeo was, for the first time in many years, afraid he might not be able to defeat this opponent. What kind of magic was going on here? Aeo wasn't one to fear powers he didn't understand, but this was beyond anything he'd ever seen before.

While he marveled, five more villagers fell to the Bok'Tarong.

His grip tightened on his sword. This man was murdering unarmed civilians. That was enough to make Aeo's blood hot with rage. But these people were also touched by the Coming Madness. Their deaths were already scripted. Unless they were stopped they would cause immense damage, and take even more lives, before their suffering came to an end.

Massacre or mercy? Aeo couldn't decide.

Three more deaths. Two of them died screaming in terror. The other looked almost joyous as the Bok'Tarong carved through his throat.

Skull-crushing pain erupted in his mind as he hesitated. He was an assassin, the king's man, here on a contract. The morality of that contract wasn't his responsibility. The king had said this man must die.

He was charging forward, sword bared, before he'd even realized he was moving. Such was the nature of the Mage General's conditioning. When the king ordered a death, Aeo had to deliver. Whether he liked it or not.

He intercepted a swing of the Bok'Tarong with his own blade. The distinctive ring of metal on metal silenced the screams for just a moment. Confusion and disbelief and anger crossed the old man's face as he disengaged from Aeo's parry. He took a step back, then glanced aside at the escaping villagers. The move opened a small space under his arm, a direct line to his ribcage and his heart.

A clear shot. Aeo could run him through here and now and be done with it.

The temptation was gone in a second. Killing a man without a fight, without a chance to defend himself, was the coward's path. Aeo was no coward.

Besides, it was the fight Aeo craved. Not the kill.

The man turned back to Aeo. He swung the Bok'Tarong. Aeo parried, then slashed downward from the left. The man cocked his wrists, turning the sharp points of the Bok'Tarong toward the slash.

Aeo realized his mistake as his blade slid into the narrow Y of the Bok'Tarong and the man rotated the blades to capture it there.

Releasing his left hand from the hilt, the man jabbed his palm upward at the base of the nearest blade, turning the Bok'Tarong in a sudden spin and ripping the trapped sword from Aeo's hand. It flew end over end, landing with a *swish* in a large fern.

In a matter of seconds Aeo, the champion assassin, was disarmed.

He was too impressed to be scared. Just how powerful was this magic? If it could allow an ancient, frail man to defeat the greatest assassin in Arata so easily, he could only imagine what a true swordsman like himself could have done with it.

It wasn't a terrible last thought to have.

Aeo stood there, defenseless, with the Bok'Tarong leveled at his throat. But the man didn't strike. He just watched Aeo with no emotion on his face. His eyes looked distant, like a man who was talking to one person but listening to another.

Aeo took a step to the side, then another, inching his way to his fallen sword. The man followed his movements, keeping Aeo in his gaze. He could have cut Aeo down at any moment, but he didn't. A man of honor, this one. Aeo could respect that.

His blade stuck out of the fern like a massive thorn. Just out of reach.

As soon as he retrieved his sword, the man would almost surely strike. Aeo would, if their places were reversed. He had to be prepared to defend as soon as he picked up his weapon.

Aeo crouched beside his sword, his eyes on his enemy. He waited there for a moment, tensing his muscles, steadying his breathing. Then he sprung sideways, grasping the hilt of his sword as he rolled over it, coming back to his feet with the blade ready. Finally, something ferns were actually good for—cushioning a sudden fall.

Not even an eyeblink later, Aeo and the man were back to the battle.

They fell into the rhythm of a well-matched fight, with neither Aeo nor the man holding a clear advantage. Aeo grinned through the strain and the sweat. At long last, he'd found a worthy opponent. Not even the weapon masters of the king's army had offered this much of a challenge.

Since Aeo couldn't force his opponent back, he gave ground willingly. A few steps here, a step there, and Aeo was pushed out of the buildings and toward the trees. The man paused, glancing back at the emptied village. Only wood and wind remained in the streets. Every living being, Madness-touched human and animal alike, had fled from the master swordsmen.

The man finally betrayed some emotion, rage and frustration that Aeo had allowed his targets to escape. Aeo used that to his advantage, taunting him farther into the trees, and the man dutifully followed.

Here Aeo had an advantage. The close-growing trees inhibited the swing of the massive Bok'Tarong, but Aeo's much smaller shortsword could still be used effectively. He dashed around the trees, breaking his opponent's line-of-sight and hoping to circle around from behind.

The man was good. His dancer-like grace aided him in the tight quarters far better than Aeo had expected. Still, Aeo was used to skulking in shadows. He'd had plenty of practice in his years as an assassin.

They engaged in a few quick scuffles, a handful of strikes and parries from behind or around the trees. Each ended with Aeo breaking off and disappearing deeper into the woods.

Finally, he saw his opportunity. A thick stand of cedars clumped together and created a patch of darker shadows up ahead. A fallen trunk, its bark long since eaten away, was wedged between two of the trees at a steep angle. Its top disappeared into the leaves overhead.

Aeo sheathed his sword and climbed up the log, his boots

slipping on the thick moss, and pulled himself into the canopy. The woody scent of cedar tickled his nose. He stifled a sneeze.

Anyone chasing him would hesitate in this tiny clearing, taking an extra moment to peer into the deep shadows. Standing perfectly still and silent... and directly beneath Aeo. He couldn't have asked for a better spot to set up an ambush.

He moved through the trees, circling back the way he'd come, and jumped down.

His opponent came to the fallen log, his eyes going to it and the branches overhead. He noted the footprints Aeo had left, following their path with his eyes, and raised his double-bladed sword toward the canopy.

Aeo smirked. He knew this man would be smart enough to sense the ambush. With the reach of the Bok'Tarong and the man's uncanny reflexes, he might have even thwarted it. Given enough time, this man might have even defeated Aeo.

He stepped up behind the man and, with a silent apology, slid his blade between the man's ribs and pierced his heart.

The Bok'Tarong fell from his hand. He looked back at Aeo, his eyes asking a thousand questions as he crumpled to the ground. He never got to ask a single one.

Aeo knelt and wiped his bloody blade on the man's trousers before returning it to his belt. He paused over the man's body, giving what respect he could. A futile gesture, he knew, but he had to do something. Death was a part of the job, but he would never be immune to its sting.

After a moment his eyes moved to the gleaming rose-gold of the Bok'Tarong and his melancholy vanished. This might not be war, but spoils still went to the victor. And this magnificent sword was a bounty fit for a king. Or the world's greatest assassin.

He didn't even try to suppress his grin as he took his new sword.

I don't belong to you, a voice said in his mind.

Aeo stared at the blade. A talking sword? That was new. "Who are you?"

I am the Bok'Tarong, the voice replied. *I demand you return me to the Taronese at once.*

"Not a chance. You belong to me now."

You have no idea what you're dealing with. I and the Taronese have a mission. One we must complete if humanity has any chance of survival.

"What is that supposed to mean?"

You couldn't possibly understand. All you need to know is that I will never be your sword. You must return me to the Taronese.

"Like hell I will! I earned you fair and square."

I would hardly call murdering a man who'd done you no wrong fair.

Aeo didn't justify that with a reply. "You should be honored to be the chosen weapon of Aeo, the finest assassin in the world."

I was honored to partner with the Taronese and fight our battles. You bring nothing but disgrace to this sword and death to your people by stealing me. You will return me!

"Don't bet on it," Aeo muttered, snatching the baldric from the dead man's shoulder and slinging it over his own. He slammed the blades into their unusual sheath to drive the point home.

I won't help you, the sword said in his mind.

He turned his feet toward the road, leaving the small village and the dead man behind. Over the next few days he would put as much distance as possible between him and his victim, especially since he was bearing the Bok'Tarong now—an easy giveaway for anyone who may harbor some notion of vengeance. Or try to take his sword back.

He couldn't help but smile at his good fortune. The king would line his pockets with gold for his success. He had fought— and defeated—an opponent as skilled as he. Even the Mage General would have to recognize this achievement. But more than that, the weapon he had gained was the real treasure. The Bok'Tarong was more valuable and of higher quality than any sword he'd ever seen before. Sure, the voice inside the blades might be a problem, but he could manage. Sooner or later it would see there was no one better to bear such a sword than Aeo.

Just before sunset he made camp well off the road in a small glen surrounded by tall cedars. Thanks to a lucky trap a pair of skinned hares roasted over a crackling fire shortly afterward.

While he waited for his dinner to cook, Aeo held the Bok'Tarong before him. It was a magnificent weapon—sharp edges, seductive curves, gleaming metal. It was as fine as any sword he'd ever owned and as beautiful as any woman he'd ever had. Even the firelight seemed attracted to the Bok'Tarong, as thousands of tiny flames gleamed in the blades' rosy gold.

He stepped away from the fire and raised the sword. Despite its unusual design and disproportionate blades, the weight and balance were perfect. Aeo took a basic stance and swung the

Bok'Tarong.

The sword laughed at him. *The finest assassin in the world? A child no older than eight could wield me better than that.*

Aeo growled. He did, however, shift his grip on the hilt and spread his stance a little wider.

When the Bok'Tarong's pursed silence dragged on, Aeo knew he'd gotten it right.

Aeo's focus narrowed. His whole world was the blade. Strong, steady, and swift—the assassin's mantra looped through his mind as he went through a few steps. Strong, steady, and swift. And each stroke was exactly that.

He practiced late into the night, paying no mind to the deepening darkness or the smoke rising from his burnt dinner. His muscles trembled with exhaustion and sweat poured from his body, but still he practiced. Only when the stars winked out and the dusky grey of predawn lit the horizon did Aeo stop to sleep.

Even then, his hand remained around the hilt of the Bok'Tarong.

CHAPTER THREE

S ummer came to Arata, scorching her forests with humid heat and blaring sunshine. Aeo passed those months in a blur of travel, mundane tasks, and the blessed moments of practice with the Bok'Tarong.

Until now. The day he'd never thought would come.

Aeo woke, groaning as the now-familiar ache of rheumy joints assaulted him. It took him several moments to gather enough strength to sit. When he did, his bones grated and his muscles screamed at each tiny motion. That simple action exhausted him so much he would have flopped back to the ground, if that wouldn't have caused even more pain.

A few weeks ago, Aeo had been average height, stocky and muscular from a life of traveling and fighting. Now he was little more than a hunchbacked, jelly-muscled, blotchy-skinned skeleton. His military-short blond hair was gone. His eyesight, once sharp enough to spot game in the dense woods of Arata, was so clouded he couldn't distinguish one toe from another. He was old and decrepit and dying, though he was hardly past his third decade.

The dreams had warned him. They had plagued his sleep every night since he'd taken up the Bok'Tarong. They were always different, yet somehow always the same. Foreign images, people and places he'd never seen, passed by in flashes. In each scenario the Bok'Tarong played a central role, slaying evil and preserving the innocent. *Take me home,* the sword would say. *Return me to my true masters.*

He watched as the double-bladed sword passed through hundreds of years—and hundreds of wielders—in the pursuit of justice.

It was not lost on Aeo that all of the wielders exhibited the same curious features as the man he'd killed. They were all emaciated, arthritic, and none of them held the Bok'Tarong for long before they died.

Just like him.

It was the curse of this bloody sword. It was punishing him for slaying its last bearer. The voice in the blades never spoke to him anymore. When he wielded the sword, strength and energy flooded his body. He felt like himself. But the rest of the time, he was a ghost of the man he'd been.

And yet, despite everything it had done to him, he couldn't help but love the damned thing.

By the time he was too sore and lethargic to continue his work as an assassin, he'd been too enthralled by the Bok'Tarong to care. All that mattered was his time with the sword. Contracts, drink, even women seemed like a waste of time. Any moment not spent with the Bok'Tarong was a moment lost.

And that had led him here, to a small glade in the middle of the forest. It wasn't too far from the road. The young Aeo could have made it in less than a day, but it had taken him more than three days to reach it in his current state.

He stood, with a monumental effort, and unsheathed the gleaming sword. He stared at the twisted blades with as much hate as he could muster for the beautiful sword, but still his heart loved the Bok'Tarong.

"You have been the death of me," Aeo whispered. "And so you shall finish the job." He placed the pointed end of the long blade before his heart.

With the last ounce of strength in his emaciated muscles, he plunged the Bok'Tarong into his heart, stopping its beat forever.

✲

RAEB CAME TO another nondescript village along the road. He was aching and filthy from traveling, and though the sun was low in the sky the heat this far south was blistering. He'd have given his last cloak for a shady tree and a skin of cold water. Perhaps it was lucky there was no such thing around, since he didn't have a cloak to trade for them anyway.

His meeting with the man in the bar those weeks ago had been the last thing to work in his favor. Since then he'd suffered long days of hard travel and nights sleeping with no blanket and a half-full belly. Aratan patrols had stopped him several times, hoping to conscript him to the war. As if there wasn't a much bigger war they all fought every day. The Aratans faced this war with the Entana—with the "Coming Madness"—and didn't even realize it. Nor did they realize opaque lenses and searching hands didn't guarantee a man was blind and unfit for battle.

Perhaps he should have let them take him. Surely a Halkronar blade could release him from this never-ending torture called life.

But death itself wasn't the answer. He could die and still lose everything.

He had to make sure he died free.

There had to be a way. He'd fled this far south, past the mountains, out of Arata and into the shrubby desert of Starek. Part of him wished to go farther, across the sea to the barbarian lands, but he'd never find an answer there. If he wanted to gain his freedom, he had to stay here.

Besides, he wasn't sure if his leash would stretch that far.

Raeb kicked the dry dust at his feet. He was constantly running to buy himself more time. But for what? He didn't have a plan. All he had was one crazed, desperate idea. Turning it into a plan that wouldn't end up with him dead, insane, or worse wasn't looking good. Especially in a parched, desolate place like this.

But if he *could* find something, maybe he could end it forever.

Raeb sighed. And maybe he could grow wings and fly away from it all, to a land where gold grew on trees and rivers flowed with wine.

He ran a weary hand across the stubble on his chin and surveyed the village. It was little more than a clump of adobe houses along the road, stuck amongst the cactus like a wart among thorns. At least he spotted a tavern among them. He would be able to get some food and a little rest before having to move on tonight. Perhaps he might even hear word of the Bok'Tarong. The double-bladed sword made for good fireside tales. With a little listening and a few ales, he could usually keep decent track of his pursuers.

The tavern's common room was mostly empty, but it was still too early for the working folk to arrive. Raeb ordered a meal and sat at one of the tables, observing the few inhabitants from behind his blind man disguise. It never ceased to amaze him how little attention the general populace paid to the blind. Wearing his black lenses, he was virtually invisible.

A serving girl brought Raeb his food. She was almost too young to be working in a place like this, but her calloused expression showed she was not new to the job. She placed the plate on the table and tried to hide the fact that she was staring at Raeb. He pretended not to notice.

He did keep an eye on her, though. Something about her wasn't quite right. Her hair was dark like the natives, almost as dark as his, but her eyes were green and her complexion light like an Aratan. It wasn't common to find people who chose to live in Starek if they weren't born to it, but it wasn't unheard of, either.

Still, it was her actions more than her looks that didn't sit well with Raeb. Why hide your stare from a man who couldn't see it?

The night wore on and more people came to the tavern. He listened in on the daily chatter of old friends, courting couples, and grizzled old men with nothing better to do than complain. A few folks spoke of the stalemate growing more tense between Arata and Halkron up north. He heard many tales and jokes, but nothing about his pursuer or the Bok'Tarong. Still safe—for now.

He left the town anyway. After so many decades of running he couldn't bear staying in one place for too long.

Now that the sun had set, a hint of coolness touched the air. The breeze smelled fresh and clean in a way it never smelled in Arata. Above him, the stars were white and brilliant against a coal-black sky.

Just for a minute, Raeb understood why people chose to live here.

Then the eerie whine-yip of coyotes set the hairs on the back of his neck tingling and broke the trance. This wasn't a place to let your guard down. The desert might be beautiful at times, but it was raw and dangerous in more ways than he could count. It didn't forgive distractions.

Raeb heightened his senses, forced himself to become more aware of his surroundings. Crickets chirruped from every direction. Ambient heat from the adobe homes wafted into the night. A slight shuffle as someone unaccustomed to hiding tried to stay out of sight.

He tensed. The Taronese couldn't have found him already. But then, this couldn't be the Taronese. If it was, he never would have heard them.

Raeb faced a nearby alley and stared into the shadows. "What are you doing here?"

A moment passed. Then the serving girl from the tavern stepped into the moonlight. "I think we can help each other."

"I doubt that."

He started walking away, but the girl grabbed his arm. "I know you aren't blind."

"Observant. Good for you. Now go away."

"Don't you want to hear me out first?"

"No."

"But…"

"I cannot and will not help you. And you have nothing that can help me," he said. He pulled his arm out of hers and walked away. He paused after a few steps. The girl had started to slink after him again. "Do not follow me."

"Why not?" she asked.

He turned toward her, scowling and not quite meeting her eyes. "Because I'm dangerous."

The girl scrutinized him with that strange stare of hers. "I don't believe you."

Raeb allowed his lenses to slip and reveal his black, peridot-pupil eyes. "Believe it." He turned to leave again.

"You don't scare me, you know."

His hand strayed to the unique weapon he wielded. If she, or anyone, knew about this, they'd be afraid. It even scared *him*. The Bok'Tarong might be the most powerful enchanted weapon in the world, but it wasn't the only one. And some enchantments were worse than others.

He kept his pace strong, refusing to look back. The night swallowed the village behind him. Out here the desert was still and silent. There was nothing but an expansive emptiness and millions of stars overhead. The silence was unnerving. He felt too exposed, too vulnerable. Too alone.

The sound of light footsteps coming from behind made him cringe. Perhaps not *too* alone.

The girl trotted up, slowing enough to keep pace with him as if she'd been invited along.

"You aren't very good at listening, are you?" he asked.

"My father always said I was too stubborn for my own good."

"I can see that," Raeb growled. "What do you want?"

"I'm coming with you." She shifted a small pack from one shoulder to the other, perhaps hoping to impress him with her forethought.

"No. You aren't."

"Yes, I am," she said, paying no mind to the authority in his voice.

"You don't know me. You don't know where I'm going or why I'm going there. And you aren't going to find out."

"You don't understand. I am coming with you."

It took all of his willpower not to lash out and hit the girl. "Go. Away."

"Look, I'm not leaving. I'm not sure what exactly you are, but I know you're different than the rest of us."

Raeb's head snapped up. "What do you mean?"

"You aren't like all the others taken by the Entana. You might have been at one time, but now you're… special."

Panic, like he was punched in the gut, choked him. "How do you know that?"

"I can tell."

Raeb glared at her. That didn't tell him anything. It could be a bluff, for all he knew. Perhaps she didn't know anything after all, and was hoping he would give something away. That would make much more sense than whatever she was suggesting.

He turned off the road, trudging through prickly cactus and shrubs dried crispy by the sun. The girl followed, continuing to chatter.

"They've lost their hold over you. They can't control you anymore, and that's what I want. I'll help you if you help me."

"How could you help me?"

He heard her footsteps stop, then clanging as she rummaged through her pack. Raeb continued to hike through the dry land. Maybe if he got far enough, she wouldn't be able to find him in the night.

A soft yellow glow cast his shadow in dark relief before him. He turned back to find the girl grinning in triumph, a lantern held high before her. "How about a light, for starters?"

She had spunk, he'd give her that. He carefully kept his face impassive.

She closed the distance between them, holding the lantern down near their feet. She stood as tall as she could, which came to Raeb's shoulder, and looked directly into his strange Entana eyes. She didn't flinch at the sight. Impressive. Most people cowered from his gaze, if they ever saw it.

"I know you're an Entana-taken," she said quietly. "You have some business with them, and I'm guessing it's something you don't want them to know about. Otherwise you wouldn't be skulking around like this. And if you're trying to hide from the Entana, then you need me. I know more about them than anyone."

"I doubt that," he muttered. She cocked her head, curious, but Raeb refused to elaborate. "Why do you believe you have this special knowledge?"

She poked a finger at her temple. "Because they're in here."

That made Raeb pause. He peered at her and began to notice the subtle signs the Entana left on their victims. Paranoia. Exhaustion. A sense of hyper-alertness even weariness couldn't dim. "You don't have the eyes of a -taken," he said.

She sighed and closed her eyes. Her shoulders slumped. Relaxation spread through her muscles, and a vague shimmering enveloped her. A glamour, sliding away like water off a rock. Once the magic was dispelled, she opened her eyes.

Entana-taken eyes. Shadowed and haunted, their color a bit off. The pupils were slightly elongated and no longer true black. The irises were more gray than white. She was indeed possessed by the Entana, and had been for a long time.

"Got some rogue mage to give you an illegal glamour charm, eh? How much did that cost you?"

"It's not a charm," she said. "It's mine."

"Yours? As in… your magic?"

She nodded.

"Entana can't take mages."

"I'm not a mage. I'm not powerful enough. My application to the Mage's Academy was rejected in record time. They wouldn't even see me. They said my power was just a fluke and that I should take up street entertainment and sleight-of-hand."

"That's the Mage's Academy for you. Bastards through-and-through."

She chuckled, but there was very little joy in the sound.

Raeb looked around, even though he couldn't see much in the darkness. It didn't matter. He wasn't really looking anyway.

"So your magic wasn't strong enough to keep the Entana at bay."

"Obviously not." Her tone was as cold and distant as the stars.

Raeb nodded, but her slight shift in position and defensive tone said much more than her words. There was more to that story she didn't want him to know. Interesting.

"The point is I have some magic power. I am a -taken, but I'm not their slave. I can slow the Entana down so they don't take me as fast. I can see them. Sometimes I can even hear them."

That piqued his attention. People couldn't defend themselves from the Entana. All they could do was wait until they were fully -taken or too lost in madness to care. The Entana were untouchable, a mystery that murdered without any way to protect against them.

But here was this girl, a minor mage at best, an Entana-taken who could see and hear her tormentors. Raeb had been researching the -taken for two centuries and never found anything like this before. If she was that in touch with the Entana, then maybe she *could* help him. She might be the key he'd been looking for to gain his freedom. If she could really do what she claimed, then she was right. He might need her.

But that also meant she was dangerous, to herself and to everyone around her.

Raeb scrubbed his face in his hands. Everything in him warned against taking this girl with him. He'd been a loner for decades now, and the last time he'd taken on a partner he'd carried the guilt of her death for years. He couldn't afford a liability like that.

But if what she said was true, he might never find a way to freedom without her. "What's your name?"

"Saydee."

"Do you have any skills?"

"I'm a really good cook."

"I meant useful skills."

"Cooking is useful!"

Well, he couldn't argue with that. "How about combat skills?"

"I can look really threatening with a dagger."

Raeb raised an eyebrow. "You're a minor mage who can cast a glamour to hide her Entana eyes and all you can do is wave a dagger around?"

She shrugged, smiling brightly.

He leveled a stare at her. *I'm going to regret this.*

He turned his back to her without a word, pushing the entire situation from his mind and focusing his attention on forging a safe path through the cactus. If only his life was as easy to navigate as the desert.

The light from Saydee's lantern danced at his back as the girl followed.

Chapter Four

Aeo groaned as consciousness returned. This had to be the worst hangover in history, and he would know. He'd had his fair share over the years.

Then he remembered. The Bok'Tarong. The strike to his heart. He remembered falling to the ground, the coldness creeping through his limbs, the blackness of oblivion swallowing him. He remembered dying.

What the hell?

For several minutes he lay still, his mind reeling. Was this what death was? Existing in nothingness? Or was he a ghost? He wasn't exactly an expert, but he didn't *feel* dead. Not entirely.

Then again, he didn't exactly feel *alive*, either. In some way he couldn't explain, he felt… less than human.

Could it get any worse? The Bok'Tarong had stolen his strength, his pride—his entire identity—but had refused to take his life. Instead it had left him in this… place… to suffer. Not quite dead, not quite alive, abandoned in an empty purgatory for the rest of time.

[Or maybe you simply don't belong here.]

The thought startled Aeo. Where had it come from? It was like someone had whispered directly into his brain.

[Hundreds of years and now *you*. You've destroyed everything.] The voice-that-wasn't-a-voice sounded quieter now. Weaker. Like it was struggling to insult Aeo one last time.

Oh shit.

He knew that voice. He'd listened to it patronize and insult him and demand to be taken home for weeks.

[Your greed has killed me. And without me, humanity is doomed.]

He wasn't dead, or a ghost, or anything he'd feared. He was in the blade.

He was the Bok'Tarong.

Now he just had to figure out of that was a good thing or a bad thing.

Hello? Aeo called. *Can you hear me?*

Silence. Aeo waited, called again, waited some more. Nothing. But this wasn't like the Bok'Tarong's stubborn refusal to answer him. He knew what that felt like. This was more like it was no longer there at all.

Damn it, don't leave me alone like this.

The voice left him alone. Horribly, maddeningly, utterly *alone*.

*
**

TIME PASSED. AEO couldn't tell if days or weeks went by. Then again, he couldn't tell much of anything inside the sword. It was dark, he was alone, and the only thing he could feel was his sanity slipping away. He would gladly trade whatever time he had left for a single scent, a solitary image, one brief touch. Anything besides the oppressive silence and blackness of the Bok'Tarong.

His greatest dream—to be one with the blade—had become his own personal nightmare.

An eternity later, a faint speck of light entered his vision. No brighter than an ember, no larger than a pinprick, but Aeo stared as if the sun itself had just risen. Was it madness setting in at last, or had something truly broken through his cage? He didn't dare look away from the light, in case it wasn't there when he looked back.

A firm hand grasped his middle and Aeo's senses exploded into being. Suddenly he could see and hear and feel and for a moment he couldn't process it all. So much sensation, so much *existence*. If metal could shed tears, Aeo would have cried.

He'd been found. He wasn't alone anymore. Someone had come along and picked him up and…

And *damn*. He'd thought the pinprick of light was beautiful?

Her hair fell in tight ringlets, warm brown mixed with fiery red. Streaks of crimson ran through her brown eyes as well. Powerful, well-trained muscles enhanced her figure rather than hid it. Her clothes were made of soft leathers and fitted to her form—hunter's garb. Around her upper arm she wore an intricate band of carved, opalescent green stone that glittered in the sunshine.

"Bok'Tarong, I have found you at last!" she breathed, raising the sword before her. Her hands were gentle, as if handling a fragile, priceless treasure. "I've followed your call for weeks." She rested her forehead on the wide face of the blade, sending a shiver through Aeo. It felt as if she'd caressed every inch of his body with silken hands and soft lips.

The warrior-woman pulled away from the blade almost instantly. Her eyes widened, then narrowed in suspicion. "You are not Taronese," she said. "Who are you?"

Aeo, he replied, not knowing whether he said or thought the word.

"I don't understand. You can't be the spirit of the blades. They are wise and instruct the bearer in the ways of the Bok'Tarong."

Aeo wouldn't have called that voice 'wise'. What had happened to it? *I think I might have evicted it,* he thought. He hadn't heard a peep from it in the time he'd been in the sword, and its ominous last words didn't bode well for its return.

The warrior-woman stared at him. "You spoke with the spirit of the blades?" She looked up, sighing and casting her eyes about. "Start from the beginning. How have you, uninitiated and unworthy, joined with the Bok'Tarong?"

Aeo could feel the rage building beneath her confusion. Her hands tightened around him as she waited for an answer. He was tiptoeing a line he dared not cross. *I won the sword from a man and later killed myself with it,* he explained.

"You won the sword?"

He'd hoped she would let him skip over this part, but he didn't dare refuse to answer that tone. *I'm the king's assassin. This man was my target.*

She pursed her lips. "Was the man your target, or the

Bok'Tarong?"

Aeo shuddered. Her voice had gone cold and quiet, like a predator before the kill. *The bearer. I was told the sword would be my reward.*

For a moment, there was no reply but frigid rage. "How did he die?"

I lured him into a trap and stabbed him when he was following a false trail.

Her grip tightened until Aeo gasped and choked. How could he choke without a throat, or the need to breathe? Nevertheless, the warrior-woman's hand felt like it was clamped around his stomach, squeezing until he'd explode. "You should have at least allowed him a death from the spirit blades. Then his life would have ended the way every Taronese warrior has prepared for. Instead you cast his life away as if it was worthless and took his place in the Bok'Tarong!" She grit her teeth, visibly trying to control the boiling rage within her. "Do you have any idea what a terrible crime you've committed?"

Aeo sat speechless before the warrior-woman's anger. He didn't know if it was possible for him to die again, but he was certain this woman would kill him if he misspoke now.

"When the bearer of the Bok'Tarong is killed, his spirit is taken into the blades. It's a process we've been trained for, one that requires a great deal of strength and submission to accomplish. How *your* worthless spirit managed it is beyond me." Her hand flexed around the hilt, as if wanting to punch him. "The knowledge of the bearer is combined with those who came before. Every single warrior to fight the Entana since the blades were created. It's a guide for the current bearer, a master and teacher with centuries of experience and knowledge. And in one selfish act you have *evicted* it?"

Sadness now mixed with the anger in her voice. Aeo wasn't often shamed, but he felt sheepish now.

"What else did you destroy when you forced your way into the spirit blades? Does the magic of the Bok'Tarong still survive? If your invasion has destroyed that, too..."

The voice's final words rang through Aeo's memory. *Your greed has killed me. And without me, humanity is doomed.* He didn't dare repeat them aloud. Not while this woman was so close to wringing the life out of him.

It can't all be lost, Aeo said. *If the magic was gone, how am I still stuck in here?*

She glared at him, as if astounded he'd dared to speak. Her crimson-streaked eyes burned with rage. "You have defiled the sacred Bok'Tarong. You have obliterated the wisest, most extensive resource on the Entana in the entire world. Because of your greed, you may have doomed every human alive to the fate of the -taken."

It was eerie, how she repeated the voice almost word-for-word. She couldn't have heard his thoughts. Could she? *I'll bet we can figure something out,* he said. Anything to lighten the mood — and her suffocating grip.

She paused, taking a deep breath to calm the anger growing in her voice. When she continued, her tone had gone cold and quiet. It was far more frightening that way. "This isn't a joke, assassin. The world is at war, and I don't just mean the Halkronar invasion in the west. Our entire race is at risk. If we don't stop the Entana, they could consume the minds of every human in existence. The Bok'Tarong is the only defense we have, and you treated it as some kind of valuable trinket to add to your collection. Now you may have destroyed it as well. The very least you could do is shut up and try not to ruin anything else."

The warrior-woman took the baldric from Aeo's body—he did his best not to look too hard—and buckled it across her back. When she slid the sword into the odd, strapless sheath and released the hilt, Aeo was locked inside the blades once again. But the steady light of her presence remained. With it he could make out shadows of the world around him, though color and sound were gone.

It was better than nothing, Aeo had to admit, though his heart ached and his mind reeled.

What had he done?

*
**

IT WAS STILL difficult for Aeo to distinguish time and distance, but the shadows gave him some idea of their surroundings. It looked like night was approaching and they were cutting through the brush, probably looking for a spot to camp.

Aeo was starting to sort through the deluge of new sensations now that the warrior-woman had found him. There was a strange kind of connection between them. He could sense her emotions and feel her heartbeat. He could even hear a few of her thoughts if he concentrated.

Can you hear me, too? Aeo thought.

"Yes." Her tone said she wasn't happy about that.

What's your name?

She didn't answer, but he heard her thoughts say, *Dragana.*

Aeo wasn't sure if he should reply to a thought. But then again, she heard his thoughts too. Fair's fair. *I'd have figured it out sooner or later. No need to be coy.*

Dragana sighed and pulled the Bok'Tarong from its sheath. Aeo could now see her clearly, and she looked directly at the blades as she spoke. "There will be little we won't share in one way or another. The relationship between the Bok'Tarong and the wielder is a partnership that binds the two souls together. Over time this bond will get stronger, until we will be two minds in one soul."

Aeo could feel her disgust. She didn't like the idea of being bonded with someone who had hijacked his place into the Bok'Tarong.

"Right now we can read emotions and a few surface thoughts. In time, as we get attuned to each other" — Aeo thought she might be sick at the thought—"our deep thoughts will be open to us both. Since I have a selfish, arrogant spirit to deal with instead of the true spirit of the Bok'Tarong—"

Hey!

"—we must set up boundaries. No digging into my thoughts. No searching for answers I will not offer. If I retreat from conversation, you do not follow me. Leave me in peace. Do you understand?"

Fine. As long as those rules apply to me, too.

"You have nothing to worry about. I already hear more of your thoughts than I care to. I will not seek out more." She lowered the blade, holding it in a loose grip at her side as she surveyed a tiny glade they'd come across. They wouldn't find a much better to spend the night, so she started clearing away the underbrush in order to make camp. "Even so, there are some things we cannot help but share. Everything we experience from now on will be experienced together. It will be useless to try to deny what we hear or feel."

All right, Aeo thought. *So why are you still hiding so much from me? Don't think I can't tell.*

"I said everything from now on is to be shared. I don't want to chat and play 'get to know you.' I don't want you to know me. And you are a disgraceful usurper. That is all I need to know of you."

You aren't the nicest girl in the world either, Dragana. You could at least pretend to sympathize with me.

She paused, stunned, then kicked a fallen branch from her path. "Sympathize! You murdered an innocent man, stole his weapon, and took his place among the honored ancestors of the Bok'Tarong. Why would I feel sorry for you?"

You never stopped to think about what the Bok'Tarong did to me, did you? It stole my health and my life. I had a place in the world that I worked very hard to gain, and I thrived there. I've been reduced to nothing because of this damned sword.

"Becoming the spirit of the Bok'Tarong is much more than nothing," Dragana replied. "It is a great honor, and one any Taronese warrior would happily accept."

I don't feel honored or happy in here.

"You earned your fate."

I guess now you'll tell me to shut up and deal with it.

"More or less."

Aeo grumbled something rude and uncomplimentary, and Dragana sent an equally scathing remark right back to him.

If he hadn't been so mad at her, he would have laughed.

All right. Since you seem incapable of being polite, why don't you tell me where we're going instead?

She dropped her pack and plopped down, halfheartedly stacking some logs for a fire. "The Taronese have heard rumors of Entana-taken being seen more often near the lines of battle. Our job is to see if the rumors are true and take care of the problem if it is."

What are Entana-taken?

Dragana growled. "The spirit of the Bok'Tarong doesn't know what the Entana are. How could this have happened?" She sighed to gather her patience before continuing. "The Entana are a race of beings that feed on the consciousness of humans. Once they invade a mind, they consume all the emotions and memories within. The person—the Entana-taken—loses their sense of self until they become nothing more than a mad vessel for spreading the Entana to others."

That sounds an awful lot like the Coming Madness.

"It is."

Aeo's mind went blank for a moment. *Wh-what?*

"What you call the Coming Madness is what happens when the Entana infect a person's mind. Those who suffer from it are the -taken."

Your people have known what the Coming Madness is all this time? Why didn't you ever tell anyone?

"Do you think it would have done any good? How do you

think people would react if they knew there were spiritual parasites waiting to possess their minds and consume their memories until they were empty of anything human, then let loose to spread those parasites to others? And that there is no way to protect yourself, or those you love, from these parasites?"

Aeo had seen the fear in people's eyes when they realized a killer was in their midst. It turned them into mindless animals, full of terror and panic and no intelligent thoughts. If they knew killers lurked in their minds...

"You see it," Dragana said, perhaps reading the images from his mind. "There would be mayhem. People would panic. They'd become paranoid, dangerous even, for no reason. They can't do anything to keep themselves safe. It's better they don't understand."

So, if there's no way to protect yourself from these Entana, what are we doing?

"We are here to kill them."

Now that sounds better. You'll be happy to have me around to help before long.

"Don't bet on it. I don't relish the company of arrogant asses. Besides, because of you, I'm not even sure we *can* kill them anymore."

What do you mean?

"The Bok'Tarong was made to destroy the Entana. The magic holding your spirit within the blades is the only thing that can truly kill one of them. So let's hope you didn't damage that magic when you stole your place into the Bok'Tarong."

How will we know if the magic is still intact? Aeo asked.

"Find me an Entana-taken. Then you can tell me."

Chapter Five

Raeb woke to the smell of breakfast and the sound of Saydee humming. The brutal, unfiltered sunshine was almost as painful as the knots in his back. He'd never enjoyed sleeping on the ground, but at least in Arata he could curl up among moss and plants. Here there was nothing but rocks, dust, and scorpions.

He cracked his neck and stretched his back as he sat. Saydee looked none the worse from a night in the open desert. She sat at the fire, cooking and singing quietly to herself, as if she'd done so a million times before. She gave no indication she was at all uncomfortable with Raeb's begrudging acceptance of her company.

As he inhaled the delicious scent of real food—not the dried, tasteless supplies he had in his pack—his decision to let her stay was a little easier to stomach.

"Good morning," she said. She piled a plate high with food and handed it to him. She even smiled.

Oh great. A morning person.

"What's your name?" Saydee asked as she sat across from him.

"Raeb," he said around a mouthful of bacon and flatbread.

"It's nice to meet you, Raeb."

He grunted.

She took a small bite. "So, are you going to tell me what you're trying to hide from the Entana?"

"Can't you leave a man to his breakfast in peace? I just woke up, you know."

"-Taken who try to act without the Entana's knowledge want one of a few things. I want to hear from you which one you're after."

He swallowed. "So that's how it's gonna be, is it?"

She just watched him, waiting for an answer.

Raeb put down his plate, searching for something to say. The truth was... complicated. More so than he wanted to admit, especially to this girl he knew nothing about. Even admitting the truth to himself was dangerous. You never knew when the Entana would decide to pay your juiciest thoughts a visit.

But if he didn't tell her, he couldn't use her. He'd proven time and time again he couldn't do this alone.

Besides, maybe he owed her a little something for the food.

"I'm going to destroy the Entana." Saying it aloud made his still-undigested breakfast roil.

Saydee laughed, and Raeb was surprised at the bitterness in it. "You and every other newly -taken. It's a hopeless dream."

"Not for me. I'm going to do it."

She returned to her breakfast, less than impressed. "And I'm sure you have a brilliant plan no one's ever thought of before."

"Something like that."

She glanced at him, not turning away from her plate. Something in his face must have convinced her, because a hint of curiosity snuck into the cynicism. "How are you going to do it?"

"Let's just say I'm onto something. I haven't been able to find a way to make it work until now. But I think you're right." The words left a sour taste in his mouth. "I need your help."

Saydee's eyes sparkled. Raeb could almost hear the "I told you so" in that expression. Now he remembered why he always traveled alone.

She put down her plate. "What do you need me to do?"

He stalled for a minute, looking around in the too-bright morning. Nothing but desert scrub all the way to the mountains to the north—the mountains he'd crossed just a few weeks ago, and the ones he'd likely be crossing again soon, girl in tow. "You said you can hear the Entana?"

"What, you want me to eavesdrop on them and hope they mention how to kill them or something?"

He ignored her sarcasm. "-Taken have a one-way connection from the Entana to their minds. But if what you say is true—and I'm not sure it is—something about your magic makes your connection special. It's two-way. The Entana can get to your mind but you can do the same to them. I've never seen anything like it before."

"My magic did this?"

"It's the one thing that's special about you, so it makes sense that's what caused it." Saydee scowled, but Raeb ignored it. "If you'd allow me to ride that connection, I might find a way to destroy them."

"What do you mean?"

"The Entana aren't physical beings. They're spiritual parasites. That's why we can't find them or remove them. If I sent my spirit along the connection from your mind to the Entana infecting you, I might be able to find them and their weakness."

Saydee stopped him with an upraised hand. "Wait a minute," she said, closing her eyes and shaking her head. "What are you talking about? Sending your spirit along my connection? You can't do something like that."

"You'd be surprised what I can do," he replied. "I've learned a lot in my time, and I've had some... interesting teachers. They've taught me some tricks."

"That's not what I meant. I mean you can't do it because it's suicidal. Sending your spirit outside your body? You might as well give in to the Entana now."

Raeb glanced over to his pack, where his enchanted blade lay hidden. "It isn't the smartest thing to do, I'll admit. But I'm sure I can do it."

"Why?"

Because I've done it before. "I just know."

Saydee bit her lip as she sorted through his proposal. "So you would tear your spirit out of your body?"

Raeb nodded.

"And then follow this special connection in my head to the Entana."

He nodded again.

"Are you out of your mind?"

"Apparently."

She stared at him with that same unnerving, penetrating gaze she'd used in the tavern. "You know, I believe you might actually be crazy."

Raeb shrugged, picking up his plate and resuming his meal. "Stranger things have happened."

Saydee laughed, this time without the bitterness. "Ain't that the truth." She sobered quickly, looking at Raeb. "I've seen a lot of magic in my time, and a lot of horrible things magic has done. But this has got to be one of the most reckless, insane plans I've ever heard."

Raeb didn't reply right away. Her statement of seeing horrible magicks, spoken so calmly, sent a chill up his spine. This girl—for she looked like little more than that—had a darker past than Raeb would have guessed. He couldn't help but wonder what he'd gotten himself into.

"If this plan succeeds, and you don't get lost in spiritual oblivion in the process," she said, "could we really destroy the Entana?"

Raeb nodded.

"Are you sure?"

"No," he said, compelled to honesty by the intensity of Saydee's eyes. "But I'll do everything in my power to make it happen, no matter the cost."

They stared at each other for a moment, gauging the other. Then Saydee nodded. "Do it."

"Saydee, there are dangers to you as well. Even *attempting* to send my spirit along your connection could break it, and I have no idea what that would do to your mind. It could drive you insane or leave you catatonic. It could kill us both in a heartbeat. Not to mention we'll be shining a beacon on the uniqueness of your mind. If the Entana take notice of it, they will stop at nothing to eliminate it."

"What's my other option? To do nothing? Wait until I become fully -taken?" Her tone held equal parts anger and hysteria as she gestured wildly. "I'd rather die trying to get rid of this thing in my head than lose my mind and waste my last thoughts wondering if I could have prevented that from happening."

Again, that surprising strength. This girl was far more than some innocent little tavern wench. "All right. I'll need time to research and prepare. Until I'm ready, we should set aside some time each morning to spar. Our skills will need to be at their best."

"Why? We can't fight the Entana with blades and fists, Raeb."

"It isn't the Entana I'm thinking of," he replied. "We need to be able to defend ourselves from the Taronese."

"Who are they?"

"Have you heard of the Bok'Tarong?" He very carefully kept his tone neutral.

She scoffed. "Old wives' tales. There's no enchanted blade that can kill Entana."

"Yes, there is. It's real, and the Taronese are its bearers. They're likely on my trail by now, and when they find me they aren't going to hesitate to kill me and anyone with me."

A trickle of fear entered her expression. "You mean me."

"You're a -taken too. If they so much as see you, you're already dead."

"But we're trying to destroy the Entana, just like them. Shouldn't we work together, since we want the same thing?"

Raeb stood, turning his back to Saydee. If only she knew what she was saying. "They'd never believe two -taken would take action against the Entana. Even if they could believe it, we'd be dead long before we could explain our intentions." Raeb removed an overlarge dagger, vaguely leaf-shaped, from his pack and passed it to her. "If they find us, we have to be prepared to fight."

"But I don't know anything about fighting!"

"Then you'll need to learn. Otherwise, neither of us will make it very far."

Saydee's eyes spoke a world of fears as she took the dagger. "I still think we should try to convince these Taronese to work with us."

"Try saying that when the Bok'Tarong is slicing through your throat."

✳

DAWN BURST INTO glorious color when Dragana pulled Aeo from his sheath. Chirping birds filled the silence, and leaves glowing with golden light cast away the shadows. He took a deep breath, expecting the freshness of dew and morning breezes. Instead, he smelled nothing. He was still a sword, and his senses were limited. *It's better than nothing.*

"Come. It's time for practice."

Dragana sat, crossed her legs, and placed the sword in her lap. For several long moments she simply breathed, clearing her mind. Aeo had never been one for meditation, but feeling the peace suffusing Dragana's mind, he wondered if maybe he'd missed out on something.

She stood, removed her cloak, and bent into some simple stretches. Her arms were covered with tiny goosebumps. Was autumn approaching?

A breeze opened a small window in the canopy above, allowing a brief beam of sunshine to rest on Dragana. The carved stone band circling her biceps glittered in the light. Somehow Aeo knew it wasn't just a fashion choice.

What is that on your arm? Aeo asked.

"It is the carving of my spirit," she replied.

What does that mean?

Dragana growled as she grit her teeth. She didn't answer, but her memories regarding the carving surfaced. She had been drugged, as custom dictated, to prevent any conscious thought from tampering with the pureness of the carving. It was only her spirit, her true self, in control. She had woken days later with a pounding headache and incredible weakness in her body. Her arm burned where the carving of her spirit was seated.

What is it for?

Another image, this one tinged with uncertainty and a myriad of emotions, tried to form. Aeo couldn't make sense of it. It was a person—no, two people?—and some very powerful magic. Aeo sensed a lot of vulnerability surrounding that armband, and hope and fear…

A wall of anger and embarrassment blacked out the images. Dragana cursed at him, burying memories of her past under single-minded focus. She narrowed her thoughts to this moment, this task, as she swept the blades in a fluid circle. Her mind grew blank as she moved through the dance of the sword, her motions graceful and smooth. Her muscles worked in harmony to execute each step with precision. Her thoughts traveled back to her days of training, and Aeo caught glimpses of a grand wooden temple, pristine dojos, and a life of learning and fighting and perfecting. It was a life she'd loved.

But it was a life without family, with rivalries rather than friendships. A life without laughter.

Dragana focused on her routine, closing off her thoughts. Aeo didn't object—he knew how hard it was to share a past like that. His own childhood, such as it was, had never been shared with anyone. The filthy city gutters, street gangs, and fighting for survival were a far cry from Dragana's training, but both had learned the same lessons. Fight well, trust no one but yourself, always remain a warrior no matter what. His brief time in the king's army, his conditioning under the Mage General, and then his most recent life as an assassin had only emphasized those lessons.

Dragana's step faltered, and Aeo knew he'd distracted her. His own secret past had leaked into her thoughts. He felt as exposed as if he'd been caught naked in the middle of the king's court.

They both turned their thoughts from anything personal, but

Aeo didn't forget those impressions. What he'd seen and felt gave him a much clearer picture of this warrior-woman. *Who'd have thought it? We aren't that different after all.*

The morning routine was of a different style than Aeo's had been, but it felt familiar. He found himself anticipating Dragana's movements. He knew when her stance was a little too narrow or the blade held lower than it should be. A thought from him helped her guide the blades into their exact position, and his strength helped her hold him steady. He spoke his mantra—strong, steady, swift—and heard Dragana repeat it in her mind.

They were one warrior, joined in battle.

When Dragana brought the practice to a close, Aeo was filled with elation—both his and hers. The joy of being wielded by a master overwhelmed him. Aeo had never felt so complete or so content. This was what he was meant to do.

Dragana's thoughts echoed his. *This is what I was meant to do.*

They stood together, warrior and blade, sharing the moment. Dragana's thoughts lingered on the Bok'Tarong, then soured when she thought of the assassin in the sword. Aeo felt her simmering rage whenever she remembered who he was and how he'd gotten his place in the blades. Her joy curdled, the warmth she'd felt toward him turned cold, and she slipped him back into his sheath. "You don't deserve this," she whispered as she knelt to pack up her camp.

After what I've gone through, I absolutely deserve this. You may have grown up in that little temple of yours, but I clawed my way up in life. I wasn't handed my knowledge like you were. I sweat and bled for every scrap. Without my blade I had no life, so I treated it like my life.

You should be grateful you have me to help you in this damned sword.

"You think this was handed to me? Skill like this isn't just absorbed, you idiot. I sweat and bled just as much as you did. But my knowledge came with wisdom, unlike yours. You can hack and destroy on a whim, but I have a mission. A destiny. This blade is supposed to understand that. You'll never be able to fathom what that means because you can't understand the concept of battling for a cause or battling with honor."

If Aeo still had a body, he'd have reached for his sword. *How dare you accuse me of having no honor!*

She kicked dirt over the extinguished fire and slung her pack over her shoulder. "You were an assassin. You killed for money, without regard for whether your target deserved to die. That is the lowest and least honorable profession I've ever heard of."

Those who make enemies but are too weak or too stupid to defend themselves deserve to die. Dragana started to interrupt, but Aeo didn't let her. *The men I killed were murderers, unjust rulers, traitors. They knew they had enemies, and they knew their lives were in jeopardy because of what they'd done. Did they take action, hire bodyguards? No. Some of them even refused to carry weapons in their arrogance. These are the men I killed. And I didn't sneak in amongst the shadows and slaughter them in their sleep like a coward, either. Each knew I was there, and they knew my intent. They were given the opportunity to defend themselves, and they failed.*

"Oh yes, that changes everything," she said. "It isn't wrong to kill them as long as they know I'm going to do it."

I'm an assassin, Dragana, not a bloody priest! I did the best I could with what I was.

"You could have done something other than killing people for money."

Could I? By the time I was nineteen I'd made such a name for myself I drew the attention of the king himself. I was pulled from the life I'd created and trained as his personal assassin. Do you have any idea what it's like to be conditioned by the crown? Years of training, of magic remolding and retraining your brain, of being forced to carry out orders you'd never consider obeying on your own? You can't even begin to understand the compulsions they put on me. I couldn't have gotten out of that life any more than I can get out of this sword.

Even so, I never killed anyone who wasn't my target. Whatever you may think, I didn't wallow in blood and murder whoever crossed my path. My honor demanded that of me, and I kept to it.

She paused at the description of his past, but the hard knot of anger in her thoughts didn't soften. "But you'd proven yourself willing and capable to be an assassin. You can tell me you were forced into this as much as you want, but I know better. I can feel just how much you loved that life."

You're right. I did love it. That doesn't make me a monster.

"You paint a horrible life with flattering colors," she said, "but it doesn't change the truth. Honor isn't a simple matter of how you act. True honor is how you act toward those weaker than you. An assassin—however 'honorable' you'd like to believe you were—would squash them because you'd been paid to do so. A warrior of honor would defend them, protect them, and keep them safe."

Is that why you travel around the world killing those 'weak' people infected by the Entana?

"If there was any other way, I would do it. But the Entana would ravage this world if we didn't do something. The -taken are lost to us, but we can save the rest by eliminating the disease. It's a terrible sacrifice, but one we must make."

You paint a horrible life with flattering colors, Aeo mocked, *but it doesn't change the truth.*

He got the briefest hint of Dragana's anger and confusion before she unstrapped the baldric from her shoulder and flung Aeo to the ground. He was plunged into darkness, except for the distant light of his bearer's presence.

He chuckled to himself. He'd gotten under her skin and poked at something tender.

If he thought about that enough, maybe he could ignore the aches she'd inflicted when she'd gotten under *his* skin and poked at something tender.

CHAPTER SIX

Wake up, Dragana!

The warrior-woman stirred, but remained asleep.

Wake up!

She woke with a start and grasped the Bok'Tarong. "What is it?" she whispered.

That was a great question. Aeo hardly understood himself. But somehow, through the darkness and silence of his rosy gold prison, every one of his senses was pulled toward… something. As if a silent voice whispered [over there], growing more urgent the longer he delayed.

Another camp, I think, he said. *To the south.*

"How did we not see it? We came through there just a few hours ago."

They just arrived. There's something… wrong about it.

Aeo sensed Dragana's thoughts sharpen and heartbeat quicken as she forced herself into alertness. "Tell me what you feel."

Oh boy. It was like the hair standing up on the back of your neck for no reason, the twisting in your gut when you *know* something is wrong, that instinct that no matter how much your brain assures you everything is all right, you're absolutely convinced it's not.

I can't describe it. Something is just wrong over there. It's unnatural, oily. Like something's festering and rotting.

Dragana growled, deep in her throat. "Entana."

She rose from her bedroll in absolute silence and crept through the darkened trees. No moonlight reached them, but Dragana navigated with practiced skill. Twigs and pinecones barely crackled under her feet. Aeo could almost smell the sweet, earthy scent of mushrooms and loam.

Just ahead. Be careful.

Dragana knelt, then eased onto her belly. She crawled toward a faint flicker dancing on the trunks. Firelight. Despite the awkwardness, she held the Bok'Tarong and gave Aeo sight as they surveyed the area.

The camp spread out at the bottom of a hill. Two tents and a few bedrolls filled a small open space between the trees, the modest fire smoky from burning moist needles. A few people lounged around, either staring at the fire or in various stages of fitful sleep. On the surface, it looked like any other group of adventurers turning in for the night.

But Aeo knew that wasn't the case. The wrongness was so thick he could barely breathe. As he watched, the shadows skewed and stretched until there were normal shadows and there were shadow-beings. They clung to the people like leeches.

Dark tendrils snaked in and out of the peoples' heads like a nest of diseased worms. If he concentrated, he could see a thin line extending from them to the sky and out of sight. The tendrils' appearance matched Aeo's feelings—they looked oily, festering, unnatural. They made him want to gag.

"I see five people," Dragana whispered. "And more than enough weapons for everyone." Aeo felt her analyze them in her mind: *none look awkward around the blades, muscle tone, hardness of eyes and body... these people are no strangers to battle.*

Aeo couldn't argue her conclusion. He did, however, have one more thing to add. *They're -taken.*

Dragana's heartbeat raced. "Are you sure?"

His spirit-eyes remained locked on the tendrils squirming in the men's heads. *Uh, yeah. Pretty sure.*

"What do they look like?"

I don't think I can describe them.

"Then show me."

Um... how?

Aeo felt a surge of irritation from her. "The true spirit of the Bok'Tarong would know how," she mumbled.

He wasn't about to let a challenge like that pass by. He followed the instincts that had shown him how to fight as the Bok'Tarong and led him to these -taken. [Focus on them until nothing else exists.] He concentrated on the Entana tendrils. Once they were sharp and clear in his vision, he reached out to touch Dragana's thoughts.

A flash of surprise filled Dragana, quickly overwhelmed by revulsion and rage. "By the gods of Taron. They're fully -taken.

How are they still sane?" She paused. "Forget sanity, how are they even *alive*?"

Aeo had no answers to offer, and for once he didn't think gloating would be appropriate.

"There's something wrong about this," she whispered. "Entana-taken don't act like this."

What do you mean?

"Once a person is fully -taken, they lose all control of themselves. They become violent, raving lunatics. These people are fully -taken, without question, but they're acting sane."

Was that fear in Dragana's voice? It couldn't be. But then again, if Aeo had encountered someone lost to the Coming Madness but still in their right mind, he'd be frightened of them, too. *What do we do?*

"We find out what's going on."

And then kill them.

Her grip on the Bok'Tarong tightened. "Ready?"

Aeo took another look at the tendrils. *To destroy those monsters? Absolutely.*

The warrior-woman charged down the hill, leaping over a fallen log and skidding through the underbrush with hardly a sound. The shadows grew harsher, confusing Aeo's depth perception, as she neared the circle of firelight. Dragana didn't miss a step.

She burst into the camp and slashed through the first -taken's belly before he'd even noticed her presence. Aeo tasted blood—tasted!—and felt its heat wash over him. The sensations of battle filled long-dead nerves. He drank them in, reveled in them, and let them feed his bloodlust.

Dragana plowed through the defenses of the unprepared -taken. They were still fumbling with their weapons when she knocked them down with bloody, though non-fatal, wounds.

One of the two standing -taken blocked her next strike with a massive broadsword. His muscles bulged as he tried to overpower Dragana's defense. She twisted aside, letting his momentum push him forward, and came around the side. The man was back on his feet in an instant, again using all brawn and no brains.

The berserker style, where the warrior sacrifices finesse for strength, had never impressed Aeo. He'd fought several of these brutes in the past and each time, they'd been overwhelmed by the skill of a true warrior.

He would be no match for Dragana and the Bok'Tarong.

Aeo used his spirit-eyes to oversee the battle, taking on the role of master strategist and aiding Dragana's defense. Brief thoughts and suggestions helped strengthen the warrior-woman's stance or give the blades a better angle for deflecting a nasty blow. No matter how hard the berserker looked for an opening, he couldn't find one Aeo hadn't already helped close.

Still, these -taken soldiers proved more resilient than either Aeo or Dragana had expected. The two she'd bashed had regained their feet, making it four against one. Berserkers were difficult enemies, but rather than ignoring pain, these -taken didn't seem to feel it at all. They didn't hesitate to block the Bok'Tarong with a shoulder or forearm. Cuts that would have incapacitated a normal person didn't faze them. Even as Aeo watched, blood stopped flowing from one such gash in a -taken's arm, and the flesh began mending. *How are we supposed to beat these guys if they can heal any wound we give them?*

It had to be a killing blow. Nothing else would stop these monsters for long. *An instant kill against enemies who can't be tired out, terrorized into panic, or incapacitated by pain? Impossible.*

Aeo moved his spirit-eyes around the battlefield, assessing their enemies. He started to give a suggestion to Dragana when he caught sight of something on the edge of his vision. Dread flooded him. He'd been so focused on the -taken, he'd forgotten about the Entana.

The parasites' tendrils whipped around and shot out at Dragana. Her body didn't react to the stings, but Aeo could see her spirit cringe with each strike. Every hit bruised her confidence and sapped her willpower. The wounds weren't mortal, but they were devastating in their own dangerous way.

Her attacks grew slower and weaker. Her thoughts, once clear and single-mindedly focused on the battle, strayed to worries and doubt. She hesitated to take risks, staying away from more daring moves altogether. The Entana were cowing her into a corner, backing her into a position where all her advantages would be lost.

Aeo helped her against the -taken as best he could, but he could not ignore the attacks of the Entana. Dragana's spirit bled and wept. Her righteous, infuriating confidence had withered under the relentless assault. Aeo couldn't allow that. Fear was the worst enemy of a warrior.

Two soldiers charged at her, far enough apart she couldn't

avoid them both. She ducked under one blade and rose to parry the other, but she wasn't fast enough. A sword grazed her upper arm, deflecting off the carving of her spirit. It wasn't a deep cut, but in a fight like this any loss of blood or strength was devastating.

If he didn't do something, Dragana would be crushed like a flower in a stampede.

Another tendril lashed out at her, and he struck at it on instinct. A ghostly hand—his hand!—left the Bok'Tarong and snapped a shining, transparent replica of the double-bladed sword at the tendril. Aeo felt the solid contact of blade against flesh, as if both had been physical. The tendril hissed in pain. It snaked back to the -taken and cowered.

He'd hurt the tendril. He'd left the Bok'Tarong and injured the spirit attacking Dragana.

He could fight.

He stretched his spirit beyond the metal of the Bok'Tarong, tearing his arms and torso free of the golden prison. Aeo felt as if he was ripping himself apart, leaving a chunk of his soul behind in the Bok'Tarong. Not like that would stop him. Nothing could keep him from the fight now.

[You can't do that.]

Watch me.

The sword fought him, refusing to grant him any more freedom, but Aeo held steady with his upper body released from the Bok'Tarong. He stared at the tendrils waving around him. For a moment he didn't act, he just calmed his mind and breathed. Strong, steady, and swift.

Aeo burst into a flurry of motion, slicing several oily tendrils with his first swipe. He couldn't side-step into a better position, anchored in the sword as he was, but he made do and worked his spirit-blade all the harder. The Entana shrank back before his furious attacks and left Dragana's spirit alone.

The tide of battle began to change. The -taken became more cautious and seemed to finally notice their many wounds. Aeo's hope was bolstered by his freedom, and now that the Entana were leaving Dragana's spirit in peace, her confidence was returning. He wondered if his emotions were affecting hers, but he didn't have time to ponder that. The Entana were still trying to breach his defenses and get to Dragana. Her spirit was still wounded. He couldn't let them get through.

One of the -taken slashed forward, clearly hoping to take Dragana's head from her shoulders. She fell to her knees, rolling behind the -taken, and sliced clean through the muscles of his calf with a backstroke. The -taken might not feel pain the way they should, but their bodies still worked the same as anyone's. Without that muscle, the -taken toppled into one of the tents.

Aeo felt her hope swell. She pressed the -taken all the harder, ignoring the pain in her arm and doing what she'd been trained to do—kill Entana.

One -taken sank to the ground, his massive blood loss finally taking its toll. She scored a wicked hit on another, taking him out as well. An almost casual swipe at the one with the shredded leg dispatched him, too. It was now one-on-one.

With those odds, he didn't stand a chance.

Dragana knocked the -taken to his back and placed the

Bok'Tarong against his throat. She stood over him, panting and sweating, fire in her brown-and-crimson eyes. She'd never looked better.

Aeo tore his attention from Dragana and looked at the -taken. Firelight stretched the shadows and emphasized the darkness, skewing his features into something monstrous, demonic. Fitting, given the monster inhabiting his mind.

The Entana tendrils in his head squirmed and snapped at her, but Aeo held his spirit-blade at them much like Dragana did to the -taken.

"Who are you?" she demanded.

"We are agents of the Entana," the man replied. There was no trace of fear in his voice, even though the enchanted Bok'Tarong pressed against his skin. "Well met, lady warrior. We didn't expect to find you so quickly."

"What is that supposed to mean?" she asked.

"We were told you would show yourself sooner or later. Our masters have an interest in you."

Dragana's reply was to put just enough pressure on the man's neck to draw blood. It looked black in the flickering orange light.

We can't find out what's different about them if we kill him, Aeo whispered.

Dragana didn't let up on the pressure, but she didn't press any harder, either.

The man sneered at her. "You are a fool if you believe you can stop our masters."

"How about I stop you, then?" Dragana said. Her voice was quiet and dangerous enough to make Aeo shiver.

Rather than paling or babbling in fear, the man laughed in Dragana's face. "You have no idea what you're dealing with. The Entana are beyond your reach. We who accept their presence are growing, and growing strong. We have no fear. We never age. Even now, we fight a battle to bring more into the service of the Entana. Our numbers will swell and spread the Entana to the entire world. Then we will come for you."

Aeo felt the shudder race through her. "Was that supposed to frighten me?"

"It wasn't a threat. It's the truth."

"And I suppose now you'll offer me an alternative," Dragana said.

The man stared into her eyes without a hint of remorse. "If you surrender the Bok'Tarong and join us before then, you will be welcomed and rewarded. If not, you will die."

"Both options are death for the Taronese," Dragana said. "So take this message to your masters."

With a violent shove, she sliced clean through the -taken's throat.

The man never had a chance to scream, but the Entana squealed as its human vessel died. The oily tendrils thrashed and flickered in and out of Aeo's spirit vision. The Bok'Tarong's enchantment seared the Entana like hot iron cauterized a puss-filled wound.

Outside its host, the Entana looked like little more than a slimy eel. Much of its evil had been drained away — now it was just a squirming, disgusting worm.

In his normal contracts, this was the point where Aeo hated

his job. The hunt was thrilling, the fight exhilarating, and the kill was the necessary evil to finish it off. But this… this was different. This wasn't like killing a person. This was killing a monster.

For the first time, he wouldn't regret this kill in the least.

Aeo reached out with his spirit-blade, stabbing through the parasite. It tried to squeal once more, but dissipated into oily smoke before it could.

Without a word, Dragana dispatched the rest of the -taken.

When the Entana were gone, Aeo slid himself back into the Bok'Tarong's blades. It felt good to be back in the sword, like soaking in a warm bath after a hard workout. Like coming home.

Blood oozed down Dragana's arm and slid across Aeo's blades. They'd need to bind that sooner rather than later. Her spirit would need time to repair the Entana's damage, also, and Aeo was about to suggest they return to camp and get some rest when she spoke.

"What did he mean?" Aeo knew she was talking to herself more than to him, so he didn't interrupt. "'We who accept the Entana are growing.' Are people allowing the Entana into their minds of their own free will?" She rolled one of the bodies onto its back with her foot. The flickering firelight made its dead eyes looks like glass. "Why would you do that?"

Aeo stared at the lifeless -taken. Why indeed? He'd felt the evil of the Entana. Who in their right mind would take something like that in willingly?

A small insignia on the man's collar caught his attention. *Look, Dragana,* he said. *That's the crest of the Halkronar emperor.*

Dragana's eyes widened. She scanned each of the bodies, and

each wore the same clothes with the same insignia. In the darkness and heat of battle, she and Aeo had failed to notice it. "These aren't their standard military uniforms. But they're some type of uniform, don't you think?"

I do. They look like they're made to blend in with an army, but stand out enough to mark these soldiers as different.

Soldiers. Entana-taken soldiers. Both let this information sink in for a moment. "The Taronese leaders sent us here because there were rumors of an increase in -taken near the frontlines of the war. And the -taken said they were fighting a battle to enslave more to the Entana."

There's something much bigger than the Entana going on here, Aeo said.

Her fist clenched around the Bok'Tarong. "Nothing is bigger than the Entana."

These -taken are fighting in the war. Their commanders can't be oblivious to that.

Dragana stared at the insignia on the dead -taken's collar for several moments. "I think this one *was* the commander."

Aeo was silent for a moment. *The Halkron have regiments of -taken fighting us?*

"It looks that way."

Why?

"You saw how these guys fought. A fully -taken doesn't feel pain. They have no fear. The Entana have eaten so many of their thoughts and emotions they can no longer feel anything. If someone or something could control their minds and keep them sane, they would make excellent soldiers. But that's never happened before."

Dread soured Aeo's thoughts. *It looks like someone has figured out how to do it.*

"Something like that would require immense power."

And someone with that much power and an army of unfeeling, unafraid soldiers at their call would be a huge threat. They could challenge mages, kings…

"… or countries."

Aeo paused. *You can't be serious.*

She shrugged. "It makes sense. The Halkron invade after centuries of peace. Arata holds them back, barely. Since then, there have been skirmishes but little more. There was no reason for this war to start in the first place, unless someone had plans of their own."

But how could that someone convince people to accept Entana possession and fight a war for them?

Dragana was quiet. The entire night had fallen silent, Aeo realized. The animals of the forest knew death had come to visit.

We need to find whoever's behind this.

Her eyes never left the bodies, spread through the camp like discarded dolls. Their blood looked black and alien in the darkness. "I think you're right."

CHAPTER SEVEN

Aeo knew Dragana had to be exhausted, but she couldn't afford to sleep just yet. She'd washed the blood from Aeo's blades and gotten most of it off her arm, though the intricate scrollwork on the carving of her spirit was still crusted with it.

You should probably take that off, Aeo said. *Clean it, make sure—*

"No." Her voice was hard and final, and her thoughts put up a wall of absolute refusal before he could even finish the thought.

If that gets infected, you won't be able to fight.

"I'll be fine." She squeezed more water over it, the liquid running down her muscles pinkish with blood.

What's so special about that thing, anyway? The last time I asked about it you shut me out.

"It's personal." She sucked a breath between her teeth as she wound a cloth binding around it. "Ow."

And?

Silence. He couldn't read anything else from her thoughts,

either. Aeo suspected she'd pinched the wound on purpose, to force her mind away from the topic.

Dragana?

"No. I'm not discussing this with you."

That was her *push any further and I'll kill you* voice, so he let it drop.

Once her wound and armband were cleaned, Dragana leaned against a thick cedar and fiddled with the ferns and flowers growing at its roots. She didn't pluck or pull at them like most people did. She stroked them, petting the plants as others pet a puppy. Aeo figured she probably didn't even realize she was doing it.

You should get some sleep. Even the light of her presence looked dim and tired.

"I can't," she said. She took up the Bok'Tarong and placed the blades in her lap. Her emotions, overwhelming exhaustion and confusion and doubt, slammed into Aeo.

Are you all right?

"I don't know," she said. Her voice shook. "I'm just... I don't feel like myself."

Your spirit's still recovering from the Entana's attacks.

"What would you know about the Entana's attacks? Yesterday you didn't even know what the Entana were."

I watched them attack you. I even defended you from them. A little gratitude wouldn't hurt.

She took a deep breath, slipping into a meditative mindset for just a moment. "Tell me what happened."

It wasn't an apology for her outburst, or an acceptance of his abilities, but it was the best he would get. *The Entana hit your spirit like whips. They sapped your confidence, making you doubt yourself.*

"I could feel it," she whispered. She stroked a large, feathery fern through her fingers.

The -taken would have beaten you unless I did something. So I pulled myself out of the blades. Not much, just enough to give me some room to fight back.

Dragana's spine straightened, her focus sharpened. She released the fern. "You did what?"

I pulled myself out of the blades, he repeated. Why was she so attentive all of a sudden? *I didn't get all the way out, just to my stomach. But I had the Bok'Tarong in my hand, so I was able to fight the Entana while you handled the -taken.*

"But… how? No spirit has ever managed to do that before."

Aeo paused. *No one? Ever?*

"Never."

You can't know that. Maybe it happens all the time, but people don't understand until they hold the Bok'Tarong for themselves.

"The abilities of the Bok'Tarong, and the spirit inside, are very clear. Every Taronese knows them inside and out. If a spirit could do what you just did, we'd have known about it."

Well, I did it. So it's obviously not impossible.

"It's unprecedented. Which means up to now, it *has* been impossible." She started fiddling with the ferns again, without taking her eyes from the blades.

Maybe no one thought to try before. She nodded, absentmindedly, clearly not buying his argument. *Look, Dragana, all I did was pull myself out to even the odds. The Entana had the -taken and their tendrils. You needed something more than the blades, so I acted. That's it.*

"But how can you explain it? How can you, of all people, be the first one to accomplish this?"

How could those soldiers back there have been fully -taken, yet fully sane? Lots of impossible stuff has already happened tonight.

She scowled.

Maybe the rules are changing, to accommodate the danger. Did you consider that? If the Entana are -taking people who are willing, maybe the Bok'Tarong needs to adapt in order to fight them.

"Or maybe you've broken the magic, and this is a consequence of that."

If the magic was broken I couldn't have killed those Entana. You said so yourself.

"I guess," Dragana said.

You just can't accept the fact that maybe I didn't screw everything up by being in here, can you? Everything has to be my fault. Even the good things, like me saving your damn life.

Her eyes narrowed as she grit her teeth.

I'm not asking for much. Just stop judging me and accept that I'm the one in here, and that it might not be a bad thing.

"I can't accept it. You still don't understand what a sacrilege it is to have someone like you in the Bok'Tarong."

Someone like me? This is exactly what I'm talking about. You can't see me as anything other than a monster, can you? Dragana's pursed, stubborn silence told him everything. *Fine. If you won't at least try to understand, I'll have to make you see.*

Aeo dug deep into his memories, pulling Dragana's mind

with him. He was a young man, brought before the king for his accomplishments. The Mage General had taken him and poured his magic into Aeo's mind, unrelenting. Months. Years. Training with the sword during the day, his mind torn apart by the Mage General's power at night. He was molded into his role like a lump of wet clay. By the time he'd been named the king's personal assassin, he was hardly recognizable as the man he'd been.

Aeo felt a pang of sympathy from Dragana. It spurred him on, and he pulled her deeper.

He was in battle, fighting a man whose face and features shifted between his targets. He worked his blade, sweating and slashing as if he lived those moments for the first time.

His heart hammered with excitement, not exertion. He was testing his skills, proving himself to be the best once again. He was hunting, stalking, winning — the thrill never got old.

Their surroundings changed just as the man's features did. He was in a large dining hall, surrounded by stone and tapestries and horrified nobles. A moment later the walls melted away, revealing a forested clearing not unlike the one he'd so recently fought in as the Bok'Tarong. In the blink of an eye he was in a tent, deep in a Halkronar war camp.

Still he fought, consumed in a duel between master swordsman and a dead man.

The elation of battle intoxicated him. He grinned like a madman as he fought. This was what drove him. The satisfaction of victory made life worth living. What else could compare to it?

It felt like hours he fought, never tiring, always prevailing. His targets fell. And the moment came.

Sour regret twisted his gut as he leaned in for the kill.

Dragana hadn't known this. She thought he'd reveled in death, when every one of his kills was mourned. He didn't try to hide his revulsion. He let it fill him, let Dragana experience it as profoundly as Aeo did.

Aeo let his mind wander from battle, to his life between contracts. It hadn't been all about killing. He'd had plenty of time to enjoy the finer things of life, the travel and women, the joys he could buy with the king's gold. It was a good life, and Aeo showed Dragana all of it.

You see? The life of an assassin isn't as distasteful as you think.

A wave of disgust flowed over him. Dragana sneered. "Do you know what I see in that?"

Aeo watched the same images, from Dragana's perspective. He saw evil in the heart of the king and fear in the eyes of his targets. He pictured the families left fatherless and destitute, the cities torn apart by greed when a usurper took over a dead man's rule. His "honor" seemed hollow as he watched himself murder nameless faces for a handful of coins, ignoring his convictions that he could — *should* — be better than this. Even his personal life was filled with strangers, as he saw the women he'd taken to his bed without even knowing their names, often paying for their company with the very same gold he'd won with blood.

The voice of Aeo, the tiny conscience he'd buried long ago, screamed through his mind. He could have been better than this. What he could have done, who he could have been, were questions he'd long since stopped asking. But now they pounded in his thoughts like a drumbeat. He told himself he'd done the best he could, but… had he?

This man, the man the Mage General had conditioned him to become with torture and magic, wasn't an honorable assassin. He was a heartless killer, willing to play god with others' lives in order to finance his own.

Looking at himself from Dragana's perspective, he was the kind of man who'd earned his fate upon Aeo's sword.

⁎⁎

"YOU'RE QUIET TODAY," Dragana said. They had risen at sunrise and been on the road for well over an hour, but Aeo hadn't said a word since last night.

His entire world had been turned upside down. Again. He'd thought he'd had it all as an assassin. He'd been happy in that life… hadn't he? The satisfaction after each contract, the excitement of the chase, those had been real. But happiness? He couldn't say. Could he have been that wrong?

Normally Dragana's small spark of satisfaction would have flared his temper, but this morning it embarrassed him. He'd hoped he wouldn't have to share any of this with her. He didn't want to admit the possibility she might be right.

She cleared her throat.

Right. He didn't have to explain anything. As he mulled things over, she'd have heard it all. She already knew.

Aeo hadn't felt this awkward in a long, long time. He'd have adjusted a perfectly seated strap or clomped off to collect firewood he didn't need if he could have, just to avoid this.

Dragana was bad enough as it was. If she won this battle, she'd never let him live it down.

But he couldn't shake the feeling she might be right.

"Maybe there's something to you besides arrogance and greed after all," she said.

Aeo grumbled, but didn't reply.

"There's still time to right the wrongs of a past life," Dragana offered. "The spirit of Aeo doesn't have to follow the life Aeo's flesh led."

I may not have had much choice in the way I lived, but I still followed the assassin's path. Even though my body is gone, I'm still the same person.

"People can change."

Changing isn't easy, Aeo said.

"I never said it would be. I just said it was possible."

And what? Do you expect me to change overnight? To decide my past life was a waste and become all stubborn and honorable, like you? I can't do that, Dragana. I loved that life once, and part of me still does. I can't just walk away and change in a moment.

"Well, you may not become honorable like me, but you already have the stubborn part down," she said, smiling. She paused, then continued in a more serious tone. "If you'd be more willing to sacrifice, you might find that change comes quicker than you'd think."

Because giving up my life wasn't enough?

"That wasn't a sacrifice. It was cowardice and a just repayment for what you did to the Bok'Tarong."

And just like that, the fragile peace they'd forged evaporated.

Don't tell me what it was! You have no idea what it was like! It was a greater sacrifice than anything that's ever been asked of you.

"You have no idea what's been asked of me," Dragana growled. "I've made more sacrifices than you can know."

Aeo scoffed. *All you've ever wanted to do is wield the Bok'Tarong. Here I am, in your hands. What kind of sacrifice is that?*

"To wield the Bok'Tarong is both an honor and a curse. A warrior spends many years training—sometimes an entire lifetime—but once the blade is taken up, they have only a short time before it claims them."

What's that supposed to mean?

"It means in less than a year, the Bok'Tarong will take my life just as it took yours."

Aeo found himself in the rare position of being speechless. Dragana had spoken of her impending death with such calm, as easily as saying it would snow this winter. He detected the barest flutter of anxiety in her mind. *You spent your entire life earning the right to die?* Aeo asked.

"Not to die," Dragana replied, "but to fight. I trained so I could wield the Bok'Tarong and rid the world of a terrible evil. It's an honor to defend my home and my people, and one I would gladly give my life for."

I can't think of anything I'd be willing to give my life for.

"And that's why your life has always been so shallow."

Aeo couldn't find an argument for that.

Why would the blades force death upon its wielder? It would make much more sense to allow someone who trained for so long to continue fighting, rather than just killing them.

"It's the cost of the enchantment. No one, not even the makers of the Bok'Tarong, could create life from nothing. So in order to have life, the Bok'Tarong must first take life."

Then why doesn't it take the life of the people it kills, instead of its wielder?

"Because it can't steal life," Dragana clarified. "It can only take a life that is freely given, and in wielding the Bok'Tarong you're giving it your life."

Aeo thought back to the time when he'd wielded the sword and had to agree. He'd devoted himself to the blades, had given his entire life to them. At the time he hadn't known that would *literally* be the cost. But would it have even mattered? He'd been obsessed, had abandoned his lifestyle in order to wield the Bok'Tarong. Offering his actual life to the blades had been a mere technicality at that point.

"The Taronese warrior who wields the Bok'Tarong is sapped of their life energy to support the blades. During battle that energy is shared by both the warrior and the Bok'Tarong, but otherwise they age at a rapid pace. The more they fight, the faster they die. With the -taken problem we're facing, I'll be lucky to last a year."

That last statement hurt in ways Aeo never would have anticipated.

"So don't tell me I know nothing about sacrifice. You still live because I am giving you my life-force. As much as I hate it, you're alive because of me."

Aeo couldn't think of anything to say to that.

Chapter Eight

Raeb and Saydee sat across from each other, a small fire between them. They'd spent most of the afternoon clearing the area of scrub and cactus, and the rest of it pulling thorns and cactus needles from their hands. That had been the easy part of the job.

Raeb had scribed runes into the dirt with bloody hands until after sunset. Saydee had hounded him with endless questions about this ritual—questions he either could not or would not answer. He didn't know how it worked. He didn't understand why every single ingredient was important. And he would not explain to her how he'd learned it in the first place. It had taken most of the afternoon for her to realize he wouldn't give in and be quiet.

Now the only light came from their flickering fire and the sliver of moon overhead. "We can still stop this," he said.

Saydee shook her head. "I'm ready."

Given the dangers they were walking into, and the very real

chance they wouldn't learn anything helpful from Saydee's Entana, the girl was remarkably calm. Raeb wished he was half as ready as Saydee sounded.

He took a deep breath and double-checked everything. The runes were in their proper places, the fire burned low, the herbs mixed and waiting. He looked down at the last, vital key that would hopefully give him his answers.

He held the magnificent blade in a white-knuckled grip. Five dagger blades radiated from the horizontal hilt in his fist, fanning out like a half-sun. The silvery metal shone in the firelight and sparkles of magic glittered from its depths. He could feel that magic keenly, in the ice crystals creeping up his fingers and the blade's gnawing hunger begging him for release. Baring this blade was always a test of willpower. If he didn't hold the hunger in check…

That was the real danger of this blade. It wasn't the physical wounds it could inflict, terrible as those were. There was an even darker side to it that, even after all this time, terrified him. It was the reason Raeb carried it, and the reason he so despised it.

It was also why he'd been running for so many centuries.

He started chanting and threw the herbs into the fire. The smoke curled into strange patterns that reminded him of snakes and eels and almost looked like letters. He closed his eyes and gripped his enchanted blade hard—if its magic didn't work now, he might as well sign both of their death warrants.

Raeb felt ripples in the spirit-world as the Entana in Saydee's mind was roused by the scent of the herbs. He willed a little of his blade's magic into the smoke, shivering against the suddenly frigid night. Ice coated the blade as it brought the invisible magicks surrounding them into view.

Raeb repressed a shudder as the tendrils of Saydee's Entana parasite appeared. A moment later, he let out a tension-filled sigh.

He'd been right. Next to the dark connection from the Entana to her mind was a gossamer-thin strand of golden energy flowing from Saydee's mind back into the spirit world. A tenuous trail, at best, but Raeb was confident—mostly—his weightless spirit wouldn't damage it.

He was just about to separate his spirit from his body and leap out to the connection when Saydee shuddered. She grabbed her head in her hands and started to scream, but the sound was cut short. She convulsed a few times before raising her head and letting her hands drop to her lap. She looked at Raeb and grinned, but it felt more like a sneer to him.

Raeb's heart fluttered with horror. Her eyes were solid black but for a sickly brown, elongated pupil.

Full Entana eyes.

He dropped his strange blade and drew his sword. He did not need the distraction of that blade to make this encounter any worse.

"You ignore us, blade-bearer," Saydee said in a deep man's voice.

"No," Raeb said. "I defy you, Keeper of Secrets."

Saydee chuckled. The sound sent shivers down Raeb's spine, like a skeleton had dragged bony fingers along it. "I'm flattered you remember me."

"How could I forget? I still have the scars from our last

encounter."

"You bear the marks, but you seem to have forgotten the lessons."

"Forgotten, or denied?"

Murderous anger flashed in the Keeper of Secrets' expression. For a moment, the face no longer held any resemblance to Saydee's. "Either way, it was foolish to turn away from the Entana."

"Not all of us are willing to be used by them, *ambassador*."

The Keeper of Secrets' eyes glittered in the firelight. "You spit the word like a curse, when I above all -taken have been given the greatest of gifts."

"Invading our minds and delivering orders isn't a gift. It makes you a glorified carrier pigeon." He sneered, and Raeb pressed on despite the danger. "You betray your own race to serve the parasites that would consume us. That isn't an honor, Keeper of Secrets. If you were halfway sane, you would know that."

"And if you had any sense in that skull of yours, you would realize your days are numbered if you refuse to serve."

Raeb covered his fear with an angry growl. "What do you want?"

"You contacted me, blade-bearer. After such a long silence, I was beginning to think you had forgotten the mission we gave you. Is it finished?"

"No."

The Keeper of Secrets twisted Saydee's face into a scowl. "Then why did you contact me?"

"I didn't want to talk to you."

"Yet you seduced an Entana with the ritual I taught you. If you didn't want my attention, why did you use my magic?"

Raeb hoped the Keeper of Secrets couldn't feel his thoughts race as he groped for an answer—one that wouldn't reveal his intentions, and wouldn't get him killed on the spot. "Research," he said at last.

"Research?"

"Yes. This vessel has a small amount of magical power. I was trying to determine how an Entana had managed to take a minor mage."

The Keeper of Secrets paused at this, stretching Saydee's face into an expression that looked confused and, to Raeb's disbelief, a little worried.

"Does this news trouble you?" he asked, trying—and probably failing—to keep the mocking tone from his voice.

"Not at all."

Raeb didn't believe that, but he kept his thoughts to himself. "Perhaps this could begin an era where mages are no longer immune to the Entana."

"And what have you discovered?"

He hardened his glare. "Nothing. *Someone* interrupted my study before I could begin."

The Keeper of Secrets eyed Raeb. "You cannot fool me, blade-bearer. You have never had the Entana's interests in mind, and even if you did we never asked you to investigate this. What should concern you is the mission you were supposed to complete decades ago."

"I've been working on it."

"I'm not a simpleton. You've been running from it, and the Entana will not tolerate your failure for much longer."

Raeb's heart turned to ice. He forgot to breathe. "What do you mean?"

"Plans are in place that will allow the Entana free access to this world. Decades of planning, of manipulating the humans, have come to fruition. The world is ready at last. The only thing standing in our way is your mission. Once you complete it, the world will be ours."

"Well, that's great motivation for me."

The Keeper of Secrets glared daggers at him over the fire. Somewhere in the near distance, a coyote yipped. "The Entana have kept you alive, long after your lifetime should have ended, for this purpose alone."

"And here I thought it was just Entana agriculture at its finest," Raeb said. "Keep collecting memories so the Entana is fed, and you heal them from old age itself. Isn't that how it works?"

"Complete your task by the spring equinox, or we will no longer restrain the Entana in your mind. It is hungry, after all, and holding it back from the feast of your thoughts grows tiresome."

Terror clutched at Raeb's heart. "The spring equinox? But that isn't enough time."

"It's nearly half a year. You've had more than enough time already, and you're lucky we're giving you this much. Make do with what is given to you."

Raeb reached down and grasped the enchanted blade he'd dropped. He grit his teeth and wrestled its hunger into submission. The effort left him weary, but the effect was worth it. The temperature dropped and its magic pulsed in his hand. A nest of Entana tendrils came into view, hovering over Saydee. Not all of them were hers. "Maybe I will," he growled.

The Keeper of Secrets laughed. "You would threaten me with an Entana blade? Only a fool would believe a weapon we created could kill us. Nothing but the Bok'Tarong can do that."

"Then I guess I'll have to get the Bok'Tarong and be rid of you."

"After all these centuries, you still don't understand, do you? The Taronese fools waste their lives trying to eradicate the Entana by killing the -taken. But they will never succeed."

The Keeper of Secrets reached out with Saydee's hand, as if to grab Raeb around the throat. Her fingers never connected, but Raeb felt as if the Keeper of Secrets had clamped talons around his windpipe. He choked. He panicked and flailed. Then the Keeper of Secrets pulled.

Raeb's vision blurred as his spirit was extracted from his body. He resisted, but the Keeper of Secrets was too strong. The Entana ambassador towed Raeb from the physical world and zoomed through the spirit lands.

Raeb tried to absorb what he was seeing, but many of the sights were beyond his comprehension. Stars that seemed so cold and distant on earth burned just out of reach. Colors he could never describe, in every shade he'd ever dreamed, washed the blackness of space in streaks and blurs. Though he never saw another being, he wasn't alone out here. Thousands upon thousands of entities surrounded him. Emotions radiated from them, intense joy and overwhelming sadness pulsing over Raeb.

They traveled for a minute, or maybe a day, when the beauty that made Raeb weep was erased. A black, writhing knot, unbelievably massive, loomed ahead like a stain. A nest of Entana. More of the vile creatures than he'd ever imagined. They coiled and slithered around each other, some stretching out into spiritual oblivion and the physical world. Many, many more pulsed around the core like a massive tumor.

"These are your masters, blade-bearer. You are nothing compared to this."

Raeb jumped at the Keeper of Secret's voice. In all the majesty and terror of this journey, he'd forgotten about his guide.

Raeb couldn't tear his gaze from the Entana nest. His pride wanted to argue with the Keeper of Secrets, to assert his independence over these monsters, but he couldn't. Staring at the massive tangle of Entana, large as a sun, he was nothing.

"Even the Bok'Tarong cannot touch this. They think each -taken they kill hurts us. But we have plenty more Entana to send. We will always have more Entana to send."

In a flash of comprehension, Raeb saw the Entana nest with new understanding. These weren't individual creatures, living and working together. They were *one* creature in many bodies. Each tendril lurching through a -taken's mind wasn't an Entana. It was a single extension of the much larger, much more dangerous Entana hive. Killing one didn't hurt the hive—ten more would be created to fill the gap. The tendrils were expendable, just feeding tubes of the hive. All this time the Taronese had thought they were killing the Entana, when they were just stimulating its growth.

All this time Raeb had thought he would kill his creature and be gone, when in reality he had to kill the entire Entana hive to have even a hope of freedom.

"If the Taronese with their precious Bok'Tarong cannot vanquish us, what hope does a worthless -taken like you have?"

Raeb stared at the Entana hive. Its darkness threatened to drown him. "None," he admitted.

"Good. Remember that, obey your masters, and we may yet let you live."

The Keeper of Secrets released Raeb's spirit, and he went hurtling back to his body. The tendrils of the hive assaulted him the entire way, leaving his spirit battered and bruised by the time he returned to the physical world.

Saydee was lying unconscious where she'd been sitting. Raeb was just able to catch a glimpse of her steady breathing before he crumpled to the ground and lay very still.

CHAPTER NINE

Saydee sat up, clutching her head and gritting her teeth. "What happened?"

Raeb didn't even try to sit. He lay on his back, keeping his eyes closed against the blazing desert sun. They had to have slept through the night and halfway through the morning for it to be so bloody bright. "The Keeper of Secrets decided to join our party last night."

She huffed out a pained breath. "What does that mean?"

"The ritual attracted the attention of a man—at least, I think he's a man—called the Keeper of Secrets. He's a kind of ambassador between the Entana and their human slaves. He took over your body so we could have a little chat."

The silence was so deep Raeb dared to crack open an eye. Sunlight lanced into his brain. He turned his head to see Saydee staring at him, eyes wide and skin ashen. She trembled like a newborn calf.

"How...?"

"It's probably because of your magic," Raeb answered. "It must make it easier for someone like the Keeper of Secrets to reach you."

Saydee still wasn't responding, so Raeb continued. "The point is, the Entana aren't what we thought they were. They aren't independent creatures. They're one giant creature. Each tendril leads back to a hive that controls everything. Killing one person's Entana doesn't affect it." He sighed, wishing the truth wasn't so devastating. "We'll have to kill the entire hive."

"How could we do that?" she asked. Her voice was still quiet and shaken, but at least she didn't look like a corpse anymore. If only he could recover as quickly.

"I don't know. The Entana exist in the spirit world, so the hive isn't a physical place. I don't think the connection of your mind would be strong enough to carry me all the way there."

"And once you're there, you wouldn't have a way to destroy it."

Raeb nodded. The motion made his head pound.

"So what do we do?"

"I don't know. I need to think."

Saydee went about making breakfast while Raeb mulled over this new information. The thoughtless action of cooking seemed to restore Saydee's calm, while reliving his spirit-flight made Raeb more nervous.

It wasn't until they were packing up their camp that either of them spoke.

"You said the only way to kill the Entana is the Bok'Tarong," Saydee said.

"That's right."

"But if the Entana don't exist in this world, how does that work?"

"The Bok'Tarong is enchanted. Its blades are both physical and spiritual. When it's wielded by a Taronese warrior, it kills whatever's in its path, body or no body."

"That dagger-thing you have is enchanted too." She gestured toward his pack, where it was safely locked away.

"It wouldn't work."

"Why not?"

"Because it isn't the Bok'Tarong. It can't kill the Entana." Not like he hadn't considered trying it anyway.

Saydee nodded like she'd expected that answer but hoped for better. "Too bad we can't use the Bok'Tarong against the hive."

Raeb bent over, securing his threadbare blanket to his pack. "Oh, we could, in theory. There has to be a weak spot in it somewhere. A core of the creatures, or a heart. If we could find where to strike, the Entana would die. All of them." That, at least, would work in their favor. They'd only need to hit one weakness instead of thousands. "It's getting to the hive and back alive that's the issue."

"Well," Saydee said, "you have me now."

And therein lay all his problems. He had a way now—a tenuous way, for certain, but the first he'd ever found. All he needed was a way to kill them, and he could finally break free of his slavemasters.

But that would mean confronting the Bok'Tarong—the thing he'd been running from for two hundred years. If there was anything on earth he feared more than the Keeper of Secrets, it was facing the Bok'Tarong and whatever Taronese warrior was bearing it.

Saydee walked over to him, bending to put her face into Raeb's line of sight. "What's wrong?"

More than you could possibly comprehend. "We can't use the Bok'Tarong. It's too dangerous."

Saydee straightened. "And casting your spirit out to the Entana hive is safe?"

"You don't understand." He cinched the last straps a bit tighter than he should have. He stood, leaving the pack at his feet. He couldn't risk it revealing how his hands shook. "If we get close to the Bok'Tarong, the Taronese warrior bearing it will kill us before we could even blink."

"We can find a way around that. We can sneak up on them when they're asleep, or distract them, or any number of things. It can't be that hard."

"It can be. These warriors are trained from the time they can walk, and the Bok'Tarong literally has a mind of its own. These guys aren't that easy to trick."

She glanced at him, one eyebrow raised. "How do you know so much about them?"

Raeb hesitated, just for an instant. "When you've spent as long as I have running away from them, you learn a lot. Studying your enemies is often the best way to stay alive." He lifted his pack, wiping a few beads of sweat from his brow. It wasn't even midday and the heat was already building. "Come on, Saydee. We have to move."

"Where are we going?"

Where indeed? The last thing he wanted to do was find the Bok'Tarong. But this plan could actually work. He might actually taste freedom, if he followed through with it.

No. However promising it may seem, he couldn't do it. There would be another way. He wasn't the only -taken trying to destroy the Entana. Maybe it was time to see if they had done any better than he had.

Anything to avoid the rosy-gold judgment of the Bok'Tarong.

He turned his gaze north. He looked at the mountains, hardly seeing them. His thoughts were cast beyond them, to the forested lands of Arata. "We'll go north."

"Is that where we'll find the Bok'Tarong?" Saydee asked.

He shrugged. *Not if I can help it.* "It's where I'll find a friend who might give us some more information. He's been studying the -taken's connection to the Entana. Maybe he'll have a way to strengthen yours enough for us to use it." And maybe by then Raeb will have thought of a plan that didn't require the Bok'Tarong.

"Not another friend like the Keeper of Secrets?" she asked. Her attempt at humor was lost in the quiet fear behind the question.

"No. This guy really is a friend."

"And here I thought you didn't have any of those."

Camp packed, fire extinguished, Raeb led the way out of the rough desert and toward the road. They had a long way to go. No use making the trip more difficult by trudging through cactus if they didn't have to. "You got a warm cloak?" he asked.

Saydee shook her head. "No need for one down here."

Raeb grunted. "We'll have to get you one before we reach the mountains, then. It'll be awfully cold through those passes, and not much better once winter settles over Arata. Do you have any coin?"

This time, Saydee nodded. The twinkle in her eyes hinted that she had more than enough to buy herself—and maybe even Raeb—a dozen cloaks.

If she could afford to equip them with good clothes and house them at inns with real food and soft beds every now and then, maybe bringing her along wouldn't be so bad after all.

They walked in silence for a while, which suited Raeb just fine. But eventually, as would probably be the norm, Saydee broke that silence.

"If we destroy the hive, what will happen to the -taken?"

"What do you mean?"

"You know what I mean," she said. "These peoples' thoughts have been eaten away by the Entana. *Our* thoughts, Raeb. You and me. If you pull them out, what will happen?"

"Does it matter?"

Saydee stopped mid-step, her jaw hinged open. "How can you say that?"

"Killing the Entana will mean no one else will have to lose themselves or their families to the Entana. Ever. This will be over, once and for all."

"But all the people who are -taken now..."

"It doesn't matter," he repeated.

"Raeb!"

"What?"

"Just answer my question." She enunciated each word carefully. "Will destroying the Entana hive kill the -taken?"

Being confronted like that, with such stern disapproval on Saydee's face, deflated him. "I don't know."

"And you're still going forward with this?"

"It's our only chance to be rid of the Entana."

"Can you really sacrifice that many lives? Could you sacrifice mine?"

"To save thousands, even millions more? Yes."

"To save yourself, you mean."

He sighed. "I'm a -taken too, Saydee. If this kills them, it kills me." He sounded calloused and heartless, he knew, but he no longer cared. Maybe he *was* heartless by now.

She leveled that strange, penetrating gaze at him again. "But that wouldn't bother you too much, would it?"

He glanced at her, surprised and irritated she'd read him so well. "Look, Saydee, you said it yourself. You'd rather die trying to free yourself than allow the Entana to fully take you."

"But that's my decision, and my life. I can't say the same for every -taken out there, and no one should make a decision like this for them."

"So what would you have us do? Sit on our thumbs, broiling in this gods-forsaken desert, when we have a chance to destroy the Entana?"

Saydee pursed her lips, but he could see the turmoil in her eyes.

"No matter how much it might cost, we have to take the risk.

The Entana are parasites. They'll feed on humans until there aren't any of us left." He paused. "I may have my own reasons for destroying the Entana, but you couldn't let anyone else suffer your fate if you could stop it."

He turned and walked away without looking back.

His words would hit home. Saydee might have dark secrets in her past, but she still seemed to have a heart for other people. Silly girl.

Sure enough, Saydee trotted up beside him after a few steps.

CHAPTER TEN

D ragana had seen plenty of battles. Her entire life had revolved around them.

Even so, the war-ravaged lands near the border were shocking.

The wide river valley that formed the border between Arata and Halkron should have been frantic with the autumn harvest this time of year. Miles of fields and farms, stretching north and south for days on end, should be bursting with laborers and families and merchants hauling out wagonloads of produce. It was a time of hard work and harder celebration. Normally.

Dragana stood at the edge of the deep forest, her heart twisting as she looked over the river valley. Every field in sight had been stripped naked by thousands of hungry soldiers. She counted only a handful of civilians, and these were heading her way with loaded packs and families in tow. There was no celebration in their expressions. They were evacuating.

Closer to the river, shantytowns of tents and lean-tos had

grown between the farmhouses like a fungus. More organized stands of military encampments lay in the near distance. The closer they got to the Arata-Halkron border, the more crowded and more ravaged the land became.

The atmosphere shifted drastically when they entered the frontlines. Villagers were nonexistent, driven away from the fighting by force or fear. Officers shouted orders from every direction, and soldiers scurried like roaches to carry them out. Cries of pain and moans of approaching death came from a clump of medical tents somewhere to their right.

And through it all, Entana-taken soldiers in strange uniforms strolled as if they hadn't a care in the world.

Dragana drew the Bok'Tarong from its sheath. Aeo could feel each time her gaze landed on a -taken. She tensed, letting out a low breath like a snarl, and her grip on his hilt tightened until he feared she would break him in half. Whatever anger she held for him was nothing compared to the rage burning in her now.

"What in the name of all that is holy is going on here?" she asked between clenched teeth.

She wasn't looking for an answer. She was looking to rectify the situation. With blood.

Calm down, Dragana. We can't start slaughtering everyone in sight.

"I won't touch anyone who's innocent. It's only the -taken I care about."

Even so. The officers will cut you down before you can kill more than two or three of them.

"Then that will be two or three fewer abominations in the

world," she said, taking a step toward one of the nearby -taken.

Dragana, you can't do this and you know it. Someone has to find out what's going on and stop it. That's us. If you die, there's no one else. This will continue and no one will know.

Dragana stopped advancing, but her grip didn't lessen. Nor did her murder-filled gaze leave the -taken soldier. He noted it, glaring at Dragana with something between terror and hatred, and stalked off.

"I can't just let them go," she whispered. It was physically painful for her to watch him walk away.

We have to leave them be for now, Aeo said. *Until we find the one responsible.*

She released another long, low breath. Aeo felt her push the anger away and force logic to the forefront. It wasn't an easy battle.

Good. Now let's see what's really going on here.

Aeo stared at the passing -taken. At first he thought they were from the same band he and Dragana had encountered earlier, maybe Halkronar spies. But then he noticed the Aratan crest emblazoned on the uniform's collar. *The king has -taken on his side, too. Has he gone mad?*

"Looks like it."

The Halkron -taken must have driven us to desperation. There's no other explanation.

"I don't care why they did it," Dragana said. "There's no reason in the world good enough to justify this."

No argument here.

The Bok'Tarong twitched toward each -taken Dragana

passed. "How can people not know these men are -taken?"

They know, Aeo replied, noticing the frightened glances or glares of hatred from the normal soldiers. He didn't know if they understood exactly what these soldiers were, but they had to recognize the Coming Madness. No human came within arm's reach of the -taken soldiers if they could help it.

"Then why don't they do anything about it?"

This is the military. If you don't hold a position of authority, you have no right to question the decisions of those who do.

Aeo had tried to keep the bitterness from his voice, but either his tone or the memories he suppressed reached Dragana. "You were in the army?"

For a time. It didn't take.

"I was under the impression soldiers couldn't just leave at will."

You can if your commanding officer tells you to get out or die on the spot.

"You have a way with people, don't you?"

Charming and personable, that's me.

"Do I even want to ask why you were kicked out of the army?" She only paused for a second, not giving Aeo time to answer. "No, I think I know why. Arrogant, defiant, unwilling to work as a team or take orders. Believes he's always right and takes what he thinks he deserves. Doesn't give a moment's thought to the wants or needs of others."

If she hadn't spoken each statement as an accusation, Aeo might have laughed. *That's surprisingly accurate. And it was those traits that got me chosen to be the king's assassin.*

She scoffed and rolled her eyes. Before she could respond, a human soldier approached her. "Lady warrior," he said, bowing ever so slightly, "I have been instructed to escort you to the Mage General." He tried—and failed—to keep his eyes away from the Bok'Tarong.

"May I ask why?" Dragana asked.

"Your reputation precedes you. The Mage General wishes to avoid any... unpleasant interactions between you and his soldiers."

So he knows about the -taken, too, Aeo said. *I should have known.*

Dragana smiled at the soldier with more charm than Aeo would have guessed the warrior-woman had at her command. Even the crimson streaks in her brown eyes lost their fiery edge when she wasn't about to murder the person she looked at.

She motioned to the soldier. "I would be happy to meet with the Mage General."

Careful, Dragana. You keep that up and people might start mistaking you for an attractive woman.

A string of curses floated through Dragana's mind.

The Entana grew more numerous the deeper they went into the camp, until the -taken soldiers outnumbered all else ten to one. Dragana's instinct to kill surged through them both. These men and women were choosing to spread death through the world and Dragana wanted—needed—to put an end to them. Aeo found himself plotting a path through the Entana, tagging which enemies to avoid and which looked like easier targets.

"Calm down," Dragana whispered. "It's hard enough for me to keep my composure without you riling me up."

Sorry.

She cracked a smile. "No you aren't."

Aeo chuckled. No, he wasn't. *If you lost it and started slashing at these -taken, I'd be all too happy to help. But since we need diplomacy here…* With regret, he pulled his thoughts away from battle.

Dragana nodded and followed her escort toward a large tent decorated with the king's banner. Just below it flew another that belonged to the Mage General—a sword and a hand casting a spell crisscrossed in the middle.

Don't trust a word he says to you, Aeo said. *Watch yourself in there. This man will eat you for dinner if you show any weakness.*

"I've dealt with plenty of disagreeable people in my time," she replied under her breath. Aeo got the feeling she included him in that category.

Not like him. This guy is different. He gives me the creeps.

"I didn't think anyone intimidated you."

No one does. Except him.

She blew out a deep breath. "All right. Anything specific I need to know?"

He's the one who conditioned me to be the king's assassin, he replied, *and the one who orchestrated my contract to kill the last bearer of the Bok'Tarong.*

Her heartbeat raced. "Oh."

Whatever you do, don't tell him it's me in here.

Dragana stepped up to the tent, but a guard placed his hand in Dragana's path before she could enter. "No weapons allowed in the Mage General's presence," he said.

Dragana gripped the hilt of the Bok'Tarong. "Do you know

what this is?"

"I… I have an idea, lady. But the rules are clear. No weapons, no exceptions."

"My rules are clear too. Wherever I go, the Bok'Tarong goes. No exceptions." Her stare returned to the fiery, intimidating gaze Aeo was more familiar with.

A muffled voice Aeo knew all too well came from the depths of the tent. "Let her pass, lieutenant. I have nothing to fear from the Taronese."

Dragana smirked at the soldier and waved Aeo at the man in a little "I win" gesture as she passed.

The moment Dragana stepped into the Mage General's tent, Aeo's vision went black. Complete, utter blackness, like when he'd been alone and lost in the forest. Despite himself, he started to panic.

Dragana, I can't see!

Her face must have registered Aeo's fear, because a smooth male voice spoke to them both. "Forgive my caution, lady warrior. There is a magic-dampening field around my tent at all times. For security and defensive purposes, of course. It will not damage the enchantment upon your sword, I assure you, but it will render it… weakened while in my presence."

Here. Dragana sent the thought to Aeo, along with an image of what she saw. It wasn't as crisp as his spirit-vision would have been, but it was better than nothing.

Aeo sent a surge of gratitude back to her.

The Mage General's tent looked like any other command center, filled with maps and weapons and other requirements for war. The Mage General himself stood before them, back straight and arms behind him in military rest. His hair had started to gray around the temples since Aeo had last seen him. *Ha. Serves you right.*

The Mage General appraised Dragana before speaking with a bored, almost disdainful tone. "The renowned warrior of the Taronese and bearer of the Bok'Tarong. I'd heard rumors you were in the area."

Dragana nodded her head in what could have been a slight bow. "Greetings, Mage General. I assume since you know my position, you understand why I'm here."

"For your sake, I hope I'm wrong."

The Mage General remained at ease, confident his veiled threat wouldn't be acted upon. Anger tightened Dragana's muscles. Somehow she was able to keep her voice cool.

"Mage General, you must understand the nature of these people."

"I am a mage and the right hand of the King of Arata. I understand more of the world's secrets than any man alive."

Arrogant bastard. Too bad he's probably right.

If you don't shut up, I'll sheathe you. I have to concentrate. "Then I would like to know why you have allowed a large number of -taken free access your camps."

"All those in my camps are servants of the king's army and of myself."

"Then you admit to sheltering -taken without the knowledge or permission of the Taronese?"

"I wasn't aware I needed your permission to employ soldiers

for a desperate war."

Yes you were. Aeo wasn't sure whether the thought was his or Dragana's.

"Entana-taken are not to be treated as normal people, Mage General. Their minds can dissolve at any moment, making them an even greater threat than the enemies you fight."

"And yet while they possess their own thoughts, they are free of fear and pain. They can charge into a situation no other soldier would dare enter and emerge victorious. They fight on after losing limbs or bleeding from terrible wounds. Without them, this war would already have been lost. They are saving this kingdom."

"They aren't fit to be in society."

"This isn't society, my lady. This is war."

Dragana grit her teeth, forcing a semblance of calm into her voice. "Even so, they are -taken. They shouldn't be here."

"Would you stop them from fighting, knowing the greater good they do?" The Mage General started pacing the tent, never turning his back on Dragana. He gestured to a map of the area, dark chalk lines marking the tides of the war. It didn't look good for Arata. "Innocent people would be dead now if these -taken hadn't stopped the advance of the enemy. They are the reason we have fought to a stand-still instead of losing our country. If you remove them now, we *will* lose. Would you allow that to accommodate your narrow-minded principles?"

She hesitated, resisting the urge to fidget and forcing confidence back into her tone. "It isn't my call to make. I must follow the orders of the Taronese, and that means these -taken are mine."

Dark anger crept into the Mage General's eyes. "You have no right to intrude upon the way I run my army."

"I have every right. The Bok'Tarong is the only weapon that can stop the spread of the Entana. That makes them, and the safety of the world, my responsibility."

"These men and women are members of the king's military. They are protected by his decree of sanctuary for anyone who bears his crest."

Dragana took a deep breath, hoping it would cleanse her words of their venom. "Sanctuary cannot be provided to those who are a danger to themselves or those around them. None are more dangerous than the -taken. We cannot allow them to be used as weapons."

The Mage General advanced, his face inches from hers. His words came out in a vicious whisper. "My -taken warriors are granted to me by the king himself. If you wish to remove them from service, they must be released by him. The king will ask my advice on the matter, and I will inform him that my -taken are an essential part of his army. That is the truth. I cannot defeat Halkron without them, and I will not allow us to lose Arata because the Taronese cannot accept that we use the -taken to save lives."

Dragana matched the Mage General's stubborn expression. "I will take this matter to the king, if you force me to."

"Go ahead. Try all you want, but you will never get my -taken."

He's right, Aeo said, knowing the truth was dangerous but

speaking it anyway. *The king doesn't have the stones to stand up to the Mage General.*

Dragana stared at him for a moment, indignation making her tremble. The Mage General met her gaze, calm and unruffled as always. Without another spoken word, but a fair amount of silent cursing, she ducked out of the tent and stomped away.

She glared at each of the -taken they crossed on her way out of the camp, picturing their deaths in rather graphic detail. *Now isn't the time,* Aeo said, doing his best to get them both out of there alive. *There are plenty of other Entana out there. We can't do anything about them if we die here.*

They'd almost made it out when revulsion washed over Aeo, saturating him as thoroughly and suddenly as if he'd walked under a waterfall. An oily, slimy, sewage-clogged waterfall.

It's vile. Damn it, it's vile! He gagged, wishing he could scrub the filth from his soul.

"What is it?" Dragana asked. She scanned the area, every sense on high alert.

Aeo choked, dizzy with disgust. *Over there.*

"Those are the medical tents. Maybe it's the suffering of the wounded?"

No, it's more than that. Something terrible is happening in there. I want to go in there and slaughter it. I need to.

Dragana entered the nearest tent. It was dim inside, just light enough for the healers to work without disturbing the patients. Aeo could almost smell the stench of chemicals and death that always hung around places like this. There was something else in the air here, though—something repulsive lurked just out of view.

The urge to vomit grew stronger, even without a stomach to facilitate that.

Aeo's spirit-eyes peered into the tent. Doctors scurried between writhing patients and nurses prepared tables full of equipment. Around and above it all was a miasma of squirming, inky black tendrils.

As he watched, two nurses held down a man on his right. The bed and ground around him were soaked in blood. He looked like a corpse, yet still he struggled against their hold. A doctor asked him something and the man nodded, though he looked reluctant and terrified and revolted.

One of the inky tendrils broke from the rest and snaked toward the man. His eyes widened and he did his best to break free, but he was too weak from his wounds. The tendril hovered over him for a second before filtering into his mouth, ears, and eyes. The man's soul screamed, piercing Aeo's spirit like a lance of fire.

Each second lasted a year. Aeo fought against his revulsion and his urge to destroy as the Entana drowned the man's spirit in darkness. The clear spark of humanity dimmed until it was extinguished. Only the blackness of the Entana remained.

The man stopped struggling and flopped onto the bed, exhausted and pale but calm. His breathing slowed and he sank into a deep, almost drugged sleep.

"By the gods of Taron," Dragana whispered. "What hell is this?"

This is where the devils are born, Aeo said. *They're breeding -taken here. Wounded soldiers come in, Entana-taken berserkers go out.*

"Please tell me you're joking."

I wish I was. They're using the Entana to heal wounds and take away the soldiers' pain and fear.

Both stood in silence for a moment, watching the sleeping -taken. Knowing these men and women were taking on Entana willingly angered Aeo, but watching them accept the possession made him sick.

Dragana moved toward the man without a conscious thought. She raised the Bok'Tarong, hand shaking with horror and rage and fear.

She paused, poised over the man, ready to strike. Her heart burned to kill him, just as Aeo's spirit screamed to destroy the Entana. But for the briefest of moments, neither of them acted against the wounded, defenseless man.

"Excuse me, do you need attention?"

Dragana's eyes snapped to the small doctor approaching her. He appraised her with cool, analytical eyes, then noticed the sword raised over his patient. He raced to her side, yanking her arm down and pulling her away from the sleeping -taken.

Dragana used his momentum to swing around, facing him. She lashed out and grabbed him in a painful grip on the shoulder. "What are you doing here?"

To his credit, the doctor didn't whine or moan in pain. "I should be asking you the same question. We heal people in this tent. We do not kill them."

"You just condemned this man to death by doing what you did."

Everyone in the tent had gone still and quiet, their eyes

locked on Dragana and the doctor.

"We are saving lives."

"Saving lives? By infecting people with Entana? You realize this is what you call the Coming Madness, don't you?"

"The Mage General has taught us how to control the process. If properly managed, it isn't a plague. It allows us to rescue those on the very brink of death. I am a healer—I will use any means necessary to preserve a life."

"You aren't saving them. You're prolonging their death at the cost of their soul."

Her grip tightened on the man's shoulder without her realizing it. He cried out when the pressure squeezed his nerves, but he didn't cower under her fury. "None are forced to take the Entana. Each man or woman is given a choice, and it is up to them whether they accept."

Dragana's grip slackened. "Then it's true? They choose to become -taken?"

"The Entana can heal tremendous wounds and calm the mind."

"They don't calm your thoughts. They erase them."

The doctor shook his head. "Not when the person is willing. When the mind doesn't struggle, it and the Entana form a partnership. They work together, with the Entana feeding on excess emotions or sensations. Nothing more. The person's pain and fears are relieved, their sanity remains intact, and the Entana is fed. There's even evidence the Entana can keep a person alive indefinitely, healing the body of everything from illness to old age."

"Sacrificing yourself to a spiritual parasite isn't an acceptable price just to live forever."

The doctor led Dragana's gaze to the sleeping man. "Tell that to him. Without the Entana, he would be dead now. His wife would have become a widow, his children fatherless. Now he will live, fight, and return home. He has a future because of the Entana."

"I should kill them all," she said. Her voice, though, held little conviction.

The doctor straightened. "I would not allow it." Dragana released the man, who rolled his shoulder and moved to place himself between Dragana and the wounded -taken. "And now, I must ask you to leave. Our patients need rest."

Stunned, Dragana nodded and turned away. The Bok'Tarong reflected the sliver of light entering through the tent flap, illuminating the deep darkness of the Entana medical tent.

The doctor placed a gentle hand on her sword-arm. "I'm sorry. In the heat of the moment, I didn't recognize... This must be difficult for you to accept."

She paused long enough to cast one more glance around the tent. "I can never accept it," she said. "Nor should anyone."

Chapter Eleven

Autumn was brutal in the mountains. The pass from Starek to Arata was low enough they didn't run into snow yet, but the temperature was bitterly cold. The winds were even worse. There was no vegetation here to slow the gales—they barreled through the stone corridor like a river and cut through Raeb's new wool cloak as if it was a thin cotton tunic. He and Saydee would hit a brief respite from the chill when they descended into the forests of Arata, but winter was only a couple weeks off. Raeb would just have to get used to being cold until spring.

"Raeb?"

He sighed. The girl couldn't make it an hour without finding something to chatter about.

"If we don't find the Bok'Tarong, how will we kill the Entana?"

She'd been asking that question all the way through the desert, into the foothills, and now into the mountains. She'd continue into the forests if Raeb let her. He had stalled her by insisting they'd find something, but they both knew the chances of that were slim.

He stomped along the path. They only had one plan, and it wouldn't work without the Bok'Tarong. But how could he do that? He had more reasons to avoid the Bok'Tarong than she could fathom. Sometimes it seemed like his entire life revolved around that damned blade. It had always been a curse on his life. And now she expected him to waltz straight into the danger—which she only understood a tiny bit of—with some sort of bravado? Well, she wasn't going to get that. Not from him.

He slowed to say some of this to her, taking advantage of the momentary silence. It wasn't often Saydee gave him a moment to speak when she was pressing a point.

Raeb paused. It also wasn't common for the mountain pass to be completely, utterly silent. Even the wind and the birds had gone quiet.

And there was no sound of footsteps, or even breathing, behind him.

He spun back, heart hammering. Saydee had stopped following him. She stood in the road, trembling and sweating. Raeb raced back to her just as her eyes widened and she crumpled to the ground.

The Entana were attacking.

Raeb knelt by her side, slamming his knees against cold rock, and grasped her hand. "Saydee!"

Sweat already darkened her chestnut hair. "They're coming," she whispered.

Fear clenched Raeb's heart. It had been years since he was last attacked, but he'd never forget the terror of the Entana rummaging through his thoughts. There was little you could do but lock your most precious memories into your mind and pray they didn't take anything important. Had anyone taught her how to shield her mind from the Entana? Did she know how to evade their hunt and slip her consciousness into a corner, to prevent them from finding that core of personality that was *her*? "You have to hide," he whispered. He doubted she could hear him, but hopefully some part of her subconscious would recognize his words. "Get to a place the Entana won't find you."

She was hyperventilating, thrashing as if fending off invisible enemies. Her free arm slammed into his side, stealing his breath, but he didn't care. His pain was nothing compared to hers.

"Run, Saydee!"

Her eyes darted back and forth behind her eyelids. Her expression twisted with panic and genuine terror. Raeb's memories of this were so vivid, he found his breath coming too fast, sweat pooling in his palms. The utter vulnerability, the sheer terror, the horror of feeling a monster in your most intimate thoughts. Nothing Raeb had experienced in all his long years had ever come close to being as traumatic as this. And even though the Entana were leaving his mind alone—likely the Keeper of Secrets' doing, psychological warfare seemed to be a favorite of his—Raeb began to panic.

This was the reality -taken lived with—never knowing when the Entana would swoop down for a snack. Who would you be when you awoke? If the Entana didn't drive you mad, they left you broken, no longer whole. You would never know what memory they'd taken. There was just a gaping hole, a blank, with no hints of what had been there. Raeb had known people who lost all recollection of their families, their professions, even entire decades. They were never the same again.

Saydee's breathing returned to normal. Her thrashing stopped until she became so still she could have been a corpse. After such violence, the silence was unnerving. He shook from head to toe. He didn't know if she had escaped or if the Entana had caught her. All Raeb could do was wait.

He reached his fingers toward her eyelids, but changed his mind. He didn't want to know if Saydee had full Entana eyes.

*
**

NIGHT FELL, AND Raeb still waited. The wind howled through the pass like a hungry wolf. A tiny indent in the rock walls offered enough shelter for a tiny fire and little else. He leaned against frigid stone and stared at the flames, his mind far, far away.

Saydee lay next to him, sleeping fitfully. She whimpered, and he placed his hand on her shoulder. It seemed to calm her.

Why was he so worried about her? She was a stranger who interrupted his silences with mindless chatter, who was almost obnoxiously optimistic when she wasn't haunted by whatever secrets her past held. He hadn't wanted her to tag along, but her magic made their companionship a necessity. She made every day on the road a trial in patience. So why was he afraid the Entana may have pushed her into insanity?

He felt helpless. They *were* helpless against the Entana. If he didn't do something to stop them, the -taken were just biding their time until that final attack. Which meant the Entana had already won.

Saydee woke from a nightmare with a gasp, shivering and drenched in sweat. Tears streamed from her part Entana, part human eyes. Raeb wasted no time wrapping her in a blanket and then his arms. She bundled into both and wept.

She felt so small in his arms. She was so young.

He might not have anything to lose in death, but she and countless others did. He couldn't just think of himself anymore.

"This has to end," he whispered. "No more stalling. We have to let the Bok'Tarong find us."

*
**

DRAGANA, PLEASE TELL *me what's going on.*

They'd been halfway to Karim, preparing their speech to the king, when they stopped in a tiny roadside inn for supplies. A few words from the innkeeper and mention of a blind man looking for the Bok'Tarong had changed everything. She'd barreled out like an arrow from the bow, heading southeast instead of northeast.

Aeo had argued, of course. She'd spent the last weeks teaching him how important it was to destroy the Entana, and a single rumor had convinced her to drop everything. He hadn't understood. He still didn't, and Dragana's excitement made her thoughts an incoherent jumble.

Please, Aeo, just trust me.

One simple sentence stopped all his thoughts in their tracks. He couldn't believe she'd spoken it. Not the please, nor the implications of trust building between them, but the fact she'd used his name. She'd acknowledged him as a person, not just the disgraceful assassin invading the Bok'Tarong.

He may not have understood why they'd abandoned their fight with the Mage General to go after a blind man, but after hearing his name on her tongue, he'd follow Dragana anywhere.

The glow of a fire, still lit to ward off the morning's wintry chill, had led them right to the camp. It had been abandoned minutes before, and the footprints leading away from it were deep and clear through the soggy undergrowth.

It didn't make sense. From what he'd been able to gather from Dragana's scattered thoughts, this man had been hunted by the Taronese for years—uncounted bearers had followed his trail across the whole of the continent but never caught him. And now this sloppy retreat? His path through the woods would be obvious to even a novice tracker.

He tried to tell these things to Dragana, but her emotions and bloodlust were so high he couldn't get through to her. She ran after the footprints recklessly, with no regard for even her own safety.

A rampaging bear would be more subtle than she was right now. The man would have no trouble avoiding her and slipping away.

But Aeo wasn't convinced whoever left this trail *wanted* to get away.

Dragana crashed through the trees and entered a small clearing. A man stood on the other side as if—no, *because*—he'd been expecting them.

He looked different without his blind man's lenses, but Aeo still recognized him. *That's the blind man from the tavern. He's the one who led me to the Bok'Tarong.*

He imparted these thoughts to Dragana, but she still didn't hear him. Her heart pounded and the hand holding Aeo shook. Her eyes were glued to the man, her body still as a cat who'd sighted its prey.

He made no move to run. He just stared at Dragana as if he'd always known this day would come. There was peace in his strange Entana eyes. Eyes, Aeo noticed, that seemed to see just fine.

Rage boiled in Dragana's heart. She raised the blades, leveling the points at his chest. "Raeb," she hissed, as if naming a demon. "Traitor."

"Traitors choose to change sides," he said, frustration and sadness and seething anger battling in his voice. "I wasn't given a choice. Do you truly think I wanted to become a -taken? I would have given my life for the Bok'Tarong."

"Anyone who would betray the Taronese for the Entana could never be worthy of it."

Wait. Had he been a Taronese warrior?

The man drew a sword. Dragana settled into a ready stance. The air between them crackled with tension.

"Is a warrior's final test still single combat? Did you have to defeat the temple masters to prove you were ready to bear the

Bok'Tarong?" the man asked.

"You know I did."

"Then let's see which of us is the most worthy."

Dragana's smile showed more teeth than a wolf's. "Gladly."

Their swords met before Aeo had even realized the fight was on. Dragana's fury calmed with the focus of battle, her thoughts clarifying just enough for Aeo to read a bit of the history with this man. A Taronese warrior-in-training leaving the temple for the Entana. From that moment, his fate had been sealed. His name had been repeated until all knew it as well as their own. Each Taronese warrior to follow would hunt for him as they traveled the world. The one who killed him would forever be honored in the Halls of the Bearer.

Aeo's brief moment of distraction was all it took for Dragana to gain her advantage. She spun and struck, knocking the blade from Raeb's hand. She swept out her leg at his knees. The joints buckled, the man toppled, and Dragana helped him to the ground with a boot on his shoulder. He landed hard enough Aeo heard the air blasted from his lungs.

Dragana straddled him, holding the Bok'Tarong to his throat. She was so angry she literally growled. Aeo suspected she didn't even know it.

"Since I'm going to die anyway," Raeb said, his voice hoarse, "at least let me die on my feet."

Dragana's eyes narrowed, but she didn't finish him just yet.

"I've already lost. Allow me a warrior's death. Please."

"You don't deserve a warrior's death," she said. But she stood, letting Raeb regain his feet. He groaned and moved slowly.

She didn't help him.

Aeo wasn't sure what to make of this man. From Dragana's thoughts, he'd expected some kind of murderous monster. Once Aeo learned he was a -taken he'd expected a ravenous lunatic, or a horror like the fully sane -taken soldiers they'd fought weeks ago. But Raeb was none of those things. In fact, he wasn't like any other -taken Aeo had ever seen.

He turned his spirit-eyes to the man. Entana tendrils snaked through his head, more than he'd ever seen in a single person before. More than he'd seen in ten peoples' heads.

But through all of that, the light of Raeb's soul burned clean and clear.

Something wasn't right.

The Entana were evil. Aeo pitied the -taken but their souls were beyond help. He'd seen the Entana destroy them when they entered a mind.

But Aeo didn't feel that about Raeb. He was clearly -taken. Only an idiot could miss that. But he wasn't evil.

Dragana pulled back to strike, but a female voice cried out, "Wait!"

A young woman—no more than a girl—ran to them and shoved Raeb back, placing herself between the man and Aeo's blades. She too had the tendrils of the Entana, though they were fewer and far smaller.

Dragana stopped her thrust, but barely. Anger simmered in her red-streaked eyes. Her voice was deadly calm. "Step aside, girl. This is not your business."

Aeo took another look at her. She was -taken also, but

Dragana hadn't recognized that. How did she miss it?

"I told you not to interrupt," Raeb told the girl.

"I couldn't let her kill you," she replied. Then she turned back to Dragana. "He isn't what he appears to be."

"You don't know what you're talking about, girl. You're in over your head."

"You don't know what *you're* talking about! You're willing to kill him without question when he's the only one who can help you!"

"I don't need any help, especially from a traitorous -taken." She pushed the girl away and drew her elbow back, tensing her muscles, settling her weight. Preparing to strike at Raeb again.

Aeo couldn't let Dragana do this. There was more going on here than she saw — than either of them saw.

She took a breath, preparing to strike on the exhale, when Aeo set the force of his spirit against her strike. He held the blade steady as she pushed. No matter how much she fought him, Aeo wouldn't allow it. The Bok'Tarong was not moving.

[Obey your master,] the silent voice said. [The Bok'Tarong does not deny its bearer, nor does it protect the -taken.]

Yeah, well, this Bok'Tarong does. And will.

The effort to stop Dragana nearly tore Aeo in half. He couldn't help her kill this man, at least not yet. If he proved to be a normal -taken, the kill would be quick and sweet. If not…

Aeo had to ensure Raeb stayed alive long enough to find out the truth. No matter how much it hurt.

Dragana strained against the blades, her anger turning to rage as Aeo prevented her from striking. "You can't do this!" she cried.

"The Bok'Tarong cannot deny its bearer!"

Watch me, Aeo replied. It took every ounce of strength he had to restrain her. It was like holding back an avalanche with a bedsheet.

"Let the blades go and let me kill him!"

His vision started to go fuzzy around the edges. *There's something strange about this, Dragana, don't you see that? We have to find out what.*

"I'm going to kill him, whether you say it's a good idea or not! You aren't Taronese. You can't understand what he's done or how long we've been searching for him. He will die, no matter what you do. Now let go!"

I won't let you do this.

She screamed and cursed him in Taronese.

Damn it, Dragana, listen to me! he shouted back. His concentration slipped for a second, and the blades inched closer to Raeb's throat. *I didn't argue when you left the -taken breeders to chase after this guy. I trusted you when you said this was more important. Trust me now when I say don't kill him.*

"I can't. He's a traitor to my people, to the Bok'Tarong, to the human race! He serves the Entana. He must die!"

After all the times she'd forced him to listen to her, after all the ways she'd shown him his errors, she could at least accept the same from him. And if she wouldn't accept it on her own, he would make her.

Aeo focused on the man's clear soul and forced Dragana to see it. She shook her head, refusing to acknowledge it, but he kept that image forefront in her mind. *Look. Whatever Raeb did, it hasn't tarnished his spirit. His soul is free from the Entana.*

"It isn't possible," she said. She wasn't screaming anymore, but there was more than enough venom for the words to sting. "He's a -taken. My people have sworn vengeance on him. I have to kill him." She strained against the blades, but Aeo held them firmly now.

You don't kill innocent people, Dragana. If you do this, it won't be justice. It'll be murder.

"You can't murder a -taken."

"I beg to differ," Raeb said. He'd taken several steps away from Dragana, but otherwise he hadn't moved or tried to flee.

Dragana shot him a look of pure rage, the crimson streaks in her eyes burning.

He raised his hands in a half warding, half calming gesture. "I don't know what the spirit in the sword is telling you, but you should listen to it. I didn't come here for suicide-by-Bok'Tarong. I have a plan, and I need your help."

"Why should I even listen to you?" Dragana asked.

"Because I'm your best chance to rid the world of the Entana forever."

That, finally, made Dragana pause. The pain of holding her back eased, enough to allow Aeo a moment to gather what strength he had left. "That's a lie," she said. "You're a servant of the Entana. You would never plot to destroy them."

"Do you think we *enjoy* being -taken?" he asked. "You think we want to feel our minds being eaten away, slipping ever closer to insanity?" Dragana's muscles tensed again, but Raeb didn't stop his rant. "I don't care what you believe about us. But here's the truth: the -taken hate the Entana more than anyone. We despise them more than the Taronese ever have, or ever will. Not all of us are weak. Some are willing to risk death, insanity, or worse to be free from the Entana. Like I am. If you kill me, you waste an ally with more information, more motivation, and more access to your enemy than you could ever hope for. Without me, you will never get close to truly defeating the Entana, simple as that."

Dragana was trembling. She was still angry, unbelievably angry, but his words had rocked the entire foundation of her training.

"How do I know this isn't some kind of trick?"

"You don't," he said. "You have to trust me."

Dragana laughed. "I will never trust you."

Then trust me, Aeo said. I believe he's being honest, at least in his intentions. Whether or not he can pull it off... we'll have to see.

Dragana closed her eyes, and her subconscious growl returned.

Just go with it for now. See what he has to say. If you still don't believe him after he's said his piece, then we can talk about killing him.

"All right," she said at last, eying the -taken and his companion with open hostility. "But if I suspect this is a trap, I will kill you both."

"Agreed."

CHAPTER TWELVE

They went back to the abandoned campsite, which Raeb and the girl had little trouble getting back into shape. Many of their supplies had been hidden under piles of pine needles and sticks—once removed, these were used to rekindle the fire.

The two -taken moved as if they were well accustomed to this ritual, though their eyes darted from each other to Dragana in clear worry. Dragana hung back, arms crossed in front of her chest, the Bok'Tarong held in a tight grip along her left leg.

Soon a pot of stew simmered over the flames. The girl offered Dragana a bowl, which she took as if handed a venomous snake. She sat at the -takens' fire but didn't eat.

Aeo could feel how much Dragana hungered for real food. Her mouth was salivating. Pride, rather than true suspicion, kept her from eating. *If it was me, I wouldn't waste an opportunity like this. What I wouldn't give to be able to eat again…*

The girl, Saydee, forced introductions and a few moments of awkward small talk before Raeb got down to business. He explained their situation between large, greedy spoonfuls, starting with the still-unbelievable *we want to destroy the Entana* and following that up with a lot of technical details on some kind of ritual and a very elaborate plan. It left Aeo with more questions than answers. But as soon as Raeb began telling them of a journey to the spirit world, Aeo was fascinated.

"How did you get to this Entana hive?" Dragana asked.

"I was taken there by the Keeper of Secrets. He's a sort of ambassador between the Entana and the humans," he added before Dragana had to ask.

"Why did he do that?"

Raeb shifted, betraying his discomfort with the subject. "He sensed I was trying to reach the Entana. He wanted to humiliate me, I guess, for my useless attempt."

How was he trying to get to the Entana? Aeo asked. Dragana voiced his question.

"He was using me," Saydee said.

Dragana looked at her. "What?"

Saydee glanced at Raeb, who gave a tiny nod. She took a deep breath, settling into a relaxation similar to Dragana's meditation. A second later her form shimmered, like she was merely a reflection in an agitated pool. A glamour, falling.

Dragana gasped as she recognized the Entana eyes.

"Because of my magic, I have a unique connection to the Entana. I can see and hear them. Raeb was trying to use that connection to send his spirit to the Entana and find a way to destroy them."

Dragana was so overwhelmed it took her several seconds to decide which of her many questions to ask first. "How did you become -taken, if you're a mage?"

"I'm not powerful enough to be a true mage," she said. There was a distinct sense of regret and anger in her tone.

"Even so, any magic at all should have made you immune to the Entana. How did this happen?"

Saydee's voice turned cold. "I'd rather not say."

Dragana's hold on Aeo's hilt tightened. "If the Entana are learning how to take mages, I need to know how."

"Our agreement was for a truce and a proposition to work together," Raeb interrupted. His mouth was set in a stubborn, angry line. "Our personal pasts, for good or ill, weren't included in that deal."

Icy silence fell over the group.

"This could have huge repercussions," Dragana replied with forced calm. "The Entana are already changing their tactics and waging a war of their own. Knowing how they possessed a mage could help us figure out what they're up to and how to stop them."

Raeb held up a hand. "The Entana are waging a war?"

Dragana shut her mouth in an eerily similar mimic of Raeb's earlier expression.

They told us part of their story, Aeo said. *We should return the favor and tell them what we've learned.*

You are too trusting, Dragana told him.

This isn't trust, this is logic. We don't always get to choose our allies. Even if you don't like them, you have to work with them. Dragana huffed. *We'll never get anywhere if you don't share anything. Especially something as vital as this.*

Dragana, seething inside, told them about the Mage General

and the -taken berserkers in short, clipped sentences. "Not only is the king breeding -taken for his war, but these people are accepting the possession of their own free will. We were told by one of them the Entana were planning to spread to the entire world, and their willing servants were growing in strength and numbers. We think this might not be the king's war after all, but some machination of the Entana."

Raeb shuddered, and Saydee looked like she was about to lose her supper. "Why would anyone accept the Entana?" he asked.

"Many are on the brink of death when the offer is made. The Entana save their lives."

"I'd choose death. Any day," Raeb said. He took a deep breath, and Aeo could almost see his thoughts whirl in his mind. "If the Entana are working through a human army, the Keeper of Secrets must be behind it."

"And the Entana ambassador must be working with someone who has the power to command Arata's army," Dragana said. "Which means the Entana are working with the king."

With the Mage General, you mean, Aeo corrected. *The king is ruler in title alone.*

Dragana told the others Aeo's comment, and Raeb nodded. "That sounds about right."

"If the Entana are using human armies to conquer more people, the entire population will become -taken in no time," Saydee said. "There won't be anyone to stop them."

"Yes, there will," Dragana said, hefting Aeo so his blades reflected the firelight. "The Bok'Tarong and I will stop them."

"Not alone," Raeb said. "You won't get anywhere without

us."

Again, silence. Even the light was dying as the sun set, as if the group's anger darkened the world around them.

Aeo could feel Dragana's simmering rage at working with -taken. Raeb didn't seem any more pleased at the thought than she did.

Well, this should be fun, Aeo thought.

This isn't the time for jokes, Aeo.

Nor is it the time to push away possible allies, no matter how much you want to. Didn't you hear the things Raeb has done? There's no way we could do that on our own. His abilities give us the best chance of destroying the Entana. It doesn't matter where or how he got them. He's willing to let us use them. We should accept the offer.

They're -taken, Aeo. How can I trust them?

I didn't say to trust them. I said work with them. There's a difference.

Dragana clenched her teeth and her grip on the Bok'Tarong tightened. "What were you planning?" she asked Raeb. "And what do you need us for?"

"We want to get back to the hive, with the Bok'Tarong. If we take the weapon to the source, it should be able to destroy the Entana once and for all."

"Why can't we do that without you?"

"You'll need Saydee's connection to the Entana to get you there, and you'll need my help to get into the hive. The Keeper of Secrets and I have… a history. I can get us past whatever defenses the Entana might have and into the heart, where it'll be vulnerable. Besides, one warrior and a sacred blade won't be enough. You'll need another blade at your side."

Raeb drew out a blade unlike any Aeo had ever seen—a horizontal hilt surrounded by five dagger blades in a semicircle. They radiated from his fist like a deadly sunburst. Aeo sensed a great deal of magic coming from those blades, magic that was almost as oily and evil as the Entana.

The last of the sunlight disappeared, leaving the forest as dark as the dread Aeo felt.

I don't like that blade, he told Dragana. *There's something evil about it.*

She gripped the Bok'Tarong a little tighter, holding it close. "What is that?"

Raeb's eyes were glued to the blades in his hand. His eyes reflected the firelight as if they were glowing. "I call it Sunray. It reveals magic and the spirit world, absorbs magic, and unravels enchantments." He paused for a moment, and behind the admiration in his voice Aeo caught a deep hatred for the weapon.

They were silent for a while, all eyes on the dark Sunray. Finally Raeb looked up and caught Dragana's eye. "The Bok'Tarong is needed to destroy the Entana, but without a distraction, something that'll hurt the Entana enough to keep them occupied, you'll never get close enough to strike. Sunray and I will be that distraction for you."

Raeb and Saydee did their best to look casual and uninterested, though Aeo knew they were anxiously waiting for Dragana's decision.

It sounds like we really do need them, Aeo said.

The surge of bitter frustration he received in reply told him Dragana knew it, too. She just didn't want to admit it. *They're both keeping a lot of secrets,* her thoughts said.

We're all keeping secrets from each other. That's just the way these kind of things work.

Dragana glanced around, as if searching the trees for any other option. "I can't walk away from an opportunity to destroy the Entana, no matter how improbable it seems. But I also can't put my trust in two -taken, one of them being the Taronese traitor." She'd kept most of the venom from her tone, but Raeb still flinched when she named him that way. "You'll have my help, and that of the Bok'Tarong, as long as I'm sure this isn't a trick. If you betray our alliance, you will feel the sting of the spirit-blades. I can promise you that."

Aeo watched their reactions. He'd been very good at spotting cheats and traitors in his life, and he didn't see any hints of that in them. They were serious about this plan and their partnership, and their relief at Dragana's acceptance was palpable.

He conveyed this to Dragana, and she acknowledged by relaxing slightly. She left the Bok'Tarong in her lap and took a tentative bite of the stew Saydee had given her. She perked at the first taste, then took another. Soon she was eating with relish.

The new allies settled into the camp, but talk was limited to necessary questions and uncomfortable, forced chatting. When Dragana lay down to sleep, she kept Aeo close by. *Watch over me,* she said. *Make sure they don't try anything.*

Dragana might not fully trust Aeo, but she trusted him more than the -taken across the fire. It was a start.

Chapter Thirteen

Raeb would never sleep again.

He'd hoped that once they'd gotten the Bok'Tarong's help, he'd stop worrying enough to get some rest. How naïve. The Bok'Tarong glinted in the firelight, mere strides away, as if ensuring he wouldn't forget its presence. As if he could. Each time he closed his eyes, images of that sword pointed at his throat and the murderous rage in Dragana's expression jolted him awake. Every little sound was Dragana sneaking up to him, an ambush prepared to end his miserable existence.

No matter how exhausted he might be, sleep would be impossible until all this was over. One way or another.

The night dragged on, endlessly, Raeb tossing and turning but never able to let Dragana and the Bok'Tarong from his sight. He could hardly wait for dawn to break. Anything was better than this torment.

Apparently he wasn't the only one thinking these thoughts, because within moments of sunrise they were all awake and anxious to get moving.

"So what's the first step in this grand plan of yours?" Dragana asked, already cinching up her pack. Saydee shoved small flatbread sandwiches at them as they passed by.

"We have our way to reach the Entana," he nodded at Saydee as she handed him a sandwich, "and our way to kill the Entana." He took a bite and gestured to Dragana and the Bok'Tarong. "Honestly that's more than I ever thought I'd have. But Saydee's connection isn't strong enough to take us all the way to the Entana hive. We have to find some way to strengthen it."

"How do you plan to do that?"

He looked up at the trees, glowing with morning light, and breathed deeply. He was going to regret this, he just knew it. "One of the -taken I know was researching a way to separate the link between Entana and a mind. If anyone will know how to strengthen that link instead, it will be him."

Dragana snorted. "That's your plan? Hoping someone else has done all the work and then, what, praying you can find a way to make it do what you want?"

"I'd love to hear any better ideas you might have." Raeb matched the hatred in her brown-and-crimson eyes. "Even with all your lofty talk, the Taronese have never come this close to finding a way to destroy the Entana, have you?" Dragana's knuckles whitcned around the hilt of the Bok'Tarong. Her eyes narrowed. He'd hit a soft spot, but that didn't stop him. Maybe he'd needed to say this more than he'd thought. "You're more than willing to persecute the -taken and slay them on a whim, but I'm trying to *save* them, which is more than you've ever done. My idea may not be perfect, but at least it's something more than spilling the blood of every innocent -taken around."

Dragana had the Bok'Tarong at his throat—again—before Raeb could even register the motion. Maybe he'd gone too far, but he didn't regret a single word.

Her voice was deadly calm, but he could hear the tremor in it. "You of all people should understand what we do. Without the Bok'Tarong, the Entana would have turned this entire world into -taken by now. Destroying them one at a time is better than doing nothing at all."

"And how well did that work out? The Entana you *thought* you killed returned to take another person. All you've done is amuse the Entana and kill their victims."

"You can't hold us responsible for doing our best with the knowledge we had. At least we were doing something instead of running away from our people and our responsibilities."

Her words took his breath away as surely as a punch to the sternum would. Running had been all he'd done for so long, he wasn't sure he remembered when he'd had a place to call home. He'd come close once, but he'd become so frightened of staying in one place he'd run from that, too.

Which made his proposition to return that much harder.

The spirit in the Bok'Tarong must have been calming Dragana, because she lowered the sword and took a few steps back.

Saydee stepped forward, thrusting herself into the argument. "If we're going to have a truce, we can't keep fighting like this," she said. "None of us can do everything on our own, which means we have to start putting a little faith in each other. No matter what we think of each other's pasts, we need to work together."

Dragana groaned. "That's almost exactly what the Bok'Tarong said to me."

"At least we know two of us would have gotten along," Raeb muttered. He took a calming breath, forcing as much frustration out of his voice as he could. "But this is going to keep coming up, so we might as well get it out in the open now."

He locked eyes with Dragana. "You call me a traitor, but I didn't invite the Entana into my mind. My thoughts, my life, were *stolen* from me. Everything I had worked for, everything I'd ever wanted, ripped from my grasp. And the people I loved condemned me for it. So yes, I ran from the temple. What else could I do? My own people chased me out and hunted me like some kind of disease. You blame me for running when it was the only thing I could do to save my life. You name me a traitor when everything that happened was beyond my control."

Dragana was quiet for several minutes, though Raeb knew she was talking with the Bok'Tarong. He paced, hoping the spirit saw things more clearly than the bearer. It had convinced her to spare him once before. Maybe it had a bit more sense than she did.

Finally, she exhaled. "Where is this man and his research?"

Damn Taronese and their damn stubbornness. All the explanations and justifications in the world wouldn't do any good. Even if he destroyed the Entana, he'd be a traitor in their eyes for the rest of eternity.

And now he had to divulge a secret he'd kept for almost half his long lifetime. To a Taronese warrior who clearly wouldn't listen to reason or change her mind about the -taken. He'd give anything to avoid this. But there was no other choice. If he wanted to be free, she had to know. "The -taken have a sort of unofficial homeland in the north. Last time I saw him, he was there."

Dragana's eyes widened.

"You never told me about a place like that," Saydee said.

"I haven't spoken of it in decades."

"Why not?"

He pointed at Dragana. "So she wouldn't find it." He turned to the warrior-woman. "I told you this in good faith of our truce. I'm trusting you to keep your word and help us defeat the Entana — not the -taken."

Her eyes moved from Raeb to Saydee and back.

"And there is a difference," he added. "I promise you that."

*
**

DRAGANA SLOGGED AFTER Raeb and Saydee. It had started to rain just after breakfast, the kind of slow, drizzling rain that turned a simple walk into a full-body exercise. The trees offered little respite from the downpour, and the undergrowth was soaked like sponges. No matter how carefully she stepped, Dragana squished through muck or shivered under deluges of frigid water.

She was miserable, but Aeo would have gladly traded places with her. He longed to feel the rain on his face and the mud around his ankles. Being miserable made you feel alive.

It had been far too long since Aeo had felt alive.

Strange as it seemed, he didn't regret becoming the Bok'Tarong. Assassinating an emperor had been thrilling, but killing an Entana was fulfilling. Each time he banished one of the vile tendrils he felt like he'd done something worthwhile. And now they were working toward something even more incredible—destroying the entire Entana hive. It was a hero's quest, to save humanity from terrible monsters. And Aeo the assassin was part of it.

Perhaps he was starting to become the man he always wished he could be.

But there were times when the rosy gold body of the Bok'Tarong just wasn't enough. He missed sunshine and rain, tasting food and feeling a touch on his arm. Even little things, like the memory of a campfire's smell or the nip of a breeze, made him nostalgic for his old body. His spirit-eyes saw more of the world than he'd ever experienced, but he'd never felt so detached from it all.

Dragana's muttered swearing dragged him from his thoughts. *I despise this weather,* she grumbled.

Better enjoy this while you can, Aeo replied. *If Raeb's right, you'll be dealing with snow before we get to the -taken homeland.*

Her discomfort and frustration slipped away, replaced with images of hundreds and hundreds of -taken falling to the Bok'Tarong. It was the stuff of Taronese warriors' dreams.

You know we can't go in there and kill like that, he said. *We've agreed to help Raeb and Saydee destroy the Entana. Raeb's already risked a lot by telling us about this place, and taking us there shows a great deal of trust in your word.*

How many Entana are there? she asked. *Dozens? Hundreds? You can't tell me you don't want to kill them.*

He did. He wanted to kill every single one of them. The part of him that was the Bok'Tarong couldn't fathom doing anything else. But the part that remained Aeo wasn't so sure. After all, they hadn't killed Raeb and Saydee on sight—it had been close, but they'd waited long enough to hear their plan. And now they traveled together, on a crazy, noble mission hatched in the mind of a -taken.

You're a woman of honor, Dragana. If you broke your word to Raeb you'd never forgive yourself.

He felt her hesitate, just long enough to prove he spoke the truth and she knew it. *I swore to do my best to rid the world of the Entana,* she said.

That's what we're doing. You aren't breaking your promise to the Taronese. You're trying to find a better way to fulfill that promise by following Raeb and seeing if his theory would work.

Do you think it can? she asked, hope and fear warring in her tone.

I don't know. I hope so. To destroy every Entana at once, and free the whole world… Now that would be a kill to relish.

Dragana nodded absently. *And if it doesn't, I can return to the village later.* The daydream of -taken corpses resumed, even grander than before.

Bloodlust doesn't suit you, Aeo said.

Embarrassment shut the images off. *That's ironic, coming from a killer-for-hire.*

I never killed out of desire or bloodlust. I killed for money.

And that makes it so much better, **she said.** *I kill to rid the world of evil.*

You know, our lives weren't that different. Your training tells you to kill someone, so you do, no questions asked. I do — or did — the same. Our compulsions always pulled us to kill, even when our minds tell us not to.

The calm in Dragana's voice was dangerous. *You did not just compare me to a morally questionable assassin. The Entana need to be destroyed. Or have you forgotten that?*

I know. But think about what Raeb said. When a -taken dies, the Entana doesn't die with them. It goes back to the hive and waits to take someone else. So what are we doing when we kill the -taken?

Aeo felt Dragana searching for a response — or at least, one she could accept.

Are we killing innocent people? He'd intended to ask it as a question, but his tone had said it as a statement. *They aren't the monsters. They're just victims.*

Those people put the rest of us at risk, **she said.** *When the toe is infected, sometimes the only way to save the body is to cut it off. It isn't the toe's fault, but it's better to lose one toe than the entire body.*

I wonder if the toe would agree with you.

Dragana stumbled through another puddle. Aeo wasn't sure whether the curses that followed were directed at him or the frigid, muddy water filling her boots. *Since when have you taken sides with the Entana?*

I'm not taking sides. I'm just… I don't know. I'm confused. I want to kill those -taken as much as you do, but I don't think we should. Not yet, at least. You promised Raeb and Saydee we'd help them destroy the Entana hive — not the Entana-taken.

I remember, **she snapped.**

So let's give them a chance and save the massacre for the Entana.

I can't neglect my duties for long. I'll go along with this plan, but sooner or later I'll need to do something about the -taken.

Deal, **he said.** *If it comes to that, I'll be more than happy to help. But let's hope Raeb can prove he's right about this before time runs out.*

CHAPTER FOURTEEN

T he rain didn't stop for days. It turned to sleet and slush as they pushed northward, which only made them cold as well as wet. The evergreens were heavy with ice. Every footstep crunched with frost.

Raeb hadn't been this far north in decades, maybe close to a century. The time away had dulled his memories of how awful winter could be. He remembered now. Vividly.

They passed several towns and a few cities on their way, but they'd avoided them all. Townsfolk wouldn't take kindly to a pair of -taken coming to visit. Both he and Saydee could disguise their Entana eyes well enough, but travelers in this part of the world were rare and residents were suspicious. It wouldn't take long for them to decide something was wrong with these newcomers and force them out of town. Or worse.

Raeb encouraged Dragana to venture into the towns for food, or rest, or any other excuse to get her away from him, but she always refused. She wanted to be within striking distance if the

Entana raised their ugly heads.

As much as she worried, frustrated, or even scared him, he saw so much of himself in the fiery warrior-woman. He'd been just like her when he was training to bear the Bok'Tarong. At her age, he would have killed a man like him without a second thought. It would have been a glorious accomplishment and filled him with pride.

What had happened to that passion? Where had his convictions and fire gone?

They'd been swallowed by the Entana. Two centuries of being hunted by his own people and haunted by the Keeper of Secrets had destroyed that energy. It left him weary and frightened, a shell of the man he'd been.

He shivered and pulled his cloak tighter around him, but it wasn't the snow or the wind that chilled his bones. Not this time.

He refused to think about how close he was to finding a way out. Hope was even more dangerous than fear. When the Entana resisted and his plans failed, hope would drive him mad.

Even so, he couldn't quench the tiny fire kindling in his chest.

As the sleet turned to snow and their trail began marching up the mountains, Raeb's heart fluttered. He found his steps hurrying forward, as if of their own will.

Returning to the sanctuary had been a decision based on logic and, he hated to admit it, desperation. There wasn't anywhere else for them to find the information he needed, simple as that. But coming back made him feel like he was coming home. He hadn't expected that.

Hopefully a few of the -taken would welcome him back.

Saydee would fit right in. But how could they welcome his other companion?

His good intentions would mean nothing if Dragana decided they all had to die. It wouldn't matter that he'd been trying to free them. Their deaths would be on his head.

He was just about to turn back and claim he was lost, or the village had been destroyed, when the first hint of wood smoke reached them. Through the trees, Raeb could just make out the hill that shielded the -taken sanctuary from view.

He'd missed his chance. Too late to turn back now.

Raeb spun on Dragana. "You will not raise your blade against these people. There are hundreds of innocents in this village who have done nothing wrong. If you so much as touch one of them, I will personally repay you for each injury you've caused to every -taken throughout your life."

Dragana crossed her arms. Her expression begged him to try it. He almost obliged.

"Your word," Raeb demanded.

Dragana glared at him, then nodded. "My word."

"I'll go ahead and prepare everyone for your arrival. I don't want to bring the Bok'Tarong into their midst without warning and cause a panic. Wait here until I return."

Dragana stomped off without another word.

"I'll stay with her," Saydee said quietly. "Make sure she doesn't do anything stupid."

"Thank you," Raeb said.

Now if only someone could have kept him from doing something stupid, like bringing the bloody Bok'Tarong to the one place -taken should have been safe from it.

⁂

DRAGANA AND SAYDEE picked a spot a fair distance outside of town, tucked into a relatively snow-free space between some massive firs. Dragana didn't look forward to spending another night in the bitter cold, but she hoped this spot would offer at least a semblance of shelter.

She'd almost gotten used to the awkward silences that hung over their campsites, but tonight's felt different. Without Raeb there to continually remind her of... well, everything... she realized how little she knew of Saydee. They'd come this far together and they'd probably exchanged a few dozen words at most.

She seemed nice enough, and her cooking was definitely appreciated. But she was still a -taken. Dragana couldn't reconcile that in her mind. Sometimes she was surprised she'd let them live in the first place.

"I won't bite," Saydee said.

Dragana blinked and shook her head. "What?"

She nodded toward Dragana's side, where she held the Bok'Tarong.

She hadn't even realized she'd lifted it from her bedroll.

"Just because I'm a -taken doesn't mean I'm a horrible person, you know. The monster is in my head, but it's not me." She handed Dragana a bowl of stew. "If you would take some time to get to know us, you might realize that," she added under her breath as she turned away.

Heat rose in Dragana's cheeks, and she was glad of the dim

firelight to hide it.

"This is good," she said a few bites later.

"Thanks."

"It's nice to have real food. I'm a terrible cook."

"Really?"

Dragana nodded. "Unless I can beat it with my sword, I can't do a thing with it."

Saydee laughed, and Dragana cracked a smile. A silence only slightly less uncomfortable fell as they continued their meal.

"I'm sorry if I embarrassed you before," Saydee said.

"Don't worry about it," Dragana replied. "I'm not very good at this."

"At talking, or at seeing me as a human?"

Dragana cleared her throat. It was very hard to meet Saydee's eyes.

"It's all right." She paused. "Well, it's not all right, but I understand you feel that way. I'd expect nothing less from someone like you."

"And I suppose you're ready to lecture me on how I'm wrong," Dragana spat.

Saydee shook her head. "It wouldn't do any good. Why waste my breath?"

What was she supposed to say to that?

Saydee removed her cooking pot from the fire and emptied out the leftovers. "You and I aren't that different, Dragana. We're both strong willed and too stubborn for our own good. Sometimes we can't see the truth in front of our faces until it's too late. We're willing to stick to our beliefs of 'what's best' long after they start biting us in the ass."

Dragana couldn't help but chuckle at the accuracy of Saydee's description.

"If I was in your position, there isn't anything you could say to change my mind. But just maybe, you could *show* me how wrong I am. I might not accept it right away, but at some point I'd look back on this moment and realize you were right."

"And that's what you'll do?"

She shrugged.

Dragana knew exactly what that shrug meant. Saydee trusted her to already have the answer. Dragana had used that same shrug more than a few times herself.

She stoked the fire while Saydee cleaned the pot. The women slipped into their bedrolls a few moments later, but neither seemed quite ready for sleep.

Dragana lay on her back, wishing she could see the stars. The trees blocked her view, but they also kept out any snow that might fall. It wasn't such a bad trade. She scooted closer to the fire, grateful the dancing flames kept a little of the cold night at bay.

"How long have you had the Bok'Tarong?" Saydee asked from the other side of the fire.

"Not long. Since mid-autumn."

"Hmm. That's about the time I met Raeb," she said.

"I thought you two had been together for a long time." It was easier to talk like this. Almost like she was talking to the trees instead of a -taken. "How did you two meet?"

"He came into a tavern I was working at in Starek. I could see the Entana in his mind, but I could tell he wasn't controlled by them."

"How could you tell?"

"I don't know if I can explain it. His Entana feels different. It looks different, like it's clinging to him rather than absorbed into him. He doesn't act like other -taken. I... I'm not sure I can do any better than that. I just knew."

Like Aeo knew, she thought.

"I wasn't sure how he's managed it—I'm still not—but I wanted the same. So I followed him and basically ambushed him that night." She chuckled at the memory. "He was mad, but once he found out about my magic, he couldn't force me away. We needed each other to get free, and we both knew it."

Dragana couldn't imagine the kind of courage it would take to ambush a stranger and follow him halfway across the continent. The pull of freedom must be awfully tempting to someone who could only wait for the Entana madness to set in. "Do you miss your old life?"

Saydee took several heartbeats to answer. "All the time," she whispered. "Do you?"

Dragana shrugged. "I don't have an old life. This is all I've ever known."

"I'm sorry." After a pause, Saydee continued. "I think it would be easier not knowing what it's like to have an 'old life.' You don't have the memories to haunt you. All the things you can't do anymore, the people you loved who no longer love you. That's the worst one of all. They see nothing but our disease and think we're lost. But we're still the same person inside, at least for a while. We know we're going to die, soon and horribly, and no one cares. By the time the Entana finish us off, our only memories will be of terror. And people still think it's our fault, like we asked the Entana to take us. It's like we aren't even human anymore. We're just a menace to be destroyed, for the good of everyone else."

Saydee had been speaking mostly to herself, but each word hit Dragana like a punch to the gut. Everything Saydee had said, Dragana had done. It had been in the name of justice, but she'd still done it.

And coming from Saydee, it didn't sound anything like justice.

CHAPTER FIFTEEN

Raeb returned to them the next morning. He looked like he hadn't slept at all. For the first time, Aeo could see the marks several lifetimes had left on him.

He looked at Saydee, his expression unreadable, then turned to Dragana and Aeo. "Come with me. There's something I want you to see."

"Is everything all right?" Saydee asked.

"Just come."

Aeo didn't know what had happened to so affect Raeb, but he already didn't like it.

Raeb led them over the hill and into a small plaza on the outskirts of the village. A few merchants peddled their goods to the dozen or so people meandering around. Stone buildings lined the far side of the plaza, small and snug, outlining narrow streets. Smoke rose from many chimneys, and Aeo could almost smell the bread and wood smoke.

Raeb nodded at the villagers, who smiled and offered waves

in his direction. Then they saw Dragana and the Bok'Tarong. Some stared at the sword in terror, others let their gazes slide off her and scurried away. At least none of them started screaming.

One woman, short and comfortably plump, approached them. Laugh lines framed her eyes and mouth, though her expression held little joy now.

"This is Mara," Raeb introduced. "The Entana have claimed her husband, Matow."

A tear fell down Mara's cheek, but she lifted her chin and met their eyes.

"She's given me permission to take you to see him."

Dragana shifted. "I don't think it's appropriate…"

"It is," Raeb interrupted. "It's important for you to understand."

Raeb's tone left no room for argument, so Dragana nodded. It took all her strength to keep her pace steady as she followed Raeb and Mara into a low building set apart from the others. No one spoke, as if breaking the silence never crossed their minds.

Their footsteps echoed down the long, featureless corridor. Barred and locked doors lined the walls, each with a small closed window set in it. Dragana's heart pounded so fast Aeo could feel her getting dizzy and nauseous. He wanted to comfort her, but his dread left him speechless.

Mara stopped at a door and opened the window. She spoke quietly for a moment before stepping aside and motioning for Dragana to approach.

Aeo had to mentally nudge his bearer forward. She moved woodenly, her emotions a jumble. If she'd had any possible excuse to flee, she would have.

Let me see too, he requested.

Dragana, without looking into the room, turned to Mara. "May I draw the Bok'Tarong? My sword would like to see this, as well."

Mara looked nervous, but Raeb placed a reassuring hand on her shoulder. She drew an uncertain breath and nodded.

Dragana drew the Bok'Tarong, and color and definition filled Aeo's sight. The corridor didn't look any more appealing.

She breathed deeply a few times, relaxing herself, before peering through the door's tiny window.

A middle-aged man curled in the corner of a completely empty, colorless room. Convulsions wracked his body and sweat poured from his skin. He bled from hundreds of gouges his fingernails had carved in his skin. His full Entana eyes were rabid with madness and terror. When he wasn't screaming with pain or mindless rage, he whimpered and cried like a child.

This was what the Entana reduced a person to. This was why the Taronese killed them before they reached this stage—not only to stop the Entana, but the end the person's torment.

Aeo, can you show me what you see?

Are you sure? he asked. *It's pretty terrible.*

She took a deep breath, bracing herself. *I'm sure. I need to see this.*

Aeo opened his spirit-eyes and conveyed the image to Dragana. She gasped, her stomach heaving and eyes filling with tears.

Tendrils thick as a man's wrist lashed about wildly, striking the man like whips. His spirit hung in tattered shreds, faint sparks of a clean soul winking out one by one. Aeo could *feel* his pain, like a million barbed teeth gouging his flesh, like acid burning his soul. He felt like he was dissolving, forced to experience every ounce of his self be consumed.

And the Entana *laughed*. Giddy, joyous, gluttonous laughter. It was the most evil thing Aeo had ever — would ever — hear.

Dragana swallowed a surge of nausea and raised the sacred blades.

Raeb's iron grip stopped her before she could go more than a few inches. She didn't resist his touch. He moved to stand beside her and, never taking his eyes from the man, spoke. "You see the difference?" Raeb whispered. Dragana nodded. "There is a man, and there is an Entana. Only one is your real enemy."

Dragana stared at the madman, and a single tear slid down her cheek. "What will happen to him?"

"He'll be given medication to make him sleep," Mara said. "And then..."

Raeb put his arm around her shoulders as she began to sob. "There's a plant that grows in these mountains that will give him a quick, painless death. It's the only mercy we can give to the fully -taken." He paused. "We perform a ceremony when the drug is given. It's called the Freeing Ceremony. I'd like you all to attend."

It wasn't a command, Aeo noticed. When he'd brought them to this place, Raeb wouldn't accept no for an answer. But now he was inviting them to the ceremony, and Aeo could tell Raeb genuinely wanted them to be there.

Saydee, who had been quiet this whole time, nodded. "I'll come. Of course."

Dragana nodded too, holding the Bok'Tarong in a respectful gesture. "As will we."

Their walk out of the building was as somber as a funeral procession.

*
**

SHE SHOULD BE packing up their camp—Mara had offered them beds in her home while they arranged the Freeing Ceremony— but Dragana huddled before a small fire, staring at but not seeing the flames before her. Aeo didn't have to ask what occupied her mind.

He could still feel Matow's torment. The essence of the man's soul was in there, somewhere, enduring the most torturous death Aeo could imagine.

Dragana huddled closer to the fire. "I don't know what to think anymore," she whispered. "I've been told the -taken are evil my entire life. Every lesson I was taught centered around killing them. All I ever wanted to do was bear the Bok'Tarong and kill as many as I could." She stared down at her hands as if horrified by the things they'd done.

And now? Aeo asked gently.

There was a long pause while Dragana tried to sort through her emotions. "That demon wasn't Matow. It was *eating* him. Matow..."

He isn't evil. He's a victim.

"You don't think the -taken deserve to die, do you?"

No, I don't. He paused. *Do you?*

Dragana felt like a traitor for even considering it. Her training had taught her -taken were violent, uncaring, inhuman monsters. But the only monster she'd seen in the village had been the Entana devouring Matow. Everyone else had seemed so… normal. Just ordinary folks carrying on with life. Maybe that's what they were.

If anyone in that village had been monstrous, it was her. They'd cast aside their fear and allowed her into their midst—her, the bearer of the Bok'Tarong, persecutor of the -taken. It was far more generous, more humane, than she'd ever been to them.

Her voice was barely louder than the crackling of the flames. "Has my whole life been a waste?"

Why would you ask that?

"I… I don't think they deserve to die either, but that's all I know how to do. My brain tells me to go into that town and slaughter them all, but my heart won't let me." She took a deep breath, staring into the fire. "I can't do it, Aeo."

Then don't do it.

"But then what am I going to do?"

Do what you promised to do, Aeo said. *Go with Raeb and Saydee. Destroy the Entana—the real Entana—and free those people.*

She fiddled with the hem of her shirt, rubbing the fabric between her fingers. "Do you believe it's possible? You heard Raeb. Sending our spirits to the Entana hive. Can we do that?"

Would it hurt to try?

"It might kill us," she pointed out.

Aeo's pause was brief. *I'm willing to take the risk if you are.*

"And what kind of payment would Aeo the assassin ask for such a dangerous mission?"

You wouldn't be able to afford Aeo the assassin for this mission.

Dragana frowned.

But Aeo the Bok'Tarong doesn't want any payment. Destroying the Entana will be compensation enough.

Dragana cracked a tiny smile. "You can be charming at times," she said. "When you're not an arrogant ass, that is."

Long shadows and a grumbling belly told Dragana it was time to get back to town. She rose, groaning, shivering as the air away from the fire stung her lungs. "I never used to feel the cold like this," she said. "It makes my joints ache."

Fear stabbed through Aeo. With all that had happened—the -taken soldiers, Raeb's insane plan, Matow's torment—he'd forgotten the price of the enchantment that kept him alive.

"Don't mourn for me, Aeo. I've known all along this would be my fate. I'm prepared to face it."

It just doesn't seem fair, he said.

She shrugged. "Life rarely is."

Dragana, when the time comes… what happens?

"When I can no longer fight, I'll take my life with the Bok'Tarong. At that point, my spirit will be transferred to the blades and I'll wait for the next bearer to find me."

And what about my spirit? What happens to me?

For a moment, the silence was as deep as the darkness falling around them. "I don't know."

Maybe if we destroy the Entana, and the Bok'Tarong is no longer needed… maybe you wouldn't have to die anymore. It was a nice thought, no matter how unlikely it seemed. Aeo didn't want to die, but if one of them could live to see a world without the Entana, he hoped it was Dragana. *Have you ever thought… if this works, and the Entana are destroyed… what you would do?*

"You mean, if I had a whole life ahead of me?" Her voice sounded more frightened than wistful.

Yeah.

Her thoughts spun as if she could barely comprehend the question. There'd been only two ways her life could end: as an elder in the Taronese temple, or growing old before her time in service of the Bok'Tarong. She'd never had the option of a different life.

And, Aeo realized, she was terrified to even consider one.

"I… I have no idea," she whispered at last. "I don't have a trade to live on or anyone to be with. All I have is the Bok'Tarong."

Aeo ached to reach out and comfort her. Her entire identity was dependent upon the sword. Without that, who was Dragana?

He didn't know what was in store for them, or what would happen to his spirit, but he was sure of one thing. *Whatever happens, Dragana, you'll have me,* he whispered. *I'll always be here to keep you safe.*

Chapter Sixteen

Aeo had expected a ceremony that ended a person's life to be solemn, but the -taken chose to celebrate instead. The plaza was decorated with streamers and silk flowers, and every merchant in town had brought their finest wares to be displayed and sold. People chattered and ate and danced. Any tears shed were wiped away, replaced with smiles and the occasional laughter. Even Mara did her best to enjoy herself, though the tears flowed more often and more freely from her.

Dragana and Saydee stood behind and a little apart from the -taken, Dragana holding Aeo between them so he wouldn't seem like a threat.

"How can they be so cheerful?" Dragana asked. "One of them is about to die."

"Death isn't necessarily a horrible thing," Saydee replied. "At this point, it's a release."

"I understand that. But everyone here seems so happy, despite all the terrible things that have happened to them."

Saydee shrugged. "It's a choice. -Taken live every day knowing it could be our last. The Entana devour our memories, leaving us with giant blanks in our lives. Some people give up. But we refuse to. The Entana take our moments of joy, so we make new ones. Always filling our minds with memories to treasure. That way, no matter what the Entana take, we still have a foundation to build on. We continue to live."

A hush fell over the crowd, and everyone turned toward the village.

A group of men bore Matow from the hospital on a pallet covered in fine cloth. He looked peaceful, sleeping deeply thanks to the drug they'd given him. Even the Entana consuming him seemed affected by it. The tendrils waved mindlessly, like seaweed in a gentle current.

Matow was placed on a makeshift dais at the front of the plaza, and people filed past him to say goodbye. Many left offerings of food or flowers on his pallet. Mara stood at his head, thanking the people who passed, her hand resting on her husband's.

Dragana's gaze returned to that simple gesture over and over. She didn't bother hiding her tears.

At last, Raeb stepped up behind the dais. He looked at the people, then down at the sleeping man. His voice, though only slightly louder than normal, carried across the plaza. "It's my honor to free you today, Matow. I hardly remember a time when you and Mara weren't there for me. When I'd grown weary of this existence, you taught me life could continue despite being a -taken. I owe my life to you many times over, old friend. I hate to see you leave us, but I hope you do so in peace and reach a place of rest. Wait for us there, so we can be together after this life has ended for us all."

He turned to Mara and spoke with the air of ritual. "You asked me to perform the Freeing Ceremony for Matow today. Do you provide me with the means to do so?"

She nodded, choking back tears, and handed him a tiny vial.

Raeb kissed Mara on both cheeks before taking the vial. He removed the cork and sniffed the contents very carefully. "The extract of the baenlo plant. Its poison is precious for the gift it gives us. With it, we can be freed from the Entana."

He leaned over Matow and, with shaking hands, poured a few drops into his mouth.

Nothing seemed to happen for a long time, but Aeo saw when Matow died. The Entana shivered and slid from his head, fleeing into the sky and out of sight. A moment later, Matow's spirit lifted from the body. Aeo had feared there'd be nothing left after the Entana's attack, but Matow must have held himself together to the very end. His eyes lingered on Raeb and Mara. Then his spirit faded, and he was no more.

Aeo knew in that moment Matow had finally, after decades, found true peace.

Tears choked Raeb's voice. "Be free, old friend."

He stepped down from the dais, and the people began to mingle. The atmosphere was more subdued, but Aeo had a feeling no one would be going home for many, many hours.

Raeb came to stand with Dragana and Saydee, both of whom were crying. "Thank you for coming," he said. He looked down at the Bok'Tarong in Dragana's hand, including Aeo in his thanks.

The assassin had never felt so honored. That brief look made Aeo feel, just for a moment, like a man again.

"Mara has agreed to give me Matow's research," Raeb continued. "We can begin studying it as soon as we'd like."

"Matow was your researcher?" Saydee asked.

Raeb nodded. "I'd hoped to be able to work with him directly, but his notes will have to do."

⁂

AEO HAD NEVER seen so many notes in his life. The study where Matow had worked was stuffed full of parchments. Stacked on every surface, stuck to the walls, strewn about the floor. The room was already small, but this much clutter made it feel claustrophobic.

When Raeb had said they would need to rely on Matow's notes, Aeo had feared they'd never find a clue to help them. Now he wondered if they could find the clues they needed amongst all the other meaningless scribbles.

Raeb spent days hunched over the parchments, leafing through them with growing interest. Dragana and Saydee tried to help, and Aeo would have, too, but Raeb shooed them away more often than not.

Tea had just been poured one morning when Raeb bowled into Mara's kitchen, a stack of parchments in his arms, knocking over a small table and interrupting their conversation. "The baenlo plant," he said, his voice breathless with excitement. "We

168

can use the baenlo plant!"

He looked at them expectantly, clearly waiting to see the same excitement on their faces. All Aeo saw were a few very startled, very confused expressions.

"Raeb," Saydee said, "that's poison."

He dumped his load of parchments onto the table, spilling tea on some and sending others skittering across the surface or onto the floor. Raeb didn't stop to clean them up. "The distillation process makes a poison," he agreed, "but a small dose of the pure plant doesn't kill. We use a single leaf to put the fully -taken to sleep before the Freeing Ceremony. A few more would put someone into a much deeper sleep, one that simulates death, but they would wake in a few days."

Dragana picked up her overturned teacup, glancing sadly at the puddle it left behind. "How does that help us?"

Raeb shuffled through the parchments, pulling out one with an abundance of scribbling on it. Two different hands had written those notes—Raeb must have expanded on Matow's original thoughts. "We need Saydee to remain calm and stable as we travel along her connection. Errant thoughts could weaken the link, or her emotions could rouse the Entana in her mind. If either of those happen, none of us will return."

"No pressure," Saydee whispered.

"We'll give Saydee a small dose of baenlo leaves, so her thoughts can't interrupt the connection. That'll give us a measure of stability on the journey."

"But the connection still isn't strong enough," Saydee pointed out. "Putting me to sleep won't help that."

"No," Raeb agreed, pulling out another almost illegible parchment. "But this will."

He placed the parchment in front of Dragana as if presenting a priceless jewel to an emperor.

Aeo and Dragana peered at the parchment, Saydee and Mara rising to look over her shoulder. Try as he might, Aeo couldn't make sense of the lines and arrows and scribbles. "What does this mean?" Dragana asked.

Raeb's shoulders sagged and he hung his head for a moment. Then he pointed at a word. "The Bok'Tarong." His finger traced an arrow to another word. "Sunray." Then another arrow. "Saydee."

When they didn't respond Raeb sighed, working his way backwards along the path he'd just traced. "Saydee needs more magic to strengthen her connection to the Entana. Sunray can absorb magic. The Bok'Tarong has a very powerful enchantment on it. While Saydee sleeps, I use my blade to siphon some magic from the Bok'Tarong into Saydee. That will increase her powers and hopefully make her connection to the Entana hive strong enough for us to travel along it. Instead of crawling to the hive along a spiderweb, it'll be like using a bowstring."

"How comforting," Dragana said.

Have you ever tried to break a bowstring? There's a reason they can fling arrows so fast.

"Raeb," Mara said, "are you certain you want to use that blade's magic?"

The way she asked it made everyone pause. Mara knew something about Sunray — something that terrified her.

Raeb's excitement vanished, like water down a drain.

"What aren't you telling us?" Dragana asked.

"Sunray… might not cooperate," he said. "The blades won't have a problem siphoning the Bok'Tarong's magic. But I'll have to make sure they don't take too much, and that they give it up instead of consuming it. Sunray doesn't like to ration itself, and it won't be eager to return the magic it's taken."

"You make it sound like Sunray has a mind of its own," Saydee said.

He didn't reply, but the look on his face answered her more clearly than words could have.

"You're asking me to trust the Bok'Tarong's magic to a greedy, sentient blade?" Dragana asked. Aeo choked as her grip on his hilt became a death-hold.

"No. I'm asking you to trust *me* that I won't let Sunray absorb the Bok'Tarong's magic."

Dragana didn't even scoff at the idea of trusting Raeb. Aeo could hardly believe it.

So many things could go wrong. If they used too many baenlo leaves, Saydee would never wake up. If the connection failed during their journey, their spirits would be lost in oblivion. And if Sunray pulled too much magic from the Bok'Tarong… well, at least Aeo wouldn't have to worry about what would happen to him anymore.

But how else would they get to the Entana hive? They didn't have an abundance of options here.

I think we should go with it. It's dangerous, but it sounds like it'll work.

Dragana bit her lip. *It sounds like a complicated way to get ourselves killed.*

We don't have much choice, **Aeo said.** *If we don't go with this plan, we're no closer to getting to the Entana hive.*

I know. I just wish there was another option.

Don't we all.

Dragana nodded. "Let's do it," she said, without much enthusiasm.

Raeb looked to Saydee. She looked pale, but she nodded.

"It won't take long to prepare. We should get some rest," Raeb said. "We'll need to be at our best."

Aeo just hoped their best would be enough.

CHAPTER SEVENTEEN

Morning dawned, and their time arrived. Everyone was too preoccupied by their fears to do more than glance at each other.

This could be it. Or this could be the end.

Either way, Raeb just wanted it to be over already.

Saydee lay on the floor, already deep in the baenlo-induced sleep. Raeb couldn't shake the image of how she'd stared at the baenlo leaves in her shaking hand, a single tear refusing to fall from her eye. She'd fed herself the poison without a word of complaint. It was the bravest thing Raeb had ever seen.

He sat next to her now, his right hand on her shoulder, Sunray in his left. Dragana was on his other side, her right hand wrapped around his fist, left holding the Bok'Tarong. The elements of the ritual were arrayed around them, filling the air with the scent of smoke and herbs.

Raeb and Dragana nodded to each other. Ready.

Raeb drew in a deep, cleansing breath and tapped into

Sunray's magic. The blade responded eagerly, its hunger filling Raeb's mind and drowning his thoughts. Motes of icy magic floated in the air, glittering like frost. His breath crystallized as the temperature plummeted.

The motes scattered, searching out other sources of magic and clinging to them, bringing the invisible forces into view. Some settled on Dragana's armband and the Bok'Tarong. Others outlined the Entana tendrils in the -takens' heads. Throughout the rest of the room wispy shapes appeared at random, small and indistinct. The ambient magic that held the world together.

Raeb focused on the motes, feeling the magic they illuminated. He could take any of it and feed it to Sunray. The blade was hungry—Raeb felt its desire as if it was his own. He craved the sweet magic.

He pulled his thoughts from Sunray's hunger. Dwelling on it would make the temptation worse. But still, restraining the blade—and himself— took an astounding amount of willpower.

Ignoring the delicious magic tickling his skin, he reached his senses toward the Bok'Tarong. Its power was immense, even more so than he'd expected. He'd thought he'd known how strong the Bok'Tarong's magic was, and how much of a feast it would be to Sunray, but this was far beyond anything he'd ever dreamed.

It would be so easy to take that magic. Just one thought, and it would be his. Nothing could stop him. He could absorb its magic, unravel the enchantment, and be done with it all. What a relief it would be. No more running. No more hiding. It would feel so good to be free. So good...

Raeb bit his tongue, hard, to bring his mind back to himself.

That wasn't what he wanted. He'd never wanted to do it. Destroy the Bok'Tarong, and the Entana would remain. That was unacceptable.

Destroy the Entana. That was the mission.

Instead of diving into the ocean of the Bok'Tarong's magic, he dipped in a toe. Just a taste of the power, nothing more. Sunray rejoiced in it, begged for more, but Raeb denied the blade its meal. He drew the magic from Sunray before it could be devoured, channeling it into Saydee. The trickle of power rushing through him was intoxicating, empowering, maddening. He longed to feast on it. He wanted it. He needed it. To be so close, but unable to savor it. It was almost too much to bear.

He bit his tongue again and tasted blood. Sunray's lust for the magic was impossible to ignore. He did his best anyway, turning his eyes to Saydee's Entana connections.

Just as he'd hoped, the tiny golden thread that made her unique was thickening by the second. Sunray's icy motes gravitated toward it as it grew. In a few more seconds, the connection would be strong enough for him to test.

Raeb heard a distant, wailing sound. He thought he recognized it, but it seemed so far away.

Sweet, delicious magic at last. What a feast.

Raeb's head jerked up, his eyes flying open. He didn't remember closing them.

Those thoughts weren't his. They were Sunray's. He wasn't devouring magic. The blades were.

The blades were!

Dragana screamed beside him, sharp and ragged. Her hands were locked around the Bok'Tarong's hilt, bone and veins in sharp relief from the pressure. Her face contorted in profound agony.

The motes surrounding the Bok'Tarong pulsed with power as they gorged on the sword's magic.

Raeb shouted something, he didn't know what, and flung the sunburst blades from him. They hit the wall and clattered to the ground. The icy motes flickered out of existence.

Deathly silence filled the room.

Saydee lay still as death, only the too-slow rising and falling of her chest showing she lived. Dragana had fainted, still holding the Bok'Tarong. Sweat was drying on her face and pooling in the fine lines around her eyes and mouth. She hadn't had those when they'd begun.

Raeb put his elbows on his knees and slumped, laying his head in trembling hands. His head pounded, his body ached, his stomach churned with acid. He breathed deliberately, trying to compose himself. He could still hear Dragana's screams in his mind, still feel Sunray's elation in its dark feast. At least, he hoped it was Sunray's elation. If those had been his own feelings, he'd never be able to forgive himself.

Reluctantly, his eyes traveled to the Bok'Tarong. He wouldn't know how much damage he'd done to the spirit blades until Dragana awoke. He prayed he hadn't caused any permanent harm. If he had, their plan to destroy the Entana was ruined forever. The Entana would have won, and Raeb's worst nightmare will have come true.

Raeb shook from head to toe, nausea rising in his throat. His companions were comatose, possibly dead. Their plan had failed, and it was all his fault.

***

Dragana groaned. She didn't want to wake up. Pain waited for her out there. So much pain and exhaustion, even worse than when the Entana had attacked her spirit those weeks ago.

It was early, not even an hour after sunrise. The bed was soft beneath her, but this morning it made her ache. She'd slept on rocks that hurt her head less than the fluffy pillow she rested on. She tried to kick off the heavy handmade quilts piled atop her, but all she managed was a few weak flails.

Her thoughts were strangely quiet.

Her hand still gripped the Bok'Tarong. From the stiffness in her fingers, she must have been holding it ever since the ritual.

The ritual. Gods, what a disaster.

Things had been going to plan. She'd been able to feel Raeb siphoning the Bok'Tarong's magic. After that, all she remembered was pain. Lots of it. And Aeo...

She lifted the Bok'Tarong to her chest. It was slightly less exhausting than lifting a mountain. "I hope you feel better than I do," she said to the sword.

Nothing. The blades were silent.

"Aeo? Are you all right?"

Still nothing.

Dragana's heart raced. What was wrong with Aeo? He never missed an opportunity to hear his own voice, especially if he could made a jab at Dragana at the same time. For him to be silent, something had to have gone wrong.

Had Raeb taken too much of the magic holding Aeo's spirit to the blades? Had Raeb... killed Aeo?

She was surprised how much that thought distressed her.

Dragana managed to pull herself from the bed. Bok'Tarong in one hand, the other on the wall to steady herself, she tottered to the kitchen and the low voices she heard there. At least she'd been given a downstairs bedroom—if she'd had to use the stairs like Saydee did, she'd have killed herself before she'd taken three steps.

Dragana squinted and cursed the morning sunlight that poured into the room. If she wasn't so worried about Aeo, she'd have given up and gone right back to bed.

Raeb and Mara sat together at the table, nursing small cups of tea. Both looked as bad as Dragana felt, with slumped shoulders and dark circles under their exhausted eyes.

Raeb leapt from his chair when he saw her. He stepped toward her, concern in his eyes, but Dragana forced him to a stop with a hand to his chest. Her other hand gripped the Bok'Tarong so tightly her entire arm felt the strain.

"What did you do?" she asked, her teeth clenched. Her voice rasped in her throat.

Raeb had the decency to look ashamed.

Mara came up beside her, placing a gentle hand on Dragana's arm. She guided Dragana to a chair and placed a hot cup of some herbal tisane before her. She didn't have any energy left to resist—she'd used it all confronting Raeb. He sat across the small table from her, hunched and sullen like a beaten puppy.

The sweet steam coming from the cup filtered through the air. Her headache eased when she breathed it in.

"Tell me what happened," she said, too weary to maintain her anger. Without that she deflated, too exhausted and defeated and terrified for Aeo to fight anymore.

Raeb peered at her, searching for something. Some of the worry in his face faded after a moment, but not much. "Are you all right?"

"I'm fine. What happened?"

"Sunray rebelled," Raeb said. "While I was concentrating on transferring the magic, it started to absorb it. The blade got out of control and nearly devoured all of the Bok'Tarong's enchantment."

Dragana's breath grew ragged. If that damned blade had taken too much of the Bok'Tarongs's magic, that would explain why Aeo was unreachable. But was he still in there at all?

Raeb stared at her, even though she refused to meet his eyes. "Something's wrong." It wasn't a question.

Dragana stared into her cup. She would not cry. "How is Saydee?"

"She's still asleep, but Mara says she should wake in a few hours."

Dragana nodded. The steam was making her eyes water. That was all.

Raeb leaned across the table and placed his hand on her arm. "Dragana, tell me. What happened to the Bok'Tarong?"

She pulled her arm out of Raeb's. "I don't know. I can't hear Aeo anymore." She hated how hurt and vulnerable her voice sounded.

"Aeo?" Mara asked.

"The spirit in the blades. That was — is — his name."

She raised the Bok'Tarong from her lap and placed it on the table between them. Was it just her imagination, or did the rosy gold blades seem duller than normal? They were still beautiful beyond description, but they seemed... Dragana couldn't bear to think it, but she couldn't help it. *The blades look dead.*

Raeb stared at the Bok'Tarong for a long moment, then reached to his belt and unsheathed Sunray.

Despite her pain, Dragana rose and grabbed his arm before Sunray came above the table.

"I have to see if there's still enough magic in the Bok'Tarong to maintain the enchantment," he explained. "Sunray can show us that. It's the only way we can know for sure if the magic is still intact."

"Last time you used that thing it nearly destroyed the Bok'Tarong!"

"I know. But I'm not channeling any magic, I'm just revealing it. I might even be able to heal some damage."

"It's because of that blade Aeo is gone to begin with. I won't let you endanger him anymore."

Raeb raised an eyebrow and evaluated Dragana. "Is it the blade you're worried about, or the spirit inside it?"

Dragana froze. The blades were the most sacred of Taronese possessions. Their mission took priority over all else. The spirit inside the blades was a guide, a mentor, and an advisor in the ways of the Entana. Nothing more.

But Aeo was more than that. He wasn't a Taronese warrior. He'd broken nearly every rule the Taronese knew about the

Bok'Tarong and done things no ordinary spirit should have been able to. He was stubborn, arrogant, obnoxious, and an annoying pain in the ass.

And Raeb was right. She needed the magic of the Bok'Tarong to be safe—but not for the Entana's sake. For Aeo's.

Dragana released Raeb's arm and fell back into her chair.

She didn't object again as Raeb brought Sunray to the table. She shivered as its icy magic flowed forth, lingering in the air as it sought out magic. Her arm burned as frigid motes settled on her enchanted armband, the carving of her spirit. Dragana ignored it. She had to remind herself to breathe as she waited to see if they would be attracted to the Bok'Tarong.

Finally, some migrated to the double-bladed sword. It was a tentative attraction at first. A mote here, a few there. They settled on the Bok'Tarong like fireflies being drawn to the darkness. Even Dragana could interpret their sluggishness—the magic was still there, but it was badly damaged.

"I can try to infuse some magic into the sword," Raeb said. "It might help the Bok'Tarong heal."

"Are you sure your blades won't rebel again?"

Raeb paused, just for a breath. "No. I'm confident I can control their hunger, but I can't guarantee anything."

Raeb's blunt honesty assured her. He wouldn't try to show off or do anything dangerous just to preserve his pride. Dragana appreciated that. But then again, could she refuse, knowing this was the only way to save Aeo? As much as she hated to put her trust in Raeb and that damned Sunray again, if she wanted Aeo back she didn't have a choice. "Do it."

The temperature dropped as he exercised Sunray's magic. Dragana kept her eyes on the motes surrounding the Bok'Tarong, praying to every god of Taron this would work. She needed the Bok'Tarong back.

She needed Aeo back.

Motes swirled around them. The air was still, but Dragana felt a breeze blow around her. Her skin prickled as goosebumps rose on her flesh.

More magic settled on the sacred blades. It still wasn't as much as they should have, but hopefully it would be enough.

Raeb lowered his blade and the icy motes disappeared. He heaved a deep sigh, as if the brief moments wielding Sunray's magic had drained him. He looked so exhausted Dragana wouldn't have been surprised if he slumped to the table and fell asleep here and now.

All eyes remained fixed on the Bok'Tarong. It didn't look any different, of course. But still, they watched.

CHAPTER EIGHTEEN

Oh gods, it hurts.

How could it hurt? It's not like he had a body anymore. But it did, more than he had ever hurt before. Even getting stabbed in the gut—and dying as a result—hadn't compared to this. He felt like he was being ripped to pieces by a pack of wolves.

No. Not wolves. By Entana. That seemed more accurate.

Sunray... that terrible blade of Raeb's had felt like that. Vile and oily, and tearing him to shreds. Was that what it felt like to be -taken? Aeo wouldn't wish that on anyone.

He tried to piece together what had happened during the ritual. Aeo felt his strength drain little by little, as if he was bleeding out on a battlefield. It wasn't more than he could bear, but he had worried about having the strength left to fight once they reached the Entana hive.

Dragana had tensed just as the sap on his strength doubled. Suddenly he wasn't fatigued, he was exhausted to his very core. He didn't have the energy to think, or do, anything.

And then the pain started. It hit him like a battering ram, running all the way through his essence. He hadn't been able to tell where the pain began or where it ended. It was in him, surrounding him, consuming him. It *was* him.

That was it. After that, his memory went blank. How much time had passed between then and now? He had no idea.

The pinpoint light of Dragana's presence, though reassuring, was almost too bright for him. Thank goodness she wasn't holding him. It was hard enough to survive without the terrible lights and sounds of the outside world.

As if she'd heard him, the light of Dragana's presence blossomed. And of course, she didn't move slowly so he could adjust. She must have run to him, because his vision filled with light and the world burst into painful view in the span of a heartbeat.

"Aeo?"

Whoa, Dragana, not so loud.

"Sorry." Her voice didn't drop all that much. "Are you all right? We were so worried."

I'm not sure if I can say I'm 'all right,' but I'm here.

Her entire body relaxed. "Thank the gods of Taron."

Aeo squashed the sarcastic remarks skirting his thoughts. She was truly happy he wasn't hurt. He didn't want to spoil that, even if he didn't feel like thanking any gods for how he felt.

Raeb and Mara hovered behind Dragana, relief plain on their faces. Apparently everyone had been worried about him.

Where's Saydee? he asked.

"She's still sleeping off the baenlo leaves. I think she should be waking up soon."

He wasn't sure, but he thought he saw Raeb and Mara trade a worried look.

What happened to me?

Dragana's thoughts screamed *Raeb tried to kill you*, but she spoke more rationally, with an effort. "Raeb lost control of Sunray. It started absorbing the Bok'Tarong's magic. If it had taken any more, it might have destroyed you."

Chills ran through Aeo's soul.

"Raeb infused the Bok'Tarong with magic after we'd discovered what happened, hoping that would be enough to keep you alive."

Well, I guess it worked. Thanks, Raeb.

Dragana didn't relay his thanks. She stood quietly, holding Aeo close as if she could protect him by her proximity alone. Her emotions were a jumble of fear and anger, mingled with relief. She couldn't even look at Raeb without scowling.

So... now what happens?

From the way Dragana's thoughts went blank and her eyes traveled to Raeb, accusing and angry, Aeo guessed they hadn't quite figured that out yet. It wasn't all that surprising. Their only plan had just spectacularly failed.

⁂

RAEB SEARCHED AND scoured his brain. There had to be some way to fix this. Saydee was still trapped in the baenlo sleep, Dragana was still angry with him, and they no longer had any way to reach the Entana hive. He was an intelligent man, with two hundred years of life experience to his name. Surely he could find a solution to at least *one* of these problems, couldn't he?

Two days of pacing and pondering, and he'd gotten nowhere.

He'd spent every waking hour wandering around Mara's small home. His mumbling had long since driven everyone around him crazy, but he pretended not to notice. He needed time to think, to figure out a way to make all this better.

His hand strayed to the empty sheath at his hip. He hadn't carried Sunray since the disaster. It had taken a full day to cleanse his mind of Sunray's lust for the Bok'Tarong's magic, and ever since he'd feared to take the blade back. If it was up to him, he'd abandon the damned thing and be free of its influence forever.

But for some reason, he found himself missing its weight at his side.

And there was problem number four. Even if Saydee's connection to the hive had survived the disaster, he wouldn't be able to use Sunray to strengthen it again. They couldn't risk it, after it had overpowered him and the Bok'Tarong had barely survived. He had to find something else to strengthen her connection. If he couldn't, they would never get to the Entana hive.

Mara's slow, measured footsteps coming down the stairs stirred him from his thoughts. He knew what she would say even before she approached him. Her eyes were dark and haunted, far sadder than they ever should have been. Raeb's heart hurt to see her joy squashed by the weight of all this.

"It's been three days. None of the traditional remedies will wake her."

Raeb's shoulders sagged. Saydee should have woken days

ago. He and Mara had been painstakingly precise in their measurement of the leaves, so she shouldn't have been overdosed.

But she could not be roused from the baenlo sleep.

They went to Saydee's room and looked down at the sleeping woman. She seemed even younger now than she usually did. Her chest rose in slow, deep, rhythmic breaths. It was clear this wasn't a normal sleep. She was too still, lacking the twitches and shifting of everyday rest.

"What do we do?" Mara asked.

Raeb heard what she didn't say. If someone didn't wake from the baenlo sleep after this much time, they were given the distilled poison before they could waste away and starve to death. It was a mercy for them and their families.

"I have to figure out why she's still sleeping," Raeb said.

"How will you do that?"

His pause, no longer than a handful of breaths, felt like an eternity. "I have no idea."

"Sometimes people can't be saved," she whispered.

"And sometimes you can't give up until you've tried everything," he snapped back.

Mara nodded, not in agreement but to appease his outburst. After a moment she looked up at him, her eyes as fully Entana as his. "Raeb, what has happened to you?"

The simple question stunned him. "What do you mean?"

"This anger you hold, the loss of control… I worry for you now as much as I did when Matow and I first met you."

Raeb shuddered. Mara and Matow had taken him in when

he'd been at his lowest, frightened and begging the Entana for a death they would not grant him. He hadn't lied when he'd said these wonderful people had shown him how to live. They'd saved him from a misery that would have driven him insane as surely as the Entana would have.

"Things are… complicated. No matter which path I take, I'm risking much more than just my life. The pressure to do the right thing feels like too much most of the time."

Mara placed her hand on Raeb's. "You will always make the right choice, Raeb. When all is said and done, that is the man you are."

He squeezed her hand, though he looked away from her when he spoke. "I'm not sure what kind of man I am anymore. The Entana have done so much to me… forced so much on my shoulders…" He met Mara's eyes again. "I'm not the man you knew, Mara. Not anymore. And I'm not sure this man is one either of us would have liked."

She took him by the shoulders and looked at him with a gaze that saw beyond the physical and to a person's soul. Raeb would never let anyone look at him like that, except for this woman who had come to replace the mother he no longer remembered.

"I know you, Raeb. I see who you are despite all the actions that convince you you're someone else. The Entana may ravage our minds, but they can only change us if we allow them to. No matter how hard they have tried to mold you into their instrument, you remain Raeb. The Entana do not control you any more than we are controlled by the Bok'Tarong. The threat may exist, but we continue on."

Raeb had been nodding absently, wishing he could agree. He wasn't at all sure he'd remained the man he was. The Entana had changed him. He knew that in his heart as surely as he knew the threats Mara spoke of were true.

Mara's words tumbled together, mixing and stirring up in his thoughts. When they settled, his heart skipped a beat.

As surely as the Entana were a threat to them, the Bok'Tarong was a threat to the Entana.

How could he have been so stupid? The magic he'd fed into Saydee had been the pure, Entana-killing magic of the Bok'Tarong. Siphoned into a -taken. The Entana in Saydee's mind must have recognized that power, felt threatened, and shut itself away. It would have locked Saydee's mind into the tightest fortress it could have. And since she was under the influence of the baenlo, her mind was already restrained from all thought and action. Keeping her asleep would be the simplest and most defensible way for the Entana to protect itself.

"Mara," he said, leaning in to kiss her on the cheek, "you are brilliant."

The woman blushed, but her smile was radiant and filled with pride.

Raeb turned back to Saydee, brushing his hand across her arm. Perhaps—just perhaps—he may have a way to save her. It would require some drastic measures, an unhealthy share of danger, and more than a little luck, but it might work.

And he had to try. He wouldn't let Saydee die until he knew there was no way to save her.

He found Dragana meditating outside, the Bok'Tarong

resting in her lap. It was bitterly cold, but the scents of wood smoke and clean evergreens, fresh snow and baking bread made it feel heartwarming if not body-warming. He exhaled, watching his breath fog the air before him.

This was the first bit of luck he needed. He had to get Dragana to help him, and he wasn't at all sure she would. His last plan had almost destroyed the Bok'Tarong. She hadn't forgiven him.

Then again, he wasn't sure he deserved forgiveness for that.

He sat beside her in the same meditative pose. They didn't speak for a while.

Dragana's voice was calm, but distant. "What do you want, Raeb?"

"Saydee isn't waking from the baenlo. Something's keeping her asleep."

Dragana looked at him, her brown and crimson eyes staring into his. She didn't flinch from his Entana gaze. Not anymore. "I know."

"I think I might be able to help her," Raeb continued, "but it will be very dangerous. I can't even begin to guarantee it will work. But it's the only way to confirm what's happening to her."

"And what do you think is happening to her?" There was no emotion in her voice, but Raeb wasn't fooled. She kept her tone deadpan because her emotions were rioting. He could sympathize.

"We infused Saydee, a -taken, with the magic of the Bok'Tarong. It hurt the Entana. It felt threatened, so it's keeping her asleep because it sensed it was in danger. I didn't even consider something like that happening."

"What are you suggesting we do?"

Raeb smiled at the 'we.' "I need to speak with the Entana in her mind and hope I can convince it to let her wake."

"How would you speak to an Entana?"

"Instead of sending our spirits to the hive, I could use the ritual to send myself into Saydee's mind. Once there, I can find where the Entana is and talk to it."

"He can talk to the Entana," Dragana mumbled. There was a touch of disgust in her tone.

Raeb ignored her and said the hard part, before he lost his nerve. "I'd like Aeo to join me."

Her eyes narrowed and her hand rested on the Bok'Tarong. Her voice was cold as the ground freezing Raeb's backside. "Aeo's spirit is bound to the sword. He can't leave it and enter the physical world." Raeb noted a strange tone in her voice, one that hinted at something in their past. He was asking enough as it was, so he didn't push for an explanation.

"We won't be in the physical world," he replied. "We'll be in Saydee's mind."

Dragana glared at him with all-too-familiar suspicion. "Why do you need Aeo to go with you?"

"The Entana hunters are loose in her mind. They search out anything for them to feed on—thoughts, emotions, anything that holds a shred of human personality. My presence would be a feast to them. I can't fight them off on my own, and I won't be able to defend myself once I get close to the Entana. No one is better qualified to fight them than the spirit of the Bok'Tarong."

Before she could outright refuse him, he added, "Saydee is the best hope we have of reaching the Entana hive. Without her connection, we have no way to get there."

She paused, looking unhappy and a little confused.

"This could be the only way to save her life."

That melted the last of Dragana's reluctance. Raeb saw it in her deflated posture. He waited as she conferred with the Bok'Tarong.

"Very well," she said at last, sounding unhappy but not angry. "When you enter her mind, Aeo will join you."

Chapter Nineteen

They couldn't afford to rest up and regain their strength. Saydee was running out of time. Raeb prepared the ritual, again, heart heavy and exhausted. But determined. He would not let his mistake be Saydee's death. Not today.

Raeb and Mara brought Saydee from her room and laid her in front of the small fire. Dragana and Raeb sat beside her. He tried to ignore how thin and pale the girl looked.

"One of these days you'll have to tell me where you learned these rituals," Dragana said.

"You wouldn't like the answer," he replied.

Ignoring her scowl, Raeb took a deep breath and threw the herbs into the fire. They shot sparks into the air and released an earthy smell, like freshly tilled loam and burning leaves and rotting undergrowth. The smoke coiled and formed itself into writhing, eel-like shapes. The runes he'd drawn around them slithered to life. He murmured the proper incantation, in a language that sounded like hissing snakes, and his surroundings faded. His voice echoed in his ears, repeating the phrase over and over.

When the voice faded, Raeb opened his eyes. He didn't even remember closing them.

It took him several minutes to orient himself. He felt real and solid enough to be dizzy, though he was far removed from his physical body. His head pounded from the journey—even though he hadn't felt himself traveling, it still took its toll. Several long seconds passed before he felt stable enough to look around.

He'd never seen anything like this place before. It resembled a network of caves, but the walls were moist and not quite as solid as stone. Streaks of random colors slashed across them. Ambient light flickered as if from a fire. Sounds like the howls of hunting dogs and larger, more dangerous predators reached Raeb's ears. The Entana had definitely taken up residence here.

He was in Saydee's mind.

Raeb looked to his right, at his companion. The man was a little shorter than he, but his body was stocky and well-muscled. A gentle, rosy gold hue hung around him like an aura. His blond hair was cut military-short and he had sharp, hunter's eyes. In his hand he held an exact image of the Bok'Tarong.

Raeb chuckled as he recognized the man. It was the nameless assassin who'd been asking after the Bok'Tarong all those months ago. In the spirit world, he existed as any of the rest of them would, body and all. "Aeo," he greeted.

"Raeb," Aeo replied with a nod.

The men shook hands, and Raeb watched as joy filled Aeo's eyes at the touch.

"I warned you going after the Bok'Tarong was a fool's errand," Raeb said. Rather than echoing, his voice sounded flat and muffled.

Aeo laughed when he saw the smile on Raeb's face. "Guess I should have listened." He paused, a thoughtful look on his face. "But I'm sort of glad I didn't."

The piercing howls of the Entana hunters cut their conversation short before Raeb had a chance to explore that interesting little comment.

"What are those things?" Aeo asked, already crouched in a battle-ready position.

"Entana hunters," Raeb replied. "They're like the Entana's hounds. They flush out a person's memories, scaring them into the open, and making them easier for the real Entana to find and consume."

Aeo shifted his weight. "So those aren't even the real Entana?"

"Hardly. If they were, our job would be a lot simpler."

The men paused, listening to the horrible sounds of the hunters. "If they catch us, can they kill us?" Aeo asked, his gaze swiveling around him. All levity had left his voice. He was stern, focused. Ready for the hunt.

Raeb spun as howls echoed from behind him. He didn't look at Aeo as he answered. "Yes."

Aeo's fingers tightened around the Bok'Tarong. "Okay then."

They took a moment to get their bearings. As Raeb had hoped, Saydee's mind was a maze. She'd created a web full of twisting corridors, hiding the most treasured pieces of herself in a labyrinth of tunnels and dead-ends. If she hadn't done this, it would have been a short trip to madness.

The men chose tunnels at random, weapons bared and every sense alert. No regular weapon could have followed them from the physical world, so they were armed only with the spirit-blades of Sunray and the Bok'Tarong. Raeb wasn't at all sure Sunray would do him any good in here, but it was all he had.

"So what are we looking for?" Aeo asked.

"We need to find our way to the Entana infesting Saydee's mind."

"I know that," he replied. "But how?"

"Aside from wandering around and hoping we get lucky, we'll make ourselves as much of a nuisance as we can. Once the Entana is bothered enough by our presence, it will let us find it."

Aeo's steps paused for a heartbeat. "And that sounds like a good idea to you?"

"Not at all. It's rash and stupid, without any guarantee it'll do any good."

Aeo swung the Bok'Tarong toward another tunnel opening, then checked to make sure they weren't being followed. "Gee. Thanks for letting me tag along, then."

Raeb smirked, following his instincts as much as any kind of logic. He'd never navigated another's mind in this manner, but he knew enough about the -taken to recognize Saydee had done a superb job. Her magic must have helped with the complexity of the twisting paths. The Entana would have to search long and hard to find any bit of her in this maze.

But he wasn't the Entana. He was her friend, and was here to help. Saydee knew him.

"Before we get to the Entana, though, I was hoping to find…"

They turned a corner and found themselves face-to-face with a vision of Saydee. Raeb smiled.

"… her."

This was what he'd been searching for. He'd found her self-image.

His smile faded as he looked at her. She didn't look anything like the young, lovely girl he knew. This girl was emaciated and exhausted. Large black circles rimmed her eyes, and fresh wet trails showed she'd been crying. Several large, dark bruises marred her skin. She cradled her arm, and he noticed the bulge of a broken bone. The muscles in her legs shook with weariness, as if she'd be running for much longer than she should have been able to.

"Poor girl," he whispered. Saydee put up a brave face, always smiling and willing to serve, but Raeb knew she hid deep scars. He'd known her soul was battered and wounded, but he'd had no idea it was this bad. How did she manage to keep going, and keep smiling, when her very spirit was beaten beyond reason?

He motioned for Aeo to stay back, and he took a step forward. "Saydee?"

The girl's eyes turned to him, but there was no recognition in them. He could barely see the spark of life hidden behind the misery.

"Saydee? It's Raeb. Do you remember me?"

She gazed at him for several moments before giving a slight nod.

"You know I'm a friend, don't you? That's why you let us find you?"

Another nod.

Well, at least that was something. "Good. Saydee, I need to find the Entana."

A hunter howled, as if in answer to the name. Aeo tensed and turned his back to Raeb, holding the Bok'Tarong at ready. Saydee's eyes went wide in panic. She shivered in terror and turned to flee.

Raeb took a single step forward, reaching his hand toward her. "Saydee, wait!"

She turned back to him, but did not relax. She was ready to bolt at any moment.

"I won't let them hurt you. If I can talk to them, I might be able to make them leave."

She paused at that, the haunted look in her eyes growing deeper. Hope was something she'd lost a long time ago. Raeb knew that feeling all too well.

"Saydee, please. I need your help."

The battered girl chewed her lip. She met his eyes for the first time, *seeing* him instead of just looking at him. A brief shadow of her knowing, penetrating gaze came across her face.

Raeb, for his part, didn't try to put on a brave face. He just looked back at Saydee, letting her see how desperately he needed her help. The vulnerability felt strange, but somehow... appropriate.

After a moment she nodded and turned away, her steps small and quick. Raeb followed with Aeo a discreet distance behind.

Growls and snarls filled the air as they moved through cavern after cavern. Several times they passed a piece of Saydee's spirit tucked into a corner — the golden medal of her courage, tarnished and dented; the pure light of her joy, so dim Raeb could barely see it; the armor of her confidence, scattered and broken.

Raeb figured the only things that weren't mangled or destroyed in Saydee's mind were the Entana hunters. And there were no shortage of those.

They hadn't gone far before one of the hunters caught their scent. A great booming roar echoed along the corridors. Raeb could hear the excitement in it.

Many similar howls answered the first. They were far too close for comfort.

Raeb made sure Saydee was within reach, where he could defend her. This might be her mind and her Entana, but he wasn't about to let them hurt her anymore.

The shadows of the hunters appeared on the walls, dancing wildly in the fire-like light. Their already grotesque shapes were stretched and morphed into unrecognizable monstrosities.

"There are too many," Raeb said. "We'll never be able to beat them all."

Aeo shifted from foot to foot, eyes scanning the shadows on the tunnel walls. "What do we do?"

One of the hunters yipped. The sound was repeated by the others, filling Saydee's mind with the high-pitched, almost human-sounding cry. Chills of dread coursed through Raeb's body.

When the yips faded, the silence was filled with an even

worse sound—paws and hooves pounding in a charge, growing louder and closer by the second.

Raeb grabbed Saydee's arm. "Run!"

They fled through the narrow passageways, the sounds of the hunters close on their heels. Raeb's heart hammered faster than his feet. These hunters were bad news. They could rip a spirit-body to shreds in seconds, but he and Aeo could kill them all day long and do no damage to the Entana. They couldn't afford to get caught in a battle with these beasts. They had to get to the real Entana as quickly as possible—and preferably in one piece.

The turns and curves of Saydee's mind-maze passed in frantic blinks. Raeb was so lost he hadn't a clue which way they'd come from anymore. But no matter how fast they ran, or how many random turns they took, the hunters never lost their trail. They would exhaust themselves long before they were free from the pursuit.

He looked back. Not only had the hunters failed to lose their trail, they'd gained ground. They were nearly on their heels, and Raeb could finally see them. He truly wished he couldn't.

The hunters took the shape of every wild beast imaginable, drawn in inky black shadow. No light could illuminate them—instead, they seemed to suck the very light from the air around them. Writhing Entana tendrils trailed from all over their bodies, leaving great wounds that bled poison. The only thing worse than their howls was the smell of death that enveloped them.

In the brief second Raeb watched them, they gained on him. There was no way they could outrun the hunters.

Raeb swore under his breath. "I hope you're ready for a

fight."

Aeo hefted the Bok'Tarong. "Always."

They skid to a stop, turning to stand before the charging beasts, spirit-weapons readied. Raeb cleared his mind and prepared for battle as the first of the hunters sprung at them.

Aeo stepped forward and met the lunge with a magnificent sweep of the Bok'Tarong. The sacred blades sliced through the Entana hunter like it was smoke, and the beast dissipated into the air with a heavy, oily stench.

Everything fell deathly still. Aeo stared down the unmoving hunters, daring them to challenge him. Raeb, in turn, stared at the assassin.

He'd never seen anything like it. The hunter had simply vanished at the Bok'Tarong's touch, as if every defense it had melted away. Raeb had hoped the spirit of the Bok'Tarong might cause some damage to the hunters, but he'd never dared to hope it would obliterate them.

This plan might work after all.

The moment of shock lasted only a heartbeat. Then the hunters charged in earnest.

Raeb dove away from the hunters' claws and teeth and ducked under the swing of the Bok'Tarong. He came to his feet next to Saydee. He pulled her farther away, hoping Aeo would be able to hold the hunters back long enough for him to get Saydee to safety.

He couldn't understand how Aeo was still standing. He was swarmed by hunters, so outnumbered he could hardly be seen through the shadowy tendrils. Brief glints from the rosy gold

Bok'Tarong flashed through the wall of beasts—but after each glint, smoke rose from the disintegrating body of a hunter. Or two.

Saydee pulled her arm from Raeb's and ran past him. *Toward the fight.* He called out to her, tried to stop her, but she evaded his grasp and plunged into the heart of the battle. He stared at the spot where she'd disappeared into the hunters, horrified and confused.

The commotion had drawn the attention of every hunter inward, so Raeb stood unnoticed, hardly daring to breath. Should he run? Any moment the hunters could take note of him again, and he didn't have the Bok'Tarong to defend him. But he couldn't just leave his friends. *Oh Saydee, what have you done?*

A long, terrible moment passed.

Then Saydee reappeared, several new gashes on her body, pulling Aeo behind her.

The assassin stumbled behind Saydee, swinging his sword wildly behind him. As they passed Raeb, Saydee grabbed him, too. She yanked on his arm, and he followed.

So did the hunters.

They ran, the hunters' breath hot and fetid on their necks. At any moment, Raeb was sure he'd feel the sting of claws and teeth tearing into his back.

Then everything went silent.

Saydee stopped, and the men slowed a few steps later. Raeb turned back to Saydee, trying to make sense of what had just happened.

There was no tunnel, or hunters, behind them. There was

nothing but a solid wall.

Raeb looked to Saydee. Talented girl! People couldn't just change their mind-mazes like that. It took years to cultivate a system like this. Her magic may not have been powerful enough for the Mage's Academy, but it was damn strong to be able to do something like that.

He grinned at her. "Good job, Saydee."

It took her a moment, but the battered girl smiled back. The praise bolstered her spirit and helped heal some of the damage the Entana had caused. Bruises faded and her broken arm set, though badly, so she was able to let it support itself. She was still far from healed, but it was a start.

They continued deeper into her mind. The hunters hadn't given up on them, if the increasing howls and yips were any indication. A few stragglers found them, mostly by accident it seemed, but they were no match for Aeo and the massive Bok'Tarong.

After a long time of walking through twisting tunnels, their surroundings began to change. The walls lost their streaking colors and darkened to a deep, reflective black. The howls of the hunters changed to wails of pain and weeping. The path became wide and arrow-straight, which left Raeb feeling nervous and exposed after the narrow curves of Saydee's maze.

They'd arrived.

Chapter Twenty

Their steps resounded like thunderclaps, as if every echo that hadn't sounded before had been saved up for this. There was no way anyone would be allowed to sneak into the sanctuary the Entana had carved into Saydee's mind.

Raeb looked to Saydee, but she wasn't beside him anymore. She hadn't followed them into the Entana sanctuary, and he couldn't blame her. It was dangerous enough for her in the environment of her choosing. To walk into the Entana stronghold would be suicide.

"So once we get to the Entana," Aeo whispered, pausing as his words echoed back to him, "what do we do?"

"I need to confirm it's keeping Saydee asleep, and convince it to let her wake."

"How?"

Raeb shook his head. Even if he did know how he would do this, he didn't want to say. The Entana were likely listening to them. Maybe, if he worked things right, the Entana would slip and give away something important. The less they were prepared for him, the better.

They walked and walked without a single change in their surroundings. The hallway was the same as it had always been, and there was no sign of the end in sight. From the look of things, they may as well have not moved at all.

"Where is it?" Aeo asked, his voice reverberating through Raeb's bones.

When the echoes died, a deep, rumbling sound answered him. Raeb couldn't figure out where it came from, but he knew what it was. It was the laughter of an Entana.

Aeo drew in a breath to shout, but Raeb silenced him with an outstretched hand. It was never a good thing when the Entana laughed.

Well, they were already doomed. He might as well go for broke. "Show yourself!" he demanded.

"The mortal tried to command us," the Entana chuckled. "As if any creature so frail could possibly do so."

Raeb looked over at Aeo, who was still crouched in a battle stance and looking around for the Entana. "Can you hear it?" he mouthed.

Aeo shook his head.

"You have brought me a lovely gift," the Entana said. "The spirit of the cursed blades will make a fine meal indeed."

"It might not digest well," he replied. "He's a bit prickly going down."

"Perhaps I should just kill him, then?"

Raeb took a small step sideways, putting himself in front of

Aeo. "This spirit is under my protection. You will not hurt him."

"You do not understand what you deal with, mortal."

"I understand perfectly, you vile parasite. And I am not just any mortal," he said, brandishing Sunray, "I am the blade-bearer, appointed by the Keeper of Secrets. You will obey me. Now show yourself."

Once, deep in the wilderness of Taron, Raeb had encountered a half-disemboweled boar. It had been lying dead in the humid summer air for days at least. Raeb would never forget the way the boar's intestines had turned black and bloated as they pulsed with maggots.

When the Entana materialized, it looked just like those intestines. Only its tendrils were as thick as Raeb's waist and stretched from wall to wall.

"At one time, that blade showed your favor among the Entana. But I know your reputation. You are a miserable servant and a failure. The Keeper may very well reward me for doing away with you."

Raeb's heart pounded. "Are you willing to risk it?"

They stood in a brief, tense stalemate. If the Entana figured out Raeb was bluffing, or that the Keeper of Secrets likely wouldn't care if he was killed here, he and Aeo were dead. But he hoped the Keeper was as feared by Entana as he was by -taken.

"What do you want of me, blade-bearer?" the Entana asked. All humor had fled from its voice.

Raeb started breathing again. "I want you to release this mind from the baenlo sleep."

"Why would I? This mind has been a difficult meal. I often

starve before my hunters return with memories for me to feed upon."

"Forgive me if I don't shed any tears for your hunger," Raeb replied.

"But locked in this sleep, the mind cannot hide as well. After so long with barely enough to feed upon, this state has given me a feast. I have no reason to allow her to wake."

"Sure you do," Raeb said. "Let her wake, or I'll let my friend carve your ugly hide into ribbons."

Aeo smiled at Raeb's suggestion. He lifted the Bok'Tarong, testing the edge of the rosy gold blades with his thumb.

The mass of tendrils pulsed and slithered. It was laughing again, though Raeb thought he heard a hint of fear in it.

"You saw how he handled your hunters," Raeb continued. "Imagine what his magic could do to you."

"The hunters are nothing. I am so much more than them. As easily as he could defeat the hunters, I could consume him."

"His magic would eat you from the inside out."

"It could try. I would merely return to my hive, to be regenerated and be given another vessel. It, however, would be destroyed."

Raeb's stomach crawled into his throat. This wasn't going at all the way he'd hoped.

"And before I am done with you," the Entana continued, "I will consume every memory in this mind I can access. It would be lost to madness in a moment." The dark knot of the Entana quivered with laughter. "This mind, and everything within it, is mine to do with as I please. No one will take it from me."

"You have no right to it."

"Do you believe so, blade-bearer? And when you are invited into one of your feeble mortal homes, do you have no right to it, either?"

A flutter of panic rose in Raeb's throat. If this Entana was speaking the truth, and saying what he thought it was saying…

This was no time to get distracted. He had to finish this before the Entana decided it was done toying with them. "Be gone from this vessel, Entana!"

"You may be the blade-bearer, but that does not give you control over me. You cannot command me to leave a vessel."

Aeo shifted behind him. "Uh, Raeb?"

Raeb didn't dare take his eyes from the Entana, but the tension in Aeo's voice wasn't something to be ignored. Something had gone very, very wrong.

Then Raeb heard it. Footsteps. Panting. The low, threatening growl of a predator who's spotted its prey.

A hunter had scented them.

Several more growls made Raeb pause. Hunters, he amended.

Their time was just about up.

Aeo stepped out of Raeb's peripheral vision, ready for a fight. The hunters howled and charged. A second later, the sounds of battle rang through the stone corridor. Raeb kept his eyes on the vile tangle of tendrils.

"Last chance, Entana. Let her wake."

"Never. This mind is mine. And you shall be consumed along with it."

Aeo grunted, and Raeb turned just enough to see him picking

himself up off the ground, blood streaming from a wound on his arm. Three hunters hovered around him, and from the sound of it, more were on their way.

Aeo swung the spirit sword at the closest beast, and it squealed as gore and smoke spewed from a gash in its abdomen. "Raeb, get us out of here!"

Aeo was right. If they stayed any longer, they would be overrun by hunters. They'd never leave Saydee's mind alive.

But if they left now, Saydee wouldn't wake. She'd never leave the village alive.

As much as he hated it, the choice was already made for him. Saydee's life was valuable, of course, but the spirit of the Bok'Tarong couldn't be sacrificed so easily. They might still find a way to reach the hive without Saydee's connection, but if they lost the Bok'Tarong there would be no hope to defeat the Entana.

I'm sorry, Saydee. I won't give up on you just yet.

He took a few steps back, keeping the Entana well in view. They only had seconds before they, and Saydee, became the Entana's next meal. But to make their escape, he had to concentrate. No distractions. Any slip in his focus, and it would make his last disaster seem like a resounding success.

"Aeo, stay close to me. Once we're ready, we have to move."

The assassin didn't reply.

"Aeo?"

Raeb turned as much as he dared. Aeo was overrun by hunters. He fought brilliantly, but at this rate he'd be surrounded before he could get to Raeb. If they got cut off from each other, Raeb wouldn't be able to get them both to safety.

He couldn't reach the warrior in time. He didn't even have the luxury of trying. He had to open the way out of Saydee's mind, and do it now, or they were all dead. He had to hope the assassin could handle himself and somehow make his way to Raeb's side.

Raeb held Sunray before his face and unleashed its icy magic. It was a risky move—suicidal might be a more accurate term—but short of waiting until the herbs in the physical world burned out, it was their only way to escape.

Stay hidden, Saydee, he prayed. *Stay safe. I'll find some way to save you.*

As soon as the Entana magic flooded out of Sunray, every hunter in Saydee's mind started howling. They'd be drawn to it like moths to a flame.

Long seconds passed before Sunray's motes began outlining the vast web of magic surrounding them. Raeb had to pour all his strength into the blade to keep its magic active, and even more concentration to keep it from devouring the massive amounts of power it sensed. Everything in sight was teeming with life-magic. It would be a feast like none other, but Saydee would die if Sunray took even a few bites.

Aeo's desperate battle became a distant noise to him. The disgusting knot of tendrils, the obsidian walls, he pushed it all from his mind. His world was him and Sunray and the delicious magic of Saydee's mind. He fought against the impulse to feed. He refused to let Sunray gorge itself. He had to protect Saydee, and he had to get him and Aeo to safety. Nothing else mattered.

Raeb focused every shred of willpower on his ever-hungry

blade. Its magic stretched to its limit, but Raeb kept pushing. He forced more power from it, searching the life-magicks for the single thread in this massive web that would take them home.

Aeo fought a valiant, if losing, battle. Even the Bok'Tarong wouldn't be able to withstand the press of hunters bearing down on him. Sheer numbers would overwhelm the assassin, sacred blades or no.

Sunray was already beginning to feast on the nearby magic by the time he turned his mind back to the blade. He wrested Sunray from its feeding, pulling it away like he would pull a hooked fish from the water, and wrestled the blade back into submission. Reveal, do not feed.

More concentration, more energy. Raeb was almost to the end of his strength.

Aeo grunted not five feet behind him. He'd managed to fight himself here. Good.

Aeo's grunt turned to a hiss of pain. The squeal of a dying hunter followed.

Raeb's heart leapt. He saw it. The gossamer thread tethering him to his physical body. The connection that would take him and Aeo home.

Now that he knew where to keep Sunray's motes focused, Raeb reduced the torrent of energy he pumped into the blade to an almost subconscious stream—just enough to keep the thread in view. The rest of the web faded or disappeared. Only the thread home mattered.

He glanced at Aeo. The assassin was, miraculously, still standing. The oily stench of dead Entana was thick in the air.

How many hunters had Aeo killed?

He grabbed the assassin by the arm, yanking him away from the wary beasts and toward their way home.

They made it a single step before the hunters encircled them. A thick line of oily, tendril-covered monsters now stood between them and Raeb's tether.

Hungry growls echoed through the Entana sanctuary. Raeb and Aeo stood back-to-back, spirit weapons leveled at their enemies. More shadowy beasts arrived every second.

Aeo's back was turned, so he couldn't see the large beast stalk toward him. He had no defense as the beast lunged, fangs and claws aimed at the assassin's throat.

Raeb didn't think. He just reacted.

Sunray swept out in an arcing backswing. Ice trailed behind the blades. When the Entana blade touched the hunter, Raeb met with jarring resistance. They were of the same origins, made with the same magic. It was unnatural for them to meet in battle like this.

Raeb didn't pull back. He forced the blade onward, channeling his anger and the last of his strength into the thrust.

The hunter growled. Raeb screamed out in hatred and rage. "Die, you bastard!"

Resistance shattered. Sunray plunged through the hunter's shadowed body, slicing it cleanly in two. The hunter gave a pained, pathetic yowl before evaporating into smoke.

The sanctuary rumbled. The other hunters stopped their advances and cowered. Some even ran away.

The obsidian walls of the Entana's sanctuary fractured, like they'd been shifted by an earthquake. Cracks ran up and down the surfaces like lightning bolts, widening with each passing second. The floor shook so hard Raeb could barely keep on his feet. Bile rose into his throat. This could not be good.

Saydee's Entana squealed and fled, though whether in fear or in desperation to save its sanctuary, Raeb couldn't tell. A moment ago he'd have been relieved to see the Entana go—now, he dreaded it.

The presence that followed in the Entana's wake felt even more oily and evil than the parasite had. Terror flooded through Raeb. He recognized that presence.

The Keeper of Secrets. Raeb's forbidden use of Sunray had drawn his attention, and now he was hijacking Saydee's mind.

A deep sound echoed through the area, more felt than heard. After a moment it resolved itself into a sound—the roar of sheer, unadulterated rage.

The Keeper of Secret's voice boomed through the caverns of Saydee's mind. "You will receive judgment for that, blade-bearer. No servant of the Entana crosses their masters."

Raeb ignored him, sheathing Sunray. Grasping Aeo with his left hand, he reached out with his right and lunged, stretching so far his shoulders popped. His hand closed over the golden thread of his tether.

His spirit lurched, and their surroundings changed with dizzying speed. Within a heartbeat Raeb was back in his body, wavering in his seat, sweat pouring from his body.

Dragana stared at the Bok'Tarong for a few seconds, likely ensuring the spirit had returned safely. Then she turned toward

Raeb. "Are you all right? How did it go?"

"We have to leave," he replied. His heart pounded like his body had been running, rather than just his mind. "The Entana will send people after us. We have to be far away from this village before they reach us."

"What about Saydee?"

The girl stirred at her name. "I'm here," she muttered.

Relief eased the knot in his stomach. At least something had worked in their favor. The Keeper of Secret's intrusion must have jarred Saydee's Entana enough that its grip on her mind slipped, letting her wake. However it had happened, Raeb was grateful. He'd never have forgiven himself if he'd had to leave Saydee behind.

Raeb could see the questions in Dragana's expression, but she didn't stop to ask them. Everyone moved with the speed born from hunting—or being hunted—and prepared to do as Raeb commanded.

CHAPTER TWENTY-ONE

Aeo was impressed. Less than an hour after he and Raeb had returned from Saydee's mind, they'd left the -taken sanctuary behind. Even Saydee, who'd been asleep and hadn't eaten for days, had moved without complaint. Though he couldn't understand how the girl, as pale and thin as someone on her deathbed, was able to move at all.

He had no idea where Raeb was leading them. What the man followed might be considered a trail, if the travelers were mountain goats. Dragana side-stepped her way behind Saydee, sliding as often as walking. Patches of snow and loose soil didn't help her footing. He hoped none of their kicked rocks would cause an avalanche.

He doubted Raeb even had a destination in mind. Right now, he was intent on getting as far from the sanctuary as possible. Even if that meant tumbling down the side of a mountain.

As Dragana fought to keep her balance, her steps sliding on the slick, frozen underbrush, Aeo told her about their encounter with the Entana.

When he called himself the blade-bearer, the Entana started to obey him. And when he used Sunray against the hunters, it brought the Keeper of Secrets. He said Raeb had betrayed his masters.

Dragana considered this for a while. *What's so important about that blade? Why is Raeb still carrying it, if he wants to destroy the Entana?*

You sound like you don't trust him.

I'm not sure if I do or not, she replied. *I want to, but I can't believe he's really free from the Entana.*

He saved my life, Dragana. He used the Entana blade against them in order to protect me. That doesn't seem like the actions of a man who's still in the clutches of his masters.

No, but he's hiding a lot from us. I can't help but wonder what those secrets are, and why he refuses to tell us about them.

Her footing slipped. Dragana slid for several feet, knocking Saydee over and tumbling them both off the trail. Aeo panicked. He shouldn't have distracted her with the conversation. If Dragana rolled poorly, his blades would slice clean through her or Saydee.

He set his will against the magic holding him in the sheath. It held fast, but Aeo pushed against it. He demanded the magic to release. He forced himself to fall free, away from the tumbling women and their vulnerable flesh.

The sheath released him, plunging Aeo into darkness as Dragana slid away from him.

A long moment passed before he was picked up and sight returned to him. He felt disoriented and confused, even more so when he felt the hand around him and saw the face looking down at him.

It was Raeb.

[...worthy...?] The silent voice seemed confused, even as it confirmed what Aeo felt in his soul. Despite his history, his Entana possession, everything the Taronese believed of him, Raeb was a worthy bearer of the Bok'Tarong.

The man was so full of rage. He hated the Entana so desperately it was a physical pain. It permeated every bit of him, poisoning the good man Aeo could feel buried beneath it.

On top of that, Aeo could feel the horrible intrusion of the Entana. After a bare instant of exposure to that soul-rending *wrongness* he had to shut himself away to keep himself sane.

The women had rolled to a stop at the base of a huge evergreen, a cascade of dirt, leaves, and snow following in their wake. Raeb was hurrying to them, holding the Bok'Tarong in a death-grip like he either never wanted to let it go or he wanted to toss it away as soon as possible.

Raeb knelt beside Saydee, setting the sword down between him and Dragana. Aeo's vision was black for only a second before Dragana picked him up, her thoughts jumbled from the fall and... was that jealousy? Or revulsion that Raeb, the Taronese traitor, had dared to touch the Bok'Tarong?

Before he had a chance to reassure her, or check that she was unhurt, a glint of sunlight on metal shone through the underbrush.

Dragana, stop. Be silent.

She instantly obeyed, dropping flat to the ground. She

whistled a low note and Raeb followed suit, dragging Saydee down beside him. All three humans drew their weapons, though Saydee looked pale and clammy clutching an overlarge dagger.

"What is it?" Dragana whispered.

Something metal, down the hill to the right.

She repeated his warning to Raeb.

"Could it be some kind of refuse? Something abandoned on the forest floor?" he asked.

The sun was shining off it a moment ago, but now it's gone.

"So it's moving, then," Dragana said.

"It could be a hunter, or some other innocent person," Saydee said. "Not everyone in the world is out to kill us."

"Better to be cautious than dead," Raeb replied. "I'd rather have to sheathe a blade I didn't need than need a blade I hadn't unsheathed."

Dragana leaned closer to the girl so she could keep her voice low. "We'll go check it out. But we'll assume the worst, just in case."

Saydee nodded, though her face was still twisted with worry.

They advanced slowly, the sodden ferns and evergreen needles littering the ground hardly crunched under Dragana's feather-light footsteps. Raeb was equally silent, and even Saydee managed a halfway decent approach. A few skittish squirrels fled from them, but otherwise their presence remained undetected.

At the bottom of the hill, a band of perhaps a dozen -taken soldiers hid in the undergrowth. If Dragana hadn't fallen off the trail, they'd never have spotted them.

"What are they doing here?" Dragana asked. "We're weeks

away from the frontlines."

"I think they're here for us," Raeb said. He sounded like he was about to be sick. "A hunting party from the Keeper of Secrets."

"How could they be here already?"

"They had to have been in the area," Raeb said.

Which means they're expanding past the war, Aeo said. They're moving to spread the Entana beyond the frontlines, just like that -taken warned us they would.

"So this might be a coincidence," Dragana said. "They're spies, or forward scouts, and we just stumbled upon them."

"Maybe they were, but now they're almost surely after us," Raeb said. "The Keeper of Secrets won't just let us escape after what we've done."

"Can we sneak by them?" Saydee asked.

Raeb shrugged. "Probably. But would you really want to leave an enemy like this at your back?"

Saydee paled even further.

Dragana and Raeb shared a look, then nodded. They rose together and charged.

With one broad, sweeping stroke, she parted a -taken's head from his shoulders before any of them had a chance to prepare themselves.

Raeb was at her side in an instant, working his blade—not Sunray, but a straight, ordinary sword—against two -taken. He flowed through the battle like it was a dance, always appearing one step ahead of his enemies. He complimented each of Dragana's moves, and she his. Their mutual Taronese training made them step and attack in perfect sync.

Steam rose from the soldiers' spilled blood and pockets of pinkish, half-melted snow. A dozen bodies or more, dead or close to it, littered the ground. Entana tendrils squealed as Aeo's blades severed them from their hosts. There was nothing glamorous about this fight. It was brutal, gory, and not at all dignified.

And quicker than Aeo would have believed, it was over.

"We need to move on," Raeb said. He wiped the blood from his blade and sheathed it, as if nothing had happened. "We'll have to get as far from here as we can before nightfall."

He strode away, past an ashen-faced and trembling Saydee, without looking back.

*
**

RAEB SET THEIR course due south, for no better reason than to get out of this blasted snow. Maybe he'd be able to formulate some kind of plan once his brain thawed.

They walked in silence until the sun set and the trail was lit only by dim moonlight. He'd have liked to put even more distance behind them, but the forest was too dangerous to navigate in the dark and Saydee was nearly asleep on her feet. They had to stop, but Raeb feared what might happen when they did.

Maybe it was because of their terrible luck thus far, or the appearance of -taken soldiers so soon after their escape from Saydee's mind and the Keeper of Secrets. Maybe it was just Raeb's paranoia. But he *knew* something terrible would happen once they let their guard down.

Still, they couldn't go on forever, so Raeb found a secluded spot well off the trail where they could spend the night.

Saydee was asleep before they'd gotten the camp set up. Dragana helped Raeb finish, though she seemed as weary as the girl. The strain they'd put on the Bok'Tarong the last few days had sapped much more of her life force than they'd expected, and now the young woman didn't seem so young anymore. She moved as if every joint pained her and energy was a precious commodity. Raeb had seen it happen before, more times than he cared to remember, but this time it made his heart twist and his stomach churn.

He shook the thought from his mind. He'd already gotten his emotions mixed up in this. If he started caring about Dragana and Aeo too—even he couldn't think of him as just the spirit of the Bok'Tarong anymore—then he would be walking a dangerous line between feelings and duty. He couldn't afford that.

Raeb sat awake for as long as he could manage, but eventually exhaustion took over. His eyes drooped and his shoulders slumped, and before he knew it his mind drifted into dreams.

And he wasn't alone.

"So nice of you to join me," the Keeper of Secrets said. "I was beginning to think you'd deny yourself sleep forever just to avoid my presence."

Raeb turned around and around, but he stood in empty blackness. The Keeper of Secrets was nowhere to be seen. "I'd deny myself life itself if it meant I never had to speak to you again," Raeb said.

"So I remember. It takes a great deal of vigilance on your Entana's part to keep your blade from your heart. Or the poison from your mouth. Or any of the other varied ways you've tried to make good on that threat over the years."

Raeb's heart burned with fury. He shoved the rage deeper, away from his thoughts, promising himself vengeance on his tormentors. That had always given him just enough hope to continue on.

But now, that hope flickered and died. They'd tried their best and come nowhere close to reaching the hive. All of them had nearly died in the process. Vengeance had never seemed further away.

"You know the truth, don't you, blade-bearer? However clever you may think you are, you aren't a threat to the Entana. The sooner you accept that and complete your mission, the sooner we can arrange for an end to your suffering."

"To give myself over to the Entana, to feed your parasites with my thoughts and emotions? No thank you."

The Keeper of Secret's voice grew a fraction softer. Almost thoughtful. "Perhaps we could negotiate something more… direct."

Raeb had never been one for negotiations, especially with creatures like the Entana, but the hint made him pause. Maybe he *should* negotiate. A clean death was more than he'd been able to hope for in centuries. And what was left for him here? His chance at destroying the Entana was gone. Without that, the best he could ask for was an end to the running, a chance to be at peace…

and that was what the Entana were offering. The Keeper of Secrets would give it to him. He wouldn't have to fight for it any longer. How could he refuse such an offer?

His hand strayed to Sunray. The icy blades seared his fingertips. The ever-hungry magic pulsed through it, into him, begging to be released. It was tempted by the offer, too. Not just tempted—that was the blade's most fervent desire. To be free, to feed and destroy and fulfill its mission at last. It craved that opportunity the way Raeb craved oxygen.

For Raeb to reach his chance for peace, he had to wade through Sunray's trail of blood and death. To murder his allies, to turn away from humanity and follow the Entana's lead. It was a great price to pay. And, damn it all, Raeb was actually considering it. He'd hate himself for it until the moment he died, but he was considering it.

The Keeper of Secrets' laugh echoed through Raeb's mind. "You're beginning to understand. There is no way out but the path we offer. Complete your mission. Destroy the Bok'Tarong, and you will be freed."

Haven't you fought long enough?

Weariness descended on Raeb like a blanket. It smothered him, dragged him down. He was so tired of fighting, of losing. He was ready for that chance at peace. At rest.

With a sigh of release, of desperation, Raeb closed his eyes and nodded.

Chapter Twenty-Two

Raeb woke in a cold sweat. The frozen darkness of the forest couldn't compare to the frigid emptiness in his mind. He felt trapped, like the Entana had bound his soul in their slimy tendrils and squeezed until he couldn't think. He could no longer remember a time when he'd been free. Had there ever been a time like that? What had it been like?

Sunray was in his hand, though he hadn't consciously drawn it. He was approaching Dragana's sleeping form, though he hadn't even realized he was standing. He trembled and sweat like he was dying of fever, his mind foggy and delirious. He wasn't even sure if this was a dream or reality.

He only knew that he had to destroy the Bok'Tarong.

And some part of him, buried so deep it was hardly there, was sickened by the thought.

There it is. The Bok'Tarong lay beside the warrior-woman, gleaming in the moonlight. Raeb stared at the rosy gold blades, entranced by their beauty. It had once been his dream to wield them. He'd have given his life to the sword without hesitation.

But those memories belonged to another man. This man, the one who stood enslaved to the Entana, had never known such dreams. He knew only desperation, pain, loneliness. There was no end to his nightmare.

But there was. And it lay before him.

Raeb lifted Sunray, releasing its magic. Icy motes glittered as they sought out enchantments, congregating around the Bok'Tarong.

All Raeb had to do was let it feed. Simply let go and allow it to consume with abandon. It wouldn't even take any effort on his part. The effort came in holding Sunray back. Raeb just had to stop trying, give up, and it could all end.

He knelt, placing his free hand on the curved blades of the Bok'Tarong. He could feel the magic in them. It quivered at the touch of Sunray's power.

Odd, that it did so. Aeo had never seemed to fear anything.

Aeo.

A small piece of the man who had once been Raeb surfaced. He'd liked Aeo. They'd fought well together. In another life, they may have even been friends.

I must destroy the Bok'Tarong.

I cannot kill Aeo.

Raeb's hand was raised, poised to release Sunray's hunger and strike down at the sword. But he didn't.

He couldn't. To strike now would be allowing the Entana to win. He couldn't do that. Not after what they'd done to him, and to Mara, and Matow, and Saydee. The Entana had to be destroyed. The Bok'Tarong had to endure.

He lowered Sunray.

The Bok'Tarong was snatched away and Dragana crouched before him, holding the blades in a white-knuckled grip. Her voice was cold and filled with fury. "What are you doing?"

Raeb's mind snapped back to himself. He was aware of the trees around him, the glowing embers of their fire, the stars above them. He shivered from cold and fear. Dragana's words resolved in his brain, with an effort, leaving him reeling and disoriented. He stared at her as his thoughts tried — and failed — to make sense of what was happening.

Then horror hit him like a tidal wave. He staggered back, sickened as if he'd been punched in the gut. Had he just tried to destroy the Bok'Tarong?

"Oh yes," a slimy voice hissed from behind. Raeb and Dragana both spun to the voice.

Saydee sat eerily still, staring at Raeb with the inhuman gaze of a fully -taken.

Dragana swung her blades to the girl, but Raeb held her arm back. The look she shot him was so full of bloodlust and rage he almost cowered. "Don't," he whispered. "It's the Keeper of Secrets. He's taken possession of her body."

Saydee's mouth twisted in a sadistic grin. "You didn't think I would miss this, did you? My only opportunity to witness the bane of the Entana destroyed? Though it seems this is not the spectacle I thought it would be." The Keeper of Secrets turned his gaze to Raeb. "It appears this is yet another opportunity to punish my not-so-loyal servant instead."

Dragana's brown-and-crimson eyes turned back to Raeb. "What is he talking about?"

"Come now, you can figure it out," the Keeper of Secrets said. "The Taronese may be fools, but you must have enough intelligence to puzzle out this simple riddle."

She glared daggers at Saydee's smug expression before turning an equally stabbing gaze to Raeb. "That's the secret you've been keeping? That you're going to destroy the Bok'Tarong?"

"No," Raeb said. "Well, I was supposed to, but—"

Dragana cut him off before he could explain. "How could you?"

Raeb stammered. What he could say? It didn't matter, though, because Dragana was hearing nothing of it.

"I'd almost started believing you. After all the talk of destroying the Entana and fighting with us, I'd nearly forgotten what you are. But you were never one of us, were you?" Raeb heard tears choke her voice. He suspected nothing but sheer stubbornness kept them from falling. "You were never a friend to us."

"Dragana, it's not like that."

"So what is it like? You betray your allies to these monsters and leave us all to die?"

"No, I—"

"I can't believe you would do something like this! You came to us with false friendship."

"It wasn't false—"

"Seduced us with false plans."

"No!"

"All to get us to let our guard down, so you can sneak up and kill Aeo? You'd destroy him, and our hopes to be free of the Entana, without so much as a thought of what else you're hurting to do it?"

The Keeper of Secrets grinned and giggled through Saydee's mouth.

Dragana was trembling now, her eyes glittering in the firelight. "I should have expected this from a traitor," she hissed.

"Dragana, listen to me!"

"No!" She stood, back rigid as the pines around her, expression frigid as the ice crusting their needles. She held the Bok'Tarong firmly at her side. "I listened to you before and it almost cost Aeo his life. I won't endanger him again by putting my trust in the wrong person."

She sheathed the blades and spun away from Raeb. She wadded her bedroll into a clumsy lump and shoved it into her pack. With one final hurt- and hate-filled glare, Dragana marched out of the camp and into the darkness of the night.

"Ah, such sweet betrayal," the Keeper of Secrets said. "This was worth watching."

Raeb gripped Sunray until his joints ached. This bastard had ruined everything and thought it entertaining? He tensed and pounced in an instant, lunging toward Saydee and swiping the Entana blades above her head. The perilous connection the Keeper of Secrets used to tap into Saydee's mind was severed, and the girl crumpled like a discarded puppet.

He stood there, numb, for what seemed like hours.

Everything had crashed down around him in just a few moments. And, he noted with surprise, he'd lost more than just his plans for freedom. He'd lost friends.

That stung more deeply than he'd anticipated.

He sank to the ground, staring at Saydee's unconscious form, and wished he could find the same oblivion to put his turmoil to rest.

CHAPTER TWENTY-THREE

R aeb had tried to kill him. And he hadn't been able to do a thing about it.

Aeo seethed inside his metal prison. He hadn't felt trapped inside the Bok'Tarong for a long time—but today, he'd give anything to escape from the blades. His life had been threatened, and he could do nothing but stare into Raeb's haunted Entana eyes and wait for the bite of Sunray.

The last time he'd felt that useless, he'd crawled into the forest and killed himself.

He'd been bombarded by thoughts and regrets. If only he'd been a better man in his lifetime. If only he'd been able to see this through. He'd have been happy to die, if he could have taken the Entana with him. But to die like that... He wished he could stay with Dragana for just a little while longer.

He'd looked into Raeb's eyes, overwhelmed by self-loathing and helplessness, and found he wasn't the only one.

He remembered the feel of Raeb's soul when he'd held the

Bok'Tarong, the flashes of a wounded man who was only alive because his masters demanded it of him. He'd felt Raeb's hatred of them, burning inside him like an inferno, and Aeo hadn't been afraid anymore. Once he'd seen Raeb's eyes, he hadn't worried for his life. Whatever the Keeper of Secrets had done to Raeb, he despised it more than anything else in the world. And he would defy the Entana at every turn.

But looking back at how they'd controlled Raeb, Aeo shuddered. How powerful *were* the Entana, to use Raeb like a puppet and force him to turn on his friends?

Aeo wasn't even sure how he should react to this. There was anger somewhere in there, and a little fright, but at the moment he was mostly confused.

Dragana, though… her emotions rioted enough for both of them. The force of her anger was terrifying, but Aeo was more concerned with the pain burning beneath it. The warm flame of affection she'd developed for Raeb had frozen so hard and so fast the cold seared her heart. He could feel the pressure of tears in the back of her throat.

She plodded through the snow, paying no attention to where they were going or any obstacles along the way. She couldn't seem to muster the energy for anything more.

Do you want to talk? he asked.

Dragana said, "No," but her thoughts screamed *how could he do this he betrayed us it's my fault I never should have trusted a -taken.*

He was dumbstruck by the stark disconnect. Dragana had always been one to speak her mind, or at least hide her true thoughts well enough he couldn't reach them. But these were so powerful they leapt from her mind and threatened to bowl him over. *Where are we going?*

"Away." *West.*

The war, and its -taken soldiers, was in the west. He didn't need to read her thoughts to understand her intentions. *I didn't think you were going to kill -taken anymore.*

Killing -taken is all I know. "I have to do something."

Aeo started to reply, but Dragana cut him off. "I've put off my obligations for too long," she said. "I let Ra… that -taken distract me. I am a Taronese warrior and the bearer of the Bok'Tarong. It's my duty to keep the Entana from spreading. It's about time I got to it."

But Dragana, something's wrong. Why would Raeb turn on us like that?

"He's a -taken. And a traitor. This isn't the first time he's done something like this."

You can't believe he misled us this whole time on purpose, can you? Raeb is our friend. This is the Entana's fault. It must be. And if they're powerful enough to force Raeb to try something like that, then they have to be up to something.

"You aren't even a little upset at what he almost did to you?"

Sure I am. But I want to make sure I'm upset at the right people, and I don't think Raeb's the one.

"Then who is?"

The Entana.

A growl surfaced in the back of Dragana's throat. "I'm always upset at the Entana."

Then let's do something about it.

"That's what I'm doing."

You know what I mean, Aeo replied. *Let's do something meaningful, something that would stop them forever.*

"I'm not going back." An image of the Mage General flashed through her mind, followed by the hordes of willing -taken in his army. "I'm going to do what I should have done a long time ago. I'm going to stop this war from forcing innocent soldiers to accept monsters into themselves."

He had to admit, Dragana's plan sounded like a good one. There was a lot going on in the west. Breeding -taken, people willingly accepting Entana possession. The Mage General's actions could ruin Arata if he wasn't stopped.

But by leaving Raeb and Saydee, they were walking away from an opportunity they would never find again. What good would stopping the Mage General do, if the Entana were allowed to endure? The cycle would continue. More people would be -taken, more lives lost.

And what was the Keeper of Secrets up to, with his puppetry of Raeb? Aeo couldn't let that go. The churning in his gut told him this was important, maybe even more dangerous than the Mage General's plans in the west.

Dragana, I don't think...

"Aeo, if you don't shut up I'll leave you by the side of the road for some brainless assassin to pick up."

He was stunned into silence for a moment, more hurt than he'd care to admit. *Brainless assassin? Is that what I've been reduced to?*

She took a deep breath, held it for a few seconds, and blew it out noisily. She rolled her shoulders and tried to force herself to relax. "I'm sorry, Aeo. I didn't... I just..." Another breath, this one filled with regret and pain. "I gave him a chance and it almost cost us everything. I won't make that mistake again."

But Dragana...

"No. I won't hear any more about it. We're going west and we're going to stop the Mage General." Her tone had been harsh, but her thoughts were pleading and sounded near tears. *Please, Aeo, don't make this any harder than it already is.*

No matter how badly he wanted to argue, to force her to return to Raeb and figure this out together, he couldn't bear the pain in her thoughts. Pushing her would only make things worse.

All right, then, west we go.

Dragana's thoughts retreated into the chill numbness of her emotions. Aeo let her be.

Maybe it wouldn't be so bad. They could still do some good in the west, while Dragana cooled down. And maybe Aeo could figure out how to fix the mess their lives had suddenly become.

RAEB DIDN'T DARE return to sleep. He wanted nothing more than to escape the weariness of this life, even for a few hours, but sleep wouldn't give him that kind of rest. He leaned against a tree, watching the embers' glow fade, as the stars winked out and weak light preceded the dawn.

When Saydee woke, he took a long look at her eyes — pupil even more elongated, the whites surrounding them edging ever closer to true black. If the Keeper of Secrets kept hijacking her mind like this, it wouldn't be long before she became fully -taken.

She sat up slowly, rubbing at the muscles of her neck, looking around the forest with sleepy confusion. It took her a few moments to focus on Raeb, and when she did the lingering tension in her muscles eased.

She must have read the turmoil on his face, because a scowl spread across hers. "What's wrong?" She paused, taking a closer look at their half-abandoned campsite. "Where's Dragana?"

Where indeed? Far out of his reach. "They left."

"When will she be back?"

The words were a bitter poison on his tongue, but he forced himself to say them. "They won't."

Saydee scooted closer and peered at him with her keen Entana eyes. "Raeb, what happened?"

He threw a twig into the dying coals, watching it shrivel to ash in the heat. Just like his life had done.

"The Keeper of Secrets forced my hand, and Dragana discovered the nature of my mission. It didn't agree with her."

"What do you mean, 'your *mission*'?"

He'd avoided this moment for decades. He'd never told another soul what his mission from the Entana had been, in some kind of insane hope that keeping it a secret would keep it from being real. But now the secret was out. There was nothing to lose. And yet, he still wished with all his heart he didn't have to say it aloud.

He took a deep breath and plunged forward before he lost his nerve. "You knew something was different about me right from the start. You said you wanted to be free from the Entana, like I was."

Saydee nodded.

"The truth is, I'm not free. I never have been. If anything, I'm more a slave to them than you are.

"Before the Entana found me, I was a Taronese warrior-in-training. My entire life was consumed with learning to fight and praying one day I'd be chosen to bear the Bok'Tarong." He'd stopped smiling at those memories long ago. Now they were so faded they hardly even brought him sadness. "Then I was -taken."

He sank into a deep, mournful silence. No matter how many years passed, this memory would never fade. Sudden pain, like a dagger impaling your brain. Scrambled thoughts, confusion as you feel *something* stirring in your mind. Revulsion. Terror. Not knowing what was happening as your mind is torn apart... then the horror. Realization. Truth. You were now a slave of the Entana. A -taken. Never to be your own person again.

Then blurriness. Pain. Screams being ripped from your throat until you no longer sound human. Agony. Gaping holes in your mind, memories forever lost. Sickness spreading through your body as you cry and vomit and thrash against the invisible, untouchable monster in your head.

Finally, blessed quiet. But nothing remotely close to peace. Never again.

Raeb wrestled his thoughts away from the memory, nausea roiling through him. His hands were shaking. "I left the temple as soon as I could. I knew once the masters discovered what had happened, they'd kill me. I should have stayed and let them. It would have been the honorable thing to do, but I was too afraid to face death. So I ran.

"I fought against the Entana as best as I could, but you know how useless that is. And then, a few months after fleeing the temple, the Entana tried to feed on a memory of the Bok'Tarong." He paused, reliving one of the few images from his past that was still crystal clear. "I was eight, maybe ten years old, when the sword-bearer returned to the temple. I'd hid outside the dojo for hours, hoping to catch a glimpse of the sword. And when I did, every hardship I'd gone through was worthwhile. I'd never seen anything as enchanting as those rosy gold blades. From that day on, my entire existence was focused on earning the right to bear that sword."

The sweetness of the memory soured as he continued. "As soon as the image of the Bok'Tarong rose in my mind, the Entana froze. Something held it back. And that was when I met the Keeper of Secrets." This memory, too, was crystal clear, as much as Raeb wished it wasn't. "He'd seen I was once a Taronese warrior-in-training, and he wouldn't let an opportunity like that pass by. He promised me my freedom in exchange for one small task: I had to destroy the Bok'Tarong."

"And you agreed?" Saydee asked. Raeb wasn't sure if it was contempt or confusion in her voice, but he didn't care. He'd allowed the Keeper of Secrets to manipulate him into betraying everything he'd ever worked for. His own cowardice had ruined his life. He already hated himself enough for a thousand people.

"No. I refused. But the Keeper of Secrets wouldn't let me. I could either accept or endure a lingering existence on the brink of madness. He assured me he could make me suffer for an eternity, unable to do anything but kill and spread the Entana to the entire Taronese temple. And I believed him. I still do.

"So, being the coward I am, I accepted. He bound the Entana in my mind from feeding on my thoughts, gave me Sunray to devour the Bok'Tarong's enchantment, and ordered me not to fail."

Saydee stared at him, her knees to her chest and her arms wrapped around them. "How long ago was that?"

"About two hundred years."

"How have you been able to avoid it for so long?"

"At first he didn't care how long it took. The Keeper of Secrets had plans in motion that would take decades to come to fruition. Until they were ready, he didn't need the sword destroyed. And since the Bok'Tarong doesn't hurt the Entana, it wasn't important I destroy it immediately. The sword is a nuisance to them. He'd come bother me from time to time in my dreams, asking if I was any closer, but I never received more than a lecture and a few mental whippings for my excuses.

"But now, all of his plans are ready, or close to it. I've been given a deadline. And now the Keeper of Secrets knows I had my opportunity and chose not to destroy the Bok'Tarong. It won't be long before he comes after me, and when he finds me I'll be dead. My time is almost up."

He'd spoken the last words in a rush, but now he *heard* them. The truth was there, undeniable—he was out of time.

He stood and started packing up the camp, even though the

sun had barely crested the horizon. "We have to move."

Saydee stood, as if unsure whether it was the right thing to do. "Where are we going?"

Raeb turned to the west, the last direction he'd seen Dragana and Aeo going. No, it wouldn't be smart to trail them. In her mood, Dragana would be more likely to lop his head off than listen to his explanations. He turned away.

"I'm not sure," he said, shaking bits of snow and dirt from his blanket. "But we have to leave. We have to figure out what to do before something terrible happens."

Saydee swallowed and nodded.

Raeb picked a southerly direction, wandering while his mind reeled. After two centuries, he was out of time, and he had no idea what he needed to do next. He hadn't felt this lost in decades.

Raeb's thoughts returned to the previous night. The helplessness he felt, at the mercy of the Keeper of Secrets... the pain and rage in Dragana's eyes... feeling that terrible temptation to destroy the Bok'Tarong, and nearly succumbing to it...

He drew his sword, reveling in the long, straight blade. It was a relief to hold a weapon that was not Sunray. The weight of the blade was a comfort to him, and the air swishing past it soothed his nerves.

He was glad to be moving. Sitting still had been torturous. At least this way, he could walk and move and make it harder to think.

He picked up his pace, not knowing why. The faster he went, the sooner he'd have to figure out where he was going. But slowing down, stopping, would make everything worse. If he couldn't fix his life, the least he could do was keeping moving.

Something crashed through the trees to his side, landing with a soft thud a few steps ahead.

Raeb spun, his heart racing, sword held high. It hadn't sounded like an animal, but there were plenty of things that could make noises in this forest. Bandits, though they were rare, more -taken soldiers…

A snowball crashed into him, soaking his chest with ice.

He raised his eyes just as Saydee threw another at him. He lifted his arms to block, but the snow pulverized on impact and showered him with frigid water.

"What are you thinking, Saydee?" he cried, wiping snow from his eyes.

Her laughter rang through the trees. Raeb told himself it was his imagination, or the rising sun, that made the forest seem brighter.

"You should see your face right now!" she said, lobbing another snowball his way. He batted it away with his sword, but the snow exploded over him nonetheless.

He sheathed his sword, in case he started feeling tempted to use it, and scooped up a small handful of snow from the base of a nearby tree. He threw it at her, a little harder than was probably called for. She dodged it, though the action caused her to lose her balance and her next shot missed.

Saydee laughed all the harder.

"This is ridiculous," Raeb said, though even he heard the hint of laughter in his voice. He knelt and scooped up a handful of snow. When was the last time he'd simply played? Had he ever done so? After so many years alone, always running, then the stress of the last few days... he could feel the tension leaving his body. He could almost pretend there was nothing more urgent in his life than pelting Saydee with snow.

"This is ridiculous, but stomping away and brooding isn't?"

"I'm not brooding."

"Yeah. And you're not having fun right now, either."

He was prepared to deny it. He wasn't having fun, he was defending himself from assault-by-snowball.

Despite himself, he chuckled.

"You take everything so seriously," she said.

"And you smile and laugh more than anyone I've ever met, but I don't understand how you do it."

Saydee paused, her arm stopped mid-throw. Her smile darkened a few degrees. "What do you mean?"

"I've been in your mind, Saydee. I've seen how hurt you are inside. I've heard you hint at how horrible your past has been. Yet you can act like a carefree child who's never seen anything darker than a thunderstorm. How do you do it?"

She lobbed the snowball at him, but so weakly it hardly bounced against his chest. "Life has a nasty way of making everything miserable if you don't stop to enjoy it once in a while," she said with a shrug. "I'm tired of being miserable, so I try not to make it any worse."

"Sometimes there isn't much to enjoy about life," Raeb replied. His voice, and his spirit, had returned to their normal, somber state.

"Maybe you just aren't looking for it hard enough."

"Maybe it's not worth looking for in the first place."

The words came out harsher than he'd intended, but he figured that made them all the more true. Goodness knows he had enough experience to know it.

Saydee didn't reply for a few moments. When she did, her voice was soft. All wisps of levity from their snowball fight had been drained away. "If you truly believe that, then you might as well be dead. Life isn't all happiness, but it doesn't have to be all sadness, either. There's no point in living if you aren't going to live to the fullest—through the pain as well as the joy."

Raeb felt the history behind those words. He'd seen how battered her spirit was, so at odds with how frivolously she enjoyed life at times. She'd lived through enough to believe her view on life more than Raeb believed his own sentiments about it.

"What happened to you, Saydee?"

She didn't lift her eyes to his. "What do you mean?"

"After the Mage's Academy rejected you. When, and how, you were -taken. It's obvious you're speaking from experience, but I know nothing about you."

Raeb was surprised how desperately he wanted to hear her story. The night she'd followed him out of some no-name desert town, he'd thought she was just some spoiled girl with a special connection to the Entana. But she was so much more than that— and he wanted to know how much more.

Saydee, however, didn't seem enthusiastic about sharing. Her pace slowed and her eyes wandered from tree to ground to tree, never landing anywhere near Raeb.

"Raeb?"

"Hmm?"

"I think… I think we should go to Karim."

"What?" He didn't understand where this had come from, but he had a feeling it wasn't as much an evasion of the topic as a conclusion he hadn't received all the details to. "Of all the places we could go, you suggest the capital of Arata? That's the worst place on the continent to be if you're -taken. They'd kill us in a heartbeat, even with your glamour and my disguise."

"We could do it. It's not like we'd be parading through the streets and drawing attention to ourselves."

Raeb sighed. The girl really was too stubborn for her own good sometimes. "Why do you want to go to Karim?"

She clammed up. She fiddled with her fingers and stared at the ground, chewing on her lower lip. He'd never seen her look so nervous. At least, not in this world.

If Saydee insisted on going somewhere she was obviously so hesitant to go, she had to have a damn good reason.

"I want to go to the Mage's Academy," she said at last.

For a second he was sure he'd misheard her. Her lack of magical prowess was a sore spot in her past. The Academy wasn't somewhere Saydee would go to relive happy memories. Why would she want to see that collection of dusty old bastards?

"The Mage's Academy? That's slightly less suicidal than marching straight into the Taronese temple."

"Well, I don't *want* to go," she stammered, "but I think they might be able to help us. We need to strengthen the magic between me and the Entana to get to the hive. The -taken haven't been able to help. Maybe we've been looking in the wrong place."

"Saydee, you're talking about asking mages about Entana magic. It's unknown to them. Even if someone there *had* discovered the truth behind the Coming Madness, they wouldn't know the first thing about your connection."

She shrugged, trying to act casual, but Raeb wasn't fooled. "It's worth a try."

He glanced at her, trying to read her expression. "There's something you aren't telling me."

It wasn't a question, and she didn't offer any answers.

"If I'm going to march into the capital and knock at the door of the Mage's Academy, I'd better have at least an idea of what I'm there for."

Saydee hesitated. He heard her indecision in her footsteps, but he didn't push her. He just continued walking, keeping his own footsteps strong and sure.

After a few minutes, she took a deep breath. "A long time ago, there was a mage named Ashwinn. He spent years researching Entana possession in secret. He knew more about the Entana than anyone alive, maybe even to this day. If anyone had figured out something about how the connections between Entana and -taken work, it would be Ashwinn."

"Then why is this the first time I'm hearing anything about this guy?"

"I thought your plan would work," she said. "I didn't want to bring it up if we had another option."

Raeb opened his mouth—this information could have saved them from so many dangers—but he shut it without a word. He had secrets he'd withheld in the hopes they'd never have to come to light. He could at least allow her the same.

"He lived a long time ago? How long ago are we talking?"

"Longer than you've been alive."

"Great," Raeb groaned. "Sounds like he'd be a great person to ask, except for the fact he's dead."

"He would have preserved his research. If we can get in and look through it, maybe they'd have an answer."

She'd said "maybe", but her tone said otherwise. Saydee was sure this long-dead Ashwinn would know what they had to do.

Raeb could see her face sour at the thought of the Mage's Academy. There was history there that repelled her like shadows from sunlight. She looked like she was about to vomit.

"This past you don't want to face... it involves the Mage's Academy, doesn't it?"

She nodded.

"You know that, if we go, we'll be there in a week, two at most."

She gulped and nodded again.

"And you still don't want to talk about it?"

"I will tell you, Raeb. I promise. Just... can't it wait a little longer?"

If they were walking into Saydee's past, a past she refused to acknowledge but haunted her thoughts, there could be real danger waiting for them. He couldn't be prepared if he didn't know what to expect. And given the hints he'd received about her past, it could be quite dangerous, indeed.

"Does this have anything to do with why the Entana in your

mind believes it was invited in?"

Saydee stopped cold.

It had been a stab in the dark, but her reaction said enough. "Your history with the Mage's Academy is more extensive than a simple petition and rejection, isn't it?"

She paused before replying. "Did you think I'd give up after one rejection? I thought you knew me better than that by now."

Her attempt at humor was as hollow as her voice, but Raeb got her point. The woman who'd chased him down and insisted she accompany him wouldn't have walked away after a simple 'no'.

Raeb glanced at her. She looked small and scared. Whatever she was hiding, it must be horrible.

"All right," he said. "But tromping into the Academy with these secret demons hanging over you won't make it any easier. You know that, right?"

Her voice was little more than a squeak. "I know."

Chapter Twenty-Four

Raeb hardly recognized Karim, but that wasn't surprising. After a hundred years away, it was surprising he recognized it at all.

The last time he'd been here, the capital was a small fortified castle and keep on a hill just outside the forest. Only a handful of people called it home. Now, the city had engulfed the entire hill and a large network of fields around it. He couldn't even guess how many thousands of people lived there.

"This is a bad idea," he whispered.

Saydee didn't offer any argument. She stood next to him, pale-faced, staring at the capital with wide eyes. Raeb noticed the tremor she tried to hide.

"We can still turn around," he offered.

"Where else would we go?"

They both knew the answer to that. Their only hope of finding an answer lay within those gates. If they ever wanted to be free from the Entana, they had to go forward. Otherwise they were left with nothing.

Raeb had never been more reluctant to enter a city in his entire life.

He nearly jumped out of his skin when something brushed his arm. It was just Saydee, scooting closer for comfort, but that didn't relax him much. What was he supposed to do?

He stood still, holding his breath for several heartbeats before stepping forward to break away from the contact. Better to just move on.

He and Saydee joined the throng of people waiting to enter the gates. Plenty of folks glanced at the pretty young girl, but no one paid any attention to the poor blind man on her arm.

The queue may have been long, but it moved quickly. Well before Raeb was prepared to enter into the capital, they were approaching the gates.

It took all his restraint not to gasp when he saw the guards—or rather, their Entana eyes.

"Raeb," Saydee whispered.

"I see," he replied. "Stay calm. We just have to get through the gate."

The guards, bored and inattentive at first, instantly took a liking to Saydee. The taller of the two, with darker hair and skin like a Halkronar, pushed himself away from the wall and stood straight for the first time since Raeb had seen him. "Where're you headin', missy?"

"To the Mage's Academy," she replied, smiling and refusing to look into his eyes.

"Why would a pretty thing like you be goin' up there?"

"We're hoping they might be able to do something for my uncle. He took a hit on the head a few years back and hasn't seen a thing since."

The guard's eyes shifted from Saydee to Raeb, like he was gauging just how much of an obstacle this blind man would be. Raeb did his best not to react.

"This is your uncle, huh?"

"Of course."

The guard came a step closer, his eyes locked on Saydee. Raeb noticed they didn't travel much above her neck.

Raeb stuck his hand out, as if enthused to shake hands with the guard. If his aim was a bit misplaced, and his fingers a little stiffened when they hit the man's unarmored stomach, well… he couldn't be blamed. He was blind, after all.

The guard deflated with an *oomph* and took a few steps back. He eyed Raeb, his initial flash of malice fading as he looked at Raeb's impassive face.

"Right then," he said, keeping his arms crossed over his torso. "Move along."

Saydee guided Raeb through the gates.

"I could have handled him," she whispered once they were lost in the crowd.

"You could have," he agreed. "But that was much more fun."

She smiled, but the mirth faded as she glanced back toward the gates. "He was -taken. They both were."

"And they didn't try to hide it," Raeb added.

"I guess the -taken soldiers aren't only on the frontlines anymore."

Raeb nodded, but it didn't make any sense. -Taken had been scorned in Karim for longer than he'd been alive. Most citizens wouldn't suffer a -taken to beg on their streets, let alone carry on a normal life. What had changed to allow -taken to guard their city, without discrimination?

"There's no reason to have -taken soldiers here," he said. "On the frontlines they were bred and used out of desperation. But here? There aren't enemies to defeat or wars to be won on the streets of Karim."

Saydee glanced at him, her glamour-enhanced eyes dark with suspicion. "At least, not ones we can see."

He looked back at her, his mind reeling at the implications. Did she mean a political war, one fought in courts and castles, or an Entana war, fought in minds and the spiritual realm? Either way, they were far out of their depth and walking into deeper trouble than they could handle.

Dragana, why did you have to leave? We can't do this alone.

He laughed at how desperately he wished she and Aeo were here. He couldn't remember the last time he'd come to rely on someone so much. And why was the one he'd come to rely on Dragana, of all people? How did the stubborn, self-righteous bearer of the Bok'Tarong become so important to him?

Saydee led Raeb through cobbled streets, past street vendors hawking their wares, housewives bartering for supplies, and children running between carts with abandon. He was careful to keep his expression blank and face straight ahead, so he didn't give himself away, but he longed to look around and ground himself in this strange city.

The press of bodies was almost too much for Raeb. He'd never seen so many people shoved into so small a space. They poured from every opening and rushed through the streets like a river, complete with eddies and currents and rare, deep pools of stillness. At times they even sounded like white-capped rapids, or like a stream bubbling over rocks. The flow of humanity pulled him and Saydee through the capital, and if they weren't careful they'd be swept away.

He never would have admitted it, but he was grateful to have Saydee on his arm. She was much more accustomed to navigating these kinds of narrow, teeming streets. Raeb was already lost, but she strode down the road and pushed people out of her way with strength but never cruelty. He didn't know how she managed it.

Several times he spotted -taken, never alone but never more than three in a group, mingling amongst the people. A few wore uniforms, but Raeb could tell every one of them had military experience. They stood too erect, their eyes too sharp. Civilians parted before them and scurried away before those Entana eyes fell upon them.

He pulled Saydee to a stop before a small stand of sausages. They pretended to peruse, ignoring the eager merchant. Raeb felt exposed with his back to the -taken soldiers, but he hoped the press of humanity around them would offer a bit of protection.

"Have you seen them?" he whispered, quiet enough even the merchant rattling off prices and qualities couldn't hear him.

She nodded, as if approving of a sausage that smelled of garlic and onion.

"If any of them discover us, we'll be dead before we could

defend ourselves."

"Can't we blend in with them? If those -taken are tolerated…"

"No. They'll know we aren't one of them. And if Dragana was right about these willing -taken, they're taking orders from the Entana. They'll know what we're up to by now, thanks to the Keeper of Secrets. We'll be executed as traitors."

Saydee kept her expression blank, but Raeb saw the fear tighten her jaw. She handed a few small coins to the merchant, pocketing two sausages in return.

As soon as the transaction was complete, they were swept back into the current. Saydee guided them for a bit, then ducked into an alley and away from the crowd. "What do we do?" she asked.

Raeb looked into her eyes, clear green and human thanks to her glamour. "This doesn't change anything. We still have to get into the Mage's Academy unseen." He looked back into the street as two -taken wandered past. "We just have to make sure none of them notice us."

She looked down, biting her lip like she was wrestling with an important decision. At last she nodded, her face set with determination. "All right then. Come here."

Before Raeb could ask why, she placed her hands on either side of his face. Her palms were warm and clammy, her fingers shaky. She held his head steady, staring at him as if trying to bore holes through his skull with her eyes.

He felt the intensity of that gaze like a physical pressure against his body. His skin tingled and itched.

Then Saydee's cool, silky magic slid over and around him like an embrace.

She slumped against the wall, panting, but the glamour she'd placed over Raeb held steady. He could feel it like a swimmer felt water on their skin—cool and pleasant, but soon taken for granted and overlooked.

He was impressed. It took a lot more power than Saydee had hinted she had to place a glamour on someone else. "I didn't know you could do that."

Her voice shook. "Neither did I."

"What does it do?" he asked, flexing his fingers as if expecting to feel the magic stretch around him. Like any good glamour, he didn't feel a thing.

"It makes you less noticeable."

"You mean invisible?"

She took a deep breath and pushed herself away from the wall. She wobbled for a moment, but stood on her own. "No. People just won't pay attention to you. You'll walk by, they'll see you, but they won't remember anything special about you. They'll forget you as just another inconsequential part of their day."

"Impressive," he said, and he meant it. "This could come in handy."

"It does."

Raeb looked up at her and her glamour-enhanced green eyes. "Why don't you use this more often?"

"I did for a long time. But after a while, you get tired of being ignored and forgotten."

He shook his head, chuckling to himself. He would give

anything to be ignored and forgotten for a while.

He took Saydee's hand and placed it on his arm, as much for the blind man illusion as to support her. He waited for a lull in the flow of people at the mouth of the alley, and they plunged back into the flow.

Saydee led him, a bit slower now, toward the hill at the center of the city. Fewer street carts crowded these streets, and the people milling about were dressed in colorful silks instead of rough homespun wool. Several large cedars shaded the streets and ornate buildings. Raeb found it easier to breathe away from the mobs of commoners below, but still his breath caught in his chest. There were more guards here, and more -taken. He kept his eyes open for trouble, but the two groups seemed to ignore each other. Raeb wasn't sure if that was a good sign or a bad one.

Near the top of the hill, the street opened up into a grand courtyard. The trees here were even larger and more abundant. Underneath their boughs a stone-lined pond stirred with red and gold fish. The buildings surrounding them were as massive as the trees and almost as stately, but they would never feel or smell as fresh. These places reeked of government.

Raeb's attention was drawn to a large, imposing building set apart from the others. He would have known this was the Mage's Academy even if he'd never seen it before. It was huge and unwelcoming, and looked as cold and impassive as the mages within. Saydee stared up at it with undisguised fear.

"They might as well have hung a sign saying 'go away' over the door," he said. "This was a bad idea."

Saydee ignored him, squared her shoulders, and stepped

forward.

She was acting brave, but he wasn't fooled. She was terrified. Her hand trembled on his arm, and her posture was so rigid she could have been carved from stone. Perhaps most telling of all, she hadn't said a word since the imposing Academy came into view.

They joined a small, rag-tag crowd at a nondescript door tucked in a corner. A haggard and annoyed mage shielded the door from petitioners. The peasants pleaded with him for help, spells, or potions, but he may as well have been deaf for all the attention he showed them.

"We'll never get past this," Raeb whispered. "Too many people, and I'd bet my life that mage has more than one trick up his sleeve for dealing with peasants who want to force their way inside."

He began studying the area, trying to find a more nonconventional way to enter the Academy. They'd never be able to climb the smooth stone walls, and it was too far to jump from roof to roof. Perhaps the kitchens…

He leaned over to say as much to Saydee, but the girl wasn't at his side anymore. His heart leapt into his throat. Had they been discovered already? No, that couldn't be. Saydee would have made a racket, and they would have captured him as well. So where did that stubborn girl run off to?

He saw her threading her way through the peasants, straight to the guard-mage. He swore under his breath. What did she think she could accomplish by revealing themselves? Now they'd be noticed at least, more likely watched. They'd never be able to sneak in. Not anymore.

Raeb pictured the glowing smile Saydee gave the man as she got his attention. The guard never twitched a muscle. She stood on her toes and leaned toward him, whispering something. Still, no reaction.

Saydee stepped back, paused for a second, then came back to Raeb's side. He was about to scold her for drawing attention to themselves, but her grin silenced his reprimand.

"What are you so proud of?" he grumbled.

She took his arm and led him forward without a word.

He took the hint and remained quiet as they made their way back to the guard-mage. Raeb was gauging the man's size, speed, and possible weapons when he stepped aside, granting Saydee access to the Academy.

Raeb fought hard to keep his expression oblivious.

The gloom of the corridor beyond swallowed the daylight. Saydee was first into the cool, dark depths, and Raeb was pulled along behind. Shouts and protests rose from behind them as the guard-mage closed the door and resumed his impassive post.

A quick check of the corridor revealed no doors, no side passages, and no other people.

"How did you do that?" Raeb whispered. Even that low tone echoed off the barren stone walls.

"There are a few passwords that are never spoken outside the Academy and never changed. They're designed that way so no mage, however old or however long he'd been away, would ever be locked out of his own Academy."

A bit of Raeb's frustration leaked into his voice. "It would have been nice to know you had this secret password before now." She at least had the decency to blush. "So you *are* a mage, then."

"No," she spat. "At least, not in the way you're thinking."

"Then how did you come to know this secret password?"

Saydee ignored the question.

"You'll have to tell me sooner or later," Raeb said. "I won't be kept in the dark forever."

She paused. "I know."

"I wish you'd stop saying that," he grumbled. He gave her a long-suffering sigh, looked around the empty corridor, and changed the subject. "So we're in. Now what?"

Saydee stepped forward, staring at the walls. "We go in further. This will take us into one of the back libraries, and from there we make our way to Ashwinn's laboratory."

"Why the lab? Wouldn't his notes and things be filed away in an office or library somewhere?"

"Maybe. But Ashwinn would have hidden his research on the Entana. It was forbidden, after all. The mages probably wouldn't have destroyed it, but he wouldn't have risked it. He would have kept it close and locked away so it would never be lost."

"So we have to get through the library, corridors, and into a lab. Without being caught."

She nodded. "Without being caught."

"Right." Raeb took a breath. "Shouldn't be a problem."

Chapter Twenty-five

T he corridor ran straight as an arrow for thirty paces before branching out into a wider, lighter hallway. The hundreds of small noises populating a place of learning reached Raeb's ears—rustling parchment, whispered conversations, shuffling feet, clinking glassware. His footsteps no longer echoed against bare stone, but were softened by thin rugs that had once been rather plush. The walls took on a more lived-in look he couldn't explain as they entered the first of many libraries. There were a few shelves and plenty of tables scattered around, each coated with quills and inkwells and parchments both blank and scribbled upon. Most importantly, it was empty.

Two exits led out, and Saydee took the right hand door with only the slightest pause. Another corridor, this one much brighter and more comfortable, led to another room similar to the one they'd just left. Another exit, yet another library. A few small offices, another study hall. Raeb was beginning to wonder if there was anything to the Mage's Academy but stuffy rooms filled with parchments.

He and Saydee passed a few mages, but most hardly glanced at them. A few were so absorbed with their research they walked with their noses in a book and didn't seem to care that others roamed the same halls. It was just as well—the fewer people who noticed their presence, the better off they'd be.

Their small corridor merged with a larger, much busier hallway. Mages bustled around or stood in small groups, arguing more often than talking. The smell of old parchment didn't disappear so much as fade beneath the stronger scents of ink and perfumes straining to mask the reek of human sweat. His and Saydee's footsteps were no longer the only sounds heard for minutes on end.

Saydee led him with confidence, nodding and smiling to anyone who seemed to notice them. Mages and students smiled back, the benign smiles of those who want to be polite but don't actually care. Their eyes slid over Raeb and they returned to their tasks as if nothing had happened.

They could have traveled a mile or more in the time it took them to meander through the few dozen rooms and corridors to a grand foyer near the official entrance to the Academy. The ceiling rose to dizzying heights above them, the massive expanse of marble floor teeming with people. It was designed to impress, Raeb knew, and it didn't fail to do so. The sheer size of the room made Raeb feel small and insignificant.

Saydee started to lead them across, but Raeb pulled her back into the hallway. He silenced her outcry with a glare, then pointed to a group of men standing in the shadows to their left.

They swept the foyer with keen Entana eyes.

"Dear gods," she whispered, her eyes locked on them. "There are -taken in the Mage's Academy."

Raeb had no response. -Taken in Karim, he might be able to understand. They were scorned or outright killed, but at least they were found on occasion. In the Mage's Academy, though... Mages were the biggest threat to them, apart from the Bok'Tarong. A mage would kill anyone with the smallest taint of Entana in their eyes and return to accolades and applause. Any -taken with a hint of sense would run at the first sign of a mage.

So what were these -taken soldiers doing *here*?

Dread settled in Raeb's gut. He had no idea what was going on, but he didn't like it one bit.

"We have to get past them to get to Ashwinn's lab," Saydee whispered.

"All right. Stay calm, don't skulk. Let's hope we can blend in and avoid being noticed."

Forcing himself to walk as if he hadn't a care in the world was harder than he'd thought. Every step was full of stiffness and tension, as if he expected to step on a scorpion. His eyes flit back to the -taken soldiers over and over again, hoping never to make eye contact.

Once, he caught one of the soldiers watching Saydee. Raeb tensed, his free arm reaching for Sunray before he could stop it. He looked at Saydee, to see if she'd noticed. She hadn't.

When he looked back at the soldier, the man's attention had wandered to someone else.

The walk across the foyer lasted half a lifetime. By the time they reached the far side and exited into a large hallway, Raeb was shaking and clammy with sweat.

Saydee was pale and her hand clamped on Raeb's arm like a vice, but she continued to lead them through the corridors. They wound farther into the Academy, past offices and libraries and finally some laboratories. It smelled strange here, like chemicals and burnt hair and the smell of seared air after a lightning strike. Raeb couldn't help but think it smelled like magic.

Soon the hallways morphed back to the same kind of stale, neglected corridors they'd arrived in. Raeb felt uncomfortable back here, like these were parts of the Academy that were ignored or outright avoided. He'd only felt this kind of atmosphere once before, and the memory didn't help to bolster his confidence.

This place had the same sad, neglected feeling as the hospital in the -taken sanctuary, where his kind went to go mad and die.

They rounded a corner and stopped in their tracks. Blocking their way was a gate more fitting for a castle's stronghold. Iron bars longer and thicker than Raeb's entire body barricaded the doorway. Each wooden plank of the gate was more like a half-grown tree. It would take an army to breach the gate, and even so, Raeb wasn't sure they could succeed.

"What is this, Saydee? You told me we'd be sneaking into the Mage's Academy, not breaking into a gods-be-damned prison!"

Her eyes never left the gates, and her voice was small and distant. The tremor in her hands was spreading to her entire body. "I don't know whether his magic was too powerful or his mind too cunning, or both, but Ashwinn was considered a threat to himself and others. So they kept him here, where all the dangerous mages and broken experiments are contained."

"We're chasing after a long-dead mage who was too insane and too strong for his own good." Raeb glowered at her from behind his opaque lenses. "You could have mentioned something about this, you know."

"Would you still have come with me, had you known?"

"Yes."

She blinked. She obviously hadn't expected that.

"You might be too stubborn for your own good," Raeb told her, "but that doesn't mean you have to do everything on your own. You're the one who taught me and Dragana that. Why can't you follow your own lessons?"

Her eyes were still locked on the huge, ironclad doors of the mage prison. "Because everyone I ever relied on has betrayed me."

Before he could press her for answers, she turned to him. "Please, Raeb, I know I haven't been fair to you. Maybe I should have told you a long time ago. But let's just get to Ashwinn's lab first. Then I'll tell you everything. I promise."

He pointed to the massive, fortified gates. "His *lab* is in there? Where everyone who was too mad to be trusted with freedom was kept?"

"*Are* kept. And yes. Just because they were insane or dangerous didn't mean they weren't geniuses. The Mage's Academy couldn't let a resource like that escape, so the mages kept here are given access to about anything they could want. They're just heavily guarded and supervised."

Raeb stared at the massive gate, hoping to squelch the fear

rising in his stomach. "I don't suppose you have a secret password for this one, too?"

She shook her head. "No such luck."

"Then how do we get through?"

She walked up to the gate, tugging on a tiny rope Raeb hadn't noticed before. A bell tinkled on the other side. Raeb heard muffled grumbling, shuffling, and then a small window opened at eye level. Raeb was sure the gate had been solid and seamless a moment ago.

A bored and harried mage stood on the other side. He didn't look at them. He kept his eyes down, scribbling on some paperwork, and mumbled something Raeb couldn't begin to translate. It sounded like *namklaspoitmtkrgo.*

Saydee looked at him, eyebrow raised. He shrugged.

"I'm sorry?" she asked.

He sighed the kind of long-suffering sigh only men forced to deal with idiots and those stupider than he—in other words, everyone—could manage. "Name. Class. Appointment. Cargo," he enunciated.

"Oh. Uh, Saydee, wizard-servant, we don't have an appointment or cargo but we need to get to Ashwinn's lab."

He finally looked up at her, peering through the small window as if Saydee were a juicy bug that had been squashed against it. "No appointment?"

"We're here for some maintenance, and to check that everything's in order."

"But you don't have an appointment."

"No. Is that a problem?" Saydee asked in her sweetest, most

innocent voice.

"Is it a problem?" he mimicked. "You're asking to barge into the most secure place in Karim, filled with the most dangerous minds, without the courtesy of letting us know or prepare. So yes, it is a problem." He looked down, dismissing them.

Neither Raeb nor Saydee moved.

After a few seconds, he looked up again. He seemed personally offended they hadn't scampered away. "Do you have an appointment now?"

Saydee dropped the sugary sweetness, replacing it with the stubbornness she was now famous for, at least in Raeb's mind. "No. We do not have an appointment. But we are not leaving until we have gotten to Ashwinn's lab."

"Impossible. If you do not abide by the rules, I will have you removed from the Academy. By force, if needed." He sounded like he hoped that would be the case.

Raeb had heard enough. He pushed Saydee away from the window, taking her place in the mage's face. "We aren't leaving," he said. "You will let us in, or you'll regret not doing so."

Now that he'd captured this man's attention, he could feel Saydee's magic pulsing. It strained to keep him inconspicuous. The man's eyes looked at Raeb, but he was already starting to look away and forget about him.

Raeb yanked off his opaque lenses, staring hard at the man with his peridot-pupiled Entana eyes. "Look at me!"

The man's eyes, now wide and terrified, glued onto Raeb's face. Saydee's cool magic shattered. It fell from Raeb's skin like droplets of water.

"That's better," he said. "We don't care that we don't have an appointment. We need to get into Ashwinn's lab. So open this gate and let us through before things get ugly."

"Y-yes, of course," the man stammered, tripping over himself to do as Raeb commanded. "I-I must apologize, s-sir. I didn't realize what—WHO! B-beg your pardon, a thousand times over. I didn't realize who you were."

It took him three tries to get the key in the lock. He whispered a hurried incantation, his voice shaking. By the time the massive gate creaked and grated open, he was sweating and trembling from head to toe.

"Please, enter sir. I meant no disrespect." He ushered them inside with what might have been a tiny bow.

Raeb was so stunned he couldn't think of anything to say. He'd expected fear or disgust in reaction to his Entana eyes. But terrified respect, from a mage in his own Academy? What kind of revolution had happened to change this hierarchy so profoundly? It left a sour knot of dread in his stomach.

Once past the gate, the mage resumed his post and refused to look back to Raeb and Saydee. They stood for a few seconds before looking down the corridor. Saydee took a deep breath. "Ready?" she asked.

Raeb wasn't sure whether she was asking him or herself, but he answered anyway. "Ready."

She glanced at him with a small nod, and they entered the mage's prison.

Chapter Twenty-Six

The halls here were even more depressing than those they'd come from. They were old—so old Raeb could feel the weight of centuries in the walls. The air of madness was stifling, as if he waded through a fog. Raeb felt tainted just from being here. Their echoing footsteps were like a clock ticking down their last remaining seconds of sanity.

Saydee had gotten quiet and nervous again. Raeb could feel how horrified she was to find herself here as easily as a predator smelled fear in their prey. Saydee wanted nothing more than to run away screaming, and that primal fear oozed from every pore in her body.

"Saydee, what's wrong?"

She jumped at his voice. He put his hand on her shoulder, strong and comforting, hoping to calm her nerves. Her entire body trembled. Her eyes were wild with terror.

He forced Saydee to look him in the eye. At first she cowered at his Entana eyes—something she'd never done before—but she relaxed as she recognized him. She was still scared as a bunny, but the crazed madness in her eyes dimmed.

"Saydee, talk to me. What's going on?" He paused, forcing his voice into the calmest, most soothing tones he could manage. "What happened to you here?"

Tears welled in her eyes. Her voice was so quiet he could barely hear her, even in the silent corridor. "This is where I was -taken."

That explained a lot. Raeb had no idea how he would react if they returned to the Taronese temple where he trained and was -taken, but it was something he'd avoided since he first left. Probably because, deep down, he knew he'd react something like this.

Questions still burned inside him, but he didn't ask them. Now wasn't the time.

"C'mon, Saydee. We can't go back now. Let's just find the lab and get out of here. Deep breaths. One step at a time."

He held her arm and led her farther down the corridor, keeping his motions smooth and his attention on her. They passed door after door, all closed, some with the distinctive sounds of experiments being conducted coming from behind. Raeb half expected to hear cackling and explosions at any moment.

This place was a maze of identical hallways, but Saydee led them through it like—as Raeb was now sure—she had spent many years doing so. She was hardly cognizant, didn't respond to any of Raeb's comments, but her steps were sure.

They stopped in front of a door that looked just like any other. Saydee placed her hand against the wood and closed her eyes. A shimmer of magic raced across the surface, glowing with runes and every color of the rainbow. When the waves of magic receded, Saydee removed her hand and opened the door.

Raeb wasn't sure what he'd been expecting, but it wasn't this. A well-kept, innocuous-looking laboratory lay before them. Glassware and containers were arranged on every surface. None of them held any kind of interesting, glowing, bubbling mixtures. He was almost disappointed. Papers were stacked here and there, and he stepped over and paged through a few. Raeb wasn't sure he could pronounce half of the words written there, let alone define them.

"I thought you said this Ashwinn guy lived a long time ago."

"He did."

"So who does all this junk belong to? They must have given this lab to someone else."

Saydee looked at the glassware, then bent over a stack of papers. "No. This is his."

Raeb, too, looked around. There wasn't a speck of dust anywhere, let alone cracked containers or papers crumbled to dust. Nothing to indicate this lab hadn't been used in days, let alone centuries.

"One of the wards I dispelled was a preservation spell. As long as the spell held, nothing in here would age or decay."

"Handy."

"It won't help us if we can't find anything."

"Relax, Saydee. We'll find something." He wasn't as confident as he hoped he sounded, but he wasn't about to show any doubt or fear now. Saydee was starting to come back to her senses. The last thing he wanted to do was send her reeling back through panic and terror.

They shuffled through an endless stream of papers, reports, and scribbled notes. Half of the time Raeb couldn't even guess what he was looking at. There were so many strange words and formulas and things that looked more like gibberish than language. He could be holding the answers to all their questions and have no idea.

"Does any of this make sense to you?" he asked.

She squinted at the lettering. "Some of it."

"Can you tell me what we're looking for?"

"Ashwinn's research focused on enhancing magical powers and extending a mage's life. The title should say something about that."

"And he was using Entana to do this?" Raeb shuddered. He didn't even listen for a reply, if one came. This was a subject he wasn't keen to investigate any further than they had to.

He considered asking how the research would help them, but he wasn't sure he wanted the answer to that one, either.

They rifled through some more papers in silence. "What was he to you?" Raeb asked.

Saydee froze. Her eyes had gone wide again, like a startled deer. "What... what do you mean?"

"Don't take me for a fool, Saydee. I've been misleading people and withholding information long enough to know when it's being done to me. Ashwinn wasn't just some historical figure you studied."

It wasn't a question, and Saydee didn't deny it.

"So what was he to you? Father? Lover?"

She shook her head. "He was the guard at the petitioner's door. I came here every day for over a year, begging to be admitted. I showed him my glamour and promised I would learn everything, if they'd just let me in."

"And he listened to you?"

"Not at first. It took a long time before he even looked at me. It was almost a full year before he spoke to me, and then it was just a few words at a time. He'd ask me about certain things, whether I could do certain types of magic, what the extent of my powers were. He seemed interested when I admitted just how limited they were. That should have warned me, but I was too excited at the time to notice. Why would a mage be interested in someone who has so little power she can barely conjure a basic glamour?"

Saydee continued to search through Ashwinn's research, keeping her eyes away from Raeb's. "Anyway, one day he asked me to follow him inside. I was elated. A look inside the Mage's Academy! Maybe once inside, I could find a way to convince them I belonged here." She scoffed, grumbling under her breath for a moment. "He brought me to his lab—not this one, at the time he wasn't considered a danger—and ran some tests on me."

She stopped, pulling a thick sheaf of papers from a massive stack. She stared at it, reading the title over a few times, before going deathly pale.

"Saydee? What did you find?"

She handed it over without a word.

Infection or enhancement? Modifying the mage's response to the effect of the subdural implant of a secondary influence to benefit the host organism.

Raeb stumbled over the title again. "I've seen a lot of research in my time, but nothing like this. What does that even mean?"

Saydee stepped beside him, trembling. Her hands were ice cold when they brushed his. "This is Ashwinn's research—at least, this is the research he submitted to the Academy."

"So this is what we're looking for."

"No," Saydee said. "This is part of it, sure. But this is the version that won't have a single mention of the Entana in it, and no specifics about how they affect a mage's mind. This won't tell us if we can use the Entana to strengthen my connection to them."

"Great. So what good is it, anyway?"

Saydee leaned forward and turned a page, then another, scanning the cramped writing. She pointed to a paragraph. "It's good for continuing my story," she said in a tiny, childlike voice. "This is what he did to me."

Raeb started reading.

One subject underwent a subdural implantation of a biological secondary influence to assess whether an improvement in mental and physical prowess could be accomplished and maintained. Both short- and long-term mental and physical testing were performed pre- and post-implantation to assess the physical and magical capabilities of the subject. Mental stability and changes in magical ability were measured through a standardized battery of exams executed at set timepoints. Basic vital signs and other health parameters, such as response to external stimuli, were regularly measured and changes in status tracked over time.

His head spun. "I've read every word, but I don't understand. Does anyone even talk like that?"

She almost smiled. "Over the next few months, Ashwinn assaulted my system with everything he could think of to see how my magic would react. Submerged in water until I almost drowned, torched with fire until I was covered in burns, subjected to every kind of magical probing you can imagine and more. He kept asking me to perform a complex spell I'd never been able to manage after he'd finished, when I was half-conscious from torture. I never could do it, and he would punish me every time I failed."

"Why didn't you leave?" Raeb asked.

"At first I was desperate to have more magic. I thought this would do it, and then I'd be able to stay and do my own magic. After a while, though, Ashwinn wouldn't let me."

She swallowed, steadying herself with several deep breaths. "Then he came to the last experiment."

Raeb, too, felt the need to steady himself. "The Entana."

"Ashwinn ripped through my magic to force the Entana into my mind, and the monster hacked through the rest. Each second felt like an eternity, and I wished for death in every single one." She paused, looking up at him with haunted Entana eyes. "It took half a day before the Entana got hold of my mind."

Raeb was staggered into speechlessness. Being -taken was a horrifying experience, but it was over in minutes. To suffer like that for hours on end… he couldn't even begin to fathom it. His own experience was downright pleasant compared to what Saydee had gone through.

His eyes traveled back to the paper, and a single sentence stood out to him. Even if the words were unnecessarily complex, the intent was clear.

The results showed a statistically significant augmentation of magical ability without deleterious effects to the physical being.

Raeb's heart burned with rage. Ashwinn hadn't seen Saydee as a person. She'd just been another experiment. He hadn't cared she'd been tortured by his hand and the Entana. Her magic was increased, and that was all that mattered. How could someone be so callous? If Ashwinn were here…

Saydee continued. "Once it was clear I was -taken, Ashwinn asked me to do that complex magic one more time. This time, if I couldn't do it, it would mean the experiment had failed and I would be useless to him."

She held out her hand, palm up, and closed her eyes. After a moment, a glowing sigil appeared in the air above her hand. Raeb had never seen anything like it.

"So it worked," he said.

Saydee nodded. "And I was allowed to live."

The bitterness in her voice shocked Raeb. He'd never heard Saydee speak so harshly about anything before.

"Since I was now a living, successful experiment, Ashwinn couldn't let me go. He had to continue studying me, to see if the effects lasted or had any kind of consequences on my sanity. So he bound me to him, forcing me to stay, and kept me here as his assistant."

"You mean slave," Raeb said.

Saydee nodded. "Anything and everything from cleaning equipment to scribing reports to... well, he was a creative person. I'll let you imagine the rest." She paused, as if swallowing bile. "Whatever he wanted, he took from me. If I fought him, he'd let the Entana loose in my mind for a while. Then he would beat me to within an inch of my life and see how long it took me to recover."

Raeb's mouth was dry. He squeezed and twisted the crumpled report, imagining it was Ashwinn's neck.

What could he say to her? He'd thought his own past was a difficult one, but he would live it ten times over before having to experience even one day as Ashwinn's slave. Just reliving those memories to tell Raeb about them seemed painful for her. "Saydee, you don't have to... "

"Yes, I do. I promised you the truth, Raeb. After everything we've been through together, and the truth about your past, you deserve to hear about mine. Besides," she said, casting her eyes around the lab, "it's about time I faced it."

If only he was half as brave as she was, maybe Raeb could have fought against the Keeper of Secrets better. It had taken him centuries to confront the Entana ambassador, and even then he'd caved and crumbled like a beaten puppy. But here was Saydee, standing in the very place she was abused and enslaved, refusing to let it defeat her. To say he was impressed and humbled barely scratched the surface.

"You said Ashwinn did all his research before my lifetime," he said, not knowing how to phrase his question.

"I know what you want to ask," Saydee cut in. "Go ahead and ask it."

He only paused for a second. "How old *are* you?"

She looked at him, and Raeb saw the same look in her eyes he'd seen the first time they'd met. It was the jaded, calloused look of someone far older than she seemed. "I stopped counting after three hundred," she said. "I am the first of the Entana-taken mages."

"The first. Not the only?"

"Of course not. You don't think Ashwinn did all these experiments on me just because he was curious, did you?"

"He wanted the enhanced power and extended life for himself," Raeb guessed.

"But he was too cowardly to try it on himself first," Saydee continued. "So he used me instead."

"Did he go through with it?" Raeb asked.

"Did he become a -taken mage, too? Yeah. He did."

"Then how did you escape from him?"

Saydee took a breath to answer, but instead of speaking, she screamed. Her body convulsed once, twice, and her eyes morphed into those of a fully -taken.

The Keeper of Secrets twisted Saydee's head to look at Raeb. Then he laughed, the sound warped from Saydee's normal, happy laugh to something demented and terrifying.

"You can try to run," the Keeper of Secrets told him, "but it won't do any good. The mages are already on their way to kill you."

CHAPTER TWENTY-SEVEN

They were still miles from the frontlines, but Aeo and Dragana both knew something was wrong. An unnatural stillness lingered in the air, like the whole countryside had been abandoned.

The fallow fields of the river valley were covered with a perfect layer of snow. No footprints, wagon tracks, or even animal tracks marred it. They were pure, unbroken white.

It hadn't snowed in more than three days.

Dragana limped down the road. It was the best she could do after two weeks of solid travel, now that her bones had started to grate against each other. She kept her eyes open for danger, even though Aeo knew her eyesight was beginning to blur. Neither of them mentioned it. Or the fact that her face was now lined like a middle-aged woman's, and the crimson streaks in her hair were fading to maroon.

Watching Dragana age just to keep him alive was a new kind of torture for Aeo. He hated his existence for what it did to her.

Dragana was far too young and good to be dying like this, all to keep a useless assassin alive. Well, alive after a fashion. He still wasn't sure whether he could be alive if he only existed as a spirit inside a sword.

"Would you shut up already?" Dragana mumbled. "I think I liked you better as an arrogant ass."

And I liked you better as the young, fiery warrior-woman who would have beat me out of the Bok'Tarong with my own corpse if she could have.

"Don't kid yourself. I'd still do that, if I thought it would do any good."

You'd miss my charming conversation skills too much.

Dragana scoffed and grimaced, but her sour expression couldn't last. Her smile, still full of charm, broke through. "Still, you're distracting me. If you don't shut up we might miss something."

Aeo cast his gaze around. He was sheathed, so his vision was black-and-white and he couldn't hear anything besides Dragana's voice. *What are we going to miss?*

Dragana paused, stretching her limbs and groaning as several joints popped. "How about any hint as to what on earth happened here?"

She had a point there. By this time they should be seeing signs of the war raging just a few miles ahead—trampled snow, exhausted, terror-stricken peasants, wounded soldiers turned to begging or trying to get home. But there was nothing. Not even a bird in the sky.

Has the Mage General pushed back the Halkronar? Aeo

wondered. *Have the frontlines moved farther away?*

Dragana shrugged, but her thoughts were in sync with his. The war hadn't been going well the last time they were here. The Mage General and his -taken soldiers had been desperate. What could have turned the tide?

Aeo had a hunch about that, but he was too terrified it might be true to speak it.

Dragana heard him anyway. "Let's hope that isn't the case. An entire army of willing -taken would be worse than losing this war altogether."

Too bad Raeb isn't here. I'll bet he'd have some insight into all this.

"Well, he isn't here. Deal with it."

Dragana…

"No. We are not having this conversation again."

And that was as far as he'd gotten in days. After the first few disastrous attempts at salving Dragana's pain, she'd refused to even let Aeo mention what had happened. Saying Raeb's name was enough to make her retreat into her thoughts for hours on end, pointedly ignoring Aeo. No matter how subtle or sneaky he was, Dragana would not discuss it.

You can't stay mad at him forever.

"Watch me."

Aeo sighed. *This isn't going the way I'd hoped.*

"I know," Dragana said. Her voice was more weary than angry. "And I know you're just trying to help. But I can't accept what Raeb did."

Even if it wasn't his fault?

She didn't reply for several minutes. "It was just too close," she said, more to herself than to Aeo. She stopped speaking then, but Aeo heard her final thought. *I almost lost you.*

Dragana flushed and turned away. She focused on the empty landscape before them. Aeo could feel just how desperately she wished he hadn't read that.

Dragana...

She shook her head. "No. I can't... we can't go there." They suffered through an awkward pause until Dragana cleared her throat. "Let's just figure out what's going on here."

Dragana's footsteps broke through virgin snow, crusted with frost. Aeo couldn't see any evidence of life, human or animal, anywhere. Soon they reached where the outlying camp had stood, but nothing remained.

Once they arrived at the camp proper, Dragana stood on top of a small hill and drew Aeo from his sheath. Together, they stared in silence.

Nothing. Not a soul in sight. No tents, weapons, pennants, or corpses. Just a perfect blanket of snow stretching all the way to the river. And on the Halkronar side, the same. Snow and emptiness, as if they were the last living beings to walk the earth.

It was several minutes before Aeo found his voice. *What happened?*

Dragana didn't reply. She simply stared, dumbfounded.

Arata couldn't have lost — we'd have heard something by now. Run into a Halkronar occupation. Something.

"They couldn't have won, either," she whispered.

More heartbeats slipped away in silence.

So what is going on?

Dragana trudged through the snow and frozen mud beneath. Aeo wished the faint haze and stench he caught in his spirit-vision was just smoke.

There's still the taint of Entana in the air, he said. *It's like they left a stain on the land.*

"That explains why there aren't any animals," Dragana said. "How many had to have been here to leave something like that?"

Hundreds. Thousands.

Dragana shifted her weight. "Could the war have been going that badly?"

It must have. Why else would there have been so many Entana here?

Dragana's heartbeat skyrocketed, her thoughts whirling. "We'd said the person who could control the Entana and willing -taken could challenge kings and countries."

Right. The Mage General. He was the one doing this.

"And you said he's the true power behind the throne of Arata."

He's the king in all but name. Aeo paused. *You think being the silent power wasn't good enough for him anymore?*

"You know him better than I do," Dragana said.

Aeo didn't doubt it. The Mage General could have the entire world under his thumb and he'd still be greedy for more.

"What if he was ready to make his move, but he needed more loyal soldiers? Soldiers willing to fight their own countrymen, without fear?"

More -taken soldiers, Aeo said. *You don't think...*

Dragana's thoughts filled in the images Aeo couldn't bear to conjure himself. The Mage General, ordering his soldiers forward. An attack against the fortified Halkronar line. Thousands would be injured, dying, ready to accept the Entana.

"He could have built his own personal army out of this," she continued, "with no fear, no pain… and no morals."

He didn't like it at all, mostly because it made complete sense. *And with that many, he could take Arata with hardly a fight.* He thought back to the -taken soldiers they'd killed in the mountains, so very far from here. *And then start expanding. Halkron, Starek… even Taron.*

"The Mage General gets his army and his kingdoms, and the Entana get their people." Dragana shuddered. "And there's no one to stop them."

Yes there is, Aeo said.

Dragana nodded. "Where would he go?"

Karim. The Mage General will want to gloat over his victory, at least for a little while. He won't be able to resist sitting on the Aratan throne.

She turned away from the empty battlefield and set a brisk pace to the northeast.

*
**

RAEB PACED. ONE, two, three, four, five steps. Wall. Turn. One, two, three, four, five steps. Wall. Turn.

Days had passed since the Keeper of Secrets had hijacked Saydee's mind again. He'd been right—the mages were indeed on their way. And running didn't help. Even if he hadn't been burdened with Saydee's unconscious body, he never would have escaped. He was lost in a labyrinth of corridors and labs.

But the Keeper of Secrets had been wrong, too. The mages hadn't killed them. It looked like they were going to, at first, but then they'd been ordered to wait. So they'd thrown Raeb and Saydee into this bedroom prison—the same tiny room where Saydee had been imprisoned and beaten a thousand times over. Their captors didn't stop to search them, or even remove their weapons. They'd just shoved them in here and left them to wait. But to wait for what?

When Saydee had woken, she'd panicked. It had taken Raeb hours to calm her, to convince her Ashwinn was gone and he would protect her. She'd been so skittish she hadn't sit still for him to check her Entana eyes. It had taken many covert stares to assure himself she hadn't been fully -taken by that last possession. She was still sane, as best as could be expected in her current state, but it had been a close call. Saydee's pupils were almost completely elongated, peridot-green, the irises stormy gray.

Even now, days later, Saydee huddled in the corner like a rabbit with nowhere else to run. She was making herself as small as possible until the wolf came to devour her. She still wouldn't let him touch her. Nothing he could say would calm her down, so Raeb resorted to pacing.

The only good thing was the discovery he'd made. During one of his long, fruitless searches for an escape he'd found a small stronghold built into the wall. It had taken a fair amount of Sunray's magic and a lot of prying to force it open, but inside lay the treasure they'd come for.

Even now, the thick report lay on the bed. Raeb read the title one more time: *Infection or enhancement? Modifying the mage's response to an Entana cohabitation to benefit the host organism.* It was exactly what they'd hoped to find—Ashwinn's unedited research, detailing every little tidbit he'd learned about the Entana.

A lot of good it did him, though. No matter how many times he'd tried to read it, he couldn't make sense of the thing. Even if there was a way to strengthen Saydee's connection to the Entana in there, Raeb wouldn't ever be able to find it.

It had been close to four days, he thought. Maybe five. It was hard to tell in this windowless cell. The mages kept them fed— barely—and clean—almost—but Raeb was starting to unravel. He'd never enjoyed small spaces. And he hated to admit it, but he'd rather be alone than have to deal with Saydee's traumatized silence. It hurt to look at her. He knew that somewhere deep inside she was grateful for his presence, but he found himself wishing to get away from her more and more.

Raeb paused in his pacing. He could hear muffled footsteps and feel the press of whatever magic the mages used to unlock the doors. Whether from lack of food or motivation, he'd lost the energy to keep trying to escape days ago. He retreated to the far corner and stood in front of Saydee, waiting for the mages to deposit their meager meals.

The door swung wide open, but nobody entered. Raeb stared into the lab—it seemed empty, but he knew better—and wondered what kind of trick this was.

"To hell with this." He stepped forward. Trying to think around these twisted bastards wouldn't get him anywhere. Going out there would.

The lab seemed expansive and painfully bright after his confinement in the cramped, semi-dark bedroom. A handful of steps into the room were enough to make his muscles tremble with weariness. That did not bode well for daring escapes.

Besides him and Saydee, who had kept close to his heels, there was only one other person present. A man, his features hardened by responsibility and harshness, his hair slightly grey around the temples. He stared at them with an unsettling sense of excitement. A massive sheath hung from his belt, seeming out of place against his plain magician's tunic.

Raeb and the man stared at each other. He'd expected some kind of reaction to his Entana eyes. Most people cringed, or backed up, or fled from Raeb's gaze. This man didn't show the slightest hint of fear. There wasn't even surprise in his expression.

The man's eyes slid to the girl cowering behind Raeb. His smile quirked at the corner. "Saydee," he purred. "My most successful test, and my favorite assistant. I've missed having you beside me."

Hatred flared in Raeb's chest. "Ashwinn."

He gave an exaggerated bow. "I'd say I'm pleased to meet you, but discovering you skulking through my laboratory isn't the most auspicious of meetings."

"Being confronted by a sadistic torturer who should be long dead doesn't count so well in my book, either."

"This coming from a two-hundred-year-old coward who doesn't understand the concepts of duty or loyalty to his masters."

Raeb's mind went blank. How did this man know about him? He tried not to let his surprise or fear show, but Ashwinn laughed.

"We are both servants of the Entana. You'd be surprised how

often our paths have crossed over the years."

Ashwinn turned away from him, focusing a predatory gaze on Saydee. He stalked toward her. Saydee whimpered and drew back, but that only spurred him on.

Raeb stepped in Ashwinn's way, raising Sunray. The mage quirked an eyebrow at him. "You? Being chivalrous?"

"Don't touch her," Raeb growled through clenched teeth.

Ashwinn leaned in, ignoring the blade at his throat. "You can't stop me."

He struck a heavy backhand to Raeb's head. Raeb stumbled to the side, and Ashwinn followed his first strike with a vicious kick. Raeb tumbled to the ground, his head spinning and body aching.

He saw a flash of ugliness in Ashwinn's eyes as he grabbed Saydee. He held her uncomfortably close, one hand pressing her against him, the other grabbing her chin and forcing her to look up at him. "Well, my dear, it looks like your time is just about up." He chuckled. "One more visitation from the Entana and I fear you'll be done for."

Raeb's rage flared even as icy terror clenched his heart. He staggered to his feet, his hand flying to the sword at his side. He could already picture Ashwinn's head rolling to the floor.

He tugged at the hilt of his sword, but the blade didn't pull free. He yanked harder, but was rewarded with the mage's twisted laughter.

"Tsk tsk, Raeb," he said. His eyes flashed from full brown to Entana green and back so quickly Raeb feared he'd imagined it. "I won't let this habit of threatening me slide forever, you know. I may begin to see it as a reason to let the Entana loose in your mind once and for all."

Raeb went numb. His hand slipped from the hilt, and he stood in complete shock.

The mage grinned. "Recognize me yet?"

The words fell from Raeb's lips almost by their own volition. "You're the Keeper of Secrets."

A dizzying wave of hatred gripped him. The Entana may have ruined his life, but this man was the true source of his torment. If it wasn't for him, Raeb would have died a long time ago, sent into peace by the baenlo poison. But this twisted man had found him, given him Sunray, and proceeded to haunt his every moment for the next two centuries.

Raeb had despised him before, but now he was beyond that. He was numb, in the terrifying way only the purest of righteous hatred could manage. This wasn't about emotions anymore. It was the simplest, most basic logic in existence. Raeb knew and understood, down to his core, there was only one thing left to do.

Ashwinn had to die.

The Entana ambassador laughed, as if genuinely enjoying Raeb's hatred. "You think you can defeat me?" he asked. He pushed Saydee away. She stumbled, fell backward, and hit her head on a table. She landed in a heap and didn't move again.

Raeb's rage bubbled over, and he screamed a wordless challenge.

Ashwinn snapped his fingers, and Raeb's blade was loose in its scabbard. "You want to kill me? Then come try!"

Chapter Twenty-Eight

"By the gods of Taron, Aeo, have you ever seen so many -taken?"

Dragana was doing her best to seem calm, but Aeo felt the tension in her muscles as if it was his own. It took everything in her power to remain in control. If it had been Aeo in that body, he wasn't sure he'd be able to restrain himself half as well as Dragana was.

He'd first seen it when they were still hours from Karim. The roiling cloud of Entana blotted out a huge chunk of the sky. It was as if the Entana were erasing the world, replacing it with a filthy black stain, and they'd begun with the capital of Arata.

Now they stood at the edge of the forest, looking toward the gates of Karim. The city's wall was lost beneath thousands— *hundreds* of thousands—of Entana tendrils. The air stunk of rot and filth. Even in his worst nightmares, Aeo had never dreamed of anything like this.

So this is what the Entana were after. Complete domination.

Dragana nodded. "Unless we find a way to stop them, every city in the world will end up like this one."

Aeo mustered his courage and spoke into the silence of her thoughts. *We had a way, with Raeb.*

"Aeo, don't you think we have bigger issues to deal with right now?" she asked, pointing the Bok'Tarong toward the infested capital.

It's the same issue. We have to stop the Entana, and killing -taken won't get us anywhere. Even if that could slow them down, there are too many of these berserkers. We'd never survive the battle. But Raeb was on to something. If we could get to the hive, we can destroy the Entana once and for all. It's the only way we can take the capital back and stop this from happening to the rest of the world.

"I'm not going back."

He wouldn't have hurt me. I saw it.

"That's not the point."

Then what is?

She was silent. Only her thoughts conveyed her lingering pain.

Look. I know he hurt you. It was a risk befriending him, and to have him betray that can't be easy. But he was fighting the compulsion. I saw his face — he was battling whatever was controlling him with every bit of strength he had. He did that because he cares about us.

Dragana shifted her weight, keeping her eyes locked on the Entana engulfing Karim. Her thoughts were far from the besieged city, though.

I'm not any better with friendship than you are, Dragana. I'll bet Raeb and Saydee feel the same. We're all misfits and outcasts. We're all meant to fight the Entana. Call it destiny that we got together in the first place, if you want. That destiny might even be to destroy the Entana completely. If we don't belong together, then where do *we belong?*

More silence. He sensed her thinking over his words, feeling the truth in them.

Both turned their attention back to the capital. Dragana tapped into Aeo's sight, and they stared at the darkness covering the city.

"We have to do something about this," she said, not tearing her eyes from the Entana tendrils. "The Mage General has to be stopped. We can't ignore him any longer."

Stopping him won't solve the problem.

"I know, Aeo. But ignoring it will condemn Karim to the fate of the -taken." Aeo started to interrupt, but she cut him off. "We have to fix this first. Once the Mage General is taken care of, then we can talk about Raeb and Saydee."

And then we'll finish this, Aeo added.

She nodded. "And then we'll finish this."

It wasn't an actual promise, but it was more than Aeo had hoped for. Feeling more at peace than he had in weeks, the Bok'Tarong and his bearer stared down at the infested capital.

His optimism couldn't stand against the horrible scene. The Entana infestation sucked it from him like a leech gorging on blood. *Of course, now we'll have to find a way to get in there and find the Mage General.*

He felt the worry she refused to show. "Yeah."

If the Entana are in control here, it won't be safe for us, Aeo said. *They'd never let the Bok'Tarong take a stroll amongst their slaves.*

Dragana knelt, digging through her pack. She pulled out her cloak and wrapped it around herself and the sword, raising the hood to hide her still-distinctive curls. The shadows emphasized the lines on her face. A casual glance would reveal a limping woman past her prime.

She shouldered her pack again and made her way back to the road. They joined the throng of people waiting to get into the city and passed through the gates with little more than a glance from the guards.

Aeo glared at them. Both were -taken. One wore the uniform of an Aratan soldier. The other wore a Halkronar uniform.

Well, it looks like we were right, Aeo said. *I don't know whether to be proud or horrified.*

I know what you mean, Dragana replied.

Karim was teeming with -taken. They outnumbered normal people at least three to one. Citizens hurried from one destination to another, huddled into themselves as if they expected to be beaten down at any moment. The few street merchants out sulked behind their carts, hardly daring to advertise their goods and draw attention to themselves. Aeo had never seen the streets so empty, or felt them so desolate.

The Halkronar invasion, the -taking of the soldiers, it was all for this. So the Entana can ignore nations and rulers and overpower the people. Aeo paused. *I'll bet the capital of Halkron is just as loaded with -taken soldiers as Karim is.*

And from there they can infiltrate every aspect of humanity, Dragana replied. *These willing -taken will spread across the world faster than gossip in a small town.*

But where does the Mage General fit into all this?

Once we find him, we can ask him. Her statement was punctuated by a vision of Aeo's blades slicing off the man's head.

Dragana threaded through the streets, doing her best to avoid bumping into any -taken. Given the sheer numbers of them, it was an impossible task.

He knew he should be preparing for their confrontation with the Mage General, but he could hardly think with so much evil assaulting him. Every time one of the -taken brushed against Dragana, Aeo had to fight the urge to reach out of the Bok'Tarong and throttle them.

They reached the bottom of the nobles' hill, where they could just make out the tall stone walls enclosing the king's keep. It looked high, lofty, out of reach from down here. Just as, Aeo knew, the king liked it.

We'll never be able to get close to the castle, let alone inside. You can't use your authority as the bearer of the Bok'Tarong with so many -taken around. And it's not like they'd let some random woman in to poke around and take a tour or anything.

We don't have a lot of choice here, Aeo.

I know, he said. *But we won't do much good by getting arrested or thrown out of the city, either.*

Then what do you suggest we do?

Aeo's mind raced. They were out of options and out of time. They had to get up to the castle before the Mage General could wreak more havoc on Karim. If he was still in his body, he'd be able to march straight up there and no one would dare to stop him…

Dragana, I need you to trust me. If I tell you to do something, you do it. No hesitations, no questions. Understand?

She nodded.

Go into the castle.

"I thought we'd just decided that was the worst thing we could do."

You hesitated, and you questioned me. This will never work if you can't trust me.

He could sense her fear and feel her hands shake. But she started walking toward the castle gates.

Faster. Stronger. Walk like no one in the world has the right to stop you.

She obeyed, mimicking Aeo's old arrogant gait so perfectly he couldn't contain his laughter.

The guards were moving to intercept her. Even from this distance, the anger and disbelief in their eyes was clear. The sun shone off their bared blades.

Dragana's heart raced. *What do I do, Aeo?*

Stay strong. Keep walking. When they try to stop you, brush them off. Tell them the king is expecting his assassin. Make it a threat.

She paused. *What if the king's already been deposed, and the Mage General is in charge?*

It'll be fine. The Mage General gave me my orders as often as the king did. If he's in charge now, he'll want to see how I survived after all this time. Either way, we get in.

But Aeo, I'm not you. I think he'll notice the difference.

Let me handle that.

He felt her nervousness, heard the thousand questions she

didn't ask. But she continued walking, straight to the guards preparing to stop her.

One raised his hand, his mouth opened to speak. She threw him a glare of such arrogant hatred he took a step back. "The king will have your head if I'm late," she growled at him. "He's expecting his assassin, not some jackass guard causing delays."

She breezed past him before he had an opportunity to reply.

I couldn't have done it better myself.

She continued forward, out of sight, before letting out the breath she'd been holding. Her posture sagged and her steps faltered, just for a moment. "I'm surprised I don't have an arrow in my back right now," she whispered.

These guys are never brave enough to question the king's assassin. Or risk the king's anger by refusing him – or her – entry. You'll be shadowed, but you'll be allowed passage.

Dragana marched into the castle, and Aeo could feel her trying not to gawk. He'd grown accustomed, or at least immune, to the king's finery. But Dragana had never seen so many rugs and tapestries and silver in one place. Even the huge gray stones in the walls and massive marble tiles on the floor were extravagant compared to her beloved Taronese temple.

"So now what?" she asked, keeping her voice as quiet as possible. Even so, it echoed through the corridor.

The guards will have sent a message to the king's personal servant warning him of your arrival. He'll meet you before you reach the throne room.

Sure enough, a tiny man scurried into view before Dragana had taken another dozen steps. He glanced up, noticed the very feminine outline of Dragana, and waved at the guards lining the hall. They stepped forward, swords bristling.

"You have five seconds to turn and leave before I order them to attack," the servant said in a surprisingly low voice. There was no trace of humor anywhere in him.

Repeat exactly what I say, he told Dragana. She nodded, the words coming from her mouth as soon as he spoke them to her mind. "The king's last assignment was for his assassin to kill the bearer of the Bok'Tarong. This was just after returning from Halkron. He will remember the occasion."

The servant stared at Dragana, saying nothing. He hardly even blinked.

"The king should have understood what that assignment entailed, instead of taking the word of the Mage General. It cost him his assassin."

Dragana held her chin high, prepared to meet the servant's glare. Instead, she met the weary eyes of a mourner. A hint of hope sparked behind his gaze. "Are you...?" His breath caught in his throat. "Are you the bearer? Do you have the Bok'Tarong?"

None of these guards had Entana eyes. Dragana decided to risk it. "I do."

His entire visage changed as he peered around her, trying to catch a glimpse of her blade. "Oh, thank the gods!"

The soldiers lowered their swords and stepped back to the wall. The servant grabbed Dragana's arm and dragged her forward. For such a small man, he had plenty of strength to keep her stumbling forward.

He led Dragana through more plush corridors, refusing to

explain. Dragana's silent question reached Aeo, but he had no answer or explanation. He hadn't a clue what had gotten into the man. He'd never seen anything more than a sneer on his face before.

They reached a lavish sitting room. The king sat in front of a room-sized fireplace, buried in a massive armchair, staring into the flames. He looked like a child playing dress-up in his velvet robe. He didn't move when the servant entered or whispered into his ear.

Once the man had discreetly moved off to a corner, the king spoke. "He took everything from me, and worst of all, I let him." The king waved a hand weakly, skin flabby and pale. "And now I have nothing left. Not even myself."

A horrible sense of foreboding chilled Aeo. He sharpened his spirit-vision, peering into the dark room.

Dragana, he whispered, unable to raise his voice any higher, *the king is -taken.*

As if in response, the king turned to look at her. His eyes were shadowed, bruise-dark circles beneath them. None of that could hide the distinctive eyes of a -taken.

After a moment he turned back to the fire, the depth of his misery permeating the room. "The Mage General may be the one to blame, but I granted him his power by not acting. So I suppose this is my just reward."

Not knowing how to respond, Dragana fell back on the basics. "Your Majesty, my name is Dragana, and I am a Taronese warrior and bearer of the Bok'Tarong." She unsheathed Aeo, bringing his rosy gold blades into the firelight. "And I believe you know the spirit within my blades."

Tell him he finally found me a contract that was a challenge.

She repeated Aeo's words. The king whipped his head away from the fire, looking first at Dragana and then at the Bok'Tarong. "This is a trick. It isn't possible."

"It is possible, Your Majesty," Dragana replied. "The Bok'Tarong carries the spirit of its former bearers in its blades."

"So he succeeded. The Mage General didn't believe anyone could."

Nice to know he'd sent me to my death.

The king peered at the Bok'Tarong, as if trying to see Aeo's face in the blades' reflection. "Is he still an impertinent ass?"

Dragana laughed. "Constantly."

A smile broke on the king's face. It looked out of place with his frowning eyes. "He always was good at what he did."

He lapsed back into silence. When he spoke again, his voice had gone sad and quiet. "The enchanted Bok'Tarong. It cannot be a coincidence that brings you here, at this time."

"That is not why we're here, Your Majesty."

"No?" The king didn't look relieved, but neither did he seem disappointed. He simply stared at Dragana as if she was another torture to be endured. "Then what do you want?"

"We're looking for the Mage General." The king's face darkened at the title. She barreled on before the king's anger built any higher. "He's been breeding -taken, acting in the Entana's interests. We're going to stop him."

"You can't. He's too powerful."

Try us, Aeo — and Dragana — said.

"Don't you think I've tried myself?" the king asked. He seemed too weary to be angry anymore. "After Aeo failed to return, I contracted a dozen assassins to stop him. Every single one failed while the Mage General grew stronger. His magic is terrifying, but his schemes are even worse."

"You underestimate us," Dragana said. "Tell us where he is, and let us show you."

"I don't know where he is. Once he made it clear he was coming for my throne he's remained hidden. And once this happened," he said, gesturing to his head and the Entana tendrils only Aeo could see, "I couldn't show myself. If Karim learned their ruler had been touched by the Coming Madness, it would only strengthen the Mage General's hold."

"We can get rid of him for you. We can get you your kingdom back, if you just help us."

"And what good will a kingdom do me?" he asked, his face flushing with anger. The spark lasted only a moment, before he sank back into his depression. "Rule of Arata does no good to a dead man."

"Death is not the only option for you," Dragana said. "We can leave you in peace, to continue living despite your condition."

Aeo could hardly believe she was counseling a -taken to live—he could feel her disbelief at the act, too—but her tone held no doubt or remorse. And he found himself agreeing with her. Aeo smiled. Raeb would be proud of them.

The king shook his head. "No. My life is done. I have nothing left. Arata is lost to the Mage General, and I no longer have any power to stand against him." He looked at Dragana, his eyes brimming with tears. "Please… I cannot endure this existence. It is the ultimate shame. I beg you to release me."

Dragana opened her mouth, prepared to argue, but closed it without a word. She saw it as well as Aeo did. The king had given up. He was already dead in his mind, and nothing would change that.

Reluctantly, Dragana brought the Bok'Tarong to the king's chest. She placed the blades over his heart. The king didn't even flinch at their touch.

"Just do me a favor," he said. "If you do find him… Kill the bastard. Free my people from the Mage General. You're the only ones who can."

"We will," she promised.

She took a deep breath, then met the king's eyes once more. Her voice was shaky with tears. "Be at peace."

She pushed. The king grunted, his eyes widened. Then a long, slow breath escaped from his mouth and his pierced lung. And then, silence.

✳
✳✳

DRAGANA WANDERED DOWN the street, away from the castle. Melancholy had settled itself deep in her soul. "Now what?"

Aeo shrugged. *We look somewhere else. The Mage General has to be close.*

"That doesn't help much," Dragana grumbled.

Hours passed as they scoured the streets and eavesdropped on the -taken soldiers, all in vain. No whisper of the Mage

298

General surfaced. By the time the sun began to set, they were no closer to finding him.

Weary and footsore, Dragana sidestepped around a pair of large Halkronar -taken and ducked behind a street vendor. She leaned against the brick wall of a store with a sigh. Aeo knew her old joints were aching, even though she refused to mention it.

She'd just gotten settled before the -taken soldiers turned on her. "Keep moving! No cloggin' the street, woman!"

Dragana levered herself off the wall with exaggerated slowness. She spoke with a rather convincing, rough country accent. "Sorry, sirs. Don't mean to be a bother."

"Course you don't. But you slow old peasants always are. Shame the Mage General don't let us get rid of y'all here 'n' now."

Dragana's spine stiffened and she clenched her fist. Otherwise, Aeo knew she would have drawn the Bok'Tarong.

The -taken guards caught her motion. "If you don't behave, woman, we'll have to take you in."

"I'd like to see you try," she replied.

Dragana, what are you doing?

The larger of the two -taken took a step toward Dragana, clearly trying to intimidate her. Instead of backing into the wall like he'd expected, Dragana stepped to the side, into a more open area at the mouth of an alley. She raised a critical eyebrow at his brutish tactics and didn't flinch.

The -taken swore and drew his blade. "One less peasant won't make no difference."

Dragana spun away from his awkward thrust. The twirl threw the hem of her cloak wide, exposing Aeo's rosy gold blades.

"Bok'Tarong!" the -taken yelled. He lunged at her while his companion drew his sword and charged.

So much for keeping a low profile, Aeo said. *Now what?*

Dragana drew the Bok'Tarong from her back. The -taken stumbled to a halt at the sight of the sacred blades.

She pushed the hood back from her face. "That's right. Take one more step and you'll meet the end of your abominable lives."

"You'll die first," the second -taken growled. He stepped forward, raising his sword.

The first -taken stopped him. "No. We can't just kill her. The Mage General will wanna talk to her, first." He glanced around, snagging a scrawny boy in a faded, oversized messenger's coat and dragging him over. "Go tell the Mage General we're coming with the Bok'Tarong." He shoved the boy away even as he turned his attention back to Dragana.

Aeo's gaze followed the boy as he disappeared into the sea of people. *I know how we can find the Mage General now.*

Dragana smirked. The -taken looked at her, confused by the action. That brief pause was all the time she needed. She leapt and cut them down in a handful of strokes.

Once the -taken were dead, Dragana raised her hood and dove into the crowd. She raced down the street, mingling with the civilians and dodging the guards, trying to catch up to the messenger boy who would lead them to the Mage General.

Did you see which way he went? she asked.

Turn left, Aeo replied.

Dragana did, ducking past a group of children and a pair of

women toting baskets of bread and game. Pursuing footsteps echoed off the cobblestones behind them, but Dragana kept well ahead of them.

Turn right.

Dragana had to skid almost to a stop to make sure she didn't miss the turn. This road marched up the hill at a steep incline, and what was left of her momentum was lost. She slowed and huffed as she stretched her endurance to its limit.

At the end of the lane, she caught sight of the boy as he fled past startled and indignant nobles. She tried to speed up, but she was out of breath and her aching joints screamed at her. She wasn't as young as she used to be.

The street opened up into a massive courtyard, shaded by huge trees. Stately buildings, some two and three stories tall, surrounded them. A large, stone-lined pond stood in the middle. People dressed in silks and fine linen milled everywhere, glaring at Dragana like she was something they'd stepped in.

The messenger was nowhere to be seen.

Where did he go?

He can't be far. Probably in one of these buildings.

Dragana and Aeo scanned the courtyard, looking for a likely place. Inns and taverns would be too easily rooted out. Someone like the Mage General would be recognized by the soldiers stationed here, so he would have to be out of sight. Somewhere he'd be protected from the leftover government, where the king had little to no influence…

He saw it just as Dragana did. She didn't even ask, and he didn't order. She just started walking toward the massive, imposing building of the Mage's Academy.

Chapter Twenty-nine

Raeb pulled his sword free and lunged, but Ashwinn was faster. He conjured a magical shield, and Raeb bounced off it as if he'd run straight into a wall. The tables and lab equipment swam together in his vision. Only sheer stubbornness kept him on his feet.

He tried a few quick attacks, hoping to find a weak spot in the shield. Nothing. No matter how low, high, fast, or awkwardly he attacked, there was nothing but solid magic.

Magic.

Raeb sheathed his sword. Ashwinn started a scathing comment on his cowardice, but Raeb ignored him. He reached for Sunray.

Ashwinn shut up.

Sunray froze his fingertips, and even holding it in two hands he couldn't stop his grip from shaking. He breathed deeply. He needed every ounce of willpower he could muster.

Sunray was ravenous in the magic-charged lab, and it begged

to feed.

So Raeb let it feed.

The room filled with icy, magic-seeking motes. For a breath all was still and quiet, like the first surreal moments of a snowfall.

Then Ashwinn howled as his magic was pulled into the vortex of Sunray's endless hunger.

Raeb could barely control the blade. It devoured with abandon, chomping through Ashwinn's shield as if it were nothing more than an appetizer. In a few seconds Sunray had moved on and begun sucking the ambient magic in the lab, the experiments, and the air itself.

Soon it would turn its hunger to the lives around it.

Could he risk holding onto it for that long? If he could direct Sunray's attention to Ashwinn, would the blade drain his life-force? Raeb smirked. What a fitting end for the Keeper of Secrets.

Raeb's smirk faded as he looked behind the mage, where Saydee lay crumpled and still. No, the Entana blade would go for her, first. She was the weakest. It would kill her before Ashwinn was even touched.

He didn't dare let Sunray feast any longer. His concentration was wavering, his control slipping. He gripped Sunray's power in his mind and pulled it back, pouring the force of his will into the demand.

Sunray refused.

The blade fed faster, insatiable. The air turned stale, jars and containers imploding or withering away as their contents vanished or crumbled. Saydee groaned weakly.

Sweat dripped into Raeb's eyes. His heart hammered wildly.

He had to control the blade. He had to make it stop.

He channeled his rage at Ashwinn, his fear for Saydee, his pain and weariness, into his resolve. Everything he was, strength and weakness, all if it fighting against Sunray. He could not let the blade best him again. He was finished with the Entana, finished with the Keeper of Secrets. Once they completed their mission, he was finished with Sunray.

The Entana blade fought him, but Raeb's hatred fought harder. He gripped Sunray's magic and wrestled it back. The blade squirmed and lashed out at him, his hands physically twitching, but Raeb held on. With a string of vicious curses, he slammed the magic back into the blade and shut it down.

Jelly-legged and dizzy, he sheathed the Entana blade and once again drew his sword. It felt like a giant's weapon, too large and clumsy for his limited strength. But he couldn't show weakness. Not now, with nothing between him and his mortal enemy. "You always stay out of reach. Are you afraid?" he asked, buying as much time as he could while he recovered.

"Why would I fear you? You can't harm me."

"Then why don't you come face me instead of cowering behind your magic?"

Ashwinn laughed, genuine amusement in his voice. "This is why I've always liked you, Raeb. You may not be very smart, but you've got a clever tongue. We could have worked well together."

"Don't kid yourself. One of us would have been dead by the end of the first day."

"Hmm. Perhaps you're right, for once." He dismissed what

little magic remained and drew the large broadsword from his belt. He handled the blade with practiced ease, while Raeb could barely lift his much smaller sword into a proper defense. Ashwinn grinned. "Did you hope to cripple me by taking away my magic? I am more than just a mage, my dear servant. You of all people should know that."

He charged and swung before Raeb could raise a defense. He deflected Ashwinn's strike, barely, but the impact of the massive sword numbed his arm halfway to the shoulder.

Exhausted as he was, Raeb fell back on his Taronese training. Endless days in the temple snapped into focus with startling clarity. For the first time in decades, Raeb could smell the clean scent of the dojo and feel the wind through the open-beamed ceiling. He heard the masters' criticism as they pushed for perfection: *Arms up! Feet apart! Breathe! Relax! Strike!*

The traits he'd seen in Dragana, her passion, conviction, fire—the same he'd lamented losing to the Entana—came flooding back to him. He remembered why he'd hated the Entana back then, long before he learned to despise them for his torment. Righteous fury, destroying evil simply to be rid of it, a longing to fight and make the world better, safer, happier... it all crashed back into him.

No new strength filled his muscles. But what he had would be enough. He would make it enough.

Moving as much from instinct as memory, Raeb flowed into battle. He met Ashwinn's blade with his own, forcing it wide. He stepped into the opening, jabbed out with his left elbow, and—missed.

Ashwinn had bent out of range, and was coming in with a fist of his own.

Raeb ducked low. The strike ruffled his hair as it flew over his head.

They danced around each other, on equal footing at last. Each impact of their blades rang through the lab. Ashwinn's massive sword wreaked havoc on his tabletops, breaking glassware and scattering papers across the floor. Now Raeb was glad for the lack of interesting liquids and experiments—if anything had been in those containers, they'd have exploded by now for sure.

Finally, Raeb scored a hit. His sword slashed through Ashwinn's forearm, a wide gash splitting the muscle. Blood splattered the lab.

"I have the full power of the Entana at my back," Ashwinn said. "A scratch like that won't slow me down." He slashed down with such a vicious slice Raeb felt wind from the passing blade. If his shoulder had been an inch farther to the left, he'd have lost his arm. Ashwinn followed that with another strike, and another, never giving Raeb an opportunity to rest.

Ashwinn showed no pain, even though holding the sword—let alone lifting and swinging it—tore his split muscles. He didn't even seem tired.

Ashwinn's strikes came harder and faster, while Raeb's strength rapidly drained. All the training and motivation in the world couldn't replace steady meals and toned muscles. Raeb might have been the better swordsman, in his prime, but weakened as he was it wasn't a contest.

The mage grinned. He knew, just as Raeb did, the fight was

already decided.

But only when Raeb was too exhausted to fight, when he'd slipped on blood and papers and no longer had the strength to stand, did Ashwinn stop toying with him.

"We let you live for far too long," the Keeper of Secrets said. His voice took on a slight hiss as the Entana inside him spoke. He walked forward, placing the tip of his sword on Raeb's throat. "Which will happen first—will you bleed to death, or will you go mad from the loss of your thoughts? Either way, it will be a delight to watch you writhe. Your death will feed us well."

Hatred burned in Raeb's heart like bile. He wanted to rise and defend Saydee from the horrors to come, to strike down this monster and be done with the Keeper of Secrets forever. He wanted to scream out his rage as he watched Ashwinn die. But he couldn't summon the strength to do any of it.

Shards of glass punctured his skin, adding his warm blood to the cooling pools underneath him. Pain and weariness coursed through him. No matter how much he wanted to fight, he was drained. There was nothing left in him. He was tempted to just lay back and let death find him, but...

... he wasn't ready to die.

Raeb could hardly believe it. After two hundred years of waiting for death, it had finally come for him—and he no longer wanted it to.

Chapter Thirty

A horde of -taken soldiers waited for Aeo and Dragana as they entered the Mages Academy. They stood in the middle of the gigantic foyer, while a sea of mages tried to scurry out of the way. Dragana advanced slowly, a predator undeterred by the prey before her.

The -taken didn't threaten her, or banter, or try to stall her. They attacked.

Dragana met them with a ready blade, fueled by rage and fear and the magic of the Bok'Tarong. Her breath came easier and her joints bent smoothly, strength pouring into her aging muscles as the sword shared her life-force. She flew through the battle as if she'd been born to do nothing but fight -taken.

They had no hope against her. The only thing they could do was fall before the Bok'Tarong and its bearer.

Dragana didn't pause after the last -taken died. She didn't even look back. She just continued through the Academy.

Karim was infested, the taint of Entana so strong it made Aeo sick. But something in the Mage's Academy felt *worse*. It pulled at him like a dowsing rod, and Dragana followed it like water barreling down a canyon. What kind of horror lurked here, to make a soul-scathing infestation seem mild in comparison?

They charged through corridor after corridor, following the stench of Entana, until a massive gate blocked their way. Dragana pounded on the wood with the hilt of the Bok'Tarong. Aeo didn't dare tell her how much that hurt.

After a brief moment, an old mage opened a window in the gate. "Name, class, appointment, cargo."

"Open this gate or I swear I will knock it down on top of you."

He looked up at Dragana, face squished like he sucked on a lemon. He seemed about to spit out a retort, saw the dangerous gleam in Dragana's battle-crazed eyes, and changed his mind.

The gate opened a moment later.

Dragana squeezed through and barreled down the corridor. The air here felt thick with madness and vile Entana. Darkness seeped into Aeo's spirit-vision until he could hardly see. Even the Entana sanctuary in Saydee's mind hadn't felt this oppressive, this terrible, this unredeemably evil.

We're close.

Dragana ran.

✹
✹✹

RAEB COULDN'T THINK of anything other than the blade at his throat, Saydee stirring in the corner, and how ironic it was that he'd found the will to live just as he was about to die.

He held his breath, eyes squeezed shut, heart racing. He

would die without explaining himself to Aeo and Dragana. He wouldn't be able to save Saydee from Ashwinn. The Entana would endure after he died, to continue torturing and terrorizing the world.

Infinite seconds passed.

Raeb peeked up at the mage. He wasn't looking at him, not anymore. He stared at the door, as if he could see what was happening beyond it. Raeb caught a hint of apprehension behind the smile on his face.

Then he heard the commotion in the hallway. Shouts of pain and rage, a familiar battle cry, a metallic clatter as a weapon dropped to the floor.

The mage looked down at Raeb and put just enough pressure on his sword to draw blood from Raeb's throat. "This should be fun," Ashwinn whispered.

Dragana, older and fiercer than ever, burst into the room. The Bok'Tarong—Aeo—was held before her, the rosy gold blades shimmering in the light.

Relief spread like wine, hot and welcome, through Raeb's muscles. "Your timing is perfect!"

Her brown-and-crimson eyes bored into his, and she pointed the Bok'Tarong at his chest. "You and I are going to have words," she said. Before he could reply, she swung the sword back to Ashwinn. "But you come first, Mage General."

Raeb groaned. "Mage General, too? How many identities do you have?"

"You don't think I've spent the last centuries wasting my time, do you?" Ashwinn chuckled. "Besides, they don't call me the Keeper of Secrets for nothing."

Dragana's eyes widened and she threw a glance at Raeb. A lot passed between them in just a few seconds. Yes, this was Raeb's tormentor. Yes, he was the one who'd compelled him to destroy the Bok'Tarong. Yes, he wanted Ashwinn dead as much—more, even—than Dragana did.

Yes, Dragana would gladly help kill him.

Dragana charged, forcing Ashwinn to free Raeb and block. She danced away as Raeb stumbled to his feet, placing herself between Ashwinn and Saydee. The girl was struggling to sit up, groaning and holding her head. She looked woozy and disoriented.

Raeb staggered into a defensive position and leveled his sword at Ashwinn. The point wavered, but he didn't back down.

Ashwinn looked obscenely pleased as he half-bowed to Dragana. "So nice of you to join us."

"As the bearer of the Bok'Tarong it is my duty to stop the spread of Entana possession," she said. Her eyes, and voice, were cold and hard as ice. "You, Mage General, have done more to infect the world than anyone in history. It will be my genuine pleasure to put an end to your tyranny." She paused for a moment, then smiled. "Aeo sends his regards."

"Aeo?" For an instant, Raeb would have sworn Ashwinn looked scared. But then his expression brightened, far more than was called for. Dread tightened Raeb's stomach. "My dear student succeeded in winning the Bok'Tarong? My, isn't this a fortuitous meeting!"

"He says it's one he's looked forward to for many years,"

Dragana said. Her tone was wolfish.

"I'm sure it is. He never was one to show gratitude." He turned his eyes to the sword, speaking directly to it like he would speak to a man. "If you are Aeo, my student, trained and conditioned by my own hand, kill this woman and then yourself. Rid the world of that damned sword." His voice rang with authority and magic — powerful, commanding, undeniable magic. Even Raeb felt the compulsion to obey.

Raeb watched the blood drain from Dragana's face. She turned corpse-pale and started shaking, eyes wide like she'd seen a ghost.

"This will be even better than I thought." Ashwinn leaned against a table, watching Dragana with feverish excitement.

Raeb hardly dared to breathe. Could Aeo be compelled to destroy the Bok'Tarong? He'd fought beside the man in Saydee's mind. He knew how much Aeo despised the Entana, how strongly the magic of the Bok'Tarong flowed in his veins. To obey the command of the Keeper of Secrets would go against his very nature.

The Bok'Tarong's enchantment was the most powerful Raeb had ever seen.

But the Keeper of Secrets had a mage's power, enhanced by the Entana possession, plus the power of the Entana hive itself. Which magic would prevail?

Raeb's heart hammered, his palms slick with sweat. *Come on, Aeo, you have to beat him.*

*
**

The Mage General's order reverberated in Aeo's mind, stronger than any he'd ever received. It tolled through his mind like a bell, each strike shaking his very core. It seeped deep into his essence, molding him, demanding he obey. The urge, the *need* to do so, consumed him.

I don't want to.

The bell chimed.

It was useless to fight. Aeo the assassin only existed because of this magic. He could no more deny it than a breeze could knock down a mountain.

He wasn't just Aeo anymore, though. He was the Bok'Tarong. Entana-slayer. The blades' magic had reformed him. Rebirthed him. His purpose was no longer to do the Mage General's bidding. It was to defend humanity.

The bell tolled, stronger this time.

He was a killer. A weapon for the Mage General to point wherever he pleased. A weapon had no control over its actions. It did what it was created to do, as efficiently as possible. It did not think, did not refuse. It killed. Nothing more.

What could he have been, if not for the Mage General? A soldier? A hunter? The Bok'Tarong had given him a second chance at life. One that followed a higher calling than the Mage General's orders.

THE BELL.

The command was his lifeblood. His entire reason for being was to obey that magic. Don't resist. Obey. The woman needs to die. Aeo wanted to make his master happy.

He looked at her, meeting those brown-and-crimson eyes.

The world stopped.

How could Aeo kill Dragana? Fighting beside her, sword and master, was ecstasy like he'd never known. Dragana had shown him purpose, life, nobility, sacrifice. The Mage General had forced him to be a weapon—Dragana had shown him how to be a man.

No power in existence could make him hurt her.

THE BELL THE BELL THE BELL.

Aeo was no longer the assassin. He was the Bok'Tarong. He was the man he'd always wanted to be. The man Dragana had believed he could be.

He reached deep inside, to the power inside the sword—his power, now—and shattered the bell.

*
**

DRAGANA FELL TO her knees, and Raeb's heart clenched. So that was it, then.

But then Dragana stood. She lifted her head and stared at Ashwinn, victorious and murderous like a vengeful angel. It chilled Raeb to the core.

"You'll have to do better than that," she said.

For a moment, Ashwinn stared at her with pure terror. Raeb would treasure that memory for the rest of his life.

He and Dragana locked eyes. She nodded, ever so slightly. Time to finish this.

They raised their swords together.

Ashwinn's momentary panic dissolved, replaced with the full fury of the Entana. "So this is how you want to play," he said. His voice had dropped, his body growing. Within a few seconds, it was clear this man was no longer human at all.

Ashwinn's skin boiled as the monster inside surfaced. Dozens of Entana tendrils, thick as Raeb's waist, sprouted from Ashwinn's limbs. His skin was streaked with oily black rot, and his eyes—feline, peridot-colored pupils on a field of inky black— were freakishly large. He grinned down on them from a height of at least eight feet.

"All right. Let's play."

CHAPTER THIRTY-ONE

A eo finally had his answer to what could be worse than an Entana-infested city. And it was far more horrific than he'd thought.

The Mage General—Keeper of Secrets, whatever you wanted to call him—had given himself so completely to the Entana he wasn't even a man anymore. The power billowing from him hit Aeo like a tsunami, filthy with rot and sewage and every vile thing imaginable. At least he finally looked like the monster Aeo had known he was.

And Aeo was finally free of him. Free to be his own man, to pursue his own desires.

Free to kill this monstrosity and repay years of torture. It was almost too good to be true.

The Mage General met their attack with a tentacle, swatting the Bok'Tarong away like a fly. A small hiss of pain was the only reward they got from the Entana's contact with the sacred sword.

Of course it wouldn't be that easy.

Dragana launched herself back at him instantly. She slashed at tendrils that passed close and inched ever closer to the mage's body, weaving through the ever-shifting maze of Entana darkness. Aeo kept his eyes open for spirit attacks like he'd witnessed before, but the Mage General didn't seem interested in wounding her spirit. From the way his tendrils lashed around, it looked like he preferred to bludgeon Dragana to death.

The Mage General roared, a sound too deep to be human, as Raeb stabbed him from behind. Not a mortal wound, but Aeo hoped it would at least slow the creature down.

No such luck. As soon as Raeb pulled out his blade, the wound started closing. A heartbeat later, the flesh was seamless.

The Mage General cackled as he turned toward Raeb. A whirlwind of lashing tendrils descended upon him. He struck at one while two others breached his defenses. He scored a hit and the Entana scored three. Blood oozed down Raeb's head and stained his pant leg. Raeb overextended on a defense and the Entana-beast threw him across the room with an almost contemptuous hit. He hit the wall hard. He wasn't knocked out, but he would be too dazed to move for a few minutes.

Aeo and Dragana sliced open a few of the tendrils while the Mage General was distracted, but it hadn't seemed to affect him. Now, though, he turned his full attention back to them and glared at Dragana with a mad gleam in his Entana eyes.

He attacked with several limbs at once—too many for them to counter. Dragana managed a ringing strike against the Mage General's sword and a deep gash in one of his tendrils, but the beast bulled forward. He broke through their defense like paper.

A tendril wrapped around her waist, trapping her free arm. Another encircled her sword-arm and pulled it as far out as it could, nearly dislocating her shoulder. One last tendril snaked forward, almost delicately, and wrapped itself around her throat. "I'll keep you for later," the abomination said. "I'll take great pleasure in breaking you."

Oh hell no.

That monster had inflicted enough horrors on him. He would not allow the same to be done to Dragana.

Aeo's battle cry ripped through his soul. He reached out of the blades and pulled himself free of the Bok'Tarong. Arms, head, torso.

Not enough.

The sword pulled him back into the blade like quicksand, but Aeo fought the agony and pushed. He felt like he peeled the skin from his bones. He tore himself apart, piece by piece, until he stepped free of the sword.

All the pain and weariness in the world couldn't dim his excitement. He felt free. He felt *alive.* He was giddy and lightheaded even as strength poured through his ghostly muscles. It was more intoxicating than the king's finest liquor.

He turned to Dragana. He couldn't hear her anymore, but her expression... she could *see* him. Joy surged through him as she stared, open-mouthed, her eyes roaming his spirit-body. He didn't need her thoughts to know what she was thinking: *How did you do that?*

He winked at her.

Then he turned to the abomination and threw himself into

battle.

Gods, he'd missed this! Each step, every thrust, the thrill of facing an opponent with nothing but wits and steel—he lived for this. He flew through the battle, dodging and leaping tendrils like an acrobat, striking and charging like a warrior. His spirit body responded to each command as if he'd spent every moment of his life training for this.

Flesh sizzled and boiled wherever his blades struck. The Entana couldn't heal these wounds—they were made with the pure magic of the Bok'Tarong.

The creature lashed out even more wildly. Aeo danced to the far side of the lab, half a step ahead of the Entana-beast, leading him away from Raeb and Saydee. His friends were both awake, both sitting up, but neither were in any position to defend themselves from the thrashing Entana. They stared at him with vague, addled expressions.

Aeo reversed suddenly, throwing himself back at the Mage General, and swept his blades in a wide arc. Aeo hit a tendril holding Dragana with such force it was half severed, hanging from a few strips of ragged flesh. The Mage General squealed and dropped her, and she rolled away to safety.

His friends were safe. Now it was just him and the Mage General.

Gods, he'd dreamed of this.

Well. Not *this*, specifically, but it would do. It would do quite nicely.

Aeo leapt onto a table and ran along its length, his spirit-body just substantial enough to send paperwork flying behind him.

Like the beast he was, the Mage General ignored the others and focused on the single being that had hurt him.

One-on-one wasn't exactly a fair fight here, but Aeo refused to give up. He fought to the best of his abilities—which were considerable—but he couldn't block every strike, let alone land many of his own. There were just too many dangerous parts to watch for. The flailing tendrils hit his spirit body as if it were flesh and blood. But until his friends recovered enough to rejoin the fight, he was their only defense. He had to keep going.

He beat back two tendrils and the Mage General's broadsword, but he didn't see a third tendril sneak around him. The tentacle wrapped itself around his body, squeezing just enough to prevent Aeo from drawing a breath. He swung the Bok'Tarong, but yet another tendril smacked the blades from his hand with such force Aeo thought his arm may have broken.

The Mage General cackled as he turned back to Aeo's friends. He bypassed Dragana's defense and grabbed her with a tendril, then knocked aside Raeb's desperate parry and wrapped him up, too. The creature held the three warriors to his face, grinning and gloating.

"How will you continue to sting me now?" he mocked. "Your bravery was admirable, though profoundly stupid. One should know better than to battle the Entana." He peered at each of them with his gigantic Entana eyes. "But where is my dear little Saydee?"

An arm shot out from behind him, wrapping itself around his throat. Before the next heartbeat an overlarge dagger, vaguely leaf-shaped, came around the other side and plunged into the creature's eye.

Saydee yanked him backwards, leaning over him as he screamed. "I'm right here, Ashwinn."

She pulled out the dagger and slit his throat from ear to ear.

The -taken mage tried to scream, but all that came out was a gurgle of blood. He thrashed on the floor, releasing his captives, bleeding out fast but not dying. Given enough time, the Entana might be able to heal even a wound like that.

Aeo and Dragana looked at each other and nodded. Time to do what they did best.

Aeo retrieved his fallen sword and stepped beside Dragana. They raised their blades. Two Bok'Tarongs—one physical, one spiritual—bore down on the Entana-beast.

The Entana squealed like a slaughtered pig. The sound shattered the remaining glass in the room and deafened everyone within. Aeo kept his blade moving, hacking through tendrils and severing any connection he could find between the creature and the man.

Blood oozed on the floor, some of it bright human red, some more like the blackened sludge at the bottom of a tavern's cooking pot. Severed tendrils smoked and dissolved, leaving little more than ash behind. The mage's body smelled like a sewer in the middle of a bloody battlefield.

Ashwinn stopped writhing. The Entana was silenced. The Mage General, the Keeper of Secrets, was finally dead.

Aeo looked up from the body to find his friends staring not at Ashwinn, but at him. "What?" he asked. The sound of his own physical voice startled everyone—including him.

"'What', he asks. As if pulling himself from the Bok'Tarong was completely unremarkable," Raeb said.

"He acted that way last time, too," Dragana said.

"Last time? You mean he's done this before?" The awe in Raeb's voice made Aeo uncomfortable.

"Come on, guys, it's just me," he said. "Well, most of me, anyway," he added, looking down at his shimmering spirit-body.

"Exactly," Dragana whispered. "It's *you*." She couldn't seem to pull her eyes from him, the way he couldn't take his eyes from the light of presence the day they'd met.

He could stare at Dragana forever, and let her stare in return, but standing over a putrid, Entana-infested corpse didn't exactly set the right mood. He looked away, only to find Raeb still staring at him, too. "Not in your wildest dreams," Aeo said.

Raeb blinked, his reverie finally breaking.

Aeo turned to Saydee. Thankfully, she wasn't staring at him. Her gaze was locked on the Mage General's corpse. "Nice job, Saydee."

The girl blushed and fidgeted, still holding the blood-soaked dagger. She looked down at it, seemed to realize what it was, and dropped it like it might bite her.

"Well done indeed," Raeb added. Aeo heard a tremendous amount of respect in those words, and he sensed there was a lot more to the story than what met the eye.

Aeo threw a half-hearted glance at the Mage General, but his attention caught on the single, glittering thread lingering in his spirit-vision. "Does anyone else see that?" he asked. "There's a connection there, but it's fading fast."

"A connection… like Saydee's?" Dragana asked.

"Yeah."

"Would it hold long enough for us to get there?" Dragana asked.

Aeo shrugged. "If anyone would have a strong enough connection to ride to the hive, it would be this bastard." He gave the corpse a kick for good measure. "There's only one way to find out."

Raeb looked at him. His strange Entana eyes made Aeo's skin crawl, but he did his best not to show it. "That's a dangerous gamble, Aeo. If it doesn't lead to the Entana, or it dissipates before we reach the hive, we'll be stranded in the spirit world without a guide home."

"Do we have a choice?" Dragana asked. "The -taken soldiers are everywhere. If we don't stop them, they'll take over the entire world. The human race will go extinct."

"This is a one-way trip," Raeb said. "If we follow this to the spirit world, we'll have to find our own way back."

"And if we miss this chance," Aeo said, "we may never find a way to the hive."

No one could argue that.

"We need some kind of protection," Raeb said. "Our bodies will be helpless here. If anyone comes while we're in the spirit world, we'll be defenseless."

"I'll stay," Saydee said. "I won't be much good up there, anyway. You three can handle the hive."

"Saydee, you deserve to see this through as much as any of us," Dragana said.

"It's all right." She stared at the mage's body for a moment. "I got what I needed."

Raeb placed a hand on her shoulder. She looked at him, Entana eyes to Entana eyes, and hugged him.

Raeb froze, his hands outstretched. His mouth opened and closed like a fish gasping for air. He looked at Dragana and Aeo as if to say *Help! What do I do?*

Aeo and Dragana looked at each other and burst out laughing.

She was a little shorter than he'd thought, the top of her head reaching to just under his chin. And she was right there. Only inches away. She was more real, more accessible, than she'd ever been before.

He reached out to touch her, maybe even pull her closer to him, but his hand passed right through her skin.

Right. He might *feel* alive now, but he was still just a spirit. No matter how close Dragana might seem, she would forever be out of his reach.

Aeo pushed the thoughts away. Focus. He couldn't let his emotions distract him, no matter how much they threatened to drown him.

"The connection's fading. If we're going to do this, we have to do it now."

Saydee released Raeb. The man looked thoroughly confused. Aeo could sympathize.

Dragana gave Saydee a brief hug before joining the men beside the corpse. It was already starting to smell.

"Ready?" Aeo asked.

Raeb and Dragana nodded. "Ready."

He looked at Saydee, gave her a brief nod of thanks and respect, and grabbed the thinning thread of Ashwinn's connection. He reached his other hand toward his companions.

Raeb and Dragana reached out with their bodies, but Aeo grabbed onto their spirits. *These,* he could touch. He held Dragana's spirit-hand, Raeb's wrapped around his wrist.

Then he looked up, willing them out of the physical world and toward the Entana hive.

CHAPTER THIRTY-TWO

Raeb didn't enjoy this trip through space and time any more than he had his last one. The cold winds buffeted his spirit, and the mind-boggling sights left him feeling small and speechless. Their task seemed more idealistic, and more idiotic, with each passing moment. How could three small spirits defeat an entity that existed in a place where stars and worlds passed in a blink? They'd barely beat Ashwinn, and he was just the Entana's slave. The hive itself would make Ashwinn look as strong and intimidating as a newborn kitten.

And then the Entana hive loomed before them.

"By the gods of Taron," Dragana whispered.

It was still as massive, still as vile, as Raeb remembered. Perhaps even more so, now that there was no stopping their journey. Raeb wouldn't just stare at the horror of the hive—he would enter it. Most likely, he wouldn't be leaving it.

Squeamishness and fear settled in Raeb's gut. They twisted in his stomach and made him nauseous. If he'd been able to take the coward's route and flee, he'd have considered it. Heavily.

Still, they sped ever closer to the hive.

There was no sensation of arrival or landing. Raeb was just there, suddenly, standing on ground that felt solid but looked like little more than mist. The air felt heavy, but not with moisture. It was soupy with dread.

Though Raeb had been preparing for this moment, he wasn't the least bit ready for it. They were *here*, in the heart of enemy territory, about to enrage the most dangerous foe in humanity's existence. Three of them, with a couple of enchanted swords.

We are idiots.

He was mildly surprised the Entana didn't attack the moment he arrived. They weren't stupid creatures, nor could they ignore a threat like Raeb and Aeo. Why didn't they just devour Raeb's thoughts, then dispatch Aeo and Dragana while they mourned? It would have been the quickest and easiest way to be rid of the spirit of the Bok'Tarong.

Unless he wasn't the soul the Entana were after.

Raeb shuddered. He'd evaded death-by-Entana through no strength of his own. It was only at the mercy—torture—of the Keeper of Secrets. Now Ashwinn was dead, and he was here. Why hadn't they already killed him?

Because they had something else in mind for him.

And that, more than anything, terrified him.

Dragana's sudden gasp pulled him from his thoughts. His heart raced as she dropped to her knees. Aeo lay there, his spirit body blinking in and out of existence. Bits of his rosy gold essence drifted from his skin like smoke, dissipating into the hive. His eyes were full of pain and fear, but even as Raeb watched they started to glaze over.

"Aeo! Can you hear me? Hold on, Aeo."

Raeb's heart hammered. Aeo could not die here. He was the spirit of the Bok'Tarong. If he died now, the magic of the sword might expire too. They'd have no power against the Entana. He and Dragana would be dead in moments, and the rest of the world would soon follow.

But more than that, Raeb couldn't sit here and let his friend die.

He watched Aeo's essence flicker. "His anchor must not be strong enough," he said. "His spirit doesn't have anything to hold itself together."

"What do you mean?"

"We have our bodies anchoring us to the world. They're strong and solid enough, *ours* enough, that our spirits remember what we are and hold together. Aeo has only the blades. This far away, the bond isn't strong enough."

Aeo's eyes were almost vacant, his spirit going grey and dull as he bled out the last of his rosy gold essence. Dragana held him by the shoulders, as if she could keep him together by force.

"Metal doesn't hold a spirit-bond as well as flesh," Raeb continued, fumbling with Aeo's arm more for something to do than truly believing it would help. "With how thoroughly he'd bonded with the Bok'Tarong's magic, I didn't think he'd have a problem."

Dragana's eyes were dry, but tears choked her voice. "He's dying! We have to do something!"

"There's nothing we can..." He left the sentence unfinished. Raeb had no way to save Aeo. But looking at Dragana, perhaps she did.

He'd never understood the magic behind the spirit-carvings of the Taronese jungle tribes, but he'd seen them before. They were powerful. Offering it would be a risk, but Aeo didn't have time for Raeb to worry about that. It would be Dragana's choice, anyway. And he was no expert in the arena of love.

Raeb placed his hand on her arm. At first she didn't seem to understand — perhaps she thought he was comforting her — but then she noticed his fingers didn't touch her skin. They rested on the cuff on her arm, the carving of her spirit. Its enchantment had carried it to the spirit world with them.

She raised her eyes to his. They were red from unshed tears.

"I've seen the way you look at him," he said. "I hear it in your voice."

She didn't ask for an explanation, and didn't deny what he implied. "Would it work?"

Raeb shrugged. "I don't know. But its magic is a kind of binding. It might give him something — some*one* — to anchor to."

Dragana's eyes unfocused. Raeb left her to her thoughts. This wasn't something to do lightly. A spirit-carving given in love was a beautiful, enchanting kind of magic. It created. It made things whole. But if that love wasn't pure, or reciprocated, the magic was dangerous. It would tear her own soul apart. If Aeo and Dragana weren't already bound to each other in their hearts, trying to force this would destroy them both.

She looked down at Aeo. The man's spirit flickered wildly,

fading into transparency. Another moment and he'd be gone.

Without another pause, Dragana removed the cuff. Its color drained from opalescent green to flat gray as it left her skin. She held it in her hands reverently, gazing at the enchanted carving. Then she leaned over Aeo, took his hand in hers, and slipped it onto his wrist.

The carving blazed like burnished bronze. Faint streaks of Dragana's opalescent green raced across its surface, until the two colors mixed and melded in perfect harmony.

Raeb smiled. It was more beautiful now than it had been on Dragana's arm. It was stronger, more solid, as if it had been created half-finished, so that one day it could become this. Just as it was meant to do.

Several long heartbeats passed. Aeo's spirit was still fading, the details of his face blowing away like fog in a breeze. Dragana cried out and gathered Aeo in her arms, weeping.

Raeb wanted to turn away from her sorrow, and his own, but his eyes were glued to Aeo. Was it his imagination, or had the spirit stopped fading? Raeb stared until his eyes hurt. Yes. Aeo was stabilizing. Bit by bit, he began to take shape again.

Dragana's tears dried as Aeo's body solidified. The rosy gold hue returned to his spirit. Raeb started breathing again.

Aeo lay in Dragana's lap for a moment before opening his eyes, recognition flooding into them.

Her smile was brittle with fragile hope. Her hands trembled as she helped Aeo sit up. The assassin cradled his head and swayed for a minute. "Worst. Hangover. Ever."

"You should be grateful you're still alive to feel it," Raeb said, tension melting from his body.

Aeo groaned. "I'm not sure if I'm ready to feel grateful yet."

He rubbed his hands over his face, then noticed the gleaming cuff on his wrist. He stared at it for a second, then at Dragana's arm. Faint shadows, with just a hint of bronze and shimmering green, traced the outline of where the cuff had once rested.

"What did I miss?" he asked.

"Your spirit was coming apart. You needed something to hold you together. To keep you alive." She gestured toward the cuff. "That will bind us, body and soul," she said. Timidity and nervousness made her voice shake. "Well, as much as it can bind a soul without a body, anyway."

Aeo looked down at the cuff, then back to Dragana. He looked confused, but Raeb could see him puzzling out the details. A spark of understanding lit his eyes and he stared at Dragana, still confused, but awed.

"I've given you my spirit," she continued, as if she couldn't bear the silence. She sounded terrified. "It means... well... our souls are bound together now. We... uh... kind of belong to each other."

Aeo was silent for a moment. "You mean you *married* me?"

Dragana blushed, as much as a spirit can, and her spine straightened. If Aeo rejected her now, Raeb would blast the man's spirit into oblivion himself.

Aeo stared at Dragana for a few seconds. Then he launched himself at her, wrapped his arms around her, and kissed her.

⁎⁎

Ecstasy. No other word could match what Aeo felt as he kissed Dragana. Here in the spirit world, he was real enough to hold her, to feel her pressed against him. To be with her.

He'd thought he was happy when he was fighting, that he was made for battle. But those memories couldn't compare to holding Dragana. *This* was what he was truly meant to do.

Somewhere in the back of his mind, he knew it couldn't last. Once they returned to the physical world, Aeo would be just a sword again. But he refused to dwell on those thoughts. As long as they were here, he wasn't about to let her go.

Raeb practically danced around them in his anxiety. Their time was limited, and they had no idea what kind of defenses the hive would erect once it detected their presence. As much as Aeo wanted to stay in Dragana's arms forever, he got to his feet. They stood together, hand in hand, and took their first look at the Entana hive.

The echoes of Entana hunters surrounded them. Dim light illuminated the room, though there didn't seem to be any source. The walls were more ethereal than real, shifting colors fading in and out of reality on a whim. Instead of echoing like the hunters', their own voices sounded flat and muted.

"Does this seem familiar to you?" he asked Raeb.

The other man nodded. "It feels like Saydee's mind."

"I think we landed in the middle of a maze," Dragana said.

Aeo had noticed that, too. Five doorways led out of the room, each corridor lost to darkness and gloom within steps of the entrance. Horrible, mangled cries echoed out of them. "Those don't sound like the hunters," he whispered.

"No," Raeb said, drawing Sunray, "they don't."

Aeo moved to unsheathe the Bok'Tarong, but found it already in his hand. He pictured it in its sheath, and it was there. A thought and it returned to his grip. *Handy thing.*

Dragana stared at the blades in his hand, then drew her own Bok'Tarong from the sheath in her back. She looked confused for a moment, then understanding spread through her features. "The Bok'Tarong is a part of me," she said, glancing from her blades to the cuff on Aeo's wrist. "In more ways than one. I suppose my spirit doesn't understand it isn't actually mine."

Aeo grinned. They had two Bok'Tarongs. Their chances had just doubled.

And they would need it—soon—if the sounds emanating from the corridors were any hint.

Aeo raised the Bok'Tarong and put his back to Raeb's and Dragana's. He scanned the corridors. The ever-shifting lights and textures made it impossible to tell if something approached.

Dragana leaned back, pressing her head against the men's shoulders. "Shouldn't they have found us by now?"

Aeo shrugged. "We don't know how far sound travels through here, or how twisted the paths are. They could be on the other side of that wall but unable to reach us, for all we know."

"Or they don't want to catch us," Raeb said. "They could be surrounding us, or corralling us, or—"

Raeb's words were cut off by a choking sound. His eyes bulged as he swayed, face turning red. Sunray clattered to the floor. Then he toppled to his knees, with the speed and inevitability of a glacier.

Dragana knelt beside him. Aeo spun in circles, keeping his eye on every entrance.

Raeb froze, holding so still he could have been a statue. "Raeb?" Dragana held his shoulders in trembling hands. "Don't you dare die before I can yell at you."

He convulsed a few times, but did not respond.

A voice echoed all around them, hissing and slithering from the walls into their minds. "You beg for death by coming here."

Aeo looked up and around, searching for the source of the voice, knowing he wouldn't find it. "I come bearing death, you mean," he called back.

He assumed the rolling, gurgling sound that followed was laughter.

"You humans and your hubris. We've never known another species to think so highly of such limited skills. It's almost endearing."

"Underestimate us all you want. But we're going to stop you."

"Stop us? How do you intend to do that? We have all the power here. You're just intruders, and weak ones at that."

"Go ahead and think that. It'll make our victory that much sweeter." Aeo smiled a wolf's smile. "Now shut up, release my friend's mind, and let us get on with the business of killing you."

"Who are you, to make demands of us?"

He squared his shoulders and raised the double-bladed sword above his head. It glowed with power, and his voice echoed down the corridors more loudly than the Entana's. "I am Aeo, the spirit of the Bok'Tarong!"

Silence.

Embarrassment crept up his spine. What did he think he was doing, standing in this absurd pose like some hero of old? But he couldn't back down now. Not until he received an answer to his challenge.

"I think you scared them," Dragana said.

"Either that, or they're giving me one last chance to slink away before I make a complete fool of myself."

Raeb huffed out something that could have been a laugh. "I think the time for that has passed."

Dragana helped him back to his feet. Raeb moved stiffly, as if his next motion could shatter his entire body.

"What happened?" Aeo asked, lowering his sword.

"The Entana came by for a chat." The strain in his voice betrayed his casual words.

"What did they want?"

He raised an eyebrow, looking at Aeo. "What do you think?"

Aeo grunted. "Did they take any memories?"

Raeb stilled for a moment. "No."

"Are you sure?"

Raeb's tone was more frigid than his glare. "You can always tell when the Entana feed on a memory. There's no ignoring the emptiness they leave behind. Feeling that sense of wrongness, but not knowing why. All you know is that you feel incomplete, violated, and terrified you've lost something dear to you." He paused, still glaring at Aeo. "You might not remember what memory it was, but you *always* know when they've taken one from you."

Aeo didn't know how to respond. He'd never given much thought to what it must feel like to be a -taken. His focus had always been on the Entana themselves. Now, though, he saw the toll being a -taken had wrought on his friend.

As if he'd needed any more motivation to destroy these monsters.

A howl from the Entana hunters roared through the corridors, fracturing the tension between the two men. The sounds of pounding feet followed, and with each second they grew louder.

"Maybe I didn't scare them after all," Aeo muttered.

Raeb picked up Sunray and they resumed their defensive position. Aeo's heart hammered. It sounded like hundreds of hunters and not-quite hunters approached. He hoped it was a trick of this strange environment amplifying the sound, but something told him it wasn't.

The first of the Entana hunters came into view, their animal-like shapes almost completely hidden underneath a tangle of Entana tendrils. They reeked of corruption.

Dragana cursed under her breath. He couldn't blame her. He'd encountered these foul beasts before, killed his fair share of them, and still they disgusted him.

But they were nothing compared to the not-quite hunters that followed.

Bile rise in Aeo's throat. His palms grew clammy, and for the first time since they'd arrived, the Bok'Tarong trembled in his hands. These hunters were everything the old, familiar ones were—only they weren't animals. They were people. Oily black, disfigured into monstrosities, tendrils trailing from heads like antennae and falling around shoulders like a mane of snakes. But undeniably people.

They shambled forward, their eyes flat and empty, worse than those Aeo had seen on corpses.

Aeo's back bumped into Dragana's. He wasn't sure which of them had tried to retreat.

The hunters, human and animal, filled the space around Aeo and his friends. Still more came, crowding each passageway beyond Aeo's sight. From the sound, even more piled in behind those.

There was no way three people, enchanted swords or no, could fight a mob like that.

Instead of despair, a rush of strength and hatred flooded through Aeo. It burned through his blood. He felt the world sharpen, clarify, crystalize. He was the Bok'Tarong, and he had never been this close to his mortal enemy before.

The blades in his hand started to glow.

Stillness settled into Aeo's soul. This was his purpose. The Entana lived to devour others' lives. He lived to avenge those lives. It was simple as that.

His muscles twitched with eagerness. If he didn't have his friends at his back, relying on him for protection, he would have leapt into the midst of the hunters. As it was, he met the first charge with a fierce grin and an enthusiastic swipe of the Bok'Tarong.

The afterimage of the double-bladed sword's glow burned in his eyes. The hunter squealed, flailed, and evaporated into oily smoke.

Another hunter, possibly a lion at one time, pounced in the other's wake. Aeo lifted his sword to block, but the hunter collided with the lingering light of the Bok'Tarong's trail. It paused there for the briefest of seconds, stuck like a fly in sap, then disappeared in a puff of smoke.

Aeo's grin widened. It wasn't an afterimage. The Bok'Tarong was trailing light, and any hunter in its path was instantly purified.

He swung the blades in wide arcs, creating barricades around him and his friends. Many hunters were able to evade the deadly light to reach them, but many more were pushed into the glow or too stupid to avoid it. The trails dimmed with each impact, their power draining as they slew hunters, but Aeo rebuilt them as fast as they fell. The air around them was soon thick with oily smoke, no matter how fast it dissipated.

Raeb and Dragana were lost in the Taronese sword-dance, weaving in and out of each other's defenses flawlessly. He noted, with some sadness, that Dragana's Bok'Tarong didn't trail the same deadly light his did. *Guess we can't expect too many miracles in one day.*

Aeo's eyes watered from the smoke and the dazzling light trails of the Bok'Tarong. His blood pulsed through his body like a drumbeat. He was too deep in the fight to feel much pain, but he knew his muscles would punish him for the exertion as soon as he stopped.

And still more hunters sought their blood.

He moved and spun and stabbed, but a small voice in Aeo's

mind insisted there was an easier way. [This is the spirit world], it seemed to say. [The rules are different here. You don't have to do everything with muscle.]

Aeo couldn't devote any concentration to the concept. There were too many enemies surrounding him. He kept killing.

[Come on, Aeo, think! Our power isn't bound by physical limitations anymore. Look at yourself. Look at what you're doing. We can extend outside the blades, just as you do. Send our power out to the enemy instead of waiting for them to come to you.]

He knew the voice. It was the tiny, niggling instinct—almost like a conscience—he'd inherited when he became the Bok'Tarong. It had said his presence had killed it, that it would be lost forever.

[Not lost. Just… suppressed. Until we could properly merge with you.]

Until I became worthy, you mean.

The voice didn't deny it.

The times he'd heard that voice, it had given him knowledge or insight that had saved his and Dragana's lives. He knew better than to ignore it now.

He didn't think about what he was doing. He just let the Bok'Tarong guide him.

Ignoring the snarls and claws of the hunters, Aeo turned the blades sideways and swung it in long, broad strokes. The Bok'Tarong's magic walled him in. It wouldn't last long, with the hunters beating—and dying—on it, but hopefully it would give him enough time.

He gathered his strength, channeling it through the power of the Bok'Tarong. His hatred of the Entana burned in him like a fever. He fueled the fire, stoking the rage with his fear, his pain, with everything he had. He let it consume him until his body shook and his vision went black and he lost all sense of anything other than the incandescent hatred.

A moment before it would devour him, he released it.

A shockwave of light and power erupted from him. It tore from his spirit like a tidal wave, blinding him and drowning everything in its wake. The hunters barely had time to squeal before the light of the Bok'Tarong's magic destroyed them.

Aeo collapsed to his knees. The world spun around him. His vision darkened, his ears rang, and without Dragana's hand on his shoulder he would have crashed to the ground.

Ominous silence, so thick he could feel it, filled the room.

"You can't get rid of me that easily," Aeo told the Entana. It took all his strength to make his voice more than a whisper.

The Entana's voice echoed through the eerily silent chamber. "Come deeper then, if you dare. The closer you get, the easier it will be to kill you."

Aeo groaned and pushed himself up, fighting the most profound sense of exhaustion he'd ever felt. Every muscle in his body felt like it had been riddled with holes.

"I have got to stop doing this to myself," he muttered.

"By the gods of Taron, Aeo, are you all right?"

He grasped Dragana's hand, hoping to encourage her. It felt like he was clinging to her for life itself. "I'm all right," he said. His throat was parched, as if he'd never before tasted water. "I'll be fine."

"What on earth *was* that?" Raeb asked.

"The power of the Bok'Tarong. It doesn't have to be confined to the blades in the spirit world. I just released it." He paused, lifting his head and looking around. Not a single hunter lurked in the shadows, and no sound of them could be heard. "I guess it worked."

Raeb and Dragana helped him to his feet. He swayed for a moment, unsure which way was up, until at last he steadied.

"It more than worked, Aeo. As soon as that pulse of light hit, the hunters just dissipated. Gone." Raeb snapped his fingers. "Poof."

Dragana glared at him from around Aeo. "He saved our lives and destroyed hundreds of Entana hunters with light and magic, and the best way you can describe it is 'poof'?"

Raeb shrugged, a satisfied grin plastered on his face.

"We shouldn't stay here, in case more hunters show up," Aeo said. He looked at each of the tunnels in turn. "Which way, intrepid leader?" he asked, looking over at Raeb.

The man stared back at him. "Since when am I the leader? You're the one with the great and powerful hunter-obliterating magic."

"But this was your idea, your plan, and you know the Entana better than any of us. If anyone could lead us to the heart of the hive, it's you."

Raeb looked stunned for a moment, but he nodded. "I guess one path will be as good as any at this point," he said, surveying their choices. "If the Entana wanted to keep us out, they could do it with a thought."

He chose a tunnel at random, one slightly to their left, and led the way down. In all this time he'd never sheathed Sunray, and he didn't seem eager to do so any time soon.

Aeo and Dragana followed. Aeo tried to be wary of their surroundings, watching for traps or more hunters, but his head throbbed and the thrill of having Dragana beside him was intoxicating. He found himself looking over at her, feeling her hand in his, reveling in the memory of their kiss. She wanted him. She'd *chosen* him. What had he done to earn the love of someone like her? Whatever it was, he was forever grateful for having done it.

He forced his thoughts back to the tunnels. If he wanted to get her out of this alive, he couldn't let himself get distracted. He had to protect her. He'd never tell her that—the warrior-woman would beat him senseless—but even so. He wasn't about to let anything happen to her. She was his.

And by every one of the gods of Taron, no matter what the cost, he was going to bring her home.

CHAPTER THIRTY-THREE

R aeb tried to ignore the fear stewing in his gut. These tunnels were not friendly. The hunters might be gone for now, but this entire place reeked of malevolence. Latent violence thrummed in the walls. It leached from them like moisture in a cave. Or saliva in a giant monster's mouth.

Great. He'd never get that last image out of his brain now.

He tightened his grip on Sunray. The Entana blade froze his fingertips, but he welcomed the pain. Anything to distract himself from where he was and what he was doing.

The Entana in his mind laughed. He heard it as a distant echo, like a memory. But he knew better. The Entana were here, closer than ever. Their little chat had proven that. Only the Keeper of Secrets had been able to hold conversations like that before. Raeb had naïvely hoped that with him dead, they would cease altogether.

Unnerving though it was, at least he didn't have to fear the Keeper's intellect anymore. With him, every word held hidden meanings and veiled threats. Raeb never knew what depths their conversation truly held. The Entana were not that subtle, so at least he knew what they were up to now.

They wanted Aeo. Of course.

They wanted Raeb to kill him. No surprise there.

And they wanted to make Raeb the new Keeper of Secrets.

He very carefully kept his mind blank. To dwell on it would tell the Entana exactly what he thought of that.

He'd fought them for so long, Raeb couldn't believe they hadn't given up on him. Declared him a lost cause and devoured him already. What were they waiting for?

For him to give up. To be so worn down, so broken, he couldn't fight anymore. He'd fallen that low once, and only barely avoided disaster. How much more could he take?

Not much. Not anything, if he was honest with himself.

Raeb was already broken. Only his friends held him together now.

And no matter what he did, the Entana would take them from him next.

The Entana repeated its promise over and over, refusing to let Raeb ignore it. *Become our ambassador and spend your eternity in peace. Refuse, and spend your eternity as a mad killer. Invincible, killing everyone in your path, and remembering nothing but their faces. Your friends will be the first to haunt your existence.*

Raeb didn't doubt for a moment they could, and would, follow through with that promise.

There was no way out. Break, give into the Entana, and despise himself for eternity.

Fight and be forced to murder his friends. Then break, give into the Entana, and despise himself for eternity.

Whatever path he chose, he and his friends were doomed.

Path. Focus on the path. Do not think of the Entana. Do not think of your friends' last moments.

He watched his feet and the tunnel ahead. The walls shifted back and forth slightly, so Raeb felt like he staggered like a drunken man. If he focused on it too much, he got dizzy.

The howls of the hunters echoed toward them. They were still distant, but all three of them tensed and froze in their steps. They didn't start moving again until several breaths had passed with no additional sound.

They came to a fork in the path. The tunnel to the right led up at a sharp angle; the left, sloping downward. At the base of the hill it curved back to the right, so it would follow the same basic direction they were going now. But was that the right direction? He had no way to know.

Something about the right, upward path caught his attention. He couldn't pinpoint it, but it felt like the right way to go.

He didn't move.

"What's wrong, Raeb?" Dragana asked.

"I don't like this."

"That isn't much of a surprise," Aeo said. "Which part of this god-awful place are you referring to, specifically?"

"The part where my instincts are pulling me toward a specific path."

"Why is that a bad thing?"

Raeb turned to the assassin. "Because I still have an Entana in my brain. If they're trying to lead me somewhere, is that a place I want to go?"

They stood, thinking, for several heartbeats. Raeb cast his eyes between the two paths, though neither looked any more inviting upon inspection.

"The Entana admitted it would be easier to kill us deeper in the hive," Dragana said. "So why would they lead us away, if it would only risk more hunters and give us the possibility of escape?"

"The Entana won't care about the hunters," Raeb replied. "They don't have any thoughts or memories left to feed upon. They're just shells. Inedible scraps left over from last night's dinner. We could kill every one of them in the entire hive and not cause the Entana to even flinch."

"Dragana's theory still seems sound to me," Aeo said. "The Entana want us dead. Better to get us to their stronghold fast as they can and be done with it."

Raeb sighed. "Right it is, then." He started down the path, following his instincts.

Hopefully, those instincts wouldn't get them killed any sooner than need be.

⁎
⁎⁎

THE PATH RAEB chose was steep. It would have been bad enough in the real world, but the way the walls and floor kept shimmering in and out of existence, it felt like climbing upstream through a river. Aeo was forced to let go of Dragana's hand just

346

so they could keep their balance.

He hadn't thought it possible, but the hive grew more sinister the farther in they went. The colors on the walls faded to black and dirty gray, when the walls were visible at all. A black, sucking void lingered in their place, one that felt hungry to Aeo. A smell like decaying meat and sulfur infused the air. The tunnels grew smaller, narrower, and more constricted. Aeo could have reached out and touched both walls from where he stood, but he didn't dare. The walls were too filmy, and oily, and gods only knew what that stuff would do to him if he got it on his skin.

The howls of the hunters had returned as well. Now there were so many, coming from so many directions, the sound never truly died. It pulsed like the heartbeat of the hive itself.

The Bok'Tarong reappeared in Aeo's hand. The blades made it more difficult to navigate the steep, congested tunnel, but he felt safer with its weight settled and ready for use.

Raeb spoke without turning back. "If we get surrounded, could you do that 'poof' thing again?"

Not a chance. "My head is still pounding from last time. If I tried to summon that much power again, I doubt I'd make it through."

Dragana grabbed his free hand in a grip that threatened to crush bones. "Could I do it instead?" she asked. "I have my own Bok'Tarong, after all."

"I don't think so. Yours doesn't seem to have the same power mine does."

Finally the tunnel started to open up, into a room far larger than any they'd passed through yet. The floor sloped downward into a large, shallow bowl, though it seemed less solid than it had in the corridor. The ceiling, though high, was strung with long, inert Entana tendrils like moss on a weeping willow. The air was warm and still.

When they stepped into the room, the howls of the hunters failed to follow them.

Aeo's foot splashed into something liquid, though it didn't feel like any kind of water or muck he'd ever trod through before. It reminded him of honey. It was warm, too, almost body temperature. The surface reflected the low light in brief sparkles, like sunshine off a wave.

Aeo looked down. Just to the side of his foot, a human face stared up at him.

He yelped and tried to jump back. The sludge pulled at his feet, making it hard to keep his balance. He splashed back in past his ankles, right atop a man's face that had popped up behind him.

Relief and revulsion swam through him as the image—only an image, thank the gods— trembled and broke apart. "What is this place?"

Raeb crouched over the liquid, peering at it and running it through his fingers. It clung to his skin, dripping off in slow, heavy globs. "It's like some kind of... memory soup." He stood, looking up at the thousands of tiny hanging tendrils. "And those look like baby Entana."

"So this is a nursery?" Dragana asked.

Raeb nodded. "This must be where they regenerate tendrils."

"Then what's with the memory soup?"

"Babies need to eat, Aeo. The hive probably distills a bunch of the emotions they steal from the -taken and dumps it in here. The tendrils can reach down and feed whenever they want." He pointed off to the left, where one of the thicker tendrils had done exactly that. Dragana grimaced at the slurping sounds it made.

Aeo nodded, but something else had drawn his attention. All around Raeb, the surface churned with colors and half-formed images. More and more specks of color raced toward him, until he stood in the epicenter of a giant starburst.

When Raeb looked down, he went deathly pale. His eyes widened as he stared at the images forming in the sludge. Aeo saw landscapes and unfamiliar buildings, faces he didn't recognize, and snatches of scenes like... like he was watching someone's memories.

Raeb's memories.

Raeb hadn't moved an inch. He drank in the images like they were life itself.

Dragana gasped and stepped forward as an image of vivid green trees and steep, jagged mountains coalesced around Raeb's feet. Nestled in the crags was a vast temple complex, connected by rope bridges and sweeping staircases. Waterfalls danced down the mountains around it, some of them disappearing into a building only to reappear at its base. Aeo couldn't understand how it was even supported—it looked as if the mountain had grown around the temple rather than the other way around.

No wonder Dragana held such love for the Taronese temple. A sense of great age radiated from the place, as if it had been built with peace and wisdom as well as wood and stone. Seeing Raeb's features twist with longing and regret, Aeo felt certain the man had loved it just as much as she had.

The image swung around, as if from the eyes of a child who was determined not to miss a detail. Aeo could even feel some of what the boy Raeb had felt: awe and wonder, excitement, a hint of fear.

Just as Dragana opened her mouth to say something, images began forming at her feet, too.

Aeo checked the soup around him. A few sparks circled him, but no images formed. Perhaps the Bok'Tarong protected his thoughts? Or maybe the sheer intensity of Dragana's emotions, and their close connection to Raeb's, allowed the soup to leech her memories.

Movement above them caught Aeo's eye. The baby Entana tendrils swayed as if stirred by a gentle breeze. He should keep watch on them, but his gaze was drawn back to the memory soup and the thoughts it showed.

Dragana's memory was also her first glimpse of the Taronese temple. It didn't look very different, even though Raeb's vision of it had been centuries earlier. Even Aeo was enchanted by the mystique and agelessness of the place.

Dragana's thoughts sped through highlights of her training and settled on the moment she was chosen to bear the Bok'Tarong. Dragana and an older man fought in the middle of a large dojo, moving so swiftly Aeo had trouble following their movements. She dodged, feinted, struck, and the man was defeated. Dragana was covered in sweat, her muscles quivering with exhaustion, but her pride overwhelmed everything. Tears dripped from her eyes. Aeo found himself beaming for her.

The tendrils above them rustled.

Raeb's memories churned in response to Dragana's. Images of him training, longing, daydreaming flashed at his feet. Aeo felt Raeb's desire for the moment Dragana had experienced. But then his memories went dark and chaotic.

A great battle, a horrible, soul-rending battle, was fought and lost. And then Raeb's tear- and sweat-streaked face appeared. He looked like he'd spent a month of nights sleepless and hunted. Aeo saw him crouched in the darkness, hiding from the world, terrified of what had just happened, agonized by what had to happen next.

The images blurred, and the next thing Aeo saw was Raeb running from the temple, sobbing. He ran until he collapsed, but even so he picked himself up and kept going. Not stopping for days, out of fear and shame of what he had become.

Aeo looked up. A few of the baby tendrils were extending themselves toward Raeb and Dragana. His friends' high emotions and stirring of memories must have smelled like a feast to them.

He sent a tiny bit of power into the Bok'Tarong, bringing it to a gentle glow. The tendrils shrunk back, but Dragana and Raeb didn't seem to notice. Their eyes were still glued to the images playing in the memory soup.

Their memories of Taron and the Bok'Tarong built off each other, spurred each other's forward, until both dwelt on a single image, from two different perspectives.

At Dragana's feet, Raeb leaned over the Bok'Tarong, Sunray in hand and murder in his eyes. The fear and betrayal she'd felt burned like a brand.

At Raeb's feet, the image of the Bok'Tarong was blurred by

tears. Aeo could feel the hopelessness and confusion permeating Raeb's mind during those moments. He *knew* there was only one way out of this hell he called life, and that was to destroy the Bok'Tarong. Otherwise he was doomed to live this curse for centuries more, or go mad and lose everything. He had no choice.

But he didn't strike. He *wouldn't* strike. Raeb's thoughts had turned to Aeo, and Dragana, and he'd refused to hurt his friends.

Aeo had been so absorbed by the images he'd let the glow of the Bok'Tarong fade. He looked up just as a large tendril reared up behind Dragana, poised to strike at her head. If that thing even touched her... "Dragana!"

Raeb beat him to it. He whipped Sunray over Dragana's head. She screamed, more from confusion than fear, and ducked.

The tendril splashed into the memory soup, severed cleanly in half.

Aeo sent power into the Bok'Tarong, making it glow even more brightly than before. The effort left him dizzy, but the remaining tendrils fled back to the ceiling.

Dragana stood cautiously, then looked at Raeb. The memory soup had gone black and still at their feet, but both glanced at it like they could still see the images.

He wished he could give them time to process all this, to come to grips with this new understanding. But the Entana wouldn't wait for them forever, and the tendrils were already testing the Bok'Tarong's glow for an opening.

He led them out of the Entana nursery in silence, but Aeo could sense the difference in their little group.

Dragana had finally forgiven Raeb.

And here, at the end, that would mean everything.

CHAPTER THIRTY-FOUR

Within moments of leaving the Entana nursery, their surroundings began to change. The labyrinthine caverns became a more solid, straightforward path. Colors grew muted before fading altogether. Aeo's time in Saydee's mind had prepared him for this, but it still set his nerves on edge.

In a dozen heartbeats they had left the moist, undulating walls behind. Now their footsteps echoed on polished obsidian. Every surface was pure black, so deep Aeo felt it could swallow him if he ventured too close. The arrow-straight corridor seemed to go on forever. A presence, like the looming of a giant consciousness, surrounded them.

They'd arrived.

The magic of the Bok'Tarong burned within Aeo. This was the culmination of generations, centuries, even millennia. The entire history of the Taronese people, and the Bok'Tarong, had led to this moment. His actions would dictate whether the thousands of lives sacrificed to bring life to the double-bladed sword would be wasted.

He could not fail that legacy.

Raeb stopped so suddenly Aeo ran into him. The two men stumbled, but kept to their feet.

Dragana opened her mouth to speak, but Raeb shushed her with a flash of his eyes. He looked around, beckoning them to do the same, then shook his head. They weren't alone.

He pulled Aeo and Dragana closer, until their faces were mere inches apart. From this distance, Raeb's Entana eyes were haunted and half-crazed. He held Sunray in a white-knuckled grip.

"We don't have much time," the man whispered. It was barely audible, little more than a breath shaping the words. "The Entana know we're here. I can only evade them for so long before they'll know what's going on."

He sighed, and Aeo heard every burden Raeb had carried throughout his long life in the sound. "I'm sorry I have to do this to you, my friends. I want you to know that. I am truly sorry. But there isn't any other way."

Aeo's stomach clenched. He wasn't sure what Raeb was saying, but he didn't like it. Not one bit.

"The Entana will appear any minute. They'll offer me a choice. And once that choice is made, they'll attack. I... " He broke eye contact, seeming very fragile and full of regret. "I have to be dead by then."

Dragana's voice rang through the corridor. "What!"

Raeb tensed like a rabbit who'd heard a fox in the bushes. "The Entana offered me a deal: kill Aeo, destroy the Bok'Tarong, and live. There's no other way for me to make it out of here alive."

"You can't be serious," she whispered, much quieter this time.

"I am. But I can't do it."

"That doesn't mean you have to die!"

"It's either that or the Entana drive me mad and set me loose to kill with abandon. I can't let the Entana torture me like that. I would rather die with my mind intact and without the burden of my friends' deaths on my heart." He looked at Aeo. "Please do me the favor of killing me first."

"By the gods, Raeb, you can't ask me to do that!"

"Your power is the only thing that can set me free." He looked Aeo straight in the eye, unblinking. Sorrow and sincerity radiated from him. "I'm asking you as a friend, Aeo. Don't leave me to die at the mercy of these monsters."

"There has to be another way," Dragana said. Aeo heard the desperation in her voice, matching his own. "What if you just refuse and fight with us?"

Raeb shook his head. "The Entana have a hold of my mind. As soon as I do anything they don't like, my thoughts turn into their next meal. And then I'll kill anyone in my path." It was clear who the first victims of that rampage would be.

They had to stop this. There had to be a way to avoid one, or all, of them dying. Something. Anything.

An insane plan formed in Aeo's mind. "Raeb, give Dragana your blade."

Both of his friends looked at him like he was the one suffering from Entana madness. Understanding dawned on Dragana's face first. She nodded and extended her free hand for Sunray. In her other hand, she offered Raeb her copy of the Bok'Tarong.

Raeb held up his hands, warding the double-bladed sword away. "No. Absolutely not."

"Dragana's Bok'Tarong holds almost as much power as mine," Aeo said. "And here, its power is increased tenfold. It's death to the Entana. It could free your mind from them, at least for now. Maybe even permanently."

"It'll never work."

"It can't hurt."

"It can't help, either," Raeb spit back. "The dangers are too great."

Aeo didn't respond. Neither did Dragana. She still held her hands out, one offering a blade and one waiting to accept another.

"Dragana, we don't know what Sunray will do to you. This damned blade is a curse in and of itself."

"We don't have much choice, do we?" Her voice was calm as a lake on a windless day. Aeo marveled at her control.

Raeb took a step back. "I can't let you do this."

They stood at an impasse, none relenting. Until Raeb clutched his head, opened his mouth in a silent scream, and crashed to his knees.

The Entana had pushed their way into Raeb's mind at last. They'd run out of time. And now they would know what he was planning. They'd know he was going to betray them, and they wouldn't go easy on their punishment.

Aeo knelt beside Raeb, pulling Dragana down with him. She

extended the hilt of the Bok'Tarong before her, right against his palm. Aeo did his best to imitate Dragana's calm confidence. "Take the sword, Raeb. Stop them."

He blinked, as if it took an immense effort to do so. Then in harsh, jerky movements, he shook his head.

"Take the Bok'Tarong, Raeb, before you go mad!"

He grimaced against the intrusion of the Entana, but he did not reach for the blades. His teeth ground together as he grunted out a strained "No."

He convulsed once, twice, and a true scream escaped his throat. It lasted impossibly long, and his eyes widened and darted around. Finally he slumped to the ground, shaking, covered in a clammy sweat.

"Take. The. Sword!"

"Can't... let you..." Raeb sounded like he hardly knew what he was saying.

Dragana cursed. She leaned forward, quicker than Aeo would have expected, and pulled Sunray from his hand. Her face twisted in pain as soon as she touched it, but she didn't let go. She thrust the Bok'Tarong into Raeb's palm, and Aeo closed the man's fingers around the hilt.

Raeb fell limp, still as death.

Complete, choking silence smothered them. An eternity passed between one heartbeat and the next.

Then Raeb took a deep breath, coughing and sputtering as if he'd been half-drowned.

Aeo sat back, lightheaded with relief and shaky with passing terror.

Dragana put a gentle hand on Raeb's shoulder. Other than the coughing, he hadn't moved. "Raeb?"

The man groaned, levering himself to a sitting position.

He looked like he'd stopped to have tea with Death himself. He was pale, with bruise-dark shadows under his Entana eyes. His hair was plastered to his head with sweat. When he looked at them, there was no spark of recognition in his eyes.

Dear gods, how much did the Entana take from him?

"Raeb? Can you hear me?"

Raeb focused on Dragana, following the sound of her voice to her face. He looked at her blankly for a moment, then his eyes fell to the blade clenched in her right fist.

Dragana's fingers were blue with frostbite. Sunray's frigid blades were coated in ice, and her skin was rimy halfway up her hand. Even as he watched, frost crawled its way toward her wrist.

Bile surged through Aeo's throat, but Dragana's face was calm. Strained, clearly fighting the pain and hunger of the blade, but at peace.

All three of them stared at Dragana's hand for several seconds. Raeb drew another breath. "Sunray." It sounded like a curse.

Aeo pulled his focus from Dragana's hand and looked at Raeb. His gut eased when he realized the man recognized him at last.

"I told you it was dangerous," Raeb said. His voice was hoarse and filled with pain.

"How much did the Entana take?" Aeo whispered.

Raeb's eyes clouded with tears. "Too much. I... don't

remember much. But I know that blade, and I know you."

"Do you remember what we're doing here?"

Raeb looked at the obsidian walls surrounding them. He seemed confused, as if the memory of this place was just beyond his reach.

Then the ominous, gurgling laughter of the Entana rolled over them. Every line in Raeb's face hardened and his eyes filled with fiery rage.

"We're here to kill."

Aeo clapped him, gently, on the shoulder. "Good enough for me."

Then he turned to Dragana. Her face was tight with pain, but she managed a smile for him. He knew better than to ask if she was all right. She wasn't, but she would never let that stop her. Not now, when they were so close. "Are you ready?"

Now she grinned, the toothy smile of a predator savoring the hunt. "Let's go kill these bastards and end this."

Aeo's smile almost hurt his face. He pulled Dragana to him and kissed her. She wrapped her free hand around the carving of her spirit, the bracer on his wrist that bound their spirits in love. It warmed at her touch and filled Aeo with the most profound sense of peace—and a powerful surge of passion. He knew, instinctively, Dragana felt the same.

This could be the last time they were together like this. Once they returned to the physical world, she'd be out of his reach. He'd return to the confines of the Bok'Tarong, never again to feel the heat of her kiss or the softness of her skin.

He kissed her again, pouring every ounce of love into it. If this was to be their last kiss, he wanted it to be one worth remembering. "Whatever happens, my love, never forget this," he whispered.

She smiled at him, though her eyes shimmered with tears. Her expression turned sad, and a single tear fell onto her cheek. "You will always have my heart, Aeo. Whatever happens."

They locked eyes once more, and there was nothing left to say.

They clasped hands and stood. Aeo helped Raeb to his feet, then summoned the Bok'Tarong into his hand.

Together, they walked down the long, black corridor leading to the Entana.

CHAPTER THIRTY-FIVE

R aeb felt like a ghost of the man he'd been. Huge swaths of his memory were gone. Only the gaping hole in his sense of self was left to show him how much he'd lost.

He did know a few things. His name was Raeb, though he hadn't remembered that until the woman—what was her name again?—had said it to him. The stocky man beside her was Aeo, the spirit of the Bok'Tarong. Dragana—that was her name!—now held Sunray, the blade that had held a huge part of his identity. So why did she have it, and why was he clutching the Bok'Tarong as if it was the only thing keeping him alive?

A sound he'd heard a million times in his mind echoed through the corridor. The Entana's laughter.

Oh, he remembered them. Nothing could make him forget the centuries they'd tormented him. The demands, the abuse, the fear and hatred and helplessness and hopelessness… he remembered it all.

He and his companions were here to kill the Entana, once and for all. If they'd had a plan, the Entana had taken that from him. But it didn't matter. He would do anything, give everything, to stop these monsters.

The corridor widened drastically, large enough to encompass an entire city. Raeb felt small as an ant in this place. He had an intense desire to kneel, give supplication, surrender to whatever presence was large enough and magnificent enough to live in this shiny black cathedral.

"If only you'd accepted our presence," the Entana said, "you could have been a god."

Raeb and his friends stopped. An image formed in front of them, shifting as if it couldn't decide what shape to take. A man, easily eighty feet tall, then an equally massive woman. Next a being Raeb didn't recognize. Another woman, wearing a wedding dress. A man in laborer's clothing. A strange mixture of the two. Every shape was grotesque and misshapen by Entana possession.

Behind the images, Raeb could see the knot of tendrils that was the true Entana. It stretched across the entire metropolis-sized room, radiating oily, parasitic darkness. This creature was far larger than anything Raeb had ever dreamed, even in his worst nightmares.

The form continued to shift, though its eyes remained fixed on Raeb. "The Entana could have given you a world free of pain, fear, and death. All you had to do was kill this man and welcome our presence in your mind. Why do you continue to reject our gift?"

The Entana took the shape of a woman, comfortably chubby with a wide, kind smile. Beside him, Dragana gasped. "It's Mara," she whispered.

The form shifted into a man, his fingers stained with ink and scribbled-upon parchments peeking from his trouser pockets. "Matow," Aeo said.

Raeb should know those names. Those people had held a special place in his heart. But he had no clue who they were anymore. His sense of loss swelled and reddened with rage. His hand tightened on the Bok'Tarong until his joints popped and his nails cut into his palm. "It's not a gift," he said, staring at the images passing before his eyes. Who were these people? They had to have some significance. But without his memories, they were strangers. "It's a curse. You take away the events—and people—that shaped us into who we are."

"You could have given us the memories you didn't want. Why do you suffer through pain and torment instead of allowing us to take them from you?"

Dragana lifted her chin, speaking so loudly her voice should have echoed throughout the chamber. It didn't. "Life isn't all about happiness. It's a balance, enjoying the good as well as the bad. Emotions are what make us human. Sadness and happiness, pain and comfort, tears and laughter. They're paired, and alone they're worthless."

The face of the Entana's image grew stern, disapproving. "Stupid humans. You refuse to accept logic. We can remove the unpleasantness from your world. You can live quiet and peaceful lives, if only you stopped fighting us."

"We'll take our lives as they come, thank you very much," Aeo said. He glanced at Raeb and Dragana. "I can't believe we're arguing morals with a spiritual parasite," he whispered.

"Just wait," Raeb said. "It hasn't even gotten started yet."

"Then let's finish it," Dragana said. She raised her voice again, cool as an icy breeze and dangerous as a sharpened knife. "We will never let you take our race." She lifted Sunray, clenched in a frozen fist. "We will stop you, even if it costs our lives. As a Taronese warrior and the bearer of the Bok'Tarong, I declare your life forfeit."

The images faded, leaving only the knotted, behemoth-sized Entana heart before them. It pulsed and writhed, tendrils as large as trees and black as midnight. It defied description. Putrid, horrific, nightmarish… nothing came close to the true horror of facing the Entana.

"So be it. You could have been gods, but you choose to be chattel."

The Entana lashed out with its many tendrils, a tornado of diseased flesh and suffocating darkness. Raeb tried to dodge, but each was thick as he was tall. A dozen tendrils or more battered him to the ground. They should have squashed him flat, but the Bok'Tarong still clenched in his fist offered him a tiny hint of protection.

It wouldn't be enough. A second wave of tendrils was already bearing down on him, and he had no way to escape them.

***

As soon as the Entana moved to attack, Aeo slashed with the Bok'Tarong. He put up as many light trails between his friends and the Entana as he could. He could only hope those shields would stand against an attack as powerful as this monstrous Entana's.

The tree-trunk tendrils slapped against the light trails with a sound like a gong. They stopped, unable to go farther, but the Bok'Tarong's light trails flickered. A few seconds later, they died completely.

Aeo didn't hesitate to put more up between Dragana and the next tendrils in line.

He glanced to his left on instinct. Raeb was there, flat on his back, a pair of massive tendrils poised above him to strike. Aeo sprinted to the man's side, spinning in a wide circle at the very last moment to set a glowing barrier over his friend.

When the tendrils recoiled he helped Raeb to his feet. The man nodded his thanks, then slashed his sword above Aeo's shoulder without so much as a blink.

The Entana tendril sneaking up behind Aeo shrieked and pulled back, its tip smoking where Raeb had cut it off.

Aeo grinned. "You're awfully good at that."

Raeb nodded. "Be glad of it, and watch your back next time."

They went on the offensive. Aeo and Raeb flew into the fight with ease, swinging their double-bladed swords expertly. Dragana was having more trouble with Sunray. Not from its unfamiliar shape, but from her arm. Frost covered it to her elbow. Aeo guessed her fingers were so frozen she couldn't have released the blade now if she tried.

She had to be in incredible pain, but she never hesitated in her attacks. Sunray gleamed with blue and white ice as it bit into the tendrils of the monster that had created it.

The tendrils—that name seemed so inadequate for the monolith-sized tentacles—slammed around him with world-shaking force. Each impact of tendril against obsidian rattled his teeth. Only their glacial slowness allowed him to leap away before they turned his bones to powder.

Aeo couldn't pass a single heartbeat without slicing, stabbing, or parrying at least one tentacle. They blasted through his light trails as fast as he could make them. Whenever he forced one away, two more came barreling in to take its place.

This battle had evolved from fight to melee to sheer chaos in a matter of seconds. Now he was separated from his friends, surrounded by tendrils, and so close to death he could feel it breathing down his neck. One misstep was all it would take.

They were the three finest fighters Aeo had ever seen, but he knew a hopeless cause when he saw one. This monstrosity was too big, too powerful. Even with their enchanted weapons, there was no way they could do more than sting the creature.

He had to get closer, into the heart of this tendril-beast.

Aeo summoned every bit of speed he could muster and flung himself forward. He batted away the tendrils in his path, savoring the hiss of seared Entana flesh.

He ducked and wove through the maze of tendrils. He sprinted through every opening he could see, working his way ever closer to the heart. The Entana flailed and swung tendrils at him from every direction. They battered him and sent him skidding along the obsidian floor or rolling forward from the impact. His momentum never stopped, even as stars swam in his vision and his body screamed with pain and bruises. The Entana would beat him to a pulp before long, but he continued to bull his way forward.

The Entana's darkness poisoned the air. It scorched his lungs and left an itchy burn on his skin. The Bok'Tarong's instinctive hatred blazed brighter and hotter than ever before. Its power shielded him from the worst of the attacks — the Entana could not abide the touch of his enchanted spirit for long.

A tentacle swooped in from the side and cuffed him across the head. He was staggered long enough for one of the massive tendrils to wrap around him, imprisoning him in oily Entana flesh. The tendril sizzled where it touched his aura, but it didn't let go.

Other tendrils reached up to smack Aeo, hitting him so hard his head rang with the impacts. Bits of his confidence were ripped away with each hit, just like when the Entana had attacked Dragana's spirit so long ago. Only this time, he couldn't rip free from the blades to defend himself.

He tried to struggle, but the helplessness pervading his system was too much and the Entana's grip was too strong. He could only watch as smaller tendrils erupted from the giant tentacle with juicy pops. They snaked toward Aeo, as if tasting the air, before touching his head. They paused there, smoke rising and ash falling, Aeo cringing with the contact. Then they plunged forward, burrowing their way deep into Aeo's skull.

Aeo screamed. This wasn't the kind of everyday agony he'd felt when he'd run himself through with a sword, or when Sunray had sapped his magic. This was deeper. More intimate — a white-hot poker stuck into his soul, foot-long talons gouging out chunks of his being. The Entana was unmaking him.

The Entana was -taking him.

You can't do this to me! his mind screamed. *I'm the Bok'Tarong!*

Smoke rose from the tendrils in Aeo's head. They burrowed deeper as the magic mingled with Aeo's soul burned them away. He barely held onto consciousness.

You are in the heart of my power, the Entana replied. *And my power is so much stronger than the feeble Bok'Tarong.*

But Aeo could feel the Entana's hesitation. It wasn't sure it *could* -take him.

More tendrils stabbed into Aeo's brain. He choked on oily smoke, his vision going black. For a moment he forgot where he was, what he was doing. There was just agony and confusion. Surrender sounded so wonderful, if only to be free from the pain.

Aeo was still screaming. The Entana was squealing. And far, far away, Dragana shouted and swore in Taronese.

He couldn't let Dragana — *his* Dragana — down. She'd devoted her entire life to beating the Entana. Even now, she fought this monstrosity while her arm froze into a block of ice. He knew, beyond doubt, she was fighting through the tendrils to reach him. And she wouldn't stop until either she or the Entana was dead. That's just the way she was. Noble, fierce, stubborn. A warrior.

He couldn't give up on her. He had to keep fighting, to use his power to destroy this parasite. He had to make her proud.

Aeo channeled what power he could muster into the Bok'Tarong. He couldn't see the blades through the tendril imprisoning him, but he felt the moment they began to glow. The magic pulsed through him, and the Entana shrieked. The tendrils in his head retreated, popping from his head like corks from a bottle. The pain was almost more terrible than when they'd burrowed in. The tendril unraveled and flung Aeo away, just as he would fling away a biting insect.

He hit the wall hard, everything going black and silent.

He returned not a moment later — any longer and he wouldn't have returned at all — and staggered to his feet. He'd have loved to take a moment to breathe, gather his strength, but the Entana had other plans. Already tendrils descended on him. Even more wove together before him, blocking any path he could take back toward the heart.

There was nowhere to go. No way to get close enough to actually hurt this beast. They could never win fighting like this.

He looked left, where Raeb battled the Entana even though he'd lost nearly all of his memories. He glanced to his right, where Dragana still fought though her arm was frozen solid. His friends were making horrible sacrifices to defeat the Entana. The least he could do was put in the same effort.

Last, he looked down at the Bok'Tarong. It was as much a part of him as his own soul. They were one and the same now. And though his heart ached and tears burned his throat, he knew what he had to do.

He might not be able to get to the heart of this Entana, but maybe he could get the deadly light of the Bok'Tarong there.

Aeo pushed away his despair and clung to the hope defeating the Entana would give him. He fought his way to Dragana's side, building up the strength he'd need for this final battle.

He couldn't spare a moment to explain his plan. He just hoped she would understand. "Cover me," he called, stepping back to remove himself from the fight as best he could.

Dragana didn't even hesitate. She simply stepped in front of him, fighting all the harder to protect him. His Dragana.

Aeo took a deep breath. It was time. Whether or not he was ready, it was time.

He wished he could say goodbye.

He raised the Bok'Tarong before him, channeling all the strength he could muster into the blade. Its glow brightened, blindingly so.

Dragana glanced behind her. That instant nearly cost her, as a tendril shot down at her head. She rolled aside at the last moment, slicing Sunray into its flesh as it impacted the ground beside her. "Aeo, what are you doing? That almost killed you last time."

"What choice do we have?"

She fought off another three tendrils, then threw another glance back at him. Her face was set in a warrior's grimace, tears leaving clear tracks in the oily ash covering her face. Even in here — *especially* in here, the spirit world — she radiated beauty that had nothing to do with her body. Strength and gentleness, stubbornness and grace. Gods, she was beautiful.

They had only a heartbeat to meet each other's eyes, but whatever she saw in him dried her tears. She nodded, whether granting permission or wishing luck he didn't know, then returned to defending him against the Entana.

The Bok'Tarong radiated magic and light. Its power thrummed through his entire being. Aeo summoned all his energy and gave it to the blades, willing them to become the instrument of destruction they were born to be.

The Bok'Tarong's light pulsed in time with his heartbeat. With each beat he poured more of himself into the blades, and they brightened even further. He held blades that glowed like rosy gold suns, warming the soul with their righteous power.

The Entana fled from the radiance. It tried to lash at him, but any tendril that entered the Bok'Tarong's light evaporated with a hiss of oily smoke and a faint squeal.

It wasn't enough. Aeo could destroy tendrils for the next hundred years and still lose this battle.

[We need more power,] the blades said. [With more strength, we may be able to kill this thing.]

Where am I supposed to get more strength? I'm giving you everything I've got.

[Your spirit is not the only resource at your disposal.]

Aeo could sense his companions beside him—not just their presence, but their lives. He could touch them. Take from them.

Damn it. I can't do that to them.

But he was out of options.

He turned his head to the left, where Raeb still battled. "Raeb, do you trust me?"

"I may not have many memories left," he called back, panting, "but I remember two things: I probably shouldn't trust you. And yet I do."

Aeo smirked. "Dragana?"

She didn't let him finish the question. "With my heart, and my life. I trust you, Aeo."

"Then, my friends, I need some of your strength."

"It's yours," Dragana said. "However much I have."

"Mine too. Whatever you need to kill these bastards. Take it."

Aeo reached out to the Bok'Tarong in Raeb's hands. He could feel the power of that other sacred blade, and through it the strength and life of Raeb. The man's hatred of the Entana surpassed even his own. It was a great source of power, and Aeo grabbed onto it and pulled.

Raeb grunted, but didn't otherwise object. His Bok'Tarong began to glow, too, far fainter than its twin.

Raeb's life-force raged through Aeo's blood like ice and fire and power, and he poured it into the Bok'Tarong before he burst. His blades flared with so much light, they were blinding even through closed eyes.

The Entana monstrosity growled and squealed. The sound was so deep, so loud, it shook every bone in his body.

[Almost enough.]

He'd hoped he wouldn't have to do this, but they didn't have a choice. They needed a little more power before Aeo was ready.

Reluctantly, he reached through the connection of Dragana's spirit carving. He felt her there, bound to him body and soul. Hatred, fear, pain, and love governed her emotions. Each was so potent Aeo couldn't understand how she could handle all of them at once.

The power he'd pulled from Raeb's hatred of the Entana had made the Bok'Tarong in his hands flare like fire. The depth of Dragana's love made it burst into flames and burn with the intensity of an exploding sun.

Aeo channeled all this and more into the Bok'Tarong, until his entire body burned with light and power and energy. The

Bok'Tarong trembled in his rock-steady hands. The blades vibrated with power.

[We're ready.]

Aeo was so consumed by the power he almost didn't hear the blades. He took a deep breath, let it out. He narrowed his focus to pour all the energy from his body, and from his friends', into the Bok'Tarong. Strength drained from his limbs. He felt hollow and empty without it, but the blades grew full and hummed with life. They burned with righteous fury.

He lifted his arms higher, above his head, bringing the blades behind him. He planted his feet and arched his back. One more deep breath, once more gathering his energy.

[Goodbye,] the blades whispered. There was such finality to the statement Aeo choked back tears.

"Goodbye," he replied.

With every bit of strength in his body, he launched the Bok'Tarong at the Entana.

The blades became a rosy gold comet, hurtling through the air like a cannonball. Its light filled the cavernous room, reflecting and redoubling off the polished obsidian surfaces. The Entana shrieked like steam escaping a kettle. It was the sound of pure, unadulterated terror.

Aeo felt the blade reach the Entana heart, penetrate the tendrils, driving itself into such utter darkness the entire cavern went black as pitch. For a second they battled, blade and Entana, churning like lava and boiling like steam.

Then the light exploded, throwing sun-bright flames in every direction. The darkness shattered, blasting shards like black crystal into the air. Several cut long gashes in Aeo's skin, but he hardly noticed. He grew weaker by the second. His muscles were shaky, his eyes so heavy he could barely keep them open. The world around him was becoming more distant and unimportant by the second. He wanted nothing more than to lie down and sleep, and maybe to never wake again. It was just too hard to stay up, keep moving, continue living.

With a final, deafening squeal, what was left of the massive Entana evaporated into smoke. The light at its heart flared once more, then winked out. Nothing was left in its place.

The Bok'Tarong was gone. The Entana was destroyed.

Aeo lost consciousness before his head hit the ground.

CHAPTER THIRTY-SIX

R aeb was weak, so very weak after Aeo had channeled his life-force into the Bok'Tarong. He could barely muster the strength to lift his head and check that the others still breathed.

The room was dissolving around him. The Entana were dead, and their hive was dying along with them. Soon there would be nothing but vast, empty space around them.

The Entana had been right about one thing. There was no way he could have made it out of here alive. But he was at peace with that. The Entana were dead, and his mind… it felt so free. Nothing lurked in the shadows, no presence in his subconscious waiting to consume his memories.

He was no longer burdened with the darkness of the Entana. He felt as light as the fires of the Bok'Tarong, as if he could fly with the same speed those blades had flown to destroy his slave-master.

This was a good way to die, he decided.

He could see stars through the floor. The shininess of the

walls fractured into galaxies and solar systems. The darkness of the obsidian was the blackness of space. He saw all this and understood it in ways he'd never thought possible. This was the spirit realm, where he would spend eternity as a wandering soul.

But a wandering soul was free, subject to no one. It was a very good way to die.

There was a light, somewhere far off. It wasn't a star. It was too bright for that, and its shape was too complicated. It wasn't the glow of the Bok'Tarong, either. That was gone. But this light was just as warm, just as full of life. The shape tickled something in his mind, a weak recognition of the sigil. It called to him, beckoning him to it.

It called his name.

He lifted his head. The light was there, but so far away. He could never make it that far. His spirit was too weak.

But she was calling to him, asking—demanding—that he return to her.

Saydee.

Memory lanced through his mind. She'd remained behind, staying in the physical world to watch over their vacant bodies. She was a mage, who could see the strands of power that linked souls and anchors. She must have seen his link flicker, as he lost his connection with life.

He reached for Saydee's light. It was too far away, and he was too weak.

Her voice reminded him of the others. Dragana. Aeo. She was calling all of them. He had to bring them home, too.

He reached out to his friends. He grasped a spirit, solid as flesh. *Aeo.*

A hand came to rest on his. *Dragana.*

He looked into the woman's eyes. They were bright as the stars around them.

They drew on whatever strength they had left. It wasn't much. Aeo had taken a lot to defeat the Entana.

But Aeo had given the most. He'd sacrificed everything to the Bok'Tarong. The least he could do was honor that and give his best to get them home.

Raeb found strength he didn't know he'd had. He gathered his spirit together, holding onto Dragana's and Aeo's as well. Then he reached to Saydee's light.

We're here, he called. *Help us.*

Saydee's light burned brighter, drew closer. Raeb reached for it.

He caught it.

Bring us home, Saydee.

✳

AEO WAS WEARY to the depths of his soul, every nerve alive with pain like lightning. His muscles hurt so much he wondered if he'd ever be able to use them again.

The lab looked blessedly mundane after the unnatural Entana hive. He'd never been so happy to feel cold, hard, uncomfortable stone beneath him. Even the smell of stale blood was almost welcome.

He reached up a hand, wiping it over his face, hoping he

could wipe away his headache as easily.

He opened his eyes. He didn't dare believe it.

Aeo wiggled his fingers. Wiggled his toes. Bit his lip, hard enough to draw blood. Scrubbed his hand through his hair, stretched his neck far enough it cracked.

He sat up. Lying next to him was the Bok'Tarong, its blades dull and lifeless. Even as he watched the rosy gold began to tarnish, and a large crack crept down the length of the blades. It was eerily similar to seeing his body decaying in the woods. He couldn't bear the sight and turned away.

Dragana sat beside him, staring as if she couldn't believe her eyes.

She punched him. Hard. "I've wanted to do that since the moment I met you," she said.

"Just couldn't wait to get your hands on me," Aeo said, rubbing his arm and grinning. "I get it."

Then she kissed him. Harder.

It was too good to be true.

After long, perfect moments, Dragana's lips left his. He stared into her brown-and-crimson eyes. Many of the age lines that had wrinkled her face were gone. The Bok'Tarong no longer needed her life-force to hold his spirit. She still looked older than she was, but she was gorgeous. And she was his. Stubborn, righteous, fierce Dragana. He'd never seen anything so breathtaking in his entire life.

His fingers traced the line of her neck, down her sword-arm. A delicate network of icy blue scars marked where Sunray had frozen her arm. Her fingers were locked in a loose fist, her wrist slightly cocked. She'd never be able to use a sword again.

He couldn't help but stare at his own hand as it lingered on Dragana's. "Not that I'm complaining," he said, watching his fingers flex, "but how is this possible?"

Dragana smiled. "The carving of my spirit bound us body and soul. Wherever my spirit went, yours was compelled to go, too."

Raeb cleared his throat. "And since the Entana are destroyed, and the magic of the Bok'Tarong with it, your spirit had nowhere else to go. It must have used the last dregs of magic to make your spirit body real."

Aeo looked up to see a very amused, very embarrassed Raeb standing above them. His eyes were no longer the black-and-peridot, vertical pupil eyes of a -taken. They were a rich, deep brown. Human. They made him look strange, but also very... normal.

Saydee stood behind Raeb, looking weary and thoroughly overjoyed. Her eyes were also brown, but as light as cinnamon.

"Magic made me a new body?"

Raeb shrugged. "We could probably find some dusty old mage to explain the metaphysical implications of power and being and whatnot, but it'd be easier to just say 'yes' and be content with that."

Aeo laughed. "I'm good with that."

He looked back to Dragana, brimming with life and joy. He pulled her to him and kissed her.

However it had happened, Aeo would not let this chance to live pass him by.

*
**

RAEB TURNED AWAY from Aeo and Dragana. They obviously needed some privacy.

He stood at one of the shattered tables in Ashwinn's laboratory, ignoring the signs of their battle. Those memories were ones the Entana had fed upon. He knew he'd been here, and he knew he'd helped with all this, but he didn't remember fighting, or defeating, the Keeper of Secrets.

Perhaps that was a good thing.

He felt Saydee come up beside him. The girl looked so young, especially with her cinnamon-colored human eyes. It was hard to remember she was older than he was, and that she'd lived through horrors he could never understand. But he did remember, and he marveled that she could still seem so innocent.

"Weren't your eyes green?" he asked. "When you used your glamour, I mean."

Saydee shrugged. "I always wanted green eyes. I thought they were much prettier than brown." She looked around the lab and shuddered. "So what are you going to do now?"

He didn't reply for a long time. He hadn't thought of the future. He'd never truly believed they could free themselves from the Entana. He certainly never thought he would live through it to *have* a future.

"I think I'll go back to the -taken sanctuary," he said at last, a little surprised by how his heart stirred at the thought. "I don't remember much of my past life, but I think that would be a good place to start over."

Saydee shifted her weight, staring at her hands. "Would you mind some company?"

He smiled, and somehow he knew it was the first time he'd smiled from his heart in a long, long time. He couldn't imagine a better way to start this life—a new life, a *free* life—than with a friend by his side. "Not at all."

About the Author

Brenda J. Pierson is just a nerd living her dream. Inspired by Brandon Sanderson and R.A. Salvatore, she writes fantasy novels brimming with magic, monsters, and epic quests to save the world. In addition to writing she's a crafter, dedicated bookworm, avid gamer, lover of tacos, and crazy cat lady. She's living the good life with her husband and kitties in her hometown of Tucson, Arizona. You can find Brenda skulking around Twitter (@bjpwrites), as long as you don't mind seeing her cats as well as her books.